THE REMNANTS
OF
REBELLION

THE REMNANTS OF REBELLION

A NOVEL

PONNU ELIZABETH MATHEW

Stay curious,
keep reading...

ALEPH

ALEPH

ALEPH BOOK COMPANY
An independent publishing firm
promoted by *Rupa Publications India*

First published in India in 2025
by Aleph Book Company
7/16 Ansari Road, Daryaganj
New Delhi 110 002

Copyright © Ponnu Elizabeth Mathew 2025

The author has asserted her moral rights.

All rights reserved.

This is a work of fiction. Names, characters, places, and incidents are either the product of the author's imagination or are used fictitiously and any resemblance to any actual persons, living or dead, events, or locales is entirely coincidental.

No part of this publication may be reproduced, transmitted, or stored in a retrieval system, in any form or by any means, without permission in writing from Aleph Book Company.

For sale in the Indian subcontinent only.

ISBN: 978-93-6523-777-1

1 3 5 7 9 10 8 6 4 2

Printed in India

This book is sold subject to the condition that it shall not, by way of trade or otherwise, be lent, resold, hired out, or otherwise circulated without the publisher's prior consent in any form of binding or cover other than that in which it is published.

*For Appicha, Appachan, Ammachi,
and for Alice Mathew*

CONTENTS

Part I / 1

Part II / 27

Part III / 63

Part IV / 95

Part V / 131

Part VI / 157

Part VII / 181

Part VIII / 197

Part IX / 227

Part X / 253

Part XI / 285

Acknowledgements / 311

The Puthenpurackel Family Tree

Puthenpurackel Thommi Tharakan = Mamma Mollykuttty
↓

Eesho (Appacha) = Kochuthresia (Ammachi)   Georgekutty

Amma = Appa   Velia Pappa   Cheria Pappa

Aleyamma

PART I

chapter 1

THE TAXI STOPS SHORT OF the vertiginous driveway. Aleyamma rolls down the window and looks up. The hill undulates towards the horizon, deep into the arms of the mist. A ring of weeping willows swaddles the chartreuse hilltop and through the shifting cracks between the leaves, she gets fleeting glimpses of her future abode—the blush of a roof, a behemothic glass window, curly plumes of smoke, a begrimed chimney. The driver cranes his neck and tuts under his breath.

'Madam, the hill is too steep. I can't drive up,' he says, glaring at her in the rearview mirror.

She gets down and pulls out her luggage from the trunk. It forms an undignified heap near the lofty gate—her life packed into shoddy boxes she has brought with her from Chennai. The taxi driver eyes the heap, tuts again, and speeds away.

Aleyamma trudges up the hill, hauling half her belongings with her, leaving the rest at the bottom. When she reaches the top, it feels like home.

A mango tree brushes its branches against the thick white walls of the house. The ginger roof leans at a reverential angle. Bougainvillea in pink and white speckle the garden. The front door is left wide open. It is her first time in Puthuloor, at the house where Appacha once briefly lived.

But there is no Appacha now.

A little over a week ago, he was buried in the land where he was born—Niranam, more than 300 kilometres away from Puthuloor. Bucolic, but disparate lands. The former, an erstwhile port in central Travancore, stands at the confluence of the rivers Manimalayar and Pamba. The latter, tucked into the blood-red soil of the Western Ghats, is ripe and ready, like a pimple on the verge of bursting. Nonetheless, both places hum with stories from the past—Niranam, one of the cradles of Christianity in Kerala, bursting with songs and legends about St Thomas and the first Christians, and Puthuloor, fecund with *Hevea brasiliensis*, para rubber trees, a testament to the rule of the British crown and their first attempts at rubber cultivation on a plantation scale.

Like Niranam, where Appacha lived for a lifetime, Puthuloor, too, was Appacha's home, though it was only for a year.

Aleyamma lugs her suitcases in through the front door. The unmistakable aroma of fish fry wafts through the room and she scrunches her nose. She leaves her suitcases near the sofa and retraces her steps to the gate where the rest of the luggage is. Her eyelids are heavy, and her mind is befogged. The past few weeks have been disquieting; she ran away from Chennai, attended Appacha's funeral, and suffered through the reading of the will. She rubs the sleep from her eyes and tries to sweep aside the day—to forget. But the more she tries to forget, the more she commits to memory.

A few days after Appacha's funeral in Niranam, when Achankunju Uppappan unveiled the contents of the will to the family, the mood among the gathered kids and grandkids was mostly effervescent—until he reached the last item on the list. Aleyamma could sense the stiffness in the air. Her family did not take Appacha's decision well, because he had decided to leave the house in Puthuloor to his artist granddaughter, who knew nothing about the price of properties, or about homestays now that it had become one, or the business of luring foreigners to an exotic land by offering them bits and pieces of Syrian Christian Malayali culture and history. They believed the artist was destined to remain a starving artist.

What Velia Pappa saw was his impeccable business melting away. He ran the homestay, but he knew it was now out of his grasp. He chewed his lips acrimoniously and looked at Aleyamma from the corner of his eye. No one could actually see his eyes because he always wore black glasses to cover his goat's eye, which he was not entirely ecstatic about. He had lost his right eye in his late teens, when a firecracker exploded just as he bent down to see if it was about to ignite. It was New Year's Eve, and the party was just beginning for him and the neighbourhood lollygaggers who hung around the village maidan, playing cards and teasing college girls.

The doctors tried to salvage his eye. But it was mangled beyond repair. 'Looks like chamanthy,' everyone said when they saw him after his surgery. Someone then told him about a goat's eye that could save him the indignity of an empty eye-socket. So, a goat was butchered, one of its eyes plucked out and then placed in the ruddy hollow of Velia Pappa's socket. After he was discharged from the hospital and his eye had healed, when he looked at himself in the mirror, to his dismay, he looked like a goat. People soon started calling him 'the goat man', shouting out at him in woeful bleats whenever he drove his booming Bullet past them. He stopped teasing the college girls. He stopped hanging out with the village sloths. He just stayed in his room and kept staring at his goat's eye with his good eye. One day, he told Appacha that he was going to pluck out his goat's eye.

Though Appacha thought that Velia Pappa was a changed man and secretly thanked the accident for also taking away his son's haughtiness, he advised him against it and gave him his pair of bronzed Ray-Ban instead. 'It makes you look like a rock star now. Just like Elvis Presley,' he said. Velia Pappa liked his new look and therefore embraced the King of Rock 'n' Roll in every form. He crooned his songs raspingly, much to the annoyance of the rest of the family; dressed like him; got an Elvis cut; and even tried growing sideburns, though they never grew fully. He also tried talking like him, putting on a phoney drawl, rolling his 'r's unconvincingly. The peculiar accent that he developed then still clung to him even after he had long outgrown Elvis.

Aleyamma could sense his one-eyed Ray-Banned gaze boring into the back of her head. She wanted to disappear from the room.

Cheria Pappa looked through her. When he realized that his pedantically devised Gulf-return retirement plan had now bitten the dust, he shared the same emotion his older brother had come upon. 'We are the sons. Everything belongs to us,' he said, gesturing to Velia Pappa with a warlike genuflection of hands and head. 'The daughter's daughter is only a distant family member. Appacha became foolish and then forgot everything.' Their wives bobbed their heads in agreement. Father-in-law's cockamamie self was finally evident.

Cheria Pappa—Small Pappa—was the right name for him, though it was a name that only she called him by. He was diminutive and smaller even than Amma by a few inches. So, he wore thick shoes with a couple of inches of height hidden within the sole. When someone once asked him where he got his shoes from, he dismissed the query by saying, 'Some shop somewhere.' He didn't want anyone to know the secret hidden in the soles of his shoes. He also craned his neck at all times and it was now disproportionate to the rest of the body. But whenever he wore a mundu, he always thought of himself as the actor Mohanlal, the maestro of the mundu, who turned the fabric into more than a garment on screen—sometimes a weapon, sometimes a harbinger of fiery emotions. Cheria Pappa also wielded the mundu to convey his feelings. Mundu unfolded meant that he was adhering to decorum, which he rarely did. Mundu doubled up slackly indicated that he was relaxed, which he most often was not. Mundu doubled up tautly meant he was getting ready for the unanticipated; for instance, the reading of the will. Mundu lifted on purpose meant mortifying the unsuspected without resorting to the aid of the fist.

He wore the mundu only during his summer breaks in Kerala. The first time he landed in Dubai, he was wearing his mundu, little aware of the consequences of wearing a flimsy garment that was despised in the foreign land. The man who was sitting at the immigration counter snickered at him. 'Labourer?' he asked him without even looking at his papers. Cheria Pappa, aghast at the accusation, held back his wrath. No one had ever called him that. He cursed himself for choosing a job that he thought would pay more than the coconuts on his father's farm. 'I pay my labourers more than what you are being paid, you filthy fat pig,' he wanted to tell him. But he knew better. He swallowed the words and bit his tongue. 'No. Chartered accountant,' he said meekly, keeping aside his Mohanlal persona. He was a nobody in a foreign land, like the many nobodies that returned as somebodies, back home with suitcases full of luxuries and minds full of stories never to be recounted as they had actually happened.

Amma sat in the corner and observed everyone through her monkey crop. Such moments of quiet, though thankworthy, were scarce affairs in Amma's life. Aleyamma couldn't read her expression. Her pale pink dress matched the pallor her skin had acquired over the years, and she sat there taking in the events without letting much transpire on her face. The dresses she wore were pretty, though the patterns were passé. She always told her tailor to leave a good four inches on either side so that she could alter them according to her growing body, as if it were that of a child's. She had never worn these dresses when she was married to Appa. After Appa left, she found a man who thought she was the most beautiful woman he had ever met. More beautiful than Juhi Chawla or Madhuri Dixit. He said he liked big women. 'I am a south Indian man. South Indian men know what beauty is. Just look at Jayalalithaa and her butyraceous thighs,' he would say. Amma would go through her old collections of *Filmfare* and try to emulate the style of the leading ladies. She would tie her hair in a high ponytail with printed silk ribbons, brush her eyebrows with black brow dust, and colour her hair a deep toffee brown. She told her lady tailor to fashion dresses tight at the bosom and flared at the knees. She picked out lipsticks of daring hues and applied rouge on the apples of her cheeks. She wore dangly silver hoops and got a monkey crop that veiled most of her eyes. Whenever she was due for a haircut, Aleyamma would have to talk to her monkey crop and try to catch her eyeballs for fleeting moments of clarity.

Even with a man with an eye missing, a miniature Mohanlal wearing hush-hush heels, and a lady whose growing bottom rendered her trapped in a chair every so often, they deemed themselves a beautiful family to look at because they owed their appearance to Biblical lands. They believed that, like the Knanayas or the Southists, they too had sailed from Sassanian Persia and landed on the shores of Kerala once upon a time. They embraced this theory with stubborn confidence despite the lack of evidence, unlike the Knanayas, who chronicled their genealogy with precision. But they liked to think of themselves as exotic—people from the land flowing with milk and honey. The larger community, though, attributed their olive blush to the long-standing belief that they were once elite Brahmans converted by St Thomas, who after landing in Muziris or Murachipattanam (a legendary port in Kodungalur that had disappeared from the map because of a massive flood in the Periyar river basin—which also changed the geography of the region, creating little islands along Cochin and bringing white silt to the lands around Niranam), made his way into Niranam to set up the seven-and-a-half churches of south India on his second and last missionary journey before he was killed in Mylapore. They, like the rest of the community, shrugged at caste politics, because, as Syrian Christian Malayalis, they were outside the chaos of caste but still fancied it theoretically, offhandedly reiterating their upper-caste status at every kudumbayogam through a pompous narration by an untrained family historian.

Appa never bought these stories. 'Look at us. Half the family is dark-skinned. The rest of us have big fat noses. We were all junglees, monkeys who once lived in trees,' he would say, pointing at Amma's nose, much to her wrath.

Appa and Amma were not in love. They didn't even like each other.

When Amma met Appa for the first time, she carried a tray with tea and biscuits, looking down at her feet. So, Appa thought Amma was like any other woman he knew. Submissive. Soft-spoken. Without opinions. Like his own mother. But she wasn't.

'But then why did you look down at your feet?' he asked her later.

'Oh, I simply didn't want to trip on my sari,' Amma said.

Appa thought that Amma had tricked him into marrying her by looking down at her feet. But Amma held the opinion that Appa was the lucky one to have married into a family of old money and status—things that could never be bought with the dinars and dirhams (new money) that plumbers, electricians, and nurses brought from the Gulf. The old money had enabled them not only to build their house in Niranam with British sensibilities (and not with cheap aluminium and glass the dinars and dirhams bought), but also to buy a brand-new house off NH 47 in Cochin.

'We were ruling over everyone when people grovelled in the dirt and had no clothes on their backs,' Amma would say about her status.

Eventually, Appa had had enough of Amma and her status. He packed a suitcase and left them. A few weeks later, Amma drove with Aleyamma and dropped her in Niranam. 'I will take her back once I sort my life out,' she told Appacha, and drove away in her Ambassador.

After the reading of the will, the beautiful-looking family decided to embrace their junglee forms. Velia Pappa removed his black glasses and stared down at Achankunju Uppappan with his goat's eye. Achankunju Uppappan wasn't sure which eye to look at. They pointed in different directions.

Cheria Pappa doubled up his mundu as if he were gearing up for a fistfight from one of the Mohanlal movies. In the tumultuous room, Aleyamma couldn't discern Cheria Pappa's intended target. Though she might have been the bigger fiend in the eyes of her truculent relatives, it was most probably the unlucky Achankunju Uppappan who would be made the scapegoat. She knew they would not hit her. They were proud of the fact that they didn't hit women, and they wore it pompously as a label on their sleeve, although, in fact—and this was a secret that was never revealed—their restraint was because they were afraid the women in their family might hit them back. Their friends would hit their wives and tell them about it. 'She deserved one.' 'She asked for it.' But the men in her family didn't do that because, though the women deserved to be struck moderately, they were better men. So, they hit only men.

The wives and children shot up abruptly from their chairs, expecting some action to unfurl before them. Amma sat in the corner, hands crossed over her chest, and watched her younger brothers, almost anticipating the turn of events. She shook her monkey crop, and her eyes rolled behind it like unruly marbles.

Achankunju Uppappan, advocate-cum-(distant)-family member, decided to play the judge that day. He believed it was best to ameliorate the air with smiles. But no one cared about his smiles. It only infuriated them even more. 'What is written is written.

And what is written stands.' He talked in an unruffled tone, at a deliberately slow pace, as if attempting to cool down the room that was beginning to boil.

In the end, they agreed to shoot the messenger. Aleyamma was left unscathed, and Achankunju Uppappan left the room, clutching his bloody nose, as Cheria Pappa's fist had once again decided to do the talking.

chapter 2

THE HOUSE ON THE HILL has fifteen rooms, leaving out the corridors, loggias, and curiously shaped spaces. Aleyamma counts them soon after she brings her luggage, for it somehow seems like the right thing to do. It is not a dak bungalow, but it is modelled after those that were once built along postal routes for British administrative officials to spend the night.

The house is almost circular, with verandas garlanding the rooms inside. The kitchen, cold room, scullery, and servants' quarters are quite a walk away from the main loop, accessible through a long-canopied corridor, once fashioned to keep apart the hallowed heart of the home and the meek world of service. Furniture in rosewood fills the rooms like rich brown chocolate. Wrought-iron lighting appurtenances adorned with candles in small stands and an electric bulb where oil and wicks once burned, float like little goblets in the air, still smelling of kerosene and soot, dribbling pasty paraffin wax onto polished red-oxide floors.

The dining room, to the left of the foyer, is the longest room of the house, with a baroque table that can seat fourteen on cushioned chairs with burnished armrests. The main hall opens through the foyer, separate from the homey portico. The room has been fashioned to make assertions—that of a bourgeois, a huntsman, a husband, a colonist, an Englishman. Cloudy sepia snapshots framed in pallid gold rest on white walls, showing a man with slicked-back hair and a clipped beard, sometimes with his wife and at other times, next to unsuspecting prey he bamboozled into woodland traps. Their heads are stuffed and mounted beside the pictures.

It is not surprising that pictures of the Englishman still adorn the walls. Velia Pappa has kept them because it is good for the business of homestays. Backpackers and Louis Vuitton jet-setters alike have swarmed not only the waterways, backwaters, and beaches of Alappuzha, Kochi, and Kovalam, but have also begun wandering down Kerala's untrodden lanes, hiding amongst nature and humidity to get away from frigid temperatures and first-world problems. Once, it was called the Estate House. It was where Appacha and Ammachi lived when he worked at the rubber estate as the superintendent. There is nothing left of the estate; the office building was broken down, and the owner sold the estate in parts a few years after Appacha left the job. The only thing left standing is the superintendent's house, which Appacha bought after the owner passed away. It stayed vacant for a long time until Velia Pappa restored it and turned it into a homestay.

Aleyamma heads towards the kitchen. On her way there, she is approached by the fetching young cook with gifted hands, whom she had heard about in many of Appacha's accounts. Appacha was a wonderful storyteller. He used to tell her stories about the estate. About the endless rubber plantations. About his Alsatian mongrel, who everyone thought was a wolf but who was only a dog that looked like a wolf. About the fetching young cook with gifted hands whose wild-boar fry led Appacha and Ammachi to add a few extra kilos. She is not young any more, but still fetching. 'You look just like her,' she says as she pulls on Aleyamma's shirt sleeves, drawing her closer to her chest. Her hands smell of kodam puli and curry leaves. Her palms are stained a vibrant yellow from turmeric, but they seem more suited to the hands of a young artist. She asks Aleyamma about her journey, her plans, her life—all in one lungful. She speaks to her like she has known her all her life, like this is a moment when she is reuniting with a long-lost daughter. She does not look at her dreadlocks or the tattoos on her arms, nor question their existence with morbid stares.

'I think I am hungry,' says Aleyamma. She is reminded of the elements that go into the making of a curry.

Elsy Chedatty releases her grip, leaving Aleyamma's sleeves tinged with a yellow stain. 'Of course! Lunch is almost ready.' Elsy Chedatty flits back to the kitchen just the way she came.

Aleyamma walks to the hall and gazes at the wall that she had missed on the way in. Too many walls. Too many doors. The house discombobulates her. But there they are, looking at her in black and white. The young Appacha and Ammachi, rubbing shoulders. Elsy Chedatty is right. Except for the neatly draped sari and the soft beehive of hair, Aleyamma takes after Ammachi. Appacha is fetching in his boots and deerstalker, and is as handsome as an actor from the black-and-white movies. Then there are faces she doesn't recognize. A young man with bony arms, another with a rifle slung across his shoulder, and an old man with thick glasses that make his eyes pop.

Appacha is smiling. Even through the cloudy photograph, she can see his laugh lines. She runs her fingers over the glass frame and remembers how much they meant to her.

∽

In Niranam, the days had always embraced her warmly. In Cochin, she longed for them. Christmases, Onams, summer vacations—these were the seasons she keenly awaited—because Appa and Amma would drop her in Niranam and only return to collect her when school resumed.

Appacha's father built the Niranam house when he was a young man. People said he was from one of the four families who were the first Christians of Niranam. The house was not far from the Marthoma church and the ghat where St Thomas is believed to have baptized people. Appa always said that the story of St Thomas coming to India was made-up and was used by the community to reinforce the idea that they were Brahmins who descended from the families that converted to Christianity. Amma, as usual, opposed everything that Appa said and called him a communist. Appacha, however, shrugged off these historical sparrings, insisting that the only truth worth considering was how people were treated in the present.

Amma was proud of the Niranam house—its high ceilings, its long verandas, the wooden ara within the house—the in-house granary once used for storing unhusked rice from the family's paddy fields; the gleaming red-oxide floor, the finest of its kind, a vestige of the legacy of Kerala's storied trade with the Portuguese and Italians.

Christmases with Appacha were especially exciting affairs. The unassuming kaatadi that stood flanking their front veranda was their designated Christmas tree. Appacha said its scientific name was *Casuarina equisetifolia*. It was a scanty-looking version of the plumped-up pine trees that appeared all decked up on the English channels on television—its humble Indian cousin.

Every Christmas she spent in Niranam, the tree became an empress as its skinny boughs filled out with glittering tassels, twisted crepe ribbons, shiny bells painted silver and gold, paper angels, and cotton-roll snowballs. Appacha would hang a white star with a glowing bulb right above the tree and tuck a crumpling clay nativity set under its drooping branchlets. Baby Jesus with open arms. Mary and Joseph with folded arms. Shepherds kneeling. A cock-eyed sheep with dirty white wool. Angel Gabriel with a broken wing. Three wise men with crooked smiles and tiny gifts. Appacha said that it was undeniable that there were more than three wise men as it was perilous for three people to take a trip by themselves in those days and that people got everything wrong about the birth of Christ.

Appacha was born on 25 December, but he said that people back in the day never had parties for birthdays; so, he never celebrated the day with cakes and balloons. Also, cakes and balloons were invented much later in Niranam. Appacha believed that Christ was not born on that day. But on Christmas morning, Aleyamma would inevitably find presents under the tree. Unruled books with pages stained an Ujala blue that turned bluer in the nude tube light, but smelled like an agreeable blend of coffee, chicory, and chilli powder; colour pencils that could be sharpened on both sides; a tin car with a plastic light on top; balloons in two colours; a toy gun with pink potash strips that went pop when placed precisely between the spring hinges that the trigger was invisibly connected to, and sickly sweet lemon candies carelessly wrapped in transparent plastic. Though she knew they came from Ramakrishnan's stationery store in town, where he sat behind a wooden half shutter, bare-chested, grey hair flecking his torso like little springs, handing out to customers bright green bottles of soda with marbles on top, smelling of sweat and of ground spices he sold in newspapers rolled up like ice cream cones, she still believed that they appeared under the tree by magic. Not least because Appacha was a magician. He could swallow coins and produce them again from behind his ears. He could make ten-rupee notes disappear and turn them into notes of a much greater denomination. He could also make the milkman's cycle disappear. At first, the milkman found the act quite perplexing, but it soon became the norm—so he would find it strange if his cycle was still parked where he had left it. 'No magic today, saar?' he would ask Appacha. 'Who said it was magic? I don't know magic. Your cycle disappears because you don't keep an eye on it,' Appacha would say, giving Aleyamma a sidelong wink.

Aleyamma was eight when Amma left her with Appacha. It was the middle of the school year and Appacha enrolled her in the local school where the roof leaked every time it rained, teachers taught English and Hindi in Malayalam, boys fashioned cricket bats from rubber chappals and footballs from dried-out coconuts, and girls wore jasmine in their hair and silver kolissu around their ankles. The frail makeshift bamboo partitions between classrooms weren't designed to sift out sounds, and the air was always filled with the cacophony of incomprehensible syllables. The kids called her a city brat and made fun of her 'American' accent. 'I'm from Cochin. Cochin is in Kerala. I have not even been to America. Then, how can I have an American accent?' she asked them. But they said all people from Cochin were like Americans; they not only spoke like them but also dressed like them; they wore smart shoes and socks and girls had such short hair that they looked like strange boys.

When she told Appacha about this, he said she could wear rubber chappals to school if it helped. She did, but still, new friendships were elusive. However, she didn't care because Manoj was all the company she needed. Manoj's father, Balan, was Appacha's cook, and they lived in a house in the same compound as them. Every morning, she would get ready and make her way to the dining table and eat with Appacha and Manoj before school.

Manoj always had intriguing information to share with them when they ate. He knew that Mohinder Amarnath's nickname was

Jimmy and Sunil Gavaskar's was Sunny. He knew that Mammootty's real name was not Mammootty and Innocent's real name was Innocent. He knew that Sudha Chandran's foot was made in Jaipur and Diego Maradona's hand was like that of God's. He knew that Rajiv Gandhi was a pilot, and that Indira Gandhi threw her favourite doll into a bonfire because it was made in England. Despite watching the same movies, following the same news, and cheering for the same cricket matches, he knew a lot more than her. Appacha was proud of him because he would ask him, hand on his chin, pupils dilating with expectancy, as soon as they sat down to eat, 'So, what new things did you learn today?'

Aleyamma held no jealousy; she knew she was Appacha's beloved. He first voiced this sentiment when she declared her intent to swim in the pond that stood in their compound. But Appacha said that the pond was too dangerous for swimming. All four of her cousins knew how to swim even though they were younger than her, she protested. But Appacha firmly declared that the pond was too treacherous for anyone to venture into, especially his favourite person. While her dreams of a swimming lesson were dashed, that she was his favourite left her smiling the whole day. And yet, on one fateful day, drawn by a twist of fate, she plunged into the pond.

∽

Appacha had always warned her about that unruly tree beside the pond, leaning over it like a drunk man teetering on the brink of a fall. He told her that it had sprouted from a discarded mango he'd flung away in his youth.

One day, when Appacha had gone out, she walked towards it. With a simian grip, she clambered up, her fingers caressing the branches heavy with golden fruit, plucking them one by one and dropping them into the plastic bag tied around her tiny waist.

The bag grew bigger and her footing more intrepid. As she ventured out onto the tapering branch that hung menacingly over the waters, it cracked like a bone-dry piece of chalk, and earthbound, she dropped, another leaf falling into the cavernous depths of the pond.

Water slapped against her mercilessly. Fishes swam around her fingers and water snakes brushed against her cheeks. The taste of the pond was that of the earth itself—moist, ripe, and bursting, as if stroked by the monsoon rains. The water touched her eardrums; its rhythm as unpredictable as the waves on Cherai beach. It slipped into her nostrils and spilled down her throat.

When Appacha pulled her out, her lips were blue, and her belly was swollen. Her body was limp, her eyes closed. Yet, she could see everything—floating above her body, she saw it all. A hundred yards away, the milkman's cycle had a puncture, and he was cursing his father for not having bought him a Bajaj scooter. Five houses down, Shankaran was up the coconut tree, watching next-door Nirmala through the bathroom window. On their porch, Krishnan Uncle—Appacha's best friend, driver, and Aleyamma's Maths tutor—was wiping down the silver Contessa Classic with the front page of the previous day's *Malayala Manorama* crumpled up into a ball, and below her, Appacha was clutching her tight, tugging at the faint tethers of her existence.

He carried her on his shoulders to the Contessa. In the back seat, she rested her head against his warm chest, the scent of Brut, Cutticura, and Radhas soap enveloping her sweetly. His fingers ran over her forehead as his heartbeat echoed in her ear—lub-dub...lub-dub...lub-dub.

That day, Krishnan Uncle made the old Contessa fly, faster than he solved Maths sums, reminding her of the car from *Chitty Chitty Bang Bang* that sprouted moth wings and soared over the knife-edged cliffs and emerald waters. 'Baby will be all right,' he told Appacha, not taking his eyes off the road.

The only people who called her Baby were Appacha and Krishnan Uncle. Though Amma had decided on the name Aleyamma, Appacha couldn't bring himself to call his granddaughter a hard-to-swallow old-woman name. 'I will call her Baby,' he told Amma. Amma found this unreasonable because there were many kinds of babies in Kerala—men babies, women babies, old babies, real babies, Baby Achayans, Baby Chedattys, Johnson's babies, Murphy babies, M. A.

Baby, Baby Shalini—and she professed to her father that the archaic handle would be back in mode in the new generation; names like Sosa, Akka, and Raca were already becoming more popular, though people warned her that only the communists chose to name their children that way.

On the hospital bed, the doctors buzzed around her while Appacha sat in the waiting room with his head in his hands. Aleyamma searched for the laugh lines on his face—the ones like the drawings the kuzhiaanas left behind in the sand. She watched his ears and waited for them to wiggle. But his laugh lines had disappeared. His ears didn't wiggle any more. Appacha was crying and Krishnan Uncle was holding his shoulders.

Krishnan Uncle could always make Appacha smile. He lived next door, and he turned up every evening after wrapping up his accounting job in town to teach Aleyamma Maths and to take Appacha wherever he needed to go—the grocer, the barber, church cell meetings. They would always come back laughing at some running joke, heads bobbing, shoulders rolling, cheeks flushed. Amma, Velia Pappa, and Cheria Pappa didn't quite approve of Appacha's friendship with Krishnan Uncle. Appacha, after all, was far too polished, too steeped in sophistication, to be forging friendships with the coarse and common villagers. But Appacha didn't care what people, especially his children, thought.

Krishnan Uncle always sat with his hands on the steering wheel, hugging them protectively like he was cradling a baby, making sure the speedometer didn't go an inch above 40 km/hr. That is why everyone said Appacha kept him around. 'Why else? Given his past,' they said. 'What is in the past?' Aleyamma once asked Appacha out of curiosity. 'He once killed a giant cockroach. That's why,' said Appacha. She imagined Krishnan Uncle engaged in the act, *Malayala Manorama* rolled up in his hand, taking sylphlike footsteps to the dark corners where cockroaches hid in musty comfort, nibbling on table scraps that escaped the reach of the broom; bringing down the newspaper on the scampering creatures, crushing their bodies with a crunch, letting white pulpy blood spill from their guts, later picking them up by the wiry antennas and discarding them under the coconut tree. But she never saw him kill a cockroach. Appacha said he didn't do that any more.

Through the half-green, half-white hospital walls, Aleyamma could see Krishnan Uncle pressing his fingers into Appacha's shoulders in an attempt to loosen them. But Appacha's shoulders were stiff, leaden with fear and pain.

Stretchers and wheelchairs squeaked past them. Nurses in angel-white saris hurried between rooms. A barefoot mother with tousled hair ran with her red-hot infant from the gate. Scalpels in hand, a doctor asked a nurse to wipe his beady forehead in the operating theatre. An old man mopped the mortuary floor with a smelly rag.

A brilliant white light beckoned her from the distance.

She heard Appacha's voice, salty, pleading, desperate.... Talitha Koum...Talitha Koum.

A soft breeze embosomed her, carrying her on its wings, away from the white light and towards Appacha. Talitha Koum.... Talitha Koum, Appacha said, rising to his feet.

Aleyamma spat out the murky green water on the crisp white sheet and went back to him.

Yet it was not the pond that made Amma take Aleyamma away from Appacha. It was something else. The pond was an accident, Amma said. What he did later wasn't.

One day, after a year of living with Appacha, Amma took her away. Just as Appacha made the milkman's cycle disappear, Amma made Appacha disappear. Amma drove her Ambassador up to the porch at a snail's pace but got out briskly. Her countenance was an unforgettable one as she stomped up the crimson steps in her Kolhapuri chappals. Amma's face was always marked by an expression that melded seriousness and petulance in equal measure. But that day, there was a great deal more ire on her face. She closed the Ambassador door with a bang. The old car reciprocated with a judder and the door kept rocking behind her without closing. The door never closed properly after that; it needed a serious shove with the knee or a display of shoulder strength to keep it from swinging back open. Once inside the house, Amma shoved Aleyamma's clothes into a bag and left, pulling her roughly by the wrist, ripping the sleeve of the dress of many colours Appacha had made for her. Aleyamma sat in the back seat of the Ambassador and cried as Amma drove perplexingly fast, unusually so, away from Appacha, not slowing down even for the potholes that shook them pitilessly every time the car ran over them. On they went in a rush. Past the sandy shores of Purakad that smelled like salt and fish cutlets. Past Alleppey and the Milma factory with its little cement store outside where they usually stopped for soft-serve vanilla ice creams that melted in the warmth of their hands. Past the trucks that said, 'sound ok horn', 'no farmer no food', 'we two ours two', 'use brain save rain'. Past the sky-blue board with chipped white paint that read, 'Welcome to Cochin, the Queen of the Arabian Sea'. Past their black gate by NH 47; they shot ahead and had to make a U-turn because, amid all the tension, Amma had forgotten where they lived.

Amma had pulled her hand so hard it left her wrist bruised for a week. The bruise turned blue-black on the first day before it became ruby red, salmon pink, and finally, a dirty tint of yellow, making her wrist look jaundiced. She wore long-sleeved dresses to hide her hideous wrist and even after the marks had faded, she could still feel the pinch on her skin and picture Appacha's pencil moustache thickened by tears. That was the last time she saw him when he was a whole man. The next time she saw him, he was not Appacha.

∽

The clay pot filled to the brim with neymeen vevichadu demonstrates Elsy Chedatty's mastery over cooking. The gentle steam caresses Aleyamma's face as she breathes in the aroma. She was secretly anticipating wild boar fry. Instead, a neymeen head gawks at her with deadpan demeanour from the old blue China plate. It reminds her of the first time she made fish curry. It was in Chennai. And it was for Roy. The fish had been chopped into curry-sized pieces at the store so she could focus on the more important dealings of the day. Its sericeous flesh was calling out to be dipped in the piquant fluid simmering on the stove as she cleaned the kitchen counter. Ammachi's recipe book, yellow with time and splattered with cooking oils, rested on the far end of the counter. She had stolen it from Amma on her previous visit to Cochin. Amma never used it anyway, as she knew the recipes by heart. Aleyamma abandoned her half-smoked cigarette in the teeming ashtray and grabbed a handful of onions.

'It's fish today,' she told Roy.

'Finally. Now we are one. It is fish and politics that unite us,' he said. She had finally passed the true test of being a Malayali. Or Bengali. Not that there seemed to be much difference between the two. Whenever Roy accompanied her to the Malayali restaurant in Anna Nagar where they made parotta and beef fry just the way they made them in the roadside eateries in Kerala and people struck up a conversation with him in Malayalam, much to his puzzlement, he would simply shrug.

'Where are you from?'

'Calcutta.'

'Oh, it's the same,' they would eventually respond and start talking to him about governments.

He picked up the abandoned stub from the ashtray and kindled it back to life. She gathered the neymeen and submersed them in the brick-red liquid, assembling the chunky pieces around the lifeless but still regal head. The smell of fish and cigarettes pervaded the house. An incongruous yet mollifying fusion. It was delightful because it was theirs. The first time she made fish curry, she relished it.

'You don't like it?' Elsy Chedatty asks her. Elsy Chedatty is standing near the doorway, watching her watch the fish. The neymeen head glowers back at Aleyamma from the plate, waiting for a commendation. Its probing eyes stare into her spirit. She takes a mouthful. The gelatinous flesh rolls down her tongue like a tease. She tries to swallow the pieces without tasting them, but they glide down her throat in a big lump.

'I don't like fish,' she tells Elsy Chedatty.

'Then I will fry some in the evening. The curry might be too spicy for you.'

'I don't like *fish*.'

Aleyamma pulls out a pack of Kings from the pocket of her cargo pants and rummages for a lighter. Her hatred for fish is newfound. She has begun to detest its slimy grey skin. The hidden bones that catch her off guard. The brightness or the paleness of the curries it drifts in. The lingering metallic taste it leaves behind.

'Do you have a matchbox?' she asks Elsy Chedatty, deciding to dissolve the rancorous taste with familiarity. Elsy Chedatty disappears and promptly appears with a pack of kitchen lights, gargantuan, worn out, damp and riddled with kitchen oil splatters, and hands it over to her.

Aleyamma jiggles the box and makes a mental note to include a lighter on her shopping list.

'Don't we have any guests today?' she asks her. She knows she must learn the economics of homestays if she is to run the show now.

'You don't belong here.' She can hear Roy whispering in her ears. 'Come back to me.'

'The Russians are coming.'

'What?' She is shaken roughly from her reverie.

'A Russian party. They will come later this week. They have booked three rooms,' Elsy Chedatty clarifies.

∽

There is a story written on the wall. A story that Velia Pappa has printed on handmade silk paper and mounted within a pallid gold frame in the living room. But it is only a slice of the real tale—a censored adaptation of the actual one which he thought was too ghastly to be told to the boarders. Velia Pappa has decided what has to be remembered and what has to be forgotten.

It is the story that began when an Englishman, Charles Hitchcock, bought land and constructed a house in the middle of a forest, almost a hundred years ago. People believe his father had sailed to the shores of Quilon with his wife and baby Hitchcock after having heard about nuggets of gold in the virgin hills of Wayanad. Around forty British companies were looking for gold along the hills of the Blue Mountains where they bought hundreds of acres of land, ran trolley rails deep into the caves, dug up the earth, hollowed out the peaks, and ploughed the valleys. But they found nothing. Father Hitchcock, too, was dismayed. He sailed back to England. But his son, a young man by now, had fallen in love with the land. While his friends planted tea and coffee along the hills of Wayanad, he and his wife moved to Puthuloor, in the neighbouring district of Calicut, now Kozhikode, cleared the forest land, and planted rubber trees. Rubber, he believed, was the future of the world. The invention of pneumatic tyres and the emergence of internal combustion engines had led to an increased demand for rubber across the world; Brazil was the only player in the market until the British Raj emerged as a contender.

After planting the rubber trees, young Hitchcock also built the house which people believe took him nine years, just enough time for the trees to give their yield. The furniture and artefacts, shipped from England or handcrafted by the finest artisans in town, were restored shortly before the house was converted into a homestay.

That is all that Velia Pappa wants to tell the boarders. What he fails to mention is the rest of the story. The grisly one that the locals tell over tea and head-shakes, honing it with as many layers of fiction that they deem fit. But at its core, the story remains unchanged. A tragedy shook the Malabar region of Kerala on 20 November 1921, now a mere slice of the past printed on the pages of history books for high school students, under the subheading, 'The Wagon Tragedy'. About a hundred years ago, when the goods wagon from Tirur en route to Coimbatore stopped at Podanur junction, sixty-four bodies spilled out of it. Mostly Muslim bodies. These were the bodies of the men who were arrested after they had clashed with the Malabar Special Police, a Nair-dominated brigade set up by the British to suppress Muslim rebellions with a communal hand. The men initially resisted British rule and the feudal system that granted power to the predominantly Nair landlords over them. Soon, it took on the undertone of the Khilafat movement, a protest against the sanctions placed on the Caliph and the Ottoman Empire after World War I, and was eventually transformed into the religious and social struggle that was later dubbed the Mopilla Rebellion. The men were arrested and brought to Tirur railway station after being hauled behind bullock carts. They were then stuffed into the tight confines of a goods wagon. Ninety bare bodies in a windowless wagon chugged along for 140 kilometres. No one cared if they had air to breathe or an inch of floor to stand on. They stood on each other's bones in the murky metal box, gasped for oxygen, and shed tears that had already dried up. Some stayed alive by drinking their own urine. Sixty-four of the ninety men perished after suffocating in the wagon.

Charles Hitchcock had nothing to do with the tragedy that took place more than a hundred kilometres away. He might have learned of it later when he read about it in the newspapers. But its ripples were felt in Puthuloor. Around this time, the nature of labour was also changing in the rubber industry. Initially, most of the tappers were Mopalas from Malabar. But the peasant classes of Cochin and Travancore were gradually eating into the labour force, and this upset many.

One night, a disgruntled tapper who worked for Hitchcock put an end to the oppression and misery he believed his people were facing at the hands of the British. Armed with a green flag and a knife, he stabbed the young Englishman and his wife in their sleep and then killed himself to avoid capture. Coincidentally, the sergeant of the Malabar police who ordered the men to be transported in the Wagon Tragedy and later settled the grievances of the families by giving them a solatium of three hundred rupees per deceased head was called Richard Harvard Hitchcock. Perhaps the frustrated worker thought that all the Hitchcocks were related. Or he was just making a point. After Independence, he was seen as a hero who turned the tables on the tyrant. He was declared a freedom fighter, and a local road was named after him—Moosa Road.

No one quite knows what exactly transpired back then, the true nature of events lost to the amnesia of time. But the general presumption is that Hitchcock was far from a dreadful man. He was kind to his workers, and they never ran out of food during the war. Everyone deemed him to be a generous man who was vocal about the perils of untouchability and child marriage. There is even a curious tale suggesting that Hitchcock was murdered for attempting to prevent the marriage of the tapper's six-year-old daughter.

∽

As it is with old houses, especially the ones where there were murders or dubious deaths, Estate House spews out stories that can be chronicled in a fat book of fables. A manor on top of a hill walled by monstrously waltzing weeping willows, lost in a chalky miasma on bitter dawns and brewing cryptic echoes on tempestuous nights is, after all, foreordained to have its share in village yarns. When Appacha bought the house, some folks in the village swore blind that the nomadic company of the sayippe was unassailable and could be caught in certain flashes—footsteps fading on the veranda, a whiff of cigar in the garden, and a frosty puff on the back of one's neck—like he rose occasionally from his grave in the backyard and went for evening walks along with his wife. 'What a stupid and scatter-brained woman!' fabulist nanas would tell the village sprogs. 'How you know? How you know?' 'Because she walks around brushing her long golden locks, gets lost in the woods, and snivels for her husband. I've heard her many times.' The peripatetic pair was not welcomed by the village folk with open arms. The local temple decided that the white people had to be kept under lock and key. The pujari lit some lamps and warbled some ditties around the derelict graves that stood by the brook. The locals hoped the incantation would be the end of the visiting couple. But the couple paid no attention and continued to go on their saunters, smoking and sobbing. Since the pujari's invocations didn't work out, the locals called the church priest who prayed over the graves and sprinkled water he said was blessed from the Holy Land. 'Let us just pray that they stay in town as good spirits,' he said.

'The sayippe is still watching over the estate. Maybe that's how his soul finds peace,' the people resolved. But the pujas and prayers continued for a few years in case the spirits turned vindictive. Perhaps they finally worked, for Aleyamma has never seen the apparitions. Only the graves remain by the stream, their headstones, now just remnants swallowed up by the earth, surrendering unwillingly to the unforgiving monsoons of Puthuloor.

PART II

chapter 3

LONG BEFORE APPACHA BECAME APPACHA, he was called Eesho. It was the night before Christmas when Mamma Mollykutty's labour pangs reached a crescendo. The night carollers crooned their way through the dusty streets with their homespun drums, petromax lamps, and a rough-hewn star, mouthing film tunes, extemporized ditties, and some Christmas choruses perfunctorily wedged in between. Twice a year, the procession would make its rounds in the neighbourhood—once during Christmas and another time during Thiruvonam—with the only distinction being the replacement of the hero of the jamborees. During the latter, a fervid man would pull off a frenzied puli kali and during Christmas, it would be a mostly skinny Christmas Appooppan.

Puthenpurackel Thommi Tharakan strode up and down the veranda of the house, oblivious to the drunken rumpus created by the revellers outside, questioning if he had imperilled his thirty-two-year-old wife by doing the deed nine months ago. She was a comely woman, and he couldn't help himself. But comprehending that it was too late to undo what he had done, he could only pray that she was resilient enough to deliver the baby. No one gave birth at that age. His mother was fifteen when she had him, and she didn't even realize she had birthed him. People said she simply got up and walked about after he came out, browning cashews and raisins for the payasam that was to be distributed to the neighbourhood that day.

His mother was nine when she married his father, and she was carried on her father's shoulders for the wedding, which she imagined to be a kind of children's play. After they got married, the newlyweds would sit and make sand cakes, digging their fingers in the dirt, and climb mango trees like all children. That was a different time. But he wasn't sure whether time could defy age.

Both Tharakan and Mollykutty had previously been married to others, but they succumbed to complications from TB. They decided to stay widow and widower until the families arranged for them to be married once more as they thought they would bond over misfortunes of a comparable kind. But the two never spoke about their other lives. They didn't like picturing their new spouse with someone else. They bonded as their families had anticipated. But it was over their unarticulated lives.

As Tharakan paced up and down, twiddling the end of his mundu and shooing away the moths that danced dangerously around the kerosene lamp kept on the veranda, he told Philipose Achen that he would donate twenty kilograms of rice to Jerusalem Marthoma church (his parish in Niranam. There were no Marthoma churches in Jerusalem) if the baby came out fine. Forty, if both the mother and the baby were in good health. He even thought of throwing in a gold (plated) baptismal font if everything went well. Philipose Achen was satisfied with his offer and kept Tharakan company as he paced up and down. Philipose Achen always visited people in times of need, especially because they could be expected to call on God and make offers that would benefit God's people. This time, what the Marthoma church needed was land for a cemetery.

Though the site where the Niranam church stood had been handpicked by St Thomas, and the bathing ghat where he baptized the men and women still flanked the old church, there was no place to bury the dead; they had to be taken all the way to the Thiruvalla parish in hired bullock carts. Philipose Achen believed it was not fair, as the people had the right to be buried in the land they had worshipped on for years. Moreover, the cemetery would look beautiful next to the church and the parsonage, and Philipose Achen could, from his sitting room, keep an eye on both the living and the dead.

'Maybe you could also buy that land that we have been considering for the cemetery,' he told Tharakan.

'Why are you talking about the dead when my wife is about to give birth? It is not right to talk about it now. It is a bad omen,' Tharakan said. But he knew that he would have to part with some more cash as he knew Philipose Achen would bring up the topic of the dead at a later stage. Philipose Achen didn't believe in invisible omens. He only believed in what could be seen. Though his father had named him after their forefather, Kayamkulam Philipose Ramban, the Syriac scholar from the Malankara church who first translated the Aramaic-Syriac Peshitta Bible into Malayalam in 1811, while growing up, Philipose Achen didn't believe in the Bible or in God. Till the day he saw God. This is the account Philipose Achen gave the people of the parish.

'I was walking home one night after visiting one of my friends who had just lost his father. It was a moonless and misty black night, and I waved my torch in the air to keep the fire going. But a gust of wind took away the fire. I knew the way home, and I kept going in the dark. Suddenly, I saw a face in front of me staring at me through the mist. It was the dead father. He was an evil man who used to beat his wife and children. So, the spirit was definitely evil. I wanted to run, but I knew one could not outrun evil spirits. So, I stood there and prayed to the God that my mother had told me about. "Our father who art in heaven...." Soon, another face appeared in the mist, and it was more powerful than that of the evil spirit. The new face gobbled up the spirit in one mouthful. That face was God's. God appeared to me as he appeared to the apostle Paul. I was blind and now I can see.'

That day, Philipose decided to become an Achen.

Though Tharakan believed in omens, visible and invisible, he never bought the story that Philipose Achen tried to sell. Tharakan knew that the yarn spinner in Philipose Achen was simply taking advantage of the spirit world.

The revelry had now grown more frenetic outside. The drunken party had now reached their compound. Thump! Thump! They struck the drum and cavorted irrepressibly to what had now become indecipherable syllables. Some of the dancers decided to pass out on the porch while the others continued.... *'Unni Yesu piranna rathri... rathri, rathri.'*

'Give them some money or they will not leave,' Tharakan told a servant.

Christmas Appooppan eagerly tucked the coins into the small fold he had fashioned at the edge of his lungi and instructed those standing to pick up the ones that had scattered on the floor. With a final spirited cheer, the intoxicated Christmas Appooppan whistled and bellowed 'Merry Christmas' with all his might. Mamma Mollykutty cried in pain and out came Eesho keening a guttural tune. He was a fine baby, and he created little or no trouble for Mamma Mollykutty upon his arrival, slipping out like a baby seal into the hands of the midwife. The clock showed a little past midnight and thus they named him Eesho—meaning Jesus. He was a miracle baby, after all. It was Philipose Achen who suggested the name. Mamma Mollykutty first questioned the choice of the name as it was distinctly Catholic, and it pricked at her Syrian Christian Marthoma pride.

'What is important is that he was born on Christmas Day. Thus, there is no name more fitting than the name of the Lord,' said Philipose Achen as he blessed the little baby boy.

When Eesho grew up, he tried emending the folly that the family had collectively made, enlightening everyone that Christmas used to be a pagan shindig and there was no real proof that Jesus was born on 25 December.

'Malankara Christians once celebrated Christmas on 7 January, as per the Julian calendar. You should remember that. So, everything we do is questionable,' he told Mamma Mollykutty.

Mama Mollykutty was irate. 'So, you have become an atheist?'

'I never said that. I said there was no proof that Jesus was born on that day.'

'It is there in the Bible. You should ask Philipose Achen. He will show you.'

'No, it actually isn't. If you read it, you will know. I'm sure he hasn't read it too.'

'Don't question your mother. I am older than you.'

'Older doesn't necessarily mean wiser.' Eesho shrugged snootily.

Though Mamma Mollykutty pondered over Eesho's statement, wondering if there was any truth to it, she didn't want any confusion to show on her face. On such occasions, she always picked up the bamboo cane from its customary corner and tested its springy and solid body with a little flexing before she engaged her flaccid arms in a whacking exercise, always leaving long scarlet streaks on Eesho's shin. But Eesho didn't mind the wallops he received. All the kids were flayed routinely, and comparing the red streaks was a habitual affair when they met in school or on the playground, even showing off the scars with a bit of pomp—'See, mine is long and red', 'Mine was black, now it's blue', 'My skin has ripped off'. But Mamma Mollykutty, later feeling bad about having flayed her favourite son, would try to regain his love by spooning extra sambar on his plate or by hiding a soft-boiled duck egg beneath a generous mound of rice. So, Eesho didn't mind the beatings at all. After all, he was spared most of the time, as his younger brother, Georgekutty, was mostly at the receiving end of Mamma Mollykutty's wrath.

When Eesho was baptized, the church had gained provisions enough for a year or so, and the shimmering, gold (plated) baptismal font that Tharakan had thrown in at the last minute became the talk of the town. Everyone came to admire its magnificence. It stood flaunting its grandeur near the humble blue wooden door that barely closed. Fearing it might be stolen, Philipose Achen ordered a new door to be brought in to preserve the prized possession. If someone could routinely steal money from the charity box, they wouldn't leave the gold alone, he surmised. So, he bolted the new (but cheap) door with a second-hand Yale lock and even locked the church gate, opening them only for weddings, funerals, baptisms, and Sunday-morning services.

The day Eesho was baptized, people from all corners had gathered at the church, eager to witness the festivities. Tharakan had bedecked the church windows with fat strings of jasmine and arranged kappa, meen curry, and payasam for everyone after the service. He had erected a large pandal in the church compound with benches and desks arranged in neat lines. Baby Eesho giggled through the service even when Philipose Achen poured a mugful of cold water on him as he sat in the shimmering new gold (plated) baptismal font, inaugurating it with his naked fat baby buttocks. But what captured everyone's attention that day was the presence of doves on the church roof. They pointed at them as they descended from the sky, while the baby was lowered into the font; it was a miracle indeed. 'Just like the baptism of Jesus,' they uttered. The ones visiting the parish for the first time did not know that the doves were perennial residents of Jerusalem Marthoma church and every so often they were keen to relieve their bowels on some unassuming Sunday-morning worshipper. Plop! would go the dove shit on the oiled heads and starched chattas of the unfortunate who would have to scurry mid-service to the bathroom to wash off the blessings from above. But Philipose Achen didn't take any trouble to rectify their assumptions. He loved the effect the doves had on the people that day.

Mamma Mollykutty was more robust than what people had expected. She was thirty-five when she gave birth to her second son, Georgekutty. Tharakan didn't promise a measure of rice or gold to the Marthoma church this time, as he was certain he would have to honour the promise again, because he had very well realized his wife's verve by then.

'My gratitude is enough for God,' he told a hopeful-looking Philipose Achen when he took Georgekutty for baptism.

∽

Georgekutty was baptized in the same shimmering gold (plated) font. It was, however, a different kind of day. The entire neighbourhood had come to watch the festivities as expected. Georgekutty acted like a typical baby, wailing and trying to claw out Mamma Mollykutty's eyeballs throughout the humdrum service. When it was time to place him in the font, it was not the doves that decided to relieve their bowels. It was Georgekutty. Philipose Achen's fine new white gown was not white any more. The shit had flown everywhere. The shimmering gold (plated) baptismal font was speckled with baby poop, and Philipose Achen nearly dropped Georgekutty in shock. Tharakan feared that he might now ask him to buy the land for the cemetery in return for this misfortune. They went through with the baptism anyway and people still ate kappa, meen curry, and payasam. But through mouthfuls of food, they all remarked on how different the two celebrations were.

Growing up, people often likened Georgekutty to a hurricane that left a trail of destruction wherever he went. So, the bamboo cane found its way to his shin on a routine basis. But the more he was flayed, the more he rebelled. Sensing the trajectory, Eesho once stood in the way of the bamboo cane that Mamma Molly brandished because Georgekutty had stolen a chicken from the neighbour and cooked it for lunch. He had crept through a hole in the coconut leaf fence, snatched the chicken from the coop, and roasted it over a fire that he had made in the backyard behind a jackfruit tree, hiding away from everyone's gaze. But the neighbour, with her exceptionally keen sense of smell, detected the aroma of roast chicken and discovered Georgekutty savouring the bones of her prized bird. She made her way to their house, beating her ample breasts, and wailing as though mourning a beloved soul, rather than a chicken she would have killed for lunch one day.

'I am a very poor woman. Money cannot compensate for my loss,' she cried before accepting the coin Mamma Mollykutty thrust hurriedly into her ready hands.

'Shame, shame. You rich people should know better. Shame shame....' she said and disappeared into the hole in the coconut-leaf fence.

Mamma Mollykutty was irate at her son's doing. 'He didn't even bother sharing it. All that was left of the chicken were some bloody guts and some worthless feathers. He even chewed up the bones like a dog.' Eesho wondered whether his mother was more concerned about his brother stealing the chicken or not sharing it. But Mamma Mollykutty found a resolute Eesho blocking her path. 'Don't hit him. Can't you see that you are only making it worse?' he said. That day, both were not spared, and they both went to bed comparing the long red streaks the old bamboo cane left on their shins.

Georgekutty caught many chickens and had them for lunch over the years. The bamboo cane left little or no emotional mark on him.

Growing up, the reigning lady in Eesho's life was Mamma Mollykutty. That was, of course, until he met Kochuthresia. When Eesho first saw Kochuthresia, he was smitten. When he laid eyes on her for the first time on the netball court at an intercollegiate sports meet, a fete where, apart from the actual competitions, love bouts were also fairly common, he knew he was hooked. He sat on the cement steps of the court, as she floated across the yard like a nymph, pallu tucked into the sari at the waist, lobbing the ball every now and then into the bleached nets, and realized that the four-hour rickety bus ride from Niranam to Trivandrum was now well worth it. He had gone to cheer for his neighbour's football team who, despite the cheering and the crowd support, had lost the game.

She was poised on the court, calling out assertively to her teammates as her bare feet played hide-and-seek beneath the sari, bunched up below her waist like a mundu. Swiftly, she passed the ball, tossing it every now and then into the nets. But it was not just Eesho who was watching her. She had garnered a little audience who appeared to be cheering for her team, when, in fact, it was mostly for her. Men whose philosophies thus far deemed that netball and hopscotch were girls' pursuits, unashamedly rectified their beliefs and magnified her every move, tootle-tooting through fingers shaped like whistles, shouting slogans of support, much like they would cheer for their village football team. They watched her, open-mouthed, absorbing her striking face and the hint of a smile that flickered playfully at the corners of her mouth as she thumped the palms of her teammates in quick, spirited exchanges every time the ball found the net.

After the game, the men made a beeline towards her. She sat on the steps and fanned herself with the end of her pallu and chatted insouciantly with them, occasionally smiling and nodding. Eesho, who didn't want to play games, strolled up to her and pluckily pronounced in one breath, 'I see a cross around your neck and I see no minne. But more importantly, would you like to marry me? We could wait if you are not yet eighteen,' to which Kochuthresia's acknowledgement was first a nonplussed gawp. Then she smiled. The men retreated to their routines, shoulders slumped, cursing their lack of forthrightness.

For the next few months, Eesho would sit on a rickety state transport bus for four hours every week to meet her in Trivandrum. She would skip the last couple of classes, slipping out stealthily from the back gate of Government Women's College. On the days they planned to meet, she would linger a little longer in front of the dormitory mirror, wearing her best sari, and tuck into her hair a magenta rose from the convent garden. She would line her eyes meticulously with her kohl pencil and adorn her forehead with a little black dot. They would walk on the beach together and buy soft steamed peanuts, laughing and holding hands like a young married couple. They made a good-looking couple—Eesho, debonair in his Sunday best, long-sleeved shirts, and Kochuthresia in her puffed-sleeve blouses and velvety-soft saris that hugged her frame. Sometimes they would go to Connie's ice cream parlour and order soft vanilla ice creams. They would take their ice creams back to the beach and watch the red sun sink gently into the Arabian Sea, sitting cross-legged, playing with the tiny seashells hidden within the many folds of the soft sands. He would tell her about his home, about Mamma Mollykutty and her well-timed coddling, Tharakan and his coconut farm, paddy fields, and cashew business, Georgekutty and his affinity for the bottle.

He also told her why he had decided to go back home after working as the manager of a rubber estate in Nilambur for more than five years. 'It was a house wrapped by the hills. It was beautiful, but I was alone. I was looking for someone to go back home to. Anyway, now, back at home, my mother makes up for all the quiet times I have had. Even so, there is something about the hills that the plains don't have. Something mysterious.'

'Like magic. Like life,' said Kochuthresia, her eyes lighting up. 'Though I was raised in the plains, my heart tells me that I belong to the mountains.'

She then told him about herself. That she was abandoned outside the gates of Pristine Convent in Trivandrum, probably a few minutes after she was born, because her umbilical cord was still attached when the nuns found her. Whoever left her had left in a hurry.

When she was eight, her class took a weekend trip to Munnar. 'It was the first time I was seeing the mountains. And my heart leapt with joy. I fell in love with the mist in the morning, the cold that made the tip of my nose numb, and the sound of a thousand crickets at night. I was happy. When I left the hills, I think I left a piece of my heart there. Why are we drawn to some things in life? Why am I so drawn to the hills? Maybe my people are from there. I don't know. Life is mysterious. And precious. More precious now because you are in it.'

At that very moment, Eesho wanted to take Kochuthresia home. There was nobody more important to him. He looked at her and saw their future—a future more beautiful than he had ever imagined. He saw their home in the hills. He saw her smiling as the mist tickled her nose. He saw their children and grandchildren—little girls strong and beautiful like her. He wanted it all. He didn't fear what Mamma Mollykutty would have to say about their union. They wedded in a cloak-and-dagger service. She took his name, and he took her home.

chapter 4

'EESHO HAS NO TIME FOR puerile romance,' Mamma Mollykutty would say whenever relatives dropped by—until she had to swallow her words when Eesho brought Kochuthresia home. Mamma Mollykutty could see them from the kitchen window, and at first, she was in denial. 'It cannot be a woman. It just looks like a woman. I am only going blind. And that is better.' Mamma Mollykutty thought she would die if Eesho ever left the family for a woman, or worse, brought home a strange woman. No one ever did that sort of thing in their family, and she supposed such acts of impropriety were not meant for an upper-caste, educated family. (Though she was not educated, as her father had never taught her to read and write like he had taught his sons, Mamma Mollykutty considered her pedigree impeccable. And although she would have bridled at being thought of as progressive, she viewed herself as reasonably modern, since she chose to wear a chatta, unlike her mother, who was more comfortable baring her upper chest for all the world to see, reserving a delicate thorthu just for those times she went to church. Mamma Mollykutty had to warn her mother every time they sat on the floor to cut jackfruits, not to slice her own low-hanging fruits by mistake. A chatta would have held things in their place. Harmless modernity had to be embraced, she believed.) But eloping was not modern. It was just wrong and tasteless. It was for little boys who thought they knew better than their mothers. But mothers knew best.

Until now, she had held the unwavering belief that Eesho was incapable of making such a grave mistake, unlike the ones Georgekutty made on a fairly consistent basis. Apart from chickens, Georgekutty had also started stealing money from Mamma Mollykutty's almirah so regularly that she had to resort to the incommodious method of keeping her notes and coins buried in her corpulent breasts, held together by her chatta. And apart from smoking like a chimney, he had also taken to the bottle. Though Eesho too smoked, he smoked a pipe. A pipe, she assumed, was classier than the Kaja bidis

Georgekutty stuck behind his ears and took out occasionally, like he was picking his ears and putting it to his mouth.

'Did you go to get groceries?' she asked Eesho casually as she heard him approach the kitchen. She still did not believe that what she was seeing was real. Then she saw them standing together like a newly married couple, near the kitchen door, him still holding her hand, which grew out of his body like a third limb. No one ever held hands. Not even married people outside the bedroom. She recalled a time when she held hands with Tharakan after they got married—he had flicked her hand away like it was an insect, laughing nervously to cover his embarrassment in front of the wedding guests. The only thing he held tenderly were his coconuts, and they could have very well been his wives. Now Eesho was holding the hand of a strange woman. A woman who was not his mother. Out of nowhere, Mamma Mollykutty was surpassed by a strange woman to whom she would have to hand over the reins of the house. A strange woman who had caught her son in a sticky web. A woman who had fallen for his wealth and his good looks and decided that he was too good to let go. So, she entranced him with her specious words and flawless skin. Her fake locks and careless whispers. And men, being men, thought of only one thing.

But Mamma Mollykutty was still in a quandary. She would have comprehended it if Georgekutty had carried out this misadventure. She had never envisaged her favourite son betraying her. Her favourite son, for whom she would hide duck eggs under a mound of rice. Her favourite son, whom she only flayed moderately. Her firstborn who showed her and the world that she could defy age, and that motherhood could bloom in the deadly thirties.

Ever since her sister and her husband had moved away from the Marthoma church and joined the Pentecostals, Mamma Mollykutty had begun to suspect that the world was going crazy and that the end was near. Eesho's act had now confirmed it. In the end, sons would rebel, and daughters would stay spinsters. At least, this is what her sister had told her. Mamma Mollykutty's sister and her husband had thrown their lot in with the fiery flock at the Pentecostal church that an American missionary of German origin, George Burg, had started in Adoor. People called them crazy, for they acted like an inebriated lot, gabbling in strange tongues and shouting 'Hallelujah' till their tongues dried out and their throats cracked. But Mamma Mollykutty's sister said the Malankara Christians had become lukewarm in their faith and what they needed was the anointing of the Holy Spirit before the rapture of the believers. 'Do you want to be left behind on earth as the Antichrist tortures you and your children? Don't you want to be taken up to the heavens while the earth shakes, the sun turns black like a sackcloth, and the moon turns red as blood, whilst God unleashes his anger on the evil people of the world?' she asked. The rapture, she said, was the first sign that the world was about to end. In the rapture, all those who believed in Christ would ascend to the heavens, leaving the heathens behind to fend for themselves in a violent godless world. But she also told Mamma Mollykutty to pray for blessings on earth as well as in heaven. Mamma Mollykutty first laughed at the irony and dismissed it as a phase that her sister was going through, but when she saw that her sister's family was growing in wealth and sway, she, too, started praying with all her might.

She prayed for blessings on earth, as well as the rapture of the believers, every night before she went to sleep, reciting the Lord's Prayer robustly and trying to remember to include everyone on the list, if it ever happened. Once she believed the rapture came to pass. It was on a Good Friday night, fitting for such a phenomenon. Mamma Mollykutty was alone in the house, but she thought her husband was in the next room, reading a newspaper, when a ghostly gust of wind seeped in through the window next to her. She called out to Tharakan. 'Ketto, when was the last time it was this windy?' They called each other Ketto, always beginning their conversation with a word that meant 'listen', because they believed that not only what they said had to be taken with utmost gravity but also because they were too polite to call each other by name. It was their language of love.

Tharakan didn't respond. 'Ketto, where are you?' Then she went to look for him. But he was nowhere to be seen. Neither was the servant who would always sit by the light of the kerosene lamp and ask Tharakan about the happenings in the world as he read the newspaper out loud. 'What did Nehru do?' 'Will Germany bomb Madras again?' 'Is the Vimochana Samaram over? Now, will EMS come back to power?' Mamma Mollykutty believed they had been taken in the rapture. All of them. Even the servant who was not a Christian. The servant who prayed to gods made of mud and stone. She never thought she would be the one left behind. It would have made more sense if Tharakan or Georgekutty were the ones left out in the cold. That is when she realized that every time she prayed, she had never included her own name on the list and thus was left behind. Disappointed by the Lord's unfair decision, she began to cry out loud, wondering what would happen to her until Tharakan came running from the gate with the servant by his side. 'You can't be the first one to go like that. Poof, into the air, like smoke. Ketto, it will be me,' she kept saying, to which Tharakan's response was, 'Yes, yes, Ketto, please go. You can go now if you want. I have no problem with it whatsoever, Ketto.'

Eesho tapped Mamma Mollykutty on the shoulder to make her snap out of the thoughts whirling through her head; he was used to her bouts of inattentiveness.

'I have brought back something far better than groceries. A daughter-in-law,' he said as he introduced Kochuthresia. Mamma Mollykutty turned around, picked up the chattukam, and deemed it better to mind the appams on the stove than to speak to her daughter-in-law. Eesho gave Kochuthresia a sidelong wink, which meant that everything would be fine soon.

That day, and for the next few days, Mamma Mollykutty walked around the house brooding, communicating with the newlyweds through veiled expressions that no one could fully comprehend. She deemed it unquestionable that she had been the most important person in his life until the swift turn of events. The extra sambar she had been serving him and the duck eggs she had been hiding under his rice were meaningless expressions of love.

Mamma Mollykutty also thought that her daughter-in-law was unnecessarily educated and unreasonably modern. But what hurt her the most was none of these. It was that her boy had married a woman who was from outside their Malankara Nasrani, Syrian Christian flock, whose history was as old as Christianity. Though, over the years, the flock had scattered into different denominations, they had a shared legacy.

A Syrian Christian Marthoma girl would have been ideal. An Orthodox or Jacobite would have hurt but still wouldn't have killed her because though the Marthomites had parted with the Jacobites for their failure to embrace reformist ideas (like not praying to the saints or venerating their idols), they were part of the same coterie. A Catholic, though, was inconceivable. A lot of them were new converts. And the rest were the people on the other side of the coonan kurishu sathyam, the leaning cross oath: persuadable people who were willing to cast aside stories built over many lifetimes and also arm-twist others to do the same, after they were coaxed into abandoning the Malankara Church by the Portuguese missionaries, whose history with Christianity was far less profound than theirs. But Mamma Mollykutty's people wouldn't give in. On 3 January 1653, the Syrian Christians who didn't want to join the Catholic church made their rebellion palpable. They gathered outside the Mattancherry church in Fort Cochin to make an oath by holding onto the large cross on the compound. But not all the people could reach the cross. So, they tied a long rope to the cross, held onto it, and made an oath to never submit themselves to Catholicism and Portuguese bullying. The cross outside the church bent due to the sheer force of the legion of rebels. But it was a rebellion that they believed was necessary to preserve history. And every time people looked at the cross, it reminded them of their story.

As Mamma Mollykutty let sentimentalism take over, her eyebrows arched forlornly above her eyes. She walked around the house with a hunched frame that shot upright whenever she found an irritant crossing her path. Unfortunately, that irritant was primarily Tharakan. Tharakan was used to his wife's temper, and he mostly ignored her frequent outbursts. He knew it was best if he took a non-aligned stance, mostly because he didn't want to embitter his wife even more. He hung around the coconut plantation, spending more time than required around his coconut trees, marking his attendance in the house only during mealtimes. It was the sensible thing to do in such a situation.

Eesho tried talking to Mamma Mollykutty. 'Ammo, you are a wonderful mother. You just show love in very radical ways. Give my Kochu half a measure of your love. That's all I'm asking.' But Mamma Mollykutty had a way of tuning out the world around her when she wanted to.

Kochuthresia was uncomplaining. She tried to embrace her newfound life with a steadfast smile, happy to have a family around her, though the matriarch hadn't spoken a single word to her since the day she had arrived in the house. She had tried engaging in conversations with her mother-in-law, but every one of these attempts had been rebuffed. Until one incident changed everything.

Mamma Mollykutty took a bath at 4 p.m. every day before her late-afternoon tea and snacks. She liked to have a hot bath as she thought cold water weakened her bones. She loved the way hot water warmed her skin, sluicing away the dust of the day, also washing away the worries that she carried around with her. She would rub warm coconut oil into her wrinkly skin and then pour mugs of hot water over herself from a giant aluminium container that the servant would keep in the bathroom. One day, Mamma Mollykutty, oiled up and ready for her bath, discovered that the hot water pot was missing. It was still on the stove, the water boiling away as the servant-in-charge had gone to the bathroom to relieve himself. Putting on her chatta and mundu, while cursing the man vociferously, Mamma Mollykutty decided to bring the water pot to the bathroom herself.

The pot was boiling away on the stove. Bubbles swam to the top and broke at the surface of the water, sending hot little droplets into the air. Had Mamma Mollykutty been paying more attention, perhaps the accident wouldn't have taken place. But she was so busy formulating in her head the roasting she would give the delinquent steward that she overestimated her ability to grip the pot of boiling water and underestimated how hot it was. As her coconut-oiled fingers clutched the pot, the searing heat and her poor grasp worked against her, causing the vessel to slip from her hands. The contents of the aluminium pot came rushing to her feet and she dropped to the ground, grimacing in pain.

Sprawled on the floor, she cursed her father-in-law for building a house so big that no one could hear her cries. 'Even if I am dead and rotting away in a corner, no one will see me. They will know I am dead only when they smell my decaying body.' But Kochuthresia heard her and came rushing in. Her mother-in-law had collapsed on the floor. Her mundu had unravelled and her eyes were red with fear and pain.

Kochuthresia helped her up, took her to bed, and brought a bucket of cold water for her to dip her feet in. She also found a tub of chicken fat in the kitchen. 'The chicken fat will heal your skin. The warden in my home once put it on me when I burnt my fingers as I tried to light a candle. I know this is much worse than a candle burn. But you will be all right. Nature has a wonderful way of healing wounds,' Kochuthresia said, gently rubbing the greasy chicken fat on Mamma Mollykutty's bruised red skin. Mamma Mollykutty was overcome with remorse. A loud cry escaped her as Kochuthresia sat on the floor, tending to her. Kochuthresia hugged her and Mamma Mollykutty's cries swelled with intensity. And there they found reconciliation.

Soon Mamma Mollykutty began to act like Kochuthresia's own mother, uttering things only mammies would say: 'Eat, my child', 'Go to sleep now', 'Why are you doing all the work?', and so on. 'Well, they look good together. Like Sheela and Nazeer,' Mamma Mollykutty began to tell everyone. 'My daughter-in-law is adept at everything. She will take care of me when I am old and can't walk any more. She will be at my bedside and not let me rot in the corner of this big house that my father-in-law built.'

chapter 5

EVERY EVENING, FOR AS LONG as Eesho could remember, Philipose Achen, the now-retired Marthoma priest, would deposit the big black umbrella that he hung on the back of his white robe in a corner of the veranda, wash his pink face and dusty feet under the tap outside, and walk into the house, leaving dark red footprints on the red oxide floor. He would stroll on the veranda for a while if Mamma Mollykutty was not around, make his way to the dining table, produce a cough from the pit of his stomach, and drag the chair noisily back to announce his presence.

'Acho...tea, coffee, or milk today?' Mamma Mollykutty would call from the kitchen, either after spotting wet footprints or hearing the announcement from the dining room.

One day, Eesho noticed that Philipose Achen's flushed pink face was a tinge rosier than usual, and his voice was rather more penetrating. He didn't cough or drag the chair. He lifted the chair from under the dining table, positioned it at an angle from where he could see the kitchen door, and sat down.

'Sit, sit,' he told Eesho, patting another chair he pulled out for him.

'I come bearing news.' He told Eesho about a job in a rubber estate and the prospect of a four-figure salary that could be his if he wanted. 'You have the experience. You will make a fitting superintendent. How long can you stay here and count coconuts and cashews with your father? It is all yours anyway. And you can come back to it anytime.'

Philipose Achen paused and waited for the information to sink in with one eye on the kitchen door.

Eesho decided to put Philipose Achen out of his misery. 'She is still taking a bath.'

Philipose Achen exhaled and sat back in his chair. 'I know she won't be happy to let you go. In fact, she will be mad at me for even telling you about this.'

'I left when I had to go to the boarding school. And for plantation classes. And for the job in the hills.'

'Yes. And I remember her crying every day. But now she is glad to have you back, as she thinks you will take over the reins of the house. I am afraid I will spoil her spirit.'

Mamma Mollykutty's most recent spell of crying had to do with Georgekutty's departure a few years ago. The last time people saw Georgekutty was when he left the local toddy shop late one night. He said he was going 'north' where he would be treated with more respect for choosing a lifestyle that didn't require roots but wings. No one knew what that meant or what 'north' meant. Whether it was the north of India or the north of Kerala, nobody knew. Mamma Mollykutty cried unremittingly after his departure, knowing well that she would have cried more if it had been Eesho. She secretly thanked God that her preferred son was still with her. When Philipose Achen told her that the Marthoma church in Nagercoil had told him about a Georgekutty who had landed from Kerala in a drunken trance, Mamma Mollykutty laughed and wiped away her tears. 'My idiot son doesn't know the difference between north and south.' The good souls of Nagercoil, to her relief, found Georgekutty a room near the parsonage.

Philipose Achen took out his flat brush and ran it through his copious whiskers, white and windblown like that of Rip Van Winkle's. Besides his prominent belly, it was this feature that most defined his physical appearance. He had started growing his beard when he was a young Achen with the hopes of becoming a thirumeni, a bishop. For that, he had to grow a beard and stay a bachelor, though he didn't want to. But he liked the idea of donning the ecclesiastical robe and headdress spun from khadi on the charkha and a big plump cross around his neck that he would bless the believers with. He pictured the flock listening to him as he delivered fiery sermons, liberating messages, and Gandhian-style independence speeches on the white sand-bed of the Pampa River at the Maramon convention. People would do a little bow before him and talk to him with the reverence people reserved for those who were pious and powerful.

Philipose Achen knew his history well. And his history was both pious and powerful. It was sometime between the ninth and the twelfth centuries that a Bible sailed across the ocean, somewhere from Tur Abdin in Turkey, landed on the shores of Travancore, and came into the possession of the Syrian Christians. Over the years, the Aramaic-Syriac Peshitta Bible and its precise reproductions were used by all the churches of the Malankara Christians. In 1498, Vasco Da Gama and the Portuguese brought with them Roman Catholicism, a plenitude of Bibles, and the perils of forced conversions. But their version of the Bible differed from the Syriac one. The Catholic missionaries were bent on converting the Syrian Christians; they wanted to distance them from the Patriarch of the East, to whom they owed their loyalties, and bring them under the Pope. The Portuguese and the Syrian Christians tussled with differences of opinion, and in 1599, Aleixo de Menezes, the Archbishop of Goa, convened a synod in Udayamperoor to address what he claimed were inaccuracies in the Peshitta Bible. He urged (through dull blandishments and severe shows of strength) the leaders of the Malankara churches to bring with them their Bibles and all their liturgical texts. But instead of correcting them, he piled them up and set fire to the pile right before their eyes. Even though all the documents relating to the history of Syrian Christians were turned to ashes in a matter of minutes, one Peshitta Bible survived. The call to the synod had not reached a tiny church tucked away in the isolated hills of North Malabar. The leaders decided to protect the last remnant of their history. They locked away the little Bible in a place that only a handful of men had access to, until the British missionary, Claude Buchanan, came along and urged Mar Dionysius, the head of the Malankara church, to get the book translated into Malayalam so that everyone could have access to the text. And thus was roped in for the purpose of a historic translation Kayamkulam Philipose Ramban, Philipose Achen's forefather (believed to be his great-great-great granduncle). Philipose Achen was proud of his history, and he knew he, too, was to carry forward the flame his forefathers had lit.

Unfortunately, he was not considered pious enough by the people in power and he never became a thirumeni. But now he knew it was too late to shave off his beard or to marry. He thought both would take away much from the character that he had now been able to acquire. The beard grew along his chin like an impenetrable weaver bird's nest, and it eclipsed the protuberant belly he had developed mainly by indulging in Mamma Mollykutty's snacks. Kids would try to play with it every time he bowed his head, sticking little paper bits in it and giggling as they tried to fish them out of the thicket, burying them deeper in their quest, as he prayed, eyes closed, prolonged prayers that put one and all to sleep.

Although the thought of marrying did cross his mind from time to time, he knew that the only women who would be interested in him would be ageing widows, a prospect that stirred little joy in his heart. Or there were ones with 'slim' psychological disquiets that no one wanted to marry. But Philipose Achen wasn't sure whether it was a commitment he wanted to enter for the rest of his life. So, after retirement, he chose to stay alone in a one-bedroom house from where he got an even better view of the church and the cemetery than from the parsonage he had once stayed in.

Philipose Achen looked at Eesho enquiringly.

'You will like it there. It is an interesting place. I have already told them about you.'

'Let me think about it. First, I have to talk to Kochu.'

'Kochuthresia will agree. She is a good woman.'

'That she is. But I did not say I agreed.'

Philipose Achen looked fearful for a moment. He sank into his chair and let out a nervous laugh. Eesho wondered if he was getting a commission on this deal.

The last time a deal fell through was when Philipose Achen had walked in holding his neighbour's puppy neatly tucked under his armpit like a Bible.

Mamma Mollykutty thought it was a Bible at first, but when it started moving, she screamed, 'Get behind me, Satan!' Philipose Achen believed she was addressing him and took a step back obediently, loosening his grip on the puppy under his arm. Duke jumped free and leapt into Eesho's arms. Later, when Eesho told Philipose Achen that he wanted to buy the puppy, he was delighted. They walked over to the house of the neighbour to whom the puppy belonged. All the way there, Philipose Achen talked about how expensive Alsatian crossbreeds were, but he was crestfallen when the family said that they wanted to give the puppy away for free. 'It's good to see the people of the parish engaged in charity,' said Philipose Achen, making light of the way the situation had developed.

'I know what you are thinking,' said Philipose Achen, jiggling his head at Duke, who was now curled up near Eesho's chair. He brushed his beard, fished a ball of fine white hair from his comb, and threw it out of the window. 'That I might be getting a commission here. But I am an Achen, you see. We don't attach ourselves to the world.'

Eesho bit his tongue. 'Of course. I promise I will let you know about the job.'

'It's a four-figure salary. I would do it if I were qualified enough. But I am not the one who went for rubber technology and plantation classes. It is worth facing Mollykutty's wrath,' he said, before gently slinking away through the side door, thus escaping Mamma Mollykutty's wrath himself.

A week before Eesho and Kochuthresia's departure, Mamma Mollykutty became a force in the kitchen. It disquieted Eesho when she was effervescent the whole week, rather like she was around Christmas or Easter, pickling and potting things with a band of adroit minions she had summoned from the neighbourhood. Eesho questioned if she had registered the fact of their imminent departure, because she did not tell him not to leave or fog him with soft-boiled egg, rice, and sambar recountals. Her penchant for Duke's affection also peaked. She let him waltz through the kitchen, fed him fried beef and coconut scraps from the counter, talked to him like she would talk to a baby, and called him a 'naughty boy' ever so often.

Her affection for Duke was unusual because ever since a stray bit her in her childhood, Mamma Mollykutty had been wary of dogs. She wasn't sure of their purpose in life. More precisely, their purpose in a human's life. Cows gave milk. Hens gave eggs. Goats and turkeys were good. So were ducks and geese. Dogs were needless beings, in her opinion. If it was about guarding the house, a turkey was befitting. 'It can peck your eyes out if it doesn't like you. Its pecks can be worse than dog-bites. Once, in my younger years, I was chased by a turkey. I ran around the house for so long that I didn't even realize the turkey was no longer behind me,' she had told Eesho when he decided to keep Duke.

But Mamma Mollykutty had grown fond of Duke. She teased him and told him that he was becoming fat because he was always eating everything that people, including strangers, fed him. 'A little stupid, but a blithe spirit. So pure,' Mamma Mollykutty told everyone. Still, making a kennel out of her kitchen was something she wouldn't do.

'Ammo, you do realize that Kochuthresia and I are not going on a picnic, right?' Eesho asked her the day before they left.

Mamma Mollykutty didn't take her eyes off the green mango she was slicing into immaculate rectangles, neatly piling them on the aluminium lid resting on her lap. Her knife feigned busyness in its tempo, but her voice was flat.

'Are you questioning your mother's understanding?'

Eesho squatted next to her on the kitchen floor and Duke jumped at the occasional mango flake that found its way into the air.

'No. I was wondering why you are so happy.'

'Who said I am happy?'

'You look happy.'

'That is how I always am. You have just seen so much of me that expressions no longer register.' Mamma Mollykutty tutted and hacked the mango with renewed energy. Eesho grinned at the old Mamma Mollykutty, who was beginning to rise again.

'I thought you would tell your favourite son not to go.'

Mamma Mollykutty stopped her hacking. She rested her knife on her mundu and looked at Eesho. A smile surfaced on her face. 'I would have told you not to go. But now I will not. You know why? Because Kochuthresia will be with you. She is a good woman. She will take care of you even after I die.'

Before they left, Mamma Mollykutty hung around the Hillman

with her adroit minions, laid newspapers in the back seat, arranged into tight rows, the tubs and crocks with the things she said would not be available in the hills, shook them a few times to check for spillage or breakage, and gave her approval. She did not cry, but Eesho knew that through the pickles, squashes, and jams, she was saying goodbye.

'Mone, when will I see you next?' she asked. Tharakan stood next to her and nodded, a gesture signifying that it was a shared query.

'Soon. I will write. And Calicut is not America, Ammo.'

'It is not Calicut. It is a place in the middle of nowhere,' Mamma Mollykutty said.

Then she looked at Kochuthresia, hoping that the middle of nowhere would be worthy enough for her favourite son and newfound daughter.

Duke nuzzled his snout against Mamma Mollykutty's toes, hopped into the backseat, and found a place among the pickles and squashes. 'Naughty boy,' she said, her voice tremulant like a song in the wind.

He saw her wiping her eyes on Tharakan's jubba as they drove away. Kochuthresia stuck out her hand and waved at them and Duke stood on the back seat and watched them till they disappeared into the distance.

chapter 6

NOT MANY WOULD HAVE SIGHTED Ousepachan sitting in the far crook of the sit-out, present, yet not present. He sat still, stretched out on a planter's chair, his meaty legs securely placed on its wooden leg-rests. His thick glasses were pushed all the way into his eyeballs but kept slipping down his nose. He kept pushing them back languorously, clearly in no haste to read the newspaper open before him. Had it not been for his wife who sat perched on the leg-rest, half tush in, half tush out, no one would have discovered his existence in the house that looked too handsome for him.

Mary greeted them with a 'How do you do?' when Eesho and Kochuthresia walked in. Eesho wondered if it was a ruse, possibly a test of his English that he had to pass before the woman who reminded him of the headmistress of an Anglo-Indian school.

'How do you do?' Eesho responded.

Mary was pleased. It was a test. And he had passed it. She smiled at Kochuthresia for she had landed herself a gentleman with a fine taste in life, unlike her, whose powdered nose and painted lips were wasted on her husband. Mary's father had gotten her married to him because he was a good man, a man he could also manipulate. Ousepachan was unlike the lads at the Calicut Club who drank, smoked, and wooed women. Her father himself did that when he was young. His philandering ways were quite legendary among both the Indian and the English women who, along with their fathers, visited the club occasionally on weekends and for the yearly planter's ball. But he wanted a good man for his only child, the heir to the estate he had bought from the blind nephew of the Englishman who had built it. People believed that Mary's father had tricked the blind man into selling him the land that he had inherited from his uncle by promising him the hand of his only daughter. But once he signed the sale deed, Mary's father forgot all about their deal. He gave the place a new name—Eastman Estate—convincing everyone that he believed it was time for the man from the East to shine. Though, in reality, it was because of his love for the movies and its latest creation, Eastmancolor. He then got Mary married to someone he could duly command. But fortuitously for Ousepachan, he didn't live long enough to do that.

Ousepachan looked like any other man from Calicut. He lived in his kaili and vest and oiled his hair with more oil than required. He seldom moved. After the partial stroke he had suffered a few years earlier, he moved even less, except for the sporadic patting of his overfed belly like he was playing with a puppy. Mary was nearly the opposite of her husband. She looked strangely English, with her mid-length rococo dress, red lips, and snipped-to-the-ear hair she dyed a deep ginger. Though she did not have any Anglo-Indian blood in her, besides looking like one, she mixed English and Malayalam in equal measure in her speech, gently killing both languages at the same time. She offered Eesho and Kochuthresia camomile tea with honey, and butter biscuits from a large tin imported from England that she held in both hands, and waited for an occasion to drop the words 'whoops-a-daisy' even when they were not required.

'Whoops-a-daisy. Such a long drive it is to the house on the hill. We could have lived there ourselves. Pakshe praayam aayi, getting old so fast,' she said, looking at her husband.

'Yes, yes,' Ousepachan agreed. 'I was just in my thirties when I took over the working of the estate. Just about your age, I presume,' he told Eesho. 'It feels like a lifetime ago. I can't go there every week and do the same things I used to do. The superintendent before you used to come here with the reports every now and then.'

'Madiyan, lazy fellow he was,' pointed out Mary from the leg-rest.

'Yes. Lazy fellow he was,' Ousepachan echoed.

Eesho smiled uneasily at the man, who was now the person to whom he would be reporting.

Ousepachan sensed Eesho's discomfort and decided to change the topic. 'I was happy when I heard about you from Philipose Achen. He visits us often. Though he is not Catholic, we are closer to him than any of the priests from our parish. I think it's time to let go of our differences in history and liturgy, you see.'

'Kothiyan, greedy fellow he is,' said Mary from her perch on the leg-rest.

Ousepachan shifted painfully in his chair. 'I don't think it was greed. I think he was just poor.'

'It was both. But mostly greed. He would appear every day just in time for lunch. He would come again in the evenings and ask for paalum vellam, milk-water, instead of tea. Have you ever heard of milk-water? Of course, I would give him milk and not milk-water. Money and milk-water. Whoops-a-daisy, that's what he liked.'

Gathering that the banter was taking an unpleasant route, Ousepachan tried to steer the conversation to safer subjects instead. 'I was once like you. Strong. Tall. Fit as a fiddle,' he said, his fingertip sketching an imaginary line in the air over Eesho's frame.

'Before he shrank. Vertically,' Mary quipped from the leg-rest.

Ousepachan patted his belly and laughed at the joke directed at him. 'But now my bones creak when I move. I'm hoping that my son can take over the estate one day. He still needs to polish his people skills though,' he said, his voice dropping to a whisper. Eesho looked around for any sign of the son, but he was nowhere in sight.

Mary was uncomfortable on the leg-rest. She didn't believe her son needed polishing of any sort. She pulled her red lips together, tucked a disobedient strand of ginger hair behind her ear, and rolled her eyes in the direction of the greenhouse where she would frequently corner visitors to give them a running commentary about the life of orchids. Her eyes rested on a movement she caught in the backseat of the Hillman parked near the greenhouse.

'You have a dog. What's its name?'

'Duke.'

'Very royal. I went to London once with my father. I was only twelve then. It was the most exciting time of my life. England is a very beautiful country. No wonder the British left India.'

'That is where she gets her style from,' said Ousepachan with a wink.

Mary turned her head sharply. Her eyes bored into her husband, who squirmed in discomfiture. Since changing the subject was second nature to Ousepachan, he looked around for a diversion and his gaze rested on the planter's chair he was sitting on. 'Do you know that someone once told me that this is actually called the Bombay Fornicator? This is the only piece of furniture that I brought from the white man's house. I couldn't leave it alone,' he said, proudly drumming one of its sturdy wooden leg-rests. 'Its once-innovative design with the extendable leg-rests seemed ideal for facilitating sexual intercourse.'

Mary shot up from the leg-rest and glowered at her husband, who appeared ready to swallow his words. He dissolved into his Fornicator like a guttering candle. 'Now I only use it for sleeping.' His meek clarification only added to the ungainliness of the situation.

Mary stalked into the house to escape the gaucherie her husband was responsible for. From the looks of it, it seemed like a habitual affair.

Ousepachan had now become as red and shiny as Mary's lipstick. He absently tapped the leg-rests of his beloved Fornicator, raked his fingers through the furrows of his lungi, produced a key from somewhere within, and held it out to Eesho. 'It is a beautiful house. You will like living there. I could have lived there myself,' he said, his voice pining for the unattainable.

Eesho beheld the bronze key, tarnished with age and warm with the heat of Ousepachan's corpulent self. Eesho tried not to picture where Ousepachan had hidden it.

'Just like my body,' said Ousepachan. 'My mind is becoming just like my body. Ancient. My body is not listening to me any more. I am becoming old. That is why I need someone like you. The house is old too. Almost fifty years. But it is still good. The Englishman was happy there.'

'Why did he sell it then?' asked Eesho, uninformed of the history.

'Oh, that. You see, he decided not to go back,' said Ousepachan, his eyes breaking away from Eesho's gaze.

'Someone decided that for him, whoops-a-daisy,' pitched in Mary from somewhere within the house, her voice still recovering from the embarrassment her husband had put her through.

'Nobody knows that for sure. Stories will always be stories,' Ousepachan clarified, not really clarifying anything. 'But there is nothing the house cannot give you.'

chapter 7

EASTMAN ESTATE—THE HEADLIGHTS CAUGHT THE words, scored into the side of the gate, as Eesho brought the Hillman to a stop down the hill. Eesho pushed the tall iron gate, and it swung open, birthing rusty notes that spliced sharply through the air, filled with the lulling sounds of the night. The house stood at the top of the hill, obscured by weeping willows. When they got out of the car, Eesho took the bronze key and held it in his hand. It was warm though it was a cold night. The heat from Ousepachan's skin still clung to it, but this time, it felt like a welcoming touch. Eesho and Kochuthresia opened the door of their new abode and walked in hand-in-hand. By morning, they had made it home.

On the morning of the first day, Eesho walked out of the house and looked around. And he was pleased. Given the elevation, he had a clear view of the valley. The red road to the left dipped towards town and to the right, weaved into the heart of the hills, unfolding before him with promises. The garden was a rush of colour and flamboyance. Bougainvillea spilled their vivid hues. Weaver birds hung their nests in unassuming nooks. The scent of roses and jasmine was thick in the air. The stone benches that dotted the grounds, though old, still looked resilient. The air was nippy, unlike the flatlands. Eesho liked the small things that he could do here, like throwing a cardigan around his shoulders in the morning and taking a stroll through the frosty air, his new gum boots crunching on gravel. He loved how the deerstalker kept his head warm.

The deerstalker was Kochuthresia's gift to him—the first gift she had given him. She had unwrapped it from the folds of her sari and pressed it onto his head as they sat on the beach in Trivandrum and watched the sun sink into the blue-green sea. On the fevered sands far away, she had been prophesying about the mountains, their home in the heart of the hills, where the cold would numb the tip of her nose and the nocturnal symphony of a thousand crickets would fill the night.

Eesho unknotted the deerstalker and let the flaps down to his ears. He lit his pipe and walked to the back of the house, which became one with the hill. Dark green ferns coiled around the land like a brood of snakes. They sprouted through everything—the cracks of the rocks, the sodden bark of trees, and around the bottle-green Willys Jeep left in a shed for estate use. In Ousepachan's observation, the Jeep was ideal for Puthuloor's punishing terrains (and also because President Eisenhower called it 'one of the three decisive weapons' the US had during WWII). He said he bought it in 1960 after he saw an advertisement in the *Times of India* when he visited Bombay, announcing that the price had dropped by 200 rupees. 'You see, it was a bargain. I got it for 12,421 rupees. And I got someone to drive it all the way from the showroom in Bombay. But so worth it, you see.'

There was a hut on the periphery of the grounds. It stood at the back of the house adjoining a brook that gurgled its way through the creamy loam. Eesho wasn't sure if the hut was abandoned. The thatched roof had crumpled in, and bright green moss enveloped the walls. The closed door and a small window offered little insight into its occupancy.

Then, the door creaked open, and a figure emerged. A green watchman's shirt hung floppily over his orange lungi. He yawned, whipped out his shrivelled penis, and peed into the brook as though he were carrying out an unremarkable morning routine. The dark yellow streak melded into the milky stream that had been pretty as a picture until then. Midway through the act, the man caught sight of Eesho. He abruptly stopped peeing. He lowered his lungi and walked over the ferns with a limp that left uneven footprints on the earth.

'Saar, this water doesn't come to the house. There is a well in the back,' he said by way of introduction. His name was Pappan, and he lived in the hut with his mother. He was the watcher of the estate.

Pappan was quick on his feet despite the lopsided gait. Still, agility was not what was required of him, as he was not a tapper, tap-tapping away at trees; he, along with the other watchers, only had to watch over the men and women who did those things, make sure no one stole the rubber from the shed, and no wild boar trampled down the replanted crops.

'I didn't know you would wake up this early, saar. I didn't want to ring the bell and disturb you,' he said as they walked back to the house.

'Isn't tapping an early morning business? I didn't want to miss the most important part of the day. I will go get ready. We can go to the office together. Do you think the Jeep has diesel?'

'I don't know, saar. It has been a few months since that Jeep was last used. The previous manager left in a hurry. But there is a can of diesel in the shed. I will fill up the tank.'

'What was the hurry?'

'What, saar?'

'Why did the previous manager leave in a hurry?'

'Ghost, saar.'

'What?' Eesho asked, wondering if he had heard him right.

That is when he noticed the graves. Two of them, lichen-covered, camouflaged, sinking into the earth with only the headstones discernible through the burst of ferns that grew around them. Eesho bent down and pulled away the weeds to discover the words that were carved out on them.

Charles Hitchcock   *Daisy Hitchcock*
1892–1921   *1897–1921*

The Englishman and his wife. They were still young when they died. 'Someone decided it for them.' He heard Mary's voice rumbling through the kitchen.

'I thought you knew about the murder,' Pappan said, stressing the word 'murder' more than required.

'What murder?' Eesho asked him.

'They were killed here. In their own house. It was during the Mopilla rebellion. A tapper stabbed the sayippe and madama in their sleep. He then committed suicide. The sayippe and madama bled to death in their own bed. Imagine! No one knew about it until the servant went to serve them tea in the morning. What she saw was a river of blood and two bodies that were whiter than their already white skin.' Pappan shook his head and clicked his tongue.

'But saar, he is still here,' Pappan hissed and looked around.
'Who is?'

'The sayippe. I have heard him many times, saar. He wears thick boots and smokes cigars. In the night, he walks around the house sometimes, his boots clacking, and smoking foreign cigars.'

'How do you know they are foreign cigars?'

Pappan scratched his head for a moment before he spoke. 'Foreign ghost, foreign cigars only, no? People say his spirit still protects the house. The previous manager ran away because he saw the spirit. But I am not scared. Because I do nothing wrong, no spirit will want to harm me. I just have to accept that this is part of life now.' His eyes gleamed with expectancy, satisfied with having presented the story well.

The graves were grey, moist, and cold, covered with weeds and shrubs, their only visitors now appearing to be beetles and daddy longlegs. He wished Ousepachan had told him the story of the land because he would have been better prepared for that moment. Eesho didn't believe in phantoms and phantasms. He didn't like the idea of them either.

'I would like you to stop now. Do not tell any of this to my wife. I don't want her to worry. Get the Jeep ready. We will go to the office in some time,' he told Pappan, and walked back to the house.

When Eesho got home, Kochuthresia was at the dining table. 'It's only bread, jam, and eggs today. We should go to Calicut to do some shopping. Your mother was right. There are no real shops here. But strangely, I like that,' she said, pulling out a chair for Eesho.

He grabbed a slice of toast off the plate and made his way out of the dining room. He knew that this would surprise her. He hadn't responded to her. Also, they always ate together; even when relatives came calling and old men sat at the table, finished the food, and left scraps on their plates for their wives, as was the custom, Eesho and Kochuthresia would sit together and eat. 'They are modern people,' Tharakan would say, smiling and nodding to justify their actions to ancient relatives who sat around the table, saucer-eyed at the behaviour of the young people.

Eesho made his way to the bedroom. The young Englishman and

his wife were everywhere, staring at him in sepia, eyes twinkling at him like young people in love. They looked happy together. Much like them.

The bed horrified him, as the watcher's tale had hit him hard. He threw the piece of toast out of the window and plucked the floral sheet off the mattress, fearing he would uncover stubborn stains from the past. But it was clean; yet, it was deceptive, a goodly apple rotten at the heart. A mosquito net showered from the top and gleamed like a halo in the morning sunlight, making an imposing statement like the rest of the knick-knacks in the house. The bronze key. The looming windows. The weeping willows.

Eesho headed to the bathroom and climbed into the bathtub. He didn't want to sit on the bed. Let alone sleep in it. The bathtub comforted him in a strange way. Its hard shell pressed into his skin and blood rushed through his veins. He sank to the bottom of the empty tub.

Kochuthresia walked in. She climbed into the bathtub with him. He held her hands and told her everything—the Englishman and his wife, their graves, their bed.

'You are stronger than me,' he said.

'But you are stronger than you think you are,' she said, running her fingers along his cheeks.

In Kochuthresia's arms, Eesho was happy. He was wrapped in love like he never imagined he would be. He sank into her arms and wondered what his life would be without her.

'You are the light of my life,' he told her as she held him.

Kochuthresia's chest rose with rapture. Then she chuckled. 'But you smell.'

Eesho laughed and Kochuthresia stroked his laugh lines.

'You want me to be just like my mother who washes away worry with a hot bath?'

'Yes, why not? But are you going to take a bath in this?' she asked, tapping the shiny bathtub.

'I don't think I will ever use one. Imagine the headache of having to take a bath in it. It is a waste of time. Unless you use it for sleeping.'

PART III

chapter 8

ALEYAMMA TAKES HER BEDDING TO the bathroom and throws it into the white-china bathtub, hoping that the plunge-bath would help her sleep. She climbs in, pulls the duvet tightly to her cold chest, and sinks to the bottom of the bathtub.

The Russian party arrived as Elsy Chedatty had told her. They occupied three of the bedrooms in the house, and the incessant palaver of those in the bedroom next to hers kept her awake all night. She tossed and turned in the resplendent four-poster bed as her neighbours unceasingly talked all through their first night in a tropical country, emptying their backpacks, lathering odouriferous mosquito repellents on their pink skin, and making themselves at home.

It is not the first time she has used the bathtub as her bed. She is used to sleeping in it. When she was a teenager, she used to lock herself in the bathroom because Amma's friend had broken the lock on her bedroom door. 'Oh, I will fix it later,' he kept telling Amma. Amma introduced him to people as her 'friend'. It was out of the ordinary. None of her friends' mothers from school had men who were friends. But he was too old to be a 'boy' friend, either. Also, boyfriends were still too uncommon a thing, even in a city like Cochin. The only people who she knew had boyfriends were the white people from the serials on satellite TV, who drank milk from cartons, kept their books in lockers at school, and ate corn dogs and popcorn at baseball games and pepperoni pizza for dinner. She also knew that Nancy Drew had a boyfriend, whom the girls in her class would speak about bashfully. 'Ned Nickerson,' they would say, tittering coyly under their breath when they huddled in the corner of the library, gossiping.

Though the word boyfriend was akin and ungraspable, she knew that he was Amma's boyfriend, although Amma never admitted to that. She knew that they went for long drives and frequented the newest ice cream parlour that had opened on Marine Drive where boyfriends and girlfriends hung out and shared frosty colourful treats in the dimly lit interiors. These were usually portrayed in Malayalam movies as places where Satan-worshipping drug dealers (like the ones from *Johnny Walker* who wore crosses on their ears) worked under a convenient canopy of darkness, spiking the ice creams of gullible customers with drugs. 'Ice cream parlours are evil. Boys are misleading girls from good Christian families to indulge in bad bad things there…. American culture it is….' often whispered the Sevika Sangam ladies from church.

When they didn't go to evil places, Amma's boyfriend would come home and hang out at their house till dinner time, and every so often, stay through the night, watching movies, drinking tea, and playing Ludo or Scrabble.

The first time she saw him was when he came home on a Sunday afternoon to have tea with them. He sat on Appa's armchair and smiled, his lips twisting into a wily grin, flashing his exceedingly misaligned teeth, which grew in all directions like the wild grass of Niranam. The result was a simper. A simper that gave him the appearance of a sly politician or a deviant innkeeper from the old movies—the ones that would goggle at women and strip them bare in their seedy heads. Appa was better-looking than him. She didn't know what Amma saw in him. But then again, Appa was the one who had left. Though Appa's replacement was a lot less fetching, he had kindled something in Amma, something that she had been looking for with Appa for a long time and obviously didn't find.

Amma's boyfriend smiled at the TV and watched the stories of *Shaktimaan* along with Aleyamma, relentlessly translating the dialogue from Hindi to Malayalam, ostensibly proud of his command over the northern language. They were not the right translations. Amma brought a tray with tea and snacks and smiled at the commentary with satisfaction. Amma's Hindi was as poor as her judgement. After a while, his eyes strayed to the sitting room shelf as he sipped on his tea. 'What is that?' he asked, pointing at a jar on the shelf.

'It's a jar,' said Amma.

'What is inside it?'

'A bladder stone.'

His eyes filled his face. 'Whose stone is that?'

'My husband's.'

Apart from the old beaten Ambassador, the solitary remnant of Appa was the stone born from his hurting bladder, after he was operated on for what he first assumed was gas. The stone was as big as a table tennis ball and Appa kept it in a glass container that he had fished out from Amma's spice rack. He had sniffed the empty containers to check if they were good enough for his bladder stone and lowered his stone into one that he found satisfactory. Clink! It fell into the container like a gigantic cherry pit. He kept the container on the centre shelf of the sitting room display case for everyone to see, along with the other knick-knacks they had collected over time.

Once he looked at it elatedly and said that it was incogitable that something so big had come from his body.

'Really? Something even bigger came out of my body,' said Amma, looking at Aleyamma.

But Appa said it could be used as a weapon if someone attacked them.

'Maybe I should buy a sling for it. A sling and a stone to slay a giant,' Appa sang facetiously.

'A weapon? Seriously?' Amma laughed. She wrinkled her nose and pulled a nauseated face. 'I don't think I will touch that unhygienic thing even if a robber tries to slit my throat.'

But the bladder stone gave Appa a new sense of well-being and belief in himself. Even after Appa left, the stone remained on the shelf. It didn't add much to the cupboard in terms of embellishment, but since Amma didn't want to touch it, it stayed there, in the glass container, leisurely picking up the dust of Cochin. Flakes thrown up by the highway trucks accumulated in its pores and soon it turned another colour. A colour that couldn't be named, like the colour of the cream buns that came fresh out of the oven from Varkeys Bakery. Was it brown? Cream? Golden perhaps? But it stood there undisturbed. Like an ugly alien egg waiting to hatch.

Amma's boyfriend didn't make a fuss about the bladder stone.

And Amma's attachment to the little rock that came from her husband's innards didn't stop his visits. Once he took Aleyamma to the ice cream parlour after school, where he ordered cassata for them without looking at the menu. He smiled a slick smile of satisfaction when the waiter reappeared with two tall glasses of rainbow-tinted ice creams cut into perfect semi-circles topped with tiny beads of jelly-like fruits. She stared at her glass with apprehension and let her ice cream melt into a pool of indecipherable hue.

'You are not going to eat it?' he asked her, scowling.

'What if they've put drugs in it?' She poked her melting ice cream with her cold metal spoon.

He jerked his head back in surprise, looked down at his own ice cream, and then clapped his palm over his mouth like he was feigning fright for the amusement of a toddler.

'Then we have to come back here.' He laughed loudly at his joke, his shoulders shaking uncontrollably, as if caught in a seizure.

At home, sometimes, he would cook, and Amma would be grateful. Sometimes he would drive Aleyamma to the dentist and the bookshops. Sometimes they would take a ferry and have a picnic in Bolgatty. They would sit on Ammachi's embroidered sheets and eat cucumber sandwiches and beef samosas. He would wipe his soiled hands on the sheets instead of washing them under the tap next to the toilets, leaving behind indelible prints which mysteriously didn't rouse Amma's ire. Sometimes they would go to the children's park and the toy museum.

He would walk around the house like it were his own, in a vest and lungi, sit on Appa's armchair, eat arrowroot biscuits and achappams from the tins in the kitchen, get groceries, water the plants, and collect the electricity bill. He knew how Amma liked her tea and coffee, where old receipts were kept, and how new memories were to be made.

But he never fixed the door. In fact, he was the one who broke it.

One day, while Aleyamma was in her room sleeping, she dreamt he had squeezed her nipples. When she woke up, she realized that her dislike for him had finally manifested in a dream that felt intensely real. So real and repulsing that she could still feel his clammy fingers on her newly acquired breasts. She had the same dream again. So, she locked the door when she went to sleep. The dreams stopped.

But one day, the latch on her bedroom door was gone. The four screws had been taken out, leaving no trace of the latch that once shielded her nights. She combed through the floor, half-believing that it might have fallen, but it was nowhere to be found. That night, she went to sleep with an unlocked door. The dreams started again.

So, she started sleeping in the bathroom. In the bathtub. The lock on the bathroom door was somehow undefeatable. She had hated her bathroom until then. It was always wet, always cold. Slugs lined the walls in an attempt to go nowhere. They were strange creatures. They were not like the snails with their mighty shells. Slugs made their appearance through the sinkhole, especially on rainy nights. They would gradually scale the walls, undecided about their final destination. Some would creep up to her. They would sit together in the bathtub till sunrise, going nowhere, finding shelter in the dark, damp bathroom from the tempest outside.

She would put on her headphones and drown out the world as she listened to the Backstreet Boys and Westlife on her Walkman. With her head resting against the cold metal tub, she would imagine she were in her room in Niranam, her head burrowed into the soft embroidered pillowcases that Ammachi had made, listening to the lulling murmur of the fan stuck to the wooden roof, falling asleep to the gentle snores from the adjoining bed dropping on her like a warm blanket.

∽

It is raining when Elsy Chedatty comes to her with a cup of tea. The raindrops bounce on the windowpanes with a ferocious energy. The monsoon in Puthuloor is a bewitching sight to behold. Bedsheets smell like the earth. Moisture hangs in the atmosphere like a damp blanket. Steady precipitation fills the air with white noise. Rainwater collects in transparent puddles over pebbles and gravel and elsewhere in red puddles, reminding one of bloodshed and violence. Elsy

Chedatty's woollen scarves emerge like magic, clinging to her as soon as the clouds swell in the sky like a warning. But the rains are also punishing. Land slips from under the unassuming. Deluges wash away houses from the hills and reduce the land to nothing but the red loam it once was. Like in the rest of the state, Mother Nature is punishing humanity for its reprehensible acts of smoothing out forests, destroying the wetlands, and civilizing the wild.

A feeling of horror washes over Elsy Chedatty when she walks into the bathroom and finds Aleyamma in the bathtub. She is reminded of the scenes in the English movies that she sometimes watches with the tourists, where the bathtub is featured as either a place of comfort overflowing with frothy white soap and champagne-filled glasses, or a final resting place, bloody and macabre. She abandons the teacup on the floor, and shakes Aleyamma savagely by the shoulder, and is relieved when she sees what looks like the beginnings of a scowl spread across her sleepy face.

She asks Aleyamma in confusion, 'Did you want to take a bath?'

Aleyamma sits up in the bathtub and rubs her eyes. She has barely slept for a couple of hours. Her temple throbs like the walls of a nightclub and she feels hungover, though she is not.

'I don't usually bathe with my clothes on.' It is a feeble attempt at cracking a joke and she knows she hasn't succeeded because Elsy Chedatty doesn't smile.

'Then why are you here?' she asks her.

Though she knows Elsy Chedatty is talking about the bathroom and, in particular, the bathtub, to her, it seems like a much larger question.

She leans back in the bathtub, takes the teacup from Elsy Chedatty, and blows on the tea to cool it down. The heady smell of the brew soothes her, and she tries to forget the crumbling world she left behind in Chennai. The one she built around Roy. It's hard because even the tea reminds her of him.

She had heard about him even before she met him; all those in her art school knew about Roy because, by thirty-nine, he had established himself as an artist who was to be recognized and admired. 'Senior artist', everyone called him, because even though he was not that old in years, they believed he was seasoned enough to deserve the term reserved for those on a different plane from mere novices. His face often graced the city supplements when journalists sought quotes from celebrities on issues or subjects, even those unrelated to art. 'What is the best ice cream joint in Chennai?' 'What is your opinion about the latest Dhanush film?' 'Capital punishment. Yes or no?' In the world of art, he was the one they always approached, perhaps because he had a face fetching enough to be printed on the front pages of newspaper supplements. He was invited to most of the events in the city—soft launches and not-so-soft launches. His appearances would manifest as tiny photographs speckled in the paper the next day, his pockmarked chin standing out like that of Batman's, a slight exhibitionism evident in his bearing.

When she saw him the first time at an art exhibit, he was standing across the room, a head taller than everyone else. An air of calculated temerity made him appear even taller as he nodded convivially to the people around him. They hissed into his ears their judgements about the art pieces on the wall, out of earshot of the artist who had made them, trying to make an impression on the senior artist with their perspicacious observations.

The photographers thought he looked good—almost like a Bollywood actor—so balancing on their toes, they went about clicking pictures of him.

She took him in the same way she took in the art around her. He didn't see her until later that night, when he, weary from playing dress-up, took a break from the assembly inside and leaned his strapping frame against the wall of the building in the back where the caterers would later wash cocktail glasses and discard the remainders of the coin-sized appetizers.

There was not much light except for a ghostly glow from a naked light bulb stuck on the wall like an afterthought. Roy removed his jacket, threw it on the floor, and decided to break wind. He was in complete command over his bowels as he let out a boisterous but dawdling one, like a slow musical number from a jazz recital, not realizing that she was near him.

After the music ended, she stepped from the shadows and faced him. 'Better out than in, as Banksy believes,' she said.

He turned his head sharply at the sound of her voice. He was different from the lassoed cut-outs. He was real and oddly vulnerable. They surveyed each other in the murky blush of the naked bulb. His eyes ran over her forehead, eyes, cheekbones, and nape. They primly stopped below her shoulder.

Then he smiled. Laugh lines surfaced from the tips of his eyes. She watched them in the golden glow and remembered stories from the past. The ears that wiggled. The faint forms the kuzhiaanas left behind in the silver sand. She watched his face as his smile stretched to his ears. 'Not just Banksy, Shrek also believes it. And good for us, because it only came with the sound this time,' he said.

They giggled together under the naked light bulb like schoolchildren, tiddly with watered-down cocktails, still hungry owing to the coin-sized appetizers, faces close together, shoulders rubbing occasionally, and body odours mingling. They got acquainted over a pack of cigarettes, while inside the air-conditioned hall, the art lovers huddled in coteries and discussed the bleak future of the artist on display. The next day, he asked her out with a simple text message: 'Dinner?' She was not surprised. Other than the flatulence, the pheromones were also powerful. She thought of his face. The comfortingly familiar lines on them. 'Sure,' she texted back.

She had never been in love before. In most of her relationships, she was apathetic. Sometimes even pitying. Once, she stayed with her boyfriend, stretching the relationship to a paper-thin stage because she feared he might do something imprudent. Then, one day, she ended it. He didn't try anything foolish only because he was too afraid of his mother, who, understanding his morbid state of mind, hid everything sharp and long in the house and took matters into her own hands, blackmailing him with threats to end her own life. Another time, she stayed with a man because she felt sorry for the way he ate. He was not poor, but the way he ate gave the impression of a man who was deprived of food for days. He always ate with his shoulders stooped, eyeing the food avidly as he dug his fork into it. It was absurd to pity him, as there was no reason to do so. But in those moments, he looked like a little boy who needed his mother, and she didn't have the heart to leave him. But she walked out on him eventually, in a coffee shop, abandoning her untouched mocha on the table. As she walked away, he melted into his open-faced sandwich and an evanescent sadness floated through her, even though she didn't love him.

Because of these quirks, she drifted in and out of people's lives, never lingering long enough to call any place home. Whenever she made love, she would do everything expected of her. Moan. Groan. Sigh. Call out their names. The men would devour her, caress her, and play with her dreadlocks, though she would hit them sharply across their faces when they tried to kiss her breasts; she hated them being touched. Some would put on their clothes and leave after they'd had sex. Some would think it was a kinky game and try to do it again till she threw their clothes out the window and told them to leave in the dead of the night.

But with Roy, it was different. He held her like he held his paintbrushes—tenderly, like it was the start of a journey, the birth of something magnificent.

'Can you wiggle your ears?' she asked him once after they had made love.

'Why?' His eyebrows arched with surprise.

'I am a fan of Charlie Chaplin,' she said. He laughed, and she watched his ears that gently moved along with his breaths.

She first loved him because he reminded her of home. The laugh lines. The ears that wiggled.

Then she began to love him a little more deeply, day by day, embracing his darkness and his light. His sunrises and sunsets. His blacks, whites, greys, and blues.

The night after he cremated his mother on the banks of Ganga, he came home to her. She held him close as he melted into her body. She could smell ash in his hair and feel the weight of his grief pressing deep into her shoulder blades. She kissed him and told him that she loved him. He wept. And then she loved him wholly.

She loved the laugh lines and the lack of them.

She loved the ears that wiggled and that didn't.

She loved the milk-warm nose that rubbed against hers when they kissed. She loved the smell he left on her skin. The paint that lastingly found its way between his fingernails. The birthmark on his left inner thigh shaped like a Henri Matisse leaf motif. His mouth with the lingering taste of stale cigarettes, beer, and vagina. The tufts of grey sprinkled across his cheeks like an accidental paint splatter. His hair, sleek and glassy, long enough to be tied above his ears like a bread roll. She loved his scars, his wounds, and his slightly receding hairline. The cellulite on his rear. The way he said her name; he got it right unlike most people. *Ale*yamma, the 'Ale' sounding just like the beer. She loved the mundane things they did together. The endless conversations. The sex. The cigarette they shared afterwards like a cliché. She loved waking up with him. She loved making tea for him before heading out to the world outside them. The first time she made him tea, he said she got it right. Strong. With a hint of cardamon. Not too sweet. Not too milky.

Not even his wife got it right.

Aleyamma sits in the bathtub and knows it is all an escape. But all she tells Elsy Chedatty is, 'I was just trying to sleep.'

∽

Aleyamma wants to shake off her lassitude. She abandons the bathtub and readies herself for a morning run. From the top of the hill, she can see the road to the right wind around the slope and fade into the highlands. She sprints down the hill and up the road. The healing dawn air drums against her face and she finds herself smiling. She doesn't miss the sweltering city sky, the putrid smell of the Cooum, or the dust that sticks to her perspiration like mucilage.

She takes in the unsoiled land that rolls past her. Ancient rubber trees plunge down sharp slopes. Crickets chirp under shaded shrubberies, unwilling to cease the songs of the night. Rubber trees stipple the land. Some tapped. Some abandoned. Some ready to be chopped down and substituted with teak or mangium. Black-eyed Susan creeps up red-roofed houses bathed in a deathly still silence. In them, somewhere, are old people living out the last days of their lives, their children making children, money, and careers abroad, after entrusting the mothers and fathers to strangers they fished out of fat directories for home nurses, and their rubber trees with relatives back in the village. The value of old age was piddling and the price of rubber, even less. When Appacha first bought the house, he also wanted to buy a few acres of land with rubber trees next to it. But Velia Pappa talked him out of it as rubber prices were plummeting due to the dearth of tappers, imports, demand, and cartelization by tyre manufacturers.

The road wends its way through the forgotten land and turns uneven. The asphalt is cracked. Her smile fades and she slackens her stride as the broken bits of tar and gravel nip the soles of her feet. But she keeps going.

It is Roy who introduced her to barefoot running. He said it was the only way human beings were meant to run. 'We are barefoot creatures. It is the most natural thing,' he said after he had discovered a book about the Tarahumara runners from the Copper Canyon, who ran barefoot. He also joined a club that ran barefoot, more for socialization and not so much for health, as he always reached for his packet of cigarettes as soon as he got into the car after a run. They got together at Anna Nagar Park, immersed themselves in back-fence talk while they did stationary stretches and then set out for long runs. And because the prospect of spending more time with him seemed good, she, too, joined him. They ran all over Chennai, sometimes unsuccessfully sidestepping the warm early morning cleansings that speckled the sides of the road like molten chocolate, coming back home with blisters, splinters, and shit under their feet. But soon, the act of running soothed her. She ran because it quietened her soul. The mundane steps were a meditation. The breaths, a release. It became her drug. Up until then, only a cigarette could do the trick.

The first time she picked up a cigarette was at Speed, the most popular nightclub in Chennai, where she tagged along with a bunch of people from her college. She had climbed over the fence of the girls' hostel and jumped into the backseat of a car filled with slumping, drunken bodies, who had had cheap liquor from the local TASMAC, as they knew it would pinch their pockets a little less when they ordered their extortionate drinks at the club. In the intoxicating fogginess of the nightclub, she sat with her pint of Kingfisher as her mates danced to Timbaland and Rihanna, their bodies loose and sinuous. Some went to the DJ console to make their requests, which the DJ promptly vetoed with a spirited shake of his head. A boy slipped into the seat next to her, cracked a toothy smile, and smoked like a chimney. He offered her a cigarette, but she rolled her eyes at him. The DJ led people down the lane of nostalgia. When the remixed version of Daniel Boone's 'Beautiful Sunday' wafted through the speakers, the dancers squealed and found his choice acceptable. Their bodies found a new energy. The lights turned red, blue, and green. The walls pulsated like aching veins. *'Sunday morning, up with the lark; I think I'll take a walk in the park; Hey, hey, hey, it's a beautiful day....'* Aleyamma remembered a voice from the past. She plucked out a cigarette from the toothy boy's pack of twenty, and then another, and kept smoking through the night.

The spalls of tar under her feet sting her like whetted blades. She slips and crashes on the road, the side of her face brushing roughly against the crumbly tar. She picks herself up and touches her cheek. It stings and her fingertips are wet and red with blood. It angers her, though she knows it is only a bruise. She questions the feasibility of running without shoes as she makes her way back to the house. Elsy Chedatty is standing on the porch, as though anticipating her arrival, and when she sees her face, she gasps. She rushes to her side and holds out her pallu to clean her cheeks, but Aleyamma takes a step back.

'It's nothing. I will stick some Band-Aids on them,' she tells her and makes her way to the study.

The Band-Aids do the job; however, they gracelessly fleck her face and leave her looking like a patchwork quilt or a porcelain doll stuck together artlessly, much like the broken face of Georgekutty

Appachan when people saw him for the last time.

Georgekutty Appachan, Appacha's younger brother, got the unfortunate nickname 'paampu' or snake, because of the way he swayed after he had a drink or two. 'How can they be brothers?' People often questioned their relationship. 'They are so unlike each other.' Georgekutty Appachan's dipsomaniac life was a much-discussed topic in the family. Whenever he visited Niranam after his boozed-up tourneys across the country, squandering money on women, weed, and whisky, some people would give him cash when he turned up asking for a loan because he was the much-respected Puthenpurackel Thommi Tharakan's son and Appacha's brother. But most others would deadbolt their doors and stay indoors soundlessly until he left after generating much hubbub on the porch.

It was around sundown when Georgekutty Appachan came knocking on Appacha's door one day. Aleyamma was making mud cakes in the garden, and he beckoned her with a flourish of his wabbly fingers.

'Where is your grandfather?'

'He has gone out. But he will be back soon.'

'You think I am stupid? You are lying, you lying liar. He owes me money and I won't let you go until he gives it to me.'

He grabbed her by the waist, lifted her off her feet, and started shaking her. Appacha's Contessa drove up to the front porch. Appacha opened his door and hopped out even before Krishnan Uncle had stopped the car. He looked his brother straight in the eye. Georgekutty Appachan put Aleyamma down and took a step back.

'Isn't it time for *DuckTales*?' Appacha turned to her and gently thrust her towards Krishnan Uncle.

Krishnan Uncle took her by the hand, and they went into the drawing room. He turned on the television and raised the volume to the maximum.

'What is happening?' she asked Krishnan Uncle.

'We're just watching TV,' he said, his voice calm, though a flicker of unease crossed his face. Whenever he sat with Aleyamma each evening, guiding her through the messy world of addition and subtraction, his eyes were always certain. 'Don't worry. You will learn to love maths. And if you don't, maybe you'll be an artist like your Ammachi,' he'd said once. He was sure of himself then, confident of his task. But this time, he didn't seem so sure.

As they watched the wonderful exploits of a parsimonious Uncle Scrooge, Aleyamma peeped through the window and saw Appacha thrash his brother on the porch. 'Don't you dare touch Baby.' His voice rose over the television.

Aleyamma turned to Krishnan Uncle. 'Is Georgekutty Appachan a bad man?'

Krishnan Uncle didn't flinch. 'No, he isn't.'

'Then why is Appacha beating him?'

His answer came slower this time. 'I don't know.'

'But you are a good man,' Aleyamma said.

'What makes you say that?' Krishnan Uncle smiled a sad smile, as if her words held both peace and pain.

'Because you are Appacha's friend, and you always laugh together. And you don't scold me when you teach me maths.'

Krishnan Uncle chuckled, but then his eyes deepened in contemplation. 'People...we are both good and bad.' His voice waned, and he became still, lost in thought.

Outside, Appacha's voice rose once more. Aleyamma's eyes followed the sound. Appacha threw a long piece of white cloth to the ground and stepped on it. 'I thought you would change. But some people never will,' he said, as Georgekutty Appachan swayed on his feet. But since Appacha still loved his brother, he washed his face with the damp end of a towel, patted him dry with the dry end, and stuck Band-Aids where he was bleeding. Georgekutty left the house shambling, holding close to his chest the white cloth now muddy and torn. He was never seen again.

Aleyamma studies her reflection in the mirror and contemplates investing in a pair of sneakers, five-finger shoes, or maybe even a treadmill when Elsy Chedatty calls to her from the bottom of the stairs and tells her that the road towards town is better. 'There is an MLA living somewhere along the way. So, the road is always good.'

∽

The day the Band-Aids leave her face, Aleyamma runs towards town. The road is smooth, but there are more people on the way. Strangers stop in their tracks and study her raptly. Some come out of their houses, brushing their teeth, eyes still heavy with sleep, trying to unravel her identity in their heads, questions brimming in their eyes as they stare at her dreadlocks, tattooed arms, and naked feet, trying to decide whether she is a homeless hippie or a drug addict. A lady elbows her heavy-eyed child, points at her head, and puts her hand over her mouth.

Until she got her dreadlocks, people said she looked like a young Indira Gandhi, with a neat head of cropped hair swept to the side and a hooked nose that is supposed to be characteristic of a clever woman. 'She was the best prime minister we've ever had,' her relatives said as they palmed her head with pride. Like the rest of the Syrian Christians, whose loyalty lay with the Congress, they chose to sweep the Emergency and forced sterilizations under the carpet, and instead pointed their fingers at the communists and their labour union activities, because some relative somewhere faced problems in their tyre factory or tea estate. They also believed that communism had made people lazy; people expected to be paid for work they never did, like the nokku kooli, 'looking charges', demanded by the loading-unloading unions where wages had been divorced from labour. 'These people sit under tarpaulins on the roadsides, eyes keenly tracking the movement of goods, pitch up in front of houses, ask for daily wages, pocket them, and walk away without even lifting a finger. And if we refuse to part with cash, they don't even allow us to unload the truck. Isn't this a free country? Don't we have rights within our own compounds? This is the aftermath of social reforms. Kerala would have been a superpower if it hadn't been for things like these,' they would often say, treating Kerala like a country.

Aleyamma kept her nose but changed her hair. She got dreadlocks because she thought she looked like a version of Bob Marley, whom they often confused with Che Guevara. She was not a communist or the least bit drawn to politics, unlike Roy and his Twitterati artist comrades who threw their opinions around, pretending they had a complete grasp over various issues—the Babri Masjid, Rath Yatra, love jihad, Islam, Islamophobia, terrorism, counter-terrorism, Putin, Xi Jinping, Siachen, Manmohan Singh, Modi, Maoists, Me Too, or whatever else was the flavour of the moment—flippantly expressing their thoughts through clipped posts with carefully chosen hashtags. She got dreadlocks only to spite her family, who, by now, were convinced that no one would marry a thirty-five-year-old woman with a rebellious streak, separated parents, and hair like that of the swamis, who bathed in ganja and dipped in the Ganga. Dreadlocks, like many other things, were a black mark in the marriage market. It was as damaging as what Bangalore did to a girl's morals or what practising law did to her temperament. Amma, though she found the hairdo contemptible, didn't agree. A relative once told Amma that she had to get Aleyamma 'married off' before she found a job and formed an opinion about the world; the rationale was simple—it would pave a smoother path for her to adapt to her new family dynamics.

But Amma said that marriages are not defined by hair or cities or vocations. It depends on whether you look down at your feet when you walk.

Aleyamma looks ahead and runs.

Petty shops mushroom from the earth. It would take a few more hours for the shutters to be pulled up, as it is still early. This is where Elsy Chedatty does all the shopping for the house and the lodgers. Rice, eggs, chicken, beef, soap, bedsheets, laptops, CDs, bifocals, and Marlboro. No one has to go to Kozhikode any more. Kerala is one big town, they say.

Elsy Chedatty is over sixty and she drives a Willys Jeep like a veteran, pallu gathered at her waist, doling out imposing hand signals with her deceptively dainty arms. The Jeep came with the house, though Velia Pappa said he almost had to sell his wife's kidney to reinstate the rust bucket to its former glory.

Elsy Chedatty does all the work around the house single-handedly. A couple of years ago, there was a man who used to help her with the housework and the shopping, till he wet his bed and fled because he said he smelled cigars in the night. According to him, it was unnerving to share space with the ghosts of white people. But Velia Pappa believes he was a man with an overactive bladder and that he left after a Chinese hospital recruited him as a test subject for a study of acupuncture on people with such a condition.

Aleyamma knows she should help Elsy Chedatty, now that the house is in her name and the business of hospitality, hers. The trouble is, she has never thought of herself as hospitable. Velia Pappa and Cheria Pappa were right in their observations. The starving artist doesn't care about money. Or properties. Or the business of homestays. All she knows is to hold tight the gift Appacha left behind.

A couple of tea shops are open. The promising smell of kadala curry grows in the air. People blow into glasses of tea and share the day's hearsay. They look over the rims as she runs past them. She wonders if she could perhaps pass off as a holidaymaker, as she knows that the moral code shifts if one is not a Malayali. An old man comes out of a tea shop and watches her. There are fly-specks of puttu trapped below his pencil moustache. Her heart stirs a little. The moustache reminds her of a face from long ago. She wants to reach out to his upper vermillion and take away the remnants of his breakfast.

Opposite the tea shop is a building. An ordinary one, two storeys high, in dire need of a coat or two of paint. She notices it first because of the saffron flags that flutter from it with an almost wilful allure and later, because of the men who watch her from the veranda that runs across the length of the first floor. Behind them, the room is grim and there is a bare bulb that emanates a dim light. Chairs and tables are scattered around. Saffron party flags with green lotuses are positioned in strategic places in the corridor. In a corner, a pile of plastic chairs forms a crooked pillar. Outside is a board with flaky orange paint that reads, 'Akhil Janata Vidyarthi Parishad Office, Puthuloor'. Alongside it is another that says 'Sports Club'. She adjusts her tank top and pinches her shorts down. As she passes by, the men lean over the railing to have a better look at her. She can feel their eyes caressing the back of her thighs.

There is only one way back, and she knows they will be awaiting her return. They would have kept their cracked lips and searching eyes on high alert. But men like these don't confound her. She is old enough not to care when people mark their territory with prying eyes and fleshly puns. She is secure in her skin but more than that, she is unscathed by the gazes she gathers. They don't perturb her any more because she thinks, by now, she has become indifferent to them.

Though she doesn't want to look at the building as she makes her way back, her eyes are drawn to the veranda. Surprisingly, the men have disappeared. No giraffe-necks around. There is a man sweeping the floor, body bowed, lost in the dust around him. He is barefoot like her, sweeping up the mess, gathering the trash punctiliously into a cardboard box in his hands.

He lifts his shoulders and looks at her over the steel railings. There are no crude caresses of her body with his eyes, but her skin prickles and a deadening weakness sputters through her veins. Much like the time in the final year of her all-girls convent school, when an old man from the Catholic Sex Education Centre gave them a lesson on sex education. The old man had rolled out a chart paper with a photograph of a woman in a blue blouse with a deep-cut back and asked them, 'What do you see? What do boys see particularly? What will they be thinking?'

Someone sensible said, 'An ingenious design.'

'Wrong. The boys will be wondering if she is wearing a bra.'

The old man walked to the next roll of chart paper, unfurled it grandly to produce a picture of a young lady wearing well-fitted jeans and asked the same question. No one dared to answer this time. He flourished yet another picture. But now, the lady's jeans had disappeared, and her bottom was naked. There was pin-drop silence in class.

'Sex,' he said triumphantly.

Aleyamma realizes that she has stopped outside the building. She finds her rhythm and runs home like a tiny child.

Her skin is still shocked as she walks through the hall. She sits on the sofa and pulls up her legs into her arms. From the dining hall, she can hear Elsy Chedatty serving breakfast to the Russian party.

'Eto ostro?' a man asks her.

'Nyet, eto nye ostro. No problem, I used mild green chillies.' Elsy Chedatty's voice resounds with clarity.

Aleyamma is beguiled. Even after living in Chennai for almost two decades, she had not got used to Tamil, which is Malayalam's closest cousin.

Elsy Chedatty is now at the door. 'Shall I serve you breakfast?'

'No. I will take a shower first.'

'How was the run?'

'The road is better, like you said,' she says and pulls a cotton throw over her legs.

Elsy Chedatty eyes the throw and says on the way out, 'One cannot always please everyone.'

∽

Elsy Chedatty is concerned about Aleyamma's sleep or rather, the lack of it, as the Russian party is still happy to roister their way through the night. She says the remedy is to put Appacha's unexploited study at the farthest end of the house to good use—where it can double as a studio cum bedroom, away from the noise the guests make on their way in and out.

No one has used the room since Appacha left the house. Velia Pappa had plans to turn Appacha's study into an entertainment room, equipped with a snooker table, flat screen television, and deep couches with fluffy pillows. But he never got around to doing it because, according to him, the renovation downstairs had left him 'without two brass farthings to rub together'.

Aleyamma takes the rosewood stairway from the foyer to the study—the solitary room on the floor above. A second floor is uncommon for a bungalow. Climbing stairs was not meant for old age. But the Hitchcocks were young. And they stayed young.

The steps have lost their lustre over the years. The upper floor is marked with a generous number of windows. Old furniture still occupies the floor—bookshelves burdened with moth-eaten hardbacks, paperbacks, and yellowing periodicals line the perimeter of the room. In the centre stands a grandiose study table and a brown Morris chair. The furniture takes up just a quarter of the floor and she knows that with a bit of dusting and reorganizing, it would be a wonderful place for her.

Other than the books on the shelves, there are cupboards with the detritus of decades, covered in dust and infested with dust mites. Silverfish-consumed photo albums, handwritten bills, a collection of rubber stamps and seals from the estate, forgotten fountain pens with dried-up blue-black ink, and a silver dog collar.

Aleyamma wipes the dust off the collar. She, too, had once had a dog named Cutlet, with fuzzy burgundy ears and a penchant for fish cutlets. Cutlet surprised everyone when he came into the world, especially Krishnan Uncle, who delivered the puppies. It was a dull afternoon when the mother dog went into labour in the kennel, and Krishnan Uncle, who was home at that time, assured Appacha that he would manage the delivery. His hands moved delicately, as though they were meant for far gentler tasks. When it was all over, he stroked the mother's brow. 'See, four healthy puppies,' he told Aleyamma, his voice gushing with affection. 'The mother was beaten and abandoned near my house. See how strong she has turned out to be.'

'Why do people beat dogs?' Aleyamma asked.

Krishnan Uncle's face clouded with thought, as if searching for truth in the great and perplexing mess of human nature. Then he finally spoke. 'Because people don't know any better.' There was a quiet sadness in his voice.

'The mother is tired now. She should rest,' he said, and went into the house to fetch fresh towels.

As Aleyamma watched the puppies, she spotted a fifth one still encased in a lucent ball of skin through which a jumble of features could be seen. The mother was in a corner conquered by the puppies trying to latch on to her nipples. Aleyamma reached out to the diaphanous sac, peeled it back with the tips of her fingers, and Cutlet dropped into her hands.

Krishnan Uncle rushed to her side when he saw her holding the tiny animal close to her chest. 'You rescued him. The mother was too exhausted to cut the sac. He wouldn't have survived in there for long.'

He watched the puppy wiggling about in her hands, his forehead heavy with contemplation. 'Life...it is precious.' He then looked at her and smiled. 'Baby should be proud,' he said, patting her on the back. No one had told her that before. The words seeped into her soul, settling there like a gentle song.

Cutlet was the spindliest one of the litter—knock-kneed and bug-ridden—but he grew in strength, drinking milk and eating fish cutlets. It was Krishnan Uncle who supplied the fish cutlets. He said he wanted to do something special for the puppy. Perhaps it was a gesture of atonement for not having spotted him in the sac. Krishnan Uncle worked as an accountant at a cooperative bank in town. Every evening, after the day's work, he would arrive, punctual as dusk, to teach Aleyamma maths. But after Cutlet was born, his tiffin box took on a new purpose. In one of its compartments, there would inevitably be two perfectly crispy fish cutlets, saved with care.

Krishnan Uncle cooked his meals himself. Amma, echoing the sly certainty of village hearsay, said he did so because no woman would have him. But she said it like it was the truth. Krishnan Uncle's house was next door, with a well and a few coconut trees. It was always neat and tidy. On the wall of the sitting room was a faded poster of an Indian Airlines aeroplane as though it would lift off at any moment and carry him somewhere far away, and in the kitchen, there were always orange candies for Aleyamma. His kitchen always smelled of fried fish and something else—something sharp, something obscure, like the stories that linger in the spaces between words.

Cutlet, for his part, was more than willing to devour what Krishnan Uncle brought him.

'Maybe he is a cat living in a dog's body,' Appacha once said as Krishnan Uncle fed Cutlet.

'Like Duke,' said Krishnan Uncle.

Appacha turned to Aleyamma. 'I too had a dog who everyone thought was a wolf.'

'Was he dangerous and fierce like a wolf?' she asked.

'No. He was as gentle as a lamb. And he was a very handsome boy.'

Krishnan Uncle nodded, a knowing smile dimpling his cheeks.

Appacha continued, 'He died a happy old man. We buried him by the sea where Appacha and Ammachi met.'

Krishnan Uncle looked down and picked up the fish cutlet he had dropped.

∽

Aleyamma spends the rest of the day reviving the room. At night, she drags a mattress up the stairway and lays it on the wooden floor.

'Will you be able to sleep all right?' Elsy Chedatty asks her, eyeing the mattress on the floor.

'Don't worry, I will be out like a light.'

Aleyamma retires to the mattress and closes her eyes. She has never slept soundly since the night when Amma abandoned her soul somewhere on the drive back from Cherai beach twenty-five years ago. It was the night she saw the last of Cutlet.

The day Amma took her away from Appacha, Aleyamma had sneaked Cutlet into her bag of clothes that Amma had packed in a frenzy. For a Pomeranian, it was exceptional that Cutlet stayed silent most of the way, but when they reached Purakad and the smell of the sea and fish sailed through the open windows, he let out a rapacious whine. Amma's hands shook on the steering wheel, but she didn't stop the car or even slow down. Maybe she couldn't imagine driving all the way back, or maybe she was too proud to go back. So, she let Aleyamma keep Cutlet.

Cutlet was a complicated dog. Whenever Aleyamma was around, he was usually well-behaved, but in her absence, his behaviour would unravel into a show of rebellion. Other than fish cutlets, he also chewed up bedsheets, made daily breakfast out of the *Malayala Manorama,* hounded the portly chickens in the next-door house, crushed their still-warm eggs, and moaned diligently every time the big trucks on the highway hooted their air horns. Amma tried her best to put up with him. But she couldn't.

On Aleyamma's tenth birthday, Amma told her that they were going for a picnic to Cherai beach. 'Some fresh air will do us good,' Amma said cheerfully. They spent the evening with their picnic basket on the golden sand, warm and powdery under their feet, sipping on sun-warmed Gold Spots, and munching on curried beef samosas and fish cutlets. Aleyamma tossed bits of her cutlet in the air and Cutlet stole them with eager hops. 'Little glutton,' Amma said. She laughed and sipped her drink noisily through her straw.

It rained on the drive back home. Dark, thick gobbets of raindrops hit the old Ambassador's windshield menacingly, threatening to conquer Cochin by nightfall. Cutlet had always been afraid of the rain. Stuck in the front seat beside Amma, he thrashed and whined as raindrops ceaselessly assaulted the windshield. He howled and tried to nip Amma's arm. Amma stopped the car abruptly on the deserted road. 'What is wrong with you, you mad dog? I've had enough,' she said. Amma opened the door and gave Cutlet a little shove. She then closed the door and drove away. Aleyamma cried, a piercing sound of distress from the pit of her stomach. She put her head out and called his name. Cutlet was scampering after the car, his little legs moving as swiftly as they could. There was no more mischief in his eyes. Only fear and sadness. Aleyamma called his name again. But the wind and the rain carried her voice away. Cutlet ran for as long as he could. But Amma was faster. She pressed her dirty-brown Kolhapuri chappals firmly down on the accelerator, with an intensity she had never shown before. He soon vanished around a bend in the road. Aleyamma never saw him again.

That night, she wept into her pillow until she had no tears left. She closed her eyes and wondered where he was. She wondered if he was hungry, wet, and trembling in the driving rain. She wondered if he was still alive. She thought about his impish eyes. His fuzzy ears. The fish cutlets he ate. The chickens he chased. The newspapers he consumed. She remembered Appacha calling him a little cat and feeding him milk, Krishnan Uncle patting her on the back for a job well done.... 'Baby should be proud.' She saw Cutlet running on the wet, deserted road. Snatched from her skin. Anguished. Repudiated. Like Appacha.

After that night, she never slept soundly again.

∽

Appacha's study is a beautiful place to greet the mornings. From the mattress on the floor, she sees the world in a scatter of green and blue. There are no curtains, and the air is crisp and warm. Daylight seeps into her world between the leaves of the mango tree by the window and falls gently on her skin. At one time, that particular variety of mango didn't even have a name. A few years ago, some people approached Velia Pappa, claiming they were from a mango tree conservation group and on a mission to identify Kerala's indigenous mango trees. They had heard about a tree in the Estate House which bore long fruits that tasted like a cross between a mango and a cashew apple. They said it was indigenous to the state and had not yet been properly classified and described. Together, they named it Eastman Maavu.

Aleyamma peels off her bedcover and walks towards the window. Xanthous florets have begun to form at the ends of the limbs of the Eastman Maavu. On tiptoe, she can reach out and touch the branches. She runs her fingertips along the tough bark and remembers the tree that leaned over the pond in Niranam and the taste the fruits left on her tongue, sweet and tart like sour candies. Her eyes stray to the unopened boxes of paints and canvases she has brought from Chennai, a motley paraphernalia she had pushed into a corner of the room. She runs her fingers over them and taps them back to life—the distressed watercolour cases, the compressed charcoal sticks, the soft crumbly pastels, the acrylic tubes, and canvases. She pushes the Morris chair to a corner and makes enough space for the easel near the big window where she can catch the best of the daylight. The easel looks like it always belonged there, like it organically grew from the unpolished wooden floor, into a beast of a frame. It is as tall as her when she stretches its legs to the last hole. It once belonged to Roy. He gave it to her three years ago when she groused that her shoddy little metallic stands kept buckling under the weight of the canvases.

The light wood has gained a murky tint over time. Vermillion hue, titanium white, and ultramarine blue marble its thick body on which his initials still remain unsullied along the edge—'SR'—Sarvamayavibhanjana Roy. Sarvamayavibhanjana—the destroyer of all magic. 'Now I can watch you when you work even if I am not there,' he said, taking the end of a compass and carving out his initials on the frame. He loved watching her work, sitting on the floor in her bedroom studio, blue lungi tucked around his slender legs, cigarette in hand, rubbing his salt and pepper stubble, and occasionally turning to whatever book he was currently reading. Once she finished a work, he would inspect it with the precision of a detective and make unembellished observations. At times, she would tear up her sketches because he found them unsatisfactory. 'To destroy is to create. I am telling you this only because I love you,' he would say, looking at the forlorn bundle of torn-up papers or beaten-up canvases on the floor and then give her a peck on the cheek.

Her art was dark against his; hers forever in line with the dismal hues of Picasso during his brief blue period, and his like a riot of colours on freshly laundered whites on Holi. When he first told her that he could sense and even taste colours, she laughed. But he said there was a technical name for it—synaesthesia. Wassily Kandinsky had it—chromaesthesia—sound to colour synaesthesia. But according to Roy, he had the all-embracing kind. Red was a rushing river in his head. Blue, an icy diamond at the tip of his tongue. Green, the crunch of fried chicken. Grey, juicy and acerbic like an onion. He believed his wires were crossed for a reason and without this condition, he perhaps might have never embraced the path of an artist. 'And then maybe I would have never met you,' he said.

He never painted in front of her, though. He would always work in his house—perhaps close the door, sit with a glass of whisky, either at peace or at war with the world, as the colours in his head tumbled out until they found suitable harmony on the canvases. She wondered if he ever let his wife watch him work.

He never talked about her. Fear and self-conflict held him hostage. But she knew he was torn—torn between the two worlds he was caught between. One world he crafted for Aleyamma, picking up her calls from the bathroom, door firmly shut, one hand over his mouth, whispering words incomprehensible in compressed susurration. And the other world an arm's length away, in his own bed, where his wife slept, probably in a floral cotton nightie, buttons undone after a night of lovemaking, bindis stuck on the bedroom dresser, surrounded by an array of her perfumes and lipsticks arranged in neat lines, the nut-brown dust of Chennai gathering around them like dutiful children.

She often pondered how his world might have been different had he encountered her first. 'You should have been my wife,' he told her once and hid his bruises under his shirt sleeve. She never told him to leave his wife. It was a decision he had to make himself.

But synaesthesia brightened his shadowy world, and she thanked the universe for the little mercies it bestowed upon him.

Roy gifted her his wooden easel on her thirty-second birthday.

The easel became her lifeline. On it, she could keep enormous canvases, and they would stay unmoving. Nobly. Faithfully. Like the boy on the burning deck from her second-standard English book, that had pictures on one side and words on the other. It was printed carelessly with colours bleeding over. It was quite unusual for a book of its kind because all the other English textbooks looked extravagant, printed in the fine presses of Delhi or Bombay. The Malayalam books were always the ones to fall apart first, with their shoddy binding and cheap paper. Nevertheless, the Malayalam-looking English book left a solid impression on her. She could not forget the picture of the little boy on the page. A boy in a striped green-and-brown shirt and neatly combed hair, who stood like a pillar on a deck that was falling apart as fire consumed the ship. He stood there unmoving because his father had told him to stay put. His name was Casabianca, and the poem was fresh in her ears.

The boy stood on the burning deck,
Whence all but he had fled;
The flame that lit the battle's wreck,
Shone round him o'er the dead.

Yet beautiful and bright he stood,
As born to rule the storm;
A creature of heroic blood,
A proud, though childlike form.

She imagined the fire that swept through the ship. The flames that consumed his skin and bones. Casabianca could have run, sailed away on a lifeboat. But he didn't. He had faith in people.

She called the easel Casabianca. At first, she thought it was a risible thing to do; naming inanimate objects was something she had done as a child, when she named all the dolls in her toy cabinet. Betty, Bunty, Spongy, Lovely. If that was all right, so was this.

Casabianca is all that is left now. She wants to tuck it away somewhere, as it is beginning to leave a repugnant taste in her mouth, like the fish-head. But she doesn't. It stays near the window, in the shadow of the Eastman Maavu, silently reminding her of all the memories—good and bad.

chapter 9

WHEN ALEYAMMA SAW HER FOR the first time, she couldn't look into her eyes. She kept staring at her big, scarlet bindi, placed between her precisely plucked eyebrows, like an emergency button. It moved in step with the utterances from her mouth. Up. Down. Up. Down. She tried to take notice of the words that tumbled from her lips. But the big scarlet dot kept her engrossed. It was a necessary aberration because she knew she couldn't look into her eyes without a sense of remorse.

Thayamma Akka, Aleyamma's part-time help, let her in after she saw her waiting outside the door of the apartment. Not knocking. Not even attempting to make a move to ring the bell. She was standing there. Waiting. Thayamma Akka always had a keen ear for things like these. She could sense the milk van before it reached their lane. She could hear the men from the electricity board walking to their apartment, eager to disconnect the fuses of the electricity delinquents. She could feel the rain before it reached them.

'Call your didi,' Aleyamma heard her tell Thayamma Akka from the next room.

As Aleyamma walked to the living room, she recognized her at once; he always carried her around in his butt pocket, an old passport-size photograph, tucked into the clear layer of his worn-out leather wallet, like a good husband, an indispensable piece of his life in case he forgot about reality. She looked older in person, but some things were the same—the dove eyes, the hair parted meticulously in the centre and tied neatly into a low ponytail, the face with the remainder of a smile, the scarlet bindi.

The wife walked into the living room and sat in the centre of the couch. She crossed her arms, and her breasts soared to the top of her round-neck salwar. Aleyamma made her way to the ottoman opposite the sofa and sat down.

'I know you,' said the wife. Her bindi furrowed along with the creases of her forehead, her eyes were sizing Aleyamma up—her unmade face, her tousled hair, her scanty clothes, and her bare feet.

Aleyamma inched to the rim of the ottoman.

'I think you know my husband.' Her tone was composed, but cold.

'Yes, I have met him a few times because of work. I am an artist too.'

'Do you know *me*?'

'Sorry?'

'You let me in without asking me who I was. Do you know me?'

'I don't think I let you in. You just walked in. And I might have seen you. In the papers, with him.'

'I have never been in the papers. Because I don't go to any parties.'

'Maybe I have heard about you from him. I think he showed me a picture of you. I know him professionally. We met a few times because I asked for help. He introduced me to the agent I now have. He also showed me some techniques that I needed to work on. Still life and figure drawing, mostly.'

'Figure drawing. Interesting, isn't it?' She didn't give her time to respond. 'Did he draw you?' It was a trick question.

'No.'

The lie slipped out of her mouth fluidly. Yet, as soon as she said it, a tautness seized her throat. There was no way she could tell the truth without letting her emotions surface on her skin. She was his subject on many days; she would be in bed with a sheet wrapped around her, hiding nothing, as his eyes traced her figure and his charcoal stick left loose lines on creamy Canson sheets. She loved seeing herself the way he saw her. It was beautiful. Pure. He kept most of the sketches with him, but she would slip a couple of them into her drawer and silently pray that he wouldn't be like Gustav Klimt, who painted his mistress—after hundreds of sketches, she became dull to him.

'I know you are fucking him,' the wife said. The sharpness of her voice took Aleyamma aback and left her skin burning.

'You have it all wrong.'

'Don't play dumb with me. I know that you have him under your spell.' The wife was now on her feet, staring down at her. The scarlet bindi disappeared into the furrows of her forehead, and her eyes burned with pure disgust.

Aleyamma's face flushed with a kind of mortification she had never felt before. She sensed disgrace rise to her skin and swallow her with an unforgiving heat. 'There is no spell,' she mumbled, hoping she could disappear.

The wife laughed from across the room. Her ponytail danced behind her. Her fists were clenched. Fists that perhaps were tough enough to give one bruises.

Aleyamma sprang to her feet from the edge of the ottoman. 'I want you to leave now,' she said, finding her voice.

The wife walked towards her. Her laugh was like the midday sun. It breathed fire into Aleyamma's skin.

'You can never have him. But you already know that,' she said, the corners of her lips curling up. She slithered away to the door, breasts bobbing, and ponytail swinging. She slammed the door behind her. The door handle had broken under the impact, and it hung crookedly from the door as if holding on to the last vestige of its dignity.

Aleyamma fell onto the sofa in a soft lump. Her heart was pounding away. She was sure even Thayamma Akka could hear it from the kitchen, where she was feigning to be busy soaping the dishes with inessential clatter. Aleyamma's face turned hot.

She curled into the sofa, hugging her chest, longing for the arms that had once pulled her out of the water and the fingers that had brushed across her forehead. She yearned for those fingers to write on the ground, like Jesus, acquitting her, and for those arms to wrap around her, offering her an ounce of mercy.

The clangour from the kitchen had stopped. Thayamma Akka walked to the sofa and stroked the top of her head like she was petting a cat. 'I'm sorry, madam. My mistake. I shouldn't have let that crazy woman in.'

Then, the phone rang. Amma's voice was unfeeling, but her words broke Aleyamma's heart. 'Appacha passed away sometime in the night. They cannot keep the body for too long. You need to come now if you want to see the body.'

PART IV

chapter 10

EESHO BLEW INTO HIS TEACUP and waited for the soliloquy to come to an end. Listening to Pappan was a kind of suffering. The watchman rasped into the air like an aged man, bowed his lopsided frame in feigned meekness, and buried his mouth in his palm in pretend-deference, which Eesho understood as a stroke of luck because it filtered the shower of spittle reaching the receiving end. Pappan spoke incessantly, barely pausing for breath, which Eesho believed even Mamma Mollykutty would consider a case of verbal excess. Pappan had already told Eesho that the people of the village called him 'hopping Pappan' for his limp that left one forgettable and one unforgettable Bata-chappal marks all over the village, especially during the monsoons when the limp turned more perceptible, such that the kids in the vicinity took on a chortling perambulation behind him as they emulated his trademark lopsided gait, chanting, 'One foot up and one foot down.' But he said he didn't protest because he was invulnerable to derision of any kind. Moreover, he basked in the beauty of attention—good or bad. Besides, he said it wasn't really his fault that he came out the wrong way, and that the midwife hauled him out as soon as he stuck out his baby foot, rendering it useless, dooming him to hop, skip, and jump wherever he went, leaving behind a fascinated string of urchins hopping, skipping, and jumping.

His disability wasn't the only thing he spoke about. He would talk about everything, leaving no matter unconsidered—the land, rubber trees, the price of rubber, his mother, his life, his midwife, tea, lukewarm tea, tea without sugar, tea without milk, curdled milk, the diabetes he feared he had, his love for sugar despite the diabetes, his fascination with people, their clothes, shoes, cars, planes, boats, goats....

Eesho put down the teacup. Kochuthresia had come outside to join him and was listening to the watcher with the sort of endurance Eesho wished he had. She kept nodding dutifully as she took small sips from her teacup.

'Did you want tea? You didn't even give me a chance to ask you?' Eesho asked Pappan.

Pappan looked pleased with the offer. But he shook his head. 'No, saar. I will drink next time. Then I will come to know how madam makes the tea.'

'I did not make it. He made it,' Kochuthresia said, pointing at Eesho.

Pappan's eyes beamed with incredulity. 'Times have changed. I forgot we are almost in the '70s. Men have become cooks now, no? Not just cooks of tea and coffee. But of everything. Women can rest as men have overtaken the kitchen too.'

He first let out a chortle, but soon, his forehead narrowed with gravity. 'But, madam, you have to be careful, because men are very careless cooks. Once, I made chicken curry. I got the chicken fresh from the market. The thing was fluttering in my hands like a bhadrakali, trying to make an escape. I walked into the house and the thing started flying away. But my mother is a smart and cold-hearted woman. She caught the chicken, strangled it, and plucked out its feathers in fistfuls. Later, I chopped it into pieces because, by then, thankfully, the thing didn't look like a bird any more. And then I cooked it. But when we dug into it, she pointed out that I had left its head on. Can you believe it? Still, we ate it, head, neck, and all. But, madam, I actually wonder why people don't eat chicken heads. It is really very enjoyable. The brain…it flows like a river in the mouth.'

Eesho thought that Kochuthresia would throw up into her teacup. He swiftly steered Pappan away, before he could bring up another topic for deliberation. 'Let's go,' Eesho told him and made his way to the shed where the Jeep was parked.

Earlier in the day, Pappan had washed it, spraying it down with the garden hose. Eesho had found the diesel in the back of the shed and filled the tank. He had also discovered a brown blazer on the front seat, likely belonging to the previous superintendent, the one who had left in a hurry after having come upon the white ghost who inhabited the house. Eesho, who had never encountered a phantom before, thought a ghostly encounter could be exciting, even enthralling. What he didn't find enthralling at all was the murderous attack on the Hitchcocks that had led them to wander the estate as apparitions. Unless, of course, Pappan, in one of his flights of fantasy, had come up with the story of their untimely demise.

Kochuthresia drew the curtain and waved at him from the dining room window with a fresh cup of tea in her hands. He smiled and waved back at her. He knew he would be fine anywhere so long as she was by his side. Be it a cardboard box, a broken room, or a bloody bed.

Eesho started the engine and Pappan got into the front seat; at the foot of which, Duke was curled up on one half of Mamma Mollykutty's bedsheet that Eesho had cut up for him. The other half lay in the hallway, outside the door of the bedroom, where Duke slept at night. Once he had climbed into the Jeep, Pappan extended his deformed leg to rest it on what seemed to be a dark, fluffy pillow. No sooner had he done so, than he shrieked and fell out of the Jeep, one hand holding his chest in consternation and the other holding on to his mundu for dignity.

'Wolf...saar, there's a wolf in the car, saar.' Pappan's eyes were fixed on Duke, who now looked at the man curiously. Duke wanted to get to know the man on the ground better. He hopped out of the Jeep and sniffed Pappan's face, ears, and the bidis stuck behind them. Pappan didn't move. Through his barely parted lips, he spoke in a murmur, like a ventriloquist in performance. 'Saar, my one leg is already useless. I don't want him to eat the other one too.'

Eesho couldn't help but laugh. Though Duke looked savage, he had bitten no one. 'This dog has false teeth. They are just for show,' Philipose Achen would point out every time he played fetch with Duke on the veranda. 'He is a toy dog living in the wrong body. But always hungry. Stealing biscuits all the time.'

Eesho whistled, and Duke hopped back into the Jeep. 'You can get in the back seat if you don't want to share a seat with him. And he is not a wolf. He is only a dog who looks like a wolf.'

Pappan still made no move to get up. 'Saar, will he bite me?'

'We will have to wait and see.'

Pappan climbed into the back seat and didn't make a sound.

Eesho drove the Jeep deep into the estate, into the thick of the trees, to the fringe of the Western Ghats, onto lands where the road was scarcely a road, through ribbons of water that overran the road like little streams, through rust-coloured puddles and bristly touch-me-nots, almost to the border where people talked in a strange tongue—a heady mix of Malayalam and Tamil that sounded like a song on their lips.

Men and women dotted the hills, armed with blades, buckets and folk songs, tap-tapping away at the bark, coaxing the trees to bleed a brilliant white resin from their fresh wounds into half-moon coconut shells placed under them. Children hung around the trees, eyes still slumberous as they watched their fathers and mothers work.

'The tappers are still out,' remarked Pappan meekly from the back seat.

'So are their kids. Do they go to school?'

'We have a school not far away from the paadi. Some children go there whenever they can. But they choose to be outside because they can learn more when they see the job being done. Ousepachan saar will not employ them because he says they are still children, though I think Mary madam disagrees.'

Eesho drove past the children and their eyes lit up with curiosity when they spotted Duke. Duke let out an affectionate growl and Pappan became silent again.

The office was imposingly perched at the edge of a cliff, with brick walls of prohibitive height. A watcher sat in a chair and paid no attention to the jeep that Eesho had stopped outside the gate.

'He is dreaming. They can be a lazy bunch sometimes, saar,' Pappan said and got out of the vehicle. He pushed the gate open and yelled at the sleeping watcher, 'Is this any time to sleep? You know what time I woke up? Get up, superend saar is here.' The man roused from his dream and saluted the jeep.

The office building looked exactly as an office building should look—dull and uninteresting.

There was an old man slumbering behind his desk. A pile of papers and books sat in front of him. He breathed into them, ruffling their edges with his dampish breath.

'He has come early to see you only, saar. Otherwise, we open the office at eight.' Pappan shook the man by his elbow. The old man stirred from his sleep, slurped his drool back into his mouth, and put on glasses as thick as soda bottles. He squinted, adjusted the frames of his spectacles, and studied Eesho before breaking into a smile.

'See why we need someone like you, saar,' said Pappan. 'We need fresh blood in this place.'

The old man waggled his head in agreement and showed no fear of Duke, who stood by his legs, mostly because he couldn't see well.

'Where is the assistant superintendent?' Eesho asked Pappan.

Pappan looked fearful for a moment and his hand rose to his mouth. He looked around the room before speaking faintly. 'Kochumuthalaly might come later today. Sometimes he does not come. That is the perk of being the owner's son, I guess.'

Markose, the kochumuthalaly, the 'small owner', was in Madras, visiting his aunt, Pappan said. 'He likes the company he has there. Life in the hills must be too boring for a young man. He will come back soon, though,' he said. But from the way he said it, Eesho knew that he would not be back for a while.

Pappan pointed at the old man. 'He usually helps kochumuthalaly with the accounts.'

'It's okay. I will manage the accounts for now. I will start going for the estate rounds only after I sort it out,' Eesho said as they walked into Eesho's office that flanked the main room.

He had already planned what his days would be like. He would drive to the office and go on foot to the closest sector to watch over the people who tapped the blocks, and check the tab on the litres of latex collected, that the conductors and writers kept with them in the rooms where they worked from. He would then help the old man with the office accounts before he left for the estate rounds again. He would drive to the farthest sectors of the estate before wrapping up the day at the factory, inspecting the daily process and checking the drums of latex, crepe rubber, and rubber sheets before they were taken away in trucks to the town. There would also be regular border checks and inspections of the replanted rubber trees; he knew he would have to plan the replanting with the assistant superintendent.

The old man was moving around in the next room, piling papers from his own desk onto that of the assistant superintendent. His bug eyes attained tranquillity when his desk was free of papers. He then opened a window for fresh air, but an unexpected gust sent the papers he had neatly arranged fluttering around like a flock of startled birds. He gathered them in no hurry, made a neat pile again, stuck his fingers into his mouth and with a moist click, loosened his dentures. He wiped the dentures on his shirt and placed them on the soaring pile of papers. Satisfied, he nodded and returned to his desk.

Pappan clucked his tongue and shuffled out of the cabin. 'If kochumuthalaly sees that smelly ugly thing from your mouth, he will shoot you and then eat you.'

'I will take it away when he comes,' said the old man, giving a toothless smile.

'You need to do it before he comes. You will not make it to the table if you wait.'

∽

Thankfully, when Markose arrived two weeks later, the dentures were back in the old man's mouth and the desk was clean because Pappan had cautioned him in time.

'It was bloody hot in Madras this time. I will have to stay indoors for at least two months to get my old colour back. Mummy says that two weeks in Madras have made me a savage. Do I look like I am from Africa?' Markose stretched out his arms and rolled back his shirt sleeves for the old man to inspect the deep orange blush his skin had gained. The old man bobbed his head in agreement, though he couldn't see much difference in Markose's appearance.

Markose was wearing grey slacks and a full-sleeved shirt with a creamy white English cricket sweater on top, which Eesho assumed

Mary had shipped out to him along with her camomile tea and butter biscuits. Over his shoulder, he carried a burnished rimfire rifle. Markose pulled out his chair and rested his rifle on his desk. 'Now, where is the boy who brings the tea? He should do something to keep it hot. By the time it reaches me, it becomes as cold as payasam.'

'It's the morning chill. Things turn cold sooner than one expects,' Eesho said, walking out of his office room.

'This is superend saar,' the old man told Markose.

Markose made no attempt to get up.

'I met your parents when I went to collect the key to the Estate House. You were not home then.'

Markose leaned back in his chair. 'Yeah, I was in Madras. How is the Estate House?'

'It's good. We are settling in well.'

'Good for you. My father never let me stay there. It is always meant for the superintendent,' he said, taking out a muslin cloth from his drawer. He ran it over his rifle in gentle sweeps.

'It's a little too big for us. But we are wonderfully comfortable there.'

'Why won't you be? The house has everything.' He dusted his rifle without looking up.

The frostiness in Markose's voice was something Eesho was familiar with. It was the same tone Georgekutty used whenever Mamma Mollykutty tried talking him out of the bottle. The tone was a defence tactic. A response to unwelcome stimuli.

'I am going for my rounds. Are you coming with me?' Eesho asked him.

Markose gazed at the old man and the pile of papers in front of him. 'I have to check the accounts before I go for rounds.'

The old man was holding a book close to his glasses. 'Blind as a bat,' Markose muttered to himself and scratched his sweater. 'You go ahead. I will join you later in the factory.'

He knocked on his desk stiffly and pointed his index finger at the old man. 'Bring me the account book. And go find that boy and tell him to bring me some tea. Piping hot this time. Who in their right mind can have payasam first thing in the morning?'

When Eesho returned from his morning rounds, they were hunched over the papers, still poring over the accounts for the week.

'Come have tea with me in the office,' Eesho told Markose. 'Kuttapan will make sure it's hot from now on.'

Markose looked up from the papers. 'Who is Kuttapan?'

'The boy who brings the tea.'

'Oh, I didn't know.' Markose rolled in his chair hesitantly.

'Nice sweater,' Eesho said.

A swift delight washed over Markose's face. He looked down at his sweater and beamed, his face as buoyant as that of a boy complimented for keeping his room neat. 'Mummy got it from England. I have a set of them. Just like the ones Geoffrey Boycott would wear. Do you like cricket too?'

'Yes, I listen to it sometimes. Thank God for the shortwave. I used to play when I was a boy. But most people played football. So, I was left to play solitary cricket, which is impossible.'

'So, you understand! I used to tie a ball to a tree and hit it because there was no one to bowl to me. Even the servant boys preferred other games, and they never listened to me. But later, I played for the university team in Ceylon. That is where Papa sent me for agriculture studies.'

Eesho wanted to understand the young man's predicament, but he couldn't because he didn't make servant boys bowl to him. He pictured Markose playing cricket near Mary's greenhouse, Ousepachan dozing off in his Fornicator in the sit-out, servant boys half-heartedly but obsequiously bowling to him, tossing the rubber ball like they were trying to fell mangoes from a tree. Eesho didn't know whether to feel sorry for Markose or for the state of affairs. But Markose reminded Eesho of Georgekutty in many ways. Young. Impetuous. Mollycoddled. And thus, a certain kind of annoying. He had not yet told Mamma Mollykutty about Georgekutty's vagabond ways which was apparent from the many postcards he sent him, the latest one being from Guntur, with a solitary sentence written with an impetuous hand. 'Inadequacy makes a man mad.' Georgekutty liked to keep it simple. He didn't waste his energy on worthless words, reserving it for the times when the liquor flowed. Eesho ripped up the straw-coloured postcard and sent him a money order. But he still missed his brother and so he empathized with the boy.

'We should play together sometime,' Eesho told him.

'Yes. We will have a batsman and a bowler at least,' Markose said, still smiling.

Though Eesho questioned if that would ever happen, he was glad that the white sweater had broken the ice between them.

∽

The old man tried hard to read the day's numbers he had written down himself that morning. He sat behind his ancient desk and squinted through his glasses like he was searching for head lice in someone's mane, the numbers and words seemed so tiny to him. He scratched the paper with his forefinger, hoping that they would come out to him in clear sight from where they were trapped. But they didn't. It was the same every day and Markose told Eesho that the old man's eyesight was getting worse.

That is when Eesho brought Krishnan into the picture. He had known all along that he would eventually find the right place within the family for the young boy whom they had all but legally adopted as one of their own a long time ago.

At the outset, it was at the insistence of Mamma Mollykutty that Eesho taught him to read and write. She had seen the boy hanging around their coconut plantation as his father climbed the tall trees and felled the green nuts one by one. 'What if a coconut falls on him?' asked Mamma Mollykutty, a sense of trepidation crossing her face as she watched him walk carelessly through the sand, digging his nose, and drawing fictional creatures in the soil with his toes, as coconuts fell around him. Eesho took him away by the hand, sat him in the portico, and gave him a book to read. Krishnan leafed through the fresh pages of the *Phantom* comic, enraptured by the man in the taut purple suit, who did stunts on a brilliant white horse, and traced his fingers over the words that made no sense to him.

'How old are you?' Eesho asked him.

'Twelve.'

'Do you go to school?'

'Acchan sent me when I was little. But the school closed because there were no children. Or teachers.' He giggled.

The next day, Eesho got him a slate and some limestone pencils. They sat in the portico cross-legged, in the same corner where Tharakan once held Eesho's finger and traced on a plate of rice, his first words—'sree Yeshuve namaha'. Eesho considered practising the same ritual for the boy, perhaps changing the words to 'Hari sree Ganapathaye namaha', but he didn't, as the boy had already gone to school once. Eesho held the slate and wrote down the letters of the English alphabet. Krishnan's eyes followed the movements of his pencil.

'What do you want to do when you grow up?' Eesho asked him.

'I want to fly,' he said.

'That is a good ambition. But humans can't fly. Not even Phantom.'

'No. I want to be an aeroplane driver.'

'A pilot, you mean. But for that, you need to go to school first.'

In a few months, Eesho took him to school, not one that he thought might fold up from a dearth of tutors or pupils, but the same one in Quilon that Eesho went to as a boy, where the students wore shoes, spoke in English, and wrote with fountain pens. It was a two-storey building, the only one of its kind in the entire territory, with a hostel on the top floor and classrooms below. Krishnan's father said that it was all too much for his son, but Eesho told him it was what he needed.

The school building was the way Eesho remembered it. The two floors were painted a sandy brown, and the ground was dark like leather. The trees that lined the edge were lush—still perfect hideouts for the times when boys decided to skip uninspiring lessons. But Father Goody could always sense them from a mile away, his nose still surprisingly sharp for his advancing years. 'Descend at once, or I'll ascend and fetch you myself,' he would threaten hoarsely from under the trees, arms on his hips. But everyone knew that was an unattainable task for him. Nevertheless, the boys still feared the long bamboo cane, buried deep within his flowing brown cassock, which he produced like clockwork before the peon struck the brass dismissal bell, finding the shin of a boy he supposed was the rabble-rouser of the day, cowing him into submission.

The passage of time had left the place largely untouched, and the compound was still teeming with kappa. When rice imports were affected after the fall of Rangoon into the hands of the Japanese during World War II, Father Goody had directed the workers to plant kappa to feed the children; rice from the sprawling Irrawaddy-Sittang delta had stopped coming to India, yet India continued to export rice to Ceylon. Famines had spread and nationalist fervour grew.

On 8 August 1942, after Mahatma Gandhi launched the Civil Disobedience Movement in Gowalia Tank Maidan in Bombay, anti-British sentiments began to trickle down south towards Travancore. One afternoon, Eesho was in class, listening to Father Goody read out a conversation between Fielding and Aziz from *A Passage to India*, when a group of people walked to the school gate, waving black flags, shouting, 'Goody go back' and 'Quit India'. Father Goody went to the gate, raised his nose into the air, and looked at the man who was leading the party. 'You tatterdemalion saddle goose, I am no Fielding, and you are no Aziz. And even if we were to ride on horseback through a monsoon-soaked Mau with the wind in our hair, we would never really be friends. The earth said it. And the sky said it,' he said, lifting his hands into the air. He then reached into his cassock, brought out his bamboo cane and whooshed it around like a rapier. The men watched the bamboo cane, and chuckled. 'Who said anything about horseback riding? He's just a crazy old man,' they said and walked away to look for another sayippe whom they could serenade with their slogans. As they walked away, the man who led the party turned to the side and spat out his paan, which by the sheer force of the act and the exceptionally soaring heat that day, became airborne and landed on Father Goody's beard. Father Goody dropped his bamboo cane and squinted down at the smear of paan nestled in his snow-white beard. He plucked a mango leaf and dabbed at it, muttering at the group of men who had now disappeared from view.

'What in heaven's name do you suppose will occur once we abandon this country, Aziz? You ruling a single day without peace? Mark my words, your own men will rip you apart like a stale crumpet.' Unlike the other Jesuit priests in India, Father Goody was British, and his oath of allegiance was more with the crown and less with Christ. On the wall behind his chair, along with a painting of Christ knocking on a door, was a portrait of King George VI, in a gilded frame.

When Eesho arrived at the school with Krishnan, the portrait of George VI had been replaced by that of the current sovereign, Queen Elizabeth.

It was recess and boys were everywhere, looking sharp in their uniforms—dark blue shorts, crisp white shirts, and black shoes, with socks pulled up all the way to their knees. Krishnan carried two sets of uniforms and a pair of shoes and socks in his shiny new tin trunk that he held close to his chest. He looked down at his chappals and pressed his bony shoulder into Eesho's side.

'You will like it here,' Eesho told him.

'I don't want to go in.'

'Why? Tell me.'

'Because I look different.' Krishnan cuddled his tin trunk, his gaze locked firmly on the ground beneath his feet, avoiding the eyes from the first floor, where boys leaned over the railings with curiosity. 'They know that I am not your son or your brother.'

Krishnan's words startled Eesho. He regretted not having bought him a set of clothes and shoes other than the uniform.

Things had changed ever since the Catholic church started the school in 1902. While Protestant missionaries primarily catered to oppressed castes, the Jesuits focused on educating the elite, though they did not entirely shun the marginalized, who still found some opportunity for education there. However, the phased removal of caste restrictions in government schools from 1911 meant that everyone could get an education. A few years later, the school became a private entity owned by a local church. Somewhere along the way, the owners became avaricious. The fees grew steeper. The air, genteel. The children, toffee-nosed.

'Why does it matter what they think? You are above such petty thoughts. You just show them what you can do. When I first came here, I didn't know anyone. But very soon, I made friends. I promise you. This is only good for you.'

Krishnan looked into Eesho's eyes, locked fingers with him determinedly and together they walked into the headmaster's office, where seventy-five-year-old Father Goody sat in his chair, polishing his long bamboo cane with a gleaming chunk of rosin, either mistaking the stick for his bow (he was an enthusiastic violinist) or because it worked on things other than the violin. People said he had begun to forget things easily. Not so long ago, he woke up one night and started looking for his lady love, who he thought had eloped with someone else. 'Daphne, my dear Daphne.... Tomorrow, I shall take your hand in matrimony. Pray, return to me,' he cried in the hallway, forgetting his Jesuit status and also his robe somewhere in his room.

'This is Krishnan, the boy I was telling you about,' Eesho told Father Goody.

Father Goody put his bamboo cane and the chunk of rosin on the table and inspected Krishnan from top to toe. 'Are you scared?' he asked in Malayalam, not because he knew that the boy wouldn't understand English, but because he believed he spoke Malayalam better than the Malayalis—rolling the 'zhas' with much effort and his tongue backwards to make plosive clicks that sounded, to others, more like the weaknesses of a man who might have lost a tooth or two at a ripe old age. But he believed he had mastered the language he had studied for so long, after having reached the land of snakes, snake charmers, mosquitos, malaria, idols, and idolaters, whom he wished to redeem from the throes of hell.

Krishnan looked at Eesho for an explanation to the query he thought had been made in a tongue they spoke in England.

'Fear not, young lad,' Father Goody continued in Malayalam. 'You find yourself within the most esteemed institution of the land. We shall mould you into a true gentleman. It is our noble endeavour to refine all Indians into the exemplary individuals they are meant to become, with a particular dedication to someone of your stature.'

Eesho was glad that Krishnan didn't understand the Father's attempt at Malayalam then, but keeping aside the why colonial environment, he knew it was still a good institution. Nevertheless, when Krishnan carried his suitcase up the steps, disquieted about a world he knew truly little of, a smidgen of regret pricked Eesho. He wanted to take his hand and drive him back to Niranam. But he looked around at the colonial structure and reasoned that the Senior Cambridge education would only be good for his future.

∽

When Eesho summoned him to Puthuloor to work at the rubber estate office, Krishnan felt a sharp surge of excitement and anticipation, and also a touch of nervousness. He set off on his journey with his tin trunk and a mango sapling. The mango sapling was Mamma Mollykutty's, which she had pressed into his hands as she wiped away a dramatic tear. 'Don't lose it even if you lose your trunk,' she had told him. Krishnan hunched over the sapling, its glossy leaves trembling as the bus jostled over bumpy roads, finally dropping him off at the solitary bus stand in Calicut. He asked a girl in a bookshop for directions to Puthuloor, and she pointed to a jeep with people waiting in it. 'That is the last jeep to the village,' she said. She didn't smile at him, but there was something amiable about the way she said it. She watched him as he walked away, and then got back to minding a table laden with books and pamphlets in English and Malayalam. From a corner of a folding table in front of the room, a shortwave radio played an unfamiliar song in an unfamiliar tongue.

Krishnan walked to the waiting jeep and found a seat in the back. Soon, more people pressed in. Men flattened their bodies to make room for the new arrivals. Women sat on the floor and piled their children on top of them. The children smelled of cardamom and jaggery. The jeep set off, packed to its limit, jingling through the hills like a piggy bank ready to explode. Krishnan sat in a corner and cradled the mango sapling as if it were a baby.

When they arrived at the estate, he had no trouble finding his way, as everyone knew the way to the paadi, where all the workers lived. The estate had few houses except for those assigned to the staff. And then there were the hutments at the fringe of the forests where the local tribals, the Kurumbars, lived in a world of their own, weeding the estate and foraging the forests. A watchman handed Krishnan a key and pointed to his room, which was at the end of the row. 'Superend saar told me that you would come. You have a good room. Usually, people with families get the bigger room,' he told him.

Krishnan liked his room as soon as he walked in. There was a bed, a chair, a table, and a woodstove next to an enclosed veranda from where the neat long rows of the paadi tumbled into the depths of the valley like a plateful of stars. There were no phone lines along the hills, but there was electricity and pipe water. He walked to the veranda and thought of Mamma Mollykutty, who would sit next to her telephone in the hall and bewail the backwardness of the country that could not make trunk calls accessible in the steep hills of Puthuloor. 'Ketto, I think our country lost hope when the British left us. Do you recall what the newspapers reported about what happened up north, back then? Friends killing friends, neighbours killing neighbours, setting each other's houses on fire, running away from their own land on trains, women, children, and old ones, not knowing where they were going. Once the British left, didn't we kill our own Bapu? Put three bullets in his bare chest? Dhishoom, dhishoom, dhishoom! That is why I think they should have never left. After all, Ketto, didn't they teach us how to read and write? Didn't they give us trains and motorcars? Didn't they tell our women that they should cover their breasts? Didn't they teach the ungodly the real ways of God? We are now left with nothing but a bunch of buffoons. Nehru was the only one who could rule the country. But he is gone. Now, my hopes are pinned on his daughter. I don't think she is a dumb doll, as people say she is. People with hooked noses are supposed to be shrewd. I believe she will surprise everyone one day. Ketto, maybe she will soon lay telephone lines into the hills of Puthuloor.'

Krishnan walked to his bed, pushed his tin trunk under it and kept the sapling on the table. He watered it from a glass bottle he had carried with him and hoped he had tended it enough on the journey for it to grow into a tall, formidable tree one day.

Krishnan was well-acquainted with trees, having spent his childhood observing his father climb them. His father would take him along when he went to work whenever he could, hoping that he would learn the ways of scaling a coconut tree and harvesting the nuts. Krishnan would watch from below, as his father climbed up the rough trunks of the coconut trees that towered over the land, silently praying that he wouldn't miss a step on the way back down. There were people who fell and didn't walk again. But his father was never fearful of heights or mindful of the gravitational strain on the joints. He was the best climber in all the land.

Krishnan knew that his father liked his job and that he was grateful to be treated with respect, unlike his forefathers, who had been treated like slaves—Thanda Pulayars, a landless, impoverished caste, who were paid a handful of unhusked rice in their thoppippala, palm-leaf hats, after working day and night in their landlord's paddy fields. He had heard stories about them while growing up—about his great-grandfather and grandfather, who were at the mercy of the landlords who owned them. His great-grandfather had two wives and after he met the missionaries, he wanted to get baptized because he was smitten by a god who loved everyone irrespective of caste. But the missionaries told him to let go of one of his wives, as polygamy was a sin and a mark of evil. So, he let go of his first wife—Krishnan's great-grandmother—and also his two young boys, who were later sold in the slave market by their landlord to different masters. The mother was kicked and spat at when she followed her children. Krishnan's grandfather grew up pining for his family, once running away only to be hunted down by men and dogs, dragged back, and burned with hot coals until he returned to work. Sold from one landlord to another, he was told he could buy his freedom, knowing full well he had no anna to his name. Traded like a piece of fish, he accepted his fate as did the rest of his clan. When the missionaries finally convinced the Travancore government to abolish slavery, the boy's life hardly changed. Since the freed slaves lacked other skills, they began to work as attached labourers. The boy moved from field to field, weeding, sowing, and harvesting paddy, eating kappa when he could, and going hungry when he couldn't. Sometimes the women in the household took pity on him and poured a ladle of kanji into a banana leaf rolled into a cone, and dug it into the earth, making sure they'd hurry back to the kitchen lest they were polluted by his touch.

But one day, a man bought him for twenty rupees and told him he could do what he wanted. The man gave him a small patch of land with a well and a few coconut trees. 'You should build a hut one day. I can pay you at the end of the week.' Though it was the Thandans that felled the coconuts, young Tharakan told him that it didn't matter who did what as long as the job was done, and the work respected. Tharakan took the boy to his farm and told his men to show the boy how to scale the coconut tree. Tharakan even found the boy's older brother after searching for his family. The father had died, and the mother had walked into the jungle, preferring the beasts to landlords who beat the workers and raped the women. But for the first time in central Travancore, a Thanda Pulayar owned land and built a hut.

Now, Krishnan's grandfather, a frail old man, lay in bed, warning Krishnan to keep 90 feet from Brahmins and 64 from Nairs to avoid polluting them, and to stay clear of the Nayadis, a 'wretched race' loathed even by the untouchables. 'If they come within a distance of 22 feet,' he warned, 'let out blood from your small finger or your gum and take a bath seven times.'

'It's all nonsense,' Krishnan's father retorted. 'Don't listen to your grandfather. He is old and is recalling the times long gone by.'

'But don't let Eesho mon ever hang his head in shame because of you,' Krishnan's father told him before he left for Puthuloor.

Krishnan nodded; he wanted to earn his father's respect. He also yearned to make Eesho proud, just as he had once devoured the English letters Eesho drew for him on the slate though they looked alien; the time he had walked into Father Goody's office with imagined courage; and the first time he drove the Hillman, with Eesho beside him and Tharakan and Mamma Mollykutty in the backseat, bobbing their heads in approval.

Krishnan switched off the light and got into bed, but he was too wound up with excitement and anxiety to go to sleep immediately. He wanted to wake up on time the next day. Promising himself to buy an alarm clock, he dozed off, intending to wake up before the sun's earliest rays graced the sky. He heard the tappers outside—the shuffling of their feet, the songs on their lips, and the chattering children following them. After a cold bath in the common bathing area outside, Krishnan opened his trunk and brought out his best shirt. A sky-blue cotton shirt with fawn paisley prints that Eesho got made for him in the best tailoring shop in Quilon.

Krishnan slipped into the shirt, looked down at his body, and smiled. The shirt clung to his torso like a crisp new wrapper. He liked the way it looked; it was stark against his skin, the colour of monsoon clouds—like that of the very god, Krishnan, after whom his parents had named him.

He picked up the mango sapling from the table and locked the door. When he walked to the office, he wondered whether he should have waited for the sun to rise. The sky was still inky with a blush of pink, but the tappers, men and women, were already at work with their children by their side.

'Tapper? Or factory worker?' one of the women asked him as he walked by. 'Accounting clerk,' Krishnan said. When he reached the office building, there was no one around except a watcher sleeping near the gate, a woollen muffler shrouding his face, a blanket enveloping the rest. Krishnan tapped on the cold metal gate with his knuckles. A pair of eyes could be seen opening unhurriedly through the slit of the muffler.

'Why are you here now? The office opens only at eight,' he said, his voice faint and muted through the layer of clothing. The watcher closed his eyes again.

'But the tappers are out. I can see them. I thought there might be work to do in the office. It is my first day today. I am joining as the clerk.'

'The tappers come to the office only to collect the salary. Otherwise, they are always around the trees or at the tapping blocks.'

Krishnan let the information soak in.

'What are tapping blocks?'

The watcher opened his eyes languidly. 'That is where they work. The area demarcated for them. The conductor and the writer also sit there.' He shifted his bottom on his chair to make himself more comfortable and closed his eyes again.

'Who are they?'

The watcher sat up and his forehead knit with suspicion as he watched Krishnan through the cold iron bars of the gate. He got up and walked towards him but kept a safe distance. 'Are you actually going to join as the clerk? Or are you here to steal from the factory?'

'If I wanted to steal something, I would just steal it. Wouldn't I?'

'What do you have in your hand?' He waved his stick at Mamma Mollykutty's mango sapling.

'It is for the superend saar. His mother gave it to me.'

The watchman's face lightened through the heavy iron bars. 'You know superend saar?'

'Yes. He has known me since I was little. My father used to work for him.'

The watchman fiddled with a set of keys that hung from his belt and smiled at Krishnan. 'Then you should have told me earlier. I will open the room for you. You can wait there. Superend saar might be doing the estate rounds now. But he will be here by eight for the general field muster. I will tell you what that is if you don't know.'

There was no sarcasm in the watchman's voice, but it made Krishnan wonder if he was suited for the job, as he knew nothing about the workings of a rubber estate. The elation he felt when he had set out for the office began to abate, but he promised himself that he would learn everything because he didn't want to let Eesho hang his head in shame.

∽

From the edge of the office, the land dropped steeply into a heavily forested valley. On occasion, Eesho could hear the wild elephants' calls and the murmurs from the bamboo pipes the Kurumbars played during Pongal and Sankranti. The office was built on the precipice of a cliff where the eastern section of the plantation ended, and the southern section began. Though the plantation stretched across 2,000 acres, only three-quarters of it was under cultivation because it was not easy to flatten the forest. But they did their best to tame the wild and stretch the border, felling trees and taming elephants to carry the fallen trees, continuing the exercise the white man had begun.

Markose looked out the window and broodingly ran his fingers along his milky white sweater. 'My father thinks we shouldn't widen our boundaries any more,' he said, drawing an imaginary circle in the air. 'He says he is happy where he is. But I actually think he is just lazy.'

'I think we should leave the rest of nature alone. Forests are essential in this part of the land. But it is your father's decision at the end of the day,' Eesho said. He rubbed Duke's coat and checked his watch. It was time for the factory visit. But he knew Markose had more to say.

'If the Englishman was happy with just the house on the hill, this place would have still been a forest. And if my grandfather was happy with what we had, none of us would be standing here today.'

Markose rested his shoulder against the window and took in the view. He ran his fingers over the tan leather straps of his rimfire rifle that was always with him, even on those days he didn't step out to hunt mountain goats or barking deer. He deemed himself a good shot. Once, when the Kurumbars asked him if he could shoot a leopard that had taken away their chickens and goats, he wasted no time and set off with a hunting party. After days and nights of combing through the thick wild, he found the cat resting on a tree, scrunching on the bones of a honey badger it had caught. He killed it with a single shot, skinned the animal, and stuffed its head. Mary took the hide and spread it out on the mosaic floor in the living room. Markose mounted its head above the door of his room. Although the Kurumbars were grateful to him, hushed whispers hinted that he relished the sport more than his duty to the locals.

'Where did you find the boy?' Markose asked Eesho. He was talking about Krishnan, though they were roughly around the same age. Eesho knew that Markose was pleased with Krishnan's work, mostly because he didn't have to spend time and energy on the old man. In two weeks, Krishnan had figured out his new world. He recorded everything. The litres of latex collected. The price of rubber for the day, week, and month. The amount of magnesium oxide and NPK bought in bulk for the replanted trees. The earth scraps collected once a month. The tree lace. The cup lumps. The daily attendance. The weekly store cash. The monthly wages. Krishnan was good with it all.

'He is from my village. I have known him since he was a child. His father used to climb coconut trees. But he cannot do so any more because of his health.'

Markose pulled out a chair and made himself comfortable in it. 'He is doing well for a Thandan's son. But how come he speaks English so well?'

'He went to a boarding school in Quilon for a while.'

'He could afford that?'

'I took him there. It is where I studied.'

'That was magnanimous.'

He rested his rifle on his lap and looked out the window.

'But imagine what will happen if all their kids go to school. It will change things. We will have no more people to climb coconut trees.'

'We should plant dwarf trees. Then no one needs to climb them.'

Markose ignored the drollery and clawed an itch through his made-in-England sweater. 'Honestly, I hope I won't live to see the day the children of tappers, tribals, and Thandans become rocket scientists and presidents.'

'I think that day is not too far away.'

'And you are fine with that?'

'Absolutely.'

Kuttapan appeared before them with a tray of tea. He gripped the glasses with a finger each on the inside and outside of the rim, lifted them off the tray, and placed them on the table.

Markose grimaced and stared down at the boy. 'Haven't I told you not to do that? I don't know where your fingers have been.' He clicked open his rifle and ran a muslin patch through the barrel.

Kuttapan gazed at the rifle and looked ready to cry.

'It's okay. He will remember next time. Right?' Eesho said and patted the boy on the back. Kuttapan was still looking at the gun. 'But now, hurry along or you will be late for school. You don't want the headmaster getting lost among the trees looking for you, right?'

Kuttapan chuckled and scurried along.

Markose blew the carbon scraps from the table and shook his head. 'You are too nice to them. We must keep these people at a distance. Otherwise, they will sit on your head and slowly nibble away at your brain. You don't understand how complicated the politics is at the estate.'

'I don't think the boy is involved in politics.'

'You are not taking me seriously. Papa had to put up with their petty politics forever. The workers are a lazy bunch—the tappers, the factory workers, and the tribals. When they don't work, we cut their wages and then they raise their flags. The previous superintendent left because he couldn't deal with these people. But Papa thinks that you will be able to handle them.' Markose took a nylon brush and began to clean the crown of the barrel.

Eesho laughed and ran his fingers over his pencil moustache. 'So, it is definitely not because of ghosts.'

'Ghosts? What are you talking about?'

'Pappan said that the previous manager ran away because he saw the ghost of the white man.'

'Pappan is mad. So are all of them. Quite an asinine bunch. Believe me, it is challenging to deal with uneducated people. They have no class.' Markose clicked the barrel back and looked at Eesho musingly. 'I heard you told the tappers not to take their children to work.'

'I told them not to take their children to work on weekdays when they have school. They can still join them on Saturdays.'

'But how much can they learn in one day?'

'One day a week for the rest of their childhood is enough, isn't it?'

Markose's forehead furrowed. He put his freshly cleaned rifle on the table and turned his eyes to the valley. 'I know what you think of me. That I do not respect people. Right?'

'I never said that.'

'Papa tells me that often.'

'Then your father knows you better than I do.' Eesho got up and walked to the door. He didn't want to put off the day's factory visit.

Markose swiftly got up from his chair and walked towards Eesho. He put his hand across his heart like he was making an oath and rapped his chest gently. 'I might be just shy of twenty and Papa says that I am immature. But I want you to know that he is wrong about me. I respect every job. If I did not, then I wouldn't even be here talking to the tribals and the Thandans.' Having said that, he left the room, rimfire rifle slung over his shoulders.

∽

Eesho walked along the road that stretched into the heart of the hills. The smell of rubber sap was in the air. It was a heady smell. Intoxicating. Sweet. Pungent. Something that one would not easily forget. Like the smell of babies. Or armpits. Or wives. Or mothers. Like the smell of ripening mangoes. Or the first rain.

It was raining, and the crimson road had begun to form little puddles resembling wounds on a child's knee. Duke joyfully jumped over them. He fancied the rains as much as the belly rubs he received. During the monsoons in Niranam, they would sit together on the cool red-oxide floor and watch the growing torrent sink into the earth,

Duke working his way through a pile of glucose biscuits that Eesho had pilfered from Mamma Mollykutty's tin, which she reserved for guests. 'Naughty dog,' Mamma Mollykutty would tell Duke when she'd see him nibbling on the biscuits, but would make no effort to retrieve the tower of treats from the table.

Eesho shielded his pipe with his palms and unfolded the umbrella he had taken from the jeep. He had left the jeep at the collection point at the western block. He liked to walk around the estate on foot, and he did so whenever he could. Walking, he believed, gave him a better perspective of the land, an intimacy that eluded him when cooped up in the vehicle. There were many things he missed when he drove. The crunch of the earth. The bite of the air. The heady scent of the rubber trees. Sometimes, he would walk about barefoot, as if forging a holy bond with the earth. Even when he was a child, he would mill about barefoot with Georgekutty around the coconut trees, much to Mamma Mollykutty's exasperation. 'I have given birth to savages,' she would bellow and chase them, wielding two pairs of chappals and a menacing bamboo stick, breasts shaking, golden kunukkus swinging wildly from her ears.

Eesho chuckled at the passing thought as he walked in the growing rain. Red earth specked his gum boots like little clots, reminding him, with every step, of the stories that bled from the soil.

It had been four months since he had begun his new adventure, and by now, he had habituated himself to the land that once belonged to young Hitchcock and had learned about the times gone by. Charles Hitchcock's father was friends with John Joseph Murphy, more fondly remembered as Murphy Sayippe, who first started the Hevea rubber plantation in Kerala on the banks of the river Periyar. Along with three others, he had formed the Periyar Syndicate in 1902 before he opted to go solo a couple of years later. When he heard of his friend's son, who had stayed back in the country after his father decided to set sail to England following his futile attempt to unearth gold in the hills of Wayanad, he knew he had to help the young man. He guided young Hitchcock in the direction of Puthuloor and even helped him acquire the land from the Malabar government and the local rajas. Murphy also supplied young Hitchcock with tappers since tapping was a skilled job and not many people had mastered it at that time.

When the young couple was stabbed to death, it left the people of the village aghast, because, like Murphy, Hitchcock was an optimist. A dreamer. He provided the children of the workers' free meals and also had plans to bring pipe water to the paadi. He spoke against untouchability and child marriage. It is believed that the entire village turned up at the couple's funeral and that Murphy Sayippe was the one who read the eulogies as young Hitchcock's father couldn't make it back to India in time. The Mopilla Rebellion was at its peak and the ships that were slated to set sail were cancelled as a cautionary measure. After the Hitchcocks' demise, the estate passed into the guardianship of Hitchcock's nephew, who was also living in India—a blind young man who remained oblivious to the intricate business of rubber and the devious devices of businessmen.

During World War II, Mary's father sensed financial opportunities. The Japanese army had captured the Malay peninsula, the largest rubber-producing area in the Far East. The production of synthetic rubber was slow. But even its arrival in the market couldn't prevent a deficit. The US Army needed rubber for their truck and airplane tyres, raincoats, boots, gloves, oxygen masks, medical equipment, and pontoon bridges. In 1939, he heard of the barter agreement where the US would barter 500,000 bales of cotton for 90,000 tonnes of British rubber. He was eager to dip his toes into this most promising industry.

He had heard about the white man's estate and the blind boy struggling to manage it. With an air of calculated charm, he approached the boy, promising him the hand of his comely daughter, Mary. In exchange, he persuaded the boy to sell the estate at a price far below its true worth. 'We will be family after all,' he told the boy. Family, they never became. Murphy had tried warning the boy of the old man's gambits, but it was too late. After the deal was signed, Mary's father got her married to Ousepachan.

But now all that mattered was to keep the rubber empire thriving, and the memories of a rebellion were just remnants—yarns laced with otherworldly flavours, ancient sepia photographs fading into time-worn walls, and two graves melding into the earth.

As he walked in the rain, Eesho thought back to the first time he'd met Ousepachan after he took charge. He noticed a fleeting ripple of embarrassment on the owner's face, evident in his reluctance to meet Eesho's eyes.

'Are you happy there?' he asked him while sinking into his Fornicator.

'Yes, we are. It's home now. And my wife believes she is at her creative best there. She loves the study on top and does all her embroidery there.'

Ousepachan inched forward and bobbed his head with relief. 'Such a young couple. So in love with each other. And I hope my son is not giving you too much trouble.'

'Everything is fine. Not even the white man's ghost is troubling me.'

Ousepachan laughed with a certain air of reticence, but Mary got straight to the point from the leg-rest. 'Ghosts? Whoops-a-daisy. Silly yammers by country people. It's not the dead that will trouble you, but the living and their trade union activities.'

The rain was beginning to ease into a drizzle. The tappers in the eastern block carried on tapping the trees. Light rains didn't interfere with the workings of the day. Eesho had inspected the tapping of the western block. He had spoken with the men in charge of the tappers and checked the numbers they had put down the previous day. Markose never accompanied him on the early-morning rounds or for the general field muster when the daily attendance was marked and work allotted to the people. Eesho passed by the road that led to Markose's cottage. The gate to the cottage was shut. He was probably still sleeping.

Duke ran ahead of Eesho and watched the tappers at work, hovering along the jagged edge of the hills like billy goats, sure-footed on their path ahead, picking up the earth scraps, and pinching out the cup lumps—dried latex from the previous day—and depositing them in colourful little baskets. Then, they made incisions upwards along the bark of the trees at twenty-five-degree angles with a knife that was shaped more like a chisel. In their skilful hands, it became a sculptor's instrument. Plastic covers adorned the top of the cuts like skirts in myriad colours. The covers prevented the rain from seeping into the fresh sap oozing into the coconut shells placed under the grooves. The shells would swell with sap in a couple of hours and the men would then tip them into aluminium buckets and take them to the collection area, where they would be weighed and written into their accounts. If the tappers collected more than the standard weight, they would get paid more. So, they worked hard, each person tapping more than 400 trees a day. The collected produce would be taken to the factory and stored in drums. Some would be processed into rubber sheets, while the earth scraps and cup lumps would be pressed into crepe rubber. The remaining drums of latex would be transported to town by the end of the day to be fashioned into various objects—chappals in blue and beige, rubber ducks that could float on water, baubles for little children to play with, squeezy bottle caps, cycle, truck and car tyres, surgical gloves, and machinery parts.

The people had finished tapping, so Eesho decided to walk back to the house for breakfast. And on the way, he met Elsy.

chapter 11

IT WAS DUKE WHO FOUND her lying on the ground. Her left ankle was twisted, swelling gradually. There were teeth marks on the nape of her neck. Blood dribbled from her neck and soaked her blouse. She grimaced in pain and moaned through clenched jaws. Duke pricked up his ears and raced down the hill in the direction of her voice. Eesho ran after him and saw the injured woman sprawled on the ground.

Elsy's house was down the road, outside the border of the estate, tucked away behind rows of pineapples that stood hidden behind neem and acacia trees that belonged to nobody. The five cents of land she owned were once her father's. Her father had no sons. So now it was hers.

That is why everyone said Avaran wanted to marry her. Also, she was beautiful. 'A fetching young woman, strangely beautiful for someone from her caste. Dark but beautiful,' they said.

When Avaran asked her father for her hand in marriage, the old man took Avaran's hand and shook it, silently giving his approval. She was sixteen, and she needed a man who could take care of her. This man had a tapping job and money was steady. Also, he was Christian. When Elsy was born, her mother, who had started attending a church in the hills, had made him promise that their daughter would be married to a suitor of the Christian faith. 'Yes, I promise,' he had told her, holding her hand as she slipped away into the darkness of the other world. 'Poor child....' people around them said. Years later, when a bolt of lightning struck him and left him paralysed waist down, they said the same thing.

Her father knew that he was making the right decision. Not many Syrian Christians would marry a Parayar Christian and here was a man who didn't even want a dowry.

Avaran moved in on the night of the wedding. The beatings started the same night.

Her father smelled arrack on his son-in-law as he walked into the house. Then there were bibulous slurs from the bedroom and his daughter's muffled sobs. When the blows landed on her, he tried to get up to go to her rescue. But his crippled body betrayed him. All he could do was lie there in his soiled clothes, awaiting his only child, a once happy child who liked to fly kites and play hopscotch.

On the night of the wedding, Avaran slapped her across the face five times when she asked him if he could be quieter with his lovemaking.

'Two steps and I will be in your father's lap. I should have thought better before I married a Parayar,' he said, slurring his words. 'You have English names, but why don't your faces match your names? And why do you still go to churches built deep in the jungles? Do you think people like us will still persecute you? Tear down your churches and set them on fire? Are you afraid of me?'

He threw her to the ground and undid his mundu. 'You stay on the ground. That is where you belong.' He passed out after he'd had sex with her.

From the adjacent room, she could hear her father calling out her name. 'Elsy, mole...I am sorry.'

But she did not go to him. She was too afraid. She curled into a corner of the room as her new husband, a splayed figure on the floor, serenaded the night with his rhythmic snores. When she went to wake her father with a glass of tea in the morning, his body was cold and stiff.

Now, all she could do was cry every time Avaran hit her. With every strike, it was her father's memory she mourned. With every slap, she heard his voice. She saw his hand sticking out limply along his cot and tears drying up on his cheeks.

This time, Avaran had bitten her too. The biting was new.

When Duke sniffed her, she first froze in horror. Then she saw his eyes. They were kind. A gentle voice called out from behind the pineapple bushes. 'Are you okay? Please let me help you.'

Avaran woke up later that day and bellowed through the wall, 'I am bleeding. Come and help me.' He rubbed his shirt, stiff and crisp with caramel-red blood, and slipped his fingers under it. His skin was damp with warm sweat, but he sensed no wound. 'Elsy, I have blood on my shirt,' he said. There was no movement. She usually answered him. Though her voice was feeble, he could hear it through the plywood wall. He got up from his cot in the front room. 'Elsy, you need to answer me when I call you.'

He kicked a broken earthen pot near the hearth. Why hadn't she swept the floor? She usually never let the house get messy. There were beads of blood on the floor, brown and parched like fallen leaves. Avaran stopped in his tracks and feared the worst. He undid his mundu and checked for wounds he feared he could not feel, worried that the spirit's potency might have numbed his senses to their presence. He had had his usual bottle in the shop in town and bought another for the man who lived next to the shop. He always did that because it made the man sleep and that meant that he could sleep with the man's sister. Last night, the man was not home. So, Avaran had had the second bottle too. 'Be careful on the way back. The trucks speed along the road without mercy,' the man's sister had told him when he left the house, swaying and stumbling along. 'I will never be crushed by a truck. When I die, I will die a glorious death. Death without any blood,' he said.

Avaran tied his mundu and went to the bedroom where Elsy usually slept. Her straw mat was rolled up and kept in a corner, but her suitcase was still there. He opened it, dug his fingers into the corner where she kept the few notes he gave her every month, pulled out a couple of them, and stuck them into a knot in his mundu.

As the growl of hunger echoed within him, he made his way to the clay hearth carved against the wall opposite his cot. There was no pot on the stove. It lay broken on the floor with pazankanji drying up around it. The previous night, he had told her that he wanted meat, but all she could serve him was old rice gruel. But now he craved the bowl of pazankanji, regretting having callously smashed it on the floor when she had held it out to him.

He walked out and searched among the pineapple bushes, where he had a vague recollection of throwing her that morning. He remembered the blood on her blouse but couldn't recall hitting her. As the alcohol cleared from his head and body, a faint sense of regret tugged at him for hitting her so savagely. He peered down at his crimson-stained shirt and recalled blood flowing down the nape of her neck. Despite the regret, he was relieved that the blood on his shirt did not belong to him.

Then his heart flooded with fear. What if he had beaten her too hard? What if she had run away? There were times he wanted to talk to her kindly, but he didn't because he feared he would turn out to be like his father. His father, who had been his mother's footman. A vassal. A doormat.

However, he didn't want to be like his mother either.

Despite their modest means, they were respectable, at least on his father's side, and from an old Syrian Christian family. His mother, he thought, on the other hand, was not quite as reputable, with her penchant for young lovers and a tongue as untamed as a fishmonger's. His mother mirrored the qualities of the family who had raised her—a family that destroyed the churches the Parayars had built. These were small churches made of coconut palm leaves and red mud. They told the Parayars that while they were happy that they had found salvation, they couldn't worship near them. How difficult would it have been to build with sticks, stones, and mud in the hills?

Avaran couldn't help but think of his uncle and cousins on his mother's side as brutes. Yet, his mother often said that he was no different when liquor took hold of him. He didn't want to believe her words, but knew she was being honest. She called his father feeble. A weakling afraid of his own shadow. And in that judgement, there lay the undeniable truth. She took all the money he brought home, hid it deep in her blouse, and struck his hand aside whenever he tried to retrieve it.

Because of the way his mother treated his father, Avaran was convinced that women always took advantage of men's infirmities.

But he was not his mother. He gave Elsy things. She was frail, and she needed a man, and he was there for her. He gave her things for the kitchen and bought her clothes and lemon candies. After her father's death, he even bought her a parrot. Though he didn't like the old cripple, he knew Elsy loved him. The day after her father died, Avaran noticed she had coiled into her body like a snail. Her flesh was stiff when he held it in his hands that night. She was unreachable. The next day, he went to the market and got her the parrot. He knew she wanted someone to talk to. She smiled when he gave it to her.

Now, the parrot was also looking for her.

'Elsy, Elsy,' it cawed from the cage she had strung to the roof outside the house.

'Tell me where she went,' he asked the bird. But it only called out her name unrelentingly. Avaran spat at it. Spittle dripped down his neck. 'Useless creature.' He wiped his neck with the back of his hand and walked towards the road. Then a passer-by told him that she was seen at the Estate House.

Avaran's body tightened. What business did she have at the Estate House? Maybe the passer-by was lying. People liked to wind him up. Some were jealous of his clout in the union. Most of the workers were part of a union. Each political party had its own trade union wing at the estate and irrespective of political differences, when their shared interests were in jeopardy, they forged an unwavering unity; the method of collective bargaining was a powerful thing. Avaran believed that, in times of need, he was the one that brought them all together. But doubts about his intentions often simmered among the workers. Some said he was doing it because he was power-mad. Some said he was eyeing the post in the union at the taluk level. Despite the kernel of truth in their statements, Avaran let the comments slide, and whenever the owners of the estate attempted to exploit the workers, he stood up for everyone, refusing to budge until their demands found a resolution. And the workers didn't mind him taking charge because he did most of the heavy lifting.

Avaran walked towards the Estate House, praying that he wouldn't find her there. He would have to drag her out if she was holed up in the safety of the old English walls. She had never tried running away. Yet, he couldn't help but remember the day she had whispered to him her secret desire to flee. He had been drunk beyond reason that day, and she had thought that nothing she said would register on him. That's why she had whispered into his ears.

'I despise you for your selfishness, vanity, and hollowness. I despise you when you are drunk and when you are not. The day I flee from your presence, I will rejoice.' She thought he had passed out, but he had heard her in his drunken stupor. And now he remembered what she'd said that day.

Avaran walked up the hill, wondering if she had summoned the courage to follow through on her promise. There was a likelihood that the superend had found her and had taken her in. But he also knew that the superend had a wife.

'Whore,' he said under his breath. She was a whore, like his mother, who took in a lover a few weeks after she had killed his father with a lifetime of sharp words. Women could never be trusted. Even Elsy, with her feigned passivity. He was the foolish one.

The house emerged from behind the ring of weeping willows. The last time he was at the Estate House was a few months ago, on the day the previous superend left the village after having accepted defeat at his hands. The man had tried relentlessly to not hand out the yearly bonuses to the workers, citing the losses that the estate was having to bear. But everyone knew the truth. There might have been no profit, but it was because the boss couple had created a new company and transferred the shares they held to the new one. Thus, it affected the overall profit and the bonuses. 'My hands are tied. I cannot do anything. I am also an employee like you,' the superend kept telling the workers who had called for a strike. He suspended Avaran and a few of his fellow workers for their disruptive activities. But nobody could be suspended that easily. The sit-out strike only gained momentum. The workers demanded that the suspended workers be reinstated. The political parties to which the workers were affiliated sent their representatives from the taluk, and rumours of violence floated in the air.

The old man who co-owned the estate was soft. It was his wife's idea to devise such devious plans in the first place. The old man gave in despite his wife's defiance. The superend had had enough, though. Once, during a meeting with the striking workers, he said it was easier managing a bunch of schoolkids. He announced the company's decision to hand out the bonuses, reinstate the suspended workers, and his resolve to leave the job. When he drove out of the Estate House with his wife and three young kids, Avaran stood near the garden drinking up the look of downfall on the man's shrunken face. He had managed to break him.

Avaran walked to the portico and called out her name. There was a shuffling of feet from somewhere inside the house. He walked closer and pressed his face against the glass, waiting for the sounds of approaching footsteps. He wanted her. She was his wife. The only woman who mattered to him. The woman in town had other men, and he wasn't important to her. Though he never paid her like the other men, she was a whore. Not his frail wife. Perhaps he would even pardon her for leaving him, for seeking refuge within the citadel. Maybe he would stop drinking. For her, he could. Maybe he would stop hitting her...maybe....

He whispered her name and looked into the hall with hope in his belly. But it was not Elsy who emerged from behind the window. 'Wolf!' he cried out as he stumbled back. He tripped over a stone near the portico, but he picked himself up in a hurry and hustled down the hill, praying that the wolf wouldn't get him.

PART V

chapter 12

WHEN AMMA DECIDES TO MAKE an appearance in Puthuloor, Aleyamma gets a little nervous. Amma never liked the house though she had never lived there. But she said she was conceived here, in one of the cold bedrooms, and that it left an ineradicable mark on her. In Amma's words, it was like a cancer that could not be cured or a beauty spot that became unsightly over time.

Amma drives her Ambassador gingerly up the hill. It makes a low growl as it snakes its way up the gravelly earth at a snail's pace, sending red nuggets of soil flying from below its tyres. Behind the wheel, Amma sits upright like a porcelain doll and squints grotesquely through her monkey crop. She pouts and purses her lips as she coaxes her beloved Ambassador to reach the crest of the hill.

Amma is a terrible driver, and Appacha, knowing her innate gift for calamity, always feared that she might meet with an accident. When Amma first started driving, Appacha told her that Krishnan Uncle could give her driving lessons. But Amma shook her head as if terrorized by the proposal. 'I am not letting that man anywhere near my car. You too shouldn't. He might kill us all one day,' she said, though Krishnan Uncle, unlike Amma, was the most watchful driver in Aleyamma's observation. It was his feet that kicked the accelerator, his hands that gripped the steering wheel after Appacha drew her from the edge of the pond. He was the one who made the Contessa fly, wispy as a dream, steady and surreal, like the car from *Chitty Chitty Bang Bang*. A few minutes more and perhaps she would have embraced the light that had begun to call her name. Aleyamma knew Amma was more capable of crashing the car and killing them than Krishnan Uncle.

Amma started driving after Appa left. When he left the house, he also left his smoke-blossoming Ambassador behind. He abandoned it because it was as old as Amma and prone to breaking down on long journeys. Smoke bellowed from its exhaust pipe and every movable part imparted ominous noises.

Whenever the Ambassador broke down on the road, Amma would have to ask passers-by for help. Men would get lost in her almond eyes and show no reluctance to push the car. Amma would press the accelerator and as the engine roared to life, she would drive off without even waving a thank you to the men who hobbled behind the Ambassador, only to lose their footing and fall face down on NH 47.

Amma loved the Ambassador. Other than the bladder stone, it was her only reminder of Appa. Though she didn't care much for Appa, she cared deeply for the remnant he left behind. She washed it every evening with a generous dollop of her own shampoo, squeezed into a plastic soap dish, and water she carried in a tin bucket from the tap in the garden. She would mutter at length about the dust and pollution of Cochin while she was at the task, sometimes even grumble for a peaceful existence in some village somewhere, forgetting for a moment that she had decided not to go back to her own, and quickly refute her words with her justification, 'City or village. Dirt is dirt.'

Amma looks exhausted when she reaches the top of the hill. She is stuck in her upright position on tiger-printed seats, perspiration embossing her temple, hands placed on the steering wheel in the ten-ten position like an Ajanta clock. The monkey crop is due for a haircut, and Aleyamma knows it would be even harder to read her now because her eyes have gone missing. People hide behind many things. For the otherwise voluble Amma, it is her monkey crop.

'Why would someone build a house on such a steep hill? Feels like I have run cross-country,' she says. 'I will get my suitcase from the boot.'

Aleyamma doesn't know how long Amma plans on staying. Ever since she retired, she has been looking for a new direction in life, trying everything from knitting to Zumba, giving up all of them because they were either too passé or too frivolous.

Amma plants her suitcase on the ground with a thud. She puts her arms over Aleyamma's neck and pulls her to her shoulder like a pugilist. That is how Amma hugs her. Her stiff organza sleeve crudely caresses Aleyamma's cheek, and her perfume stings her nostrils. Amma's dress looks like paper, ready to rip. The buttons on her top are steadfastly holding the garment together; her breasts swell within it, in folds like sand dunes. She lets out a sigh and stretches herself. The top button of her blouse explodes, rolls onto the ground and disappears. Amma either doesn't notice it or doesn't care. 'What's for lunch?' she asks.

After Appa left, Amma decided to dissolve the bitterness she felt through unfaltering resolve and furious activity. Though Amma wasn't exactly in love with Appa, life without him was different. Amma, who had never worked before, found a job at a travel agency as a ticketing officer. She would book and cancel tickets the entire day, come back home tousled-haired and fagged out, dig a burrow in her bed, and pass out. After a few days, Amma realized that the kitchen was her haven. She cooked every day like she was cooking a feast. Every evening at five, when the school bus dropped Aleyamma off, it was not Amma that greeted her at the door, but the smell of food she was diligently making in their green tiled kitchen—fat fish frying in fresh coconut oil, yellow jackfruits spilling slimy guts over the floor, crisp banana chips, mutton biryani sealed with a sheet of atta and baked in a clay pot that once belonged to Ammachi. On some nights, the steady murmurs of the Pioneer Whisky which Cheria Pappa got her from Dubai, and the clangour of aluminium pans would keep Aleyamma awake as Amma tested her baking skills in a gigantic oven she had fished out from a corner of the storeroom. It was a wedding gift from one of Appa's aunts, who had told her that her nephew's favourite sweet dish was marble cake. Amma never made it for Appa when he was around. But she made many after he left.

Amma would not only make food industriously, but also clean up her plate effortlessly. Soon Amma's dresses started becoming tight, and she couldn't slip them on effortlessly like before because they would get trapped at her breasts. She would call Aleyamma midway through her labour, arms suspended in the air like a zombie, head caught somewhere in between. 'Pull, pull. Just pull it down with all your might,' Amma would cry through the apparel mangled around her like a death snare. First, Amma thought her breasts were becoming big. She would examine them in the mirror, wedging the skin in between her fingers to see if there was more flesh than she remembered. Then she questioned the detergent's efficacy. But when she saw that Aleyamma's clothes were fine, she realized the true culprit lay elsewhere. So, to rid herself of the addiction, she embarked on a journey of self-starvation, hoping water and air would melt the flesh away. All they did was make a mad Amma madder. Her voice became more gravelly, she began to huff and puff, and her almond eyes flared more than necessary. Mercifully, those days were short-lived and soon, she made her way back to the kitchen, rattling pots and flourishing whisks, crooning, 'Eat your food with gladness. Drink your wine with a joyful heart', getting bigger clothes as a solution to the quandary she needed to resolve.

∽

Aleyamma is not sure what Amma thinks of Elsy Chedatty because Amma acts like she doesn't exist in the house. She has always maintained that servants must be kept at arm's distance. This included the utensils they ate from. Growing up, Aleyamma always stared at the dull steel plate and glass perched at the far corner of their dish rack, from which the succession of maids who passed through Amma's hands would eat and drink, seated on a low wooden stool in the utility area next to the kitchen. Once, when she asked Amma about the separate plate and glass, she shrugged and said, 'That is how it has always been.'

'But why?'

'Those are dirty plates and glasses. That's why. Now get lost.'

Once Amma caught the helper using the good plates for her lunch. 'Put those back. Use your plate,' Amma said.

'What is wrong with this plate, chechi?' the lady asked, though she already knew the answer.

'There is nothing wrong. That is the good plate.'

'Okay, chechi,' she said without putting up a fight. But that was the last Amma saw of her. She left the house with the good and the bad plates, hiding them somewhere within the copious layers of her sari.

∽

Her prejudice notwithstanding, Amma has no trouble partaking of the spread that Elsy Chedatty has laid in front of her. Her eyes sparkle with delight as she surveys the table piled high with food. In her eagerness to welcome Amma, Elsy Chedatty had gone overboard.

'This is too much,' Aleyamma says, smiling.

Elsy Chedatty is standing near the door. 'The guests have gone out for breakfast. But they will come back for lunch. So, nothing will be wasted.'

'Who said anything about wasting?' says Amma as she piles upma on her plate.

'True, there will absolutely be no waste today,' Aleyamma says. Amma shoots her a warning glance and tops her plate with chicken curry.

At the end of the meal, Amma lets out a satiated sigh. But she doesn't thank Elsy Chedatty for her labour of love.

Despite her gluttony at lunch, Amma's hunger is not satiated. Later that night, Amma hovers around the fridge. She trowels jam from a tall glass bottle with a tablespoon and puts it in her mouth. The leathery goo sticks to Amma's teeth as she licks the spoon and lets out throaty sounds of satisfaction. When she sees Aleyamma standing in the corner of the room, watching her nocturnal caper, her face stiffens. In the chalky light of the refrigerator, she mutters with a full mouth, 'It's banana jam. It's truly delicious.'

'Yes, Elsy Chedatty made it.'

'Do you want some?' She holds out the jar and swallows the last bit of jam in her mouth.

'No. I am not hungry.'

'Just like old times,' she says and screws the cap back on. 'There were times when I poured milk down your throat. You were too young. You won't remember.'

'No, I remember,' she tells her. Amma understood the importance of nutrition like any other mother, but she took it more sedulously than anyone else. Every evening, Amma would take her to the tree-lined Foreshore Road and point at the ships that sailed past them and the birds that flew above their heads. Then she would thrust open Aleyamma's mouth with her thumb and index finger and empty a tumbler of milk down her throat, which she would throw up eventually on the drive back home. But she never stopped the routine, as she believed that at least some of the milk was still left somewhere in her stomach. Her approach was unlike that of Appacha's, which was more enticing; discovering hidden duck eggs was an act that made her get to the bottom of the plate without hesitation.

'You remember me giving you the milk?' Amma asks her, smiling like that is a happy memory.

'I remember because you scarred me with the milk.'

Amma's face clouds over and her eyes roll behind her monkey crop. She has never known how to take a joke. Grumpily, she puts the jam jar back in the fridge, closes the door with a resounding thud, and makes her way to her room, licking her lips.

Aleyamma takes out the jar of jam. She sits on the edge of the dining table and sinks a spoon into the jam. Amma is right. It's delicious, yet a disquieting aftertaste lingers; this is always the case when she enters Amma's force field. Over the years, Amma has given her enough reasons to question her actions. Like the time she tore her away from Manoj and gave her a good scrub. Manoj was her best friend in Niranam, though Amma told her that a servant's son couldn't possibly assume the role of a best friend. Once, they were playing police-and-robber in the garden, with her arms around his waist and her fingers locked within his. When the police didn't let go of the robber, she noticed Amma staring down at them from the kitchen window, her lips curled in disdain. Amma walked to the garden and told her through gritted teeth that the time for playing had come to an end. She took Aleyamma to the bathroom, plucked the Radhas soap from the orange puddle it had left in the corner of the washbasin, and washed her 'dirt' away in purposeful and painful sweeps.

'You can't touch him. We don't know if he took a bath or if he dug his nose. He also might have lice in his hair. But more importantly, you don't want him to fall in love with you. Imagine the kids you'll have together. Little black things with big fat noses who will all go to hell because they will be praying to idols made of mud and stone. Do you want to have black babies with big fat noses? Do you want them to go to hell?'

'But you have a big fat nose. So, will you go to hell?' Aleyamma said, pointing her finger at Amma's face. Amma momentarily stopped the scrubbing, raised two soapy fingers to her sweeping nose bridge, and ran them along it. Her fingers spread out like vernier callipers, as though she was attempting to measure the vastness of her nose. Having done that, she walloped Aleyamma on her soapy bottom.

What Amma said brought her much disquietude, but she never told Manoj about the agonizing scrub she got that day. She had to protect Manoj, even though he was two years older than her, and she took it upon herself to shield him from Amma and others like her, especially Mouse Appachan.

Mouse Appachan was a quaint being, as was his wife, Happy Kochamma, who was Appacha's second cousin. Aleyamma didn't know what Mouse Appachan's real name was. She called him Mouse Appachan because she thought he looked like a rodent. When Appacha heard her refer to him as Mouse Appachan for the first time, he laughed and said, 'Maybe we should offer him cheese the next time he comes home.'

Unlike Mouse Appachan, Happy Kochamma's real name was Happy, a name that her parents believed would come true in her life, but most likely didn't because she was married to Mouse Appachan. She was the farthest removed from a mouse in terms of likeness, thickset like the rest of the women in the family and always breathless, huffing and puffing every step of the way. She said that it was because of the heat. But Appacha said it was really because of her weight.

Mouse Appachan had an opinion about the world. About people. And Amma agreed with him about everything. About politics. About how communism had destroyed the state and how the communists were still doing the same because they opposed everyone who wanted to do something useful, whether it was to build supermarkets, factories, or four-lane roads. About servants. And the children of servants. According to them, Manoj and Aleyamma could never be friends. And that Manoj's father, Balan, a blithe spirit, was much too close to Appacha for their liking. 'Do you see how he looks at you right in the eyes while talking to you? There was a time when people like him spoke with respect. They would shield their mouths with their hands and look at the ground. Times have changed,' he told Amma. And even when Balan tried to help Mouse Appachan after he got drunk with the grape wine Appacha had made for Christmas, and nearly passed out on the porch after underestimating the potency of the concoction, mundu discarded somewhere, penis hanging like a limp rag between scraggy legs, he swore at him like Noah swore at Ham. 'Curse you Balan, the lowest of slaves. God made you and your forefathers as black as soot for a reason. You are a cursed generation.'

Amma was there, too, when Mouse Appachan sang verses from the Bible in his drunken stupor. Amma did not curse. But she did not stop the cursing either. She watched, her stoic face not softening even when Manoj pulled his father away from the drunken mêlée, their eyes welling with tears.

So, it is not surprising that Amma does not acknowledge the presence of Elsy Chedatty.

chapter 13

VELIA PAPPA'S VOICE IS GENTLE, and his Elvis Presley drawl is more pronounced over the phone. He rarely called; that wasn't his style. There were the impersonal messages on her birthdays, the perfunctory 'Happy New Year' texts, nothing more. But as Amma's brother, some familial duty gnawed at him, urging him to check on a niece left fatherless by a man who had vanished into thin air. After Appa left, Amma didn't like to speak about him. Appa never called or wrote them letters. When someone told Amma that he had shacked up with his secretary in Goa and that there were rumours that she was with child, Amma laughed hard and said, 'Poor woman.'

Aleyamma could never bring herself to delete Velia Pappa's messages though they were nothing more than obligatory; there was something strangely reassuring in knowing they were tucked away in her memory card, as if their mere presence staved off a yawning loneliness. Perhaps it was the unbroken silence from Appa that made her cling to these fleeting notes from an uncle who, though a stranger in every other way, still sought a connection.

It is the first time he is reaching out to her after the reading of the will, which had ended in resentment.

'How are things there? Has chechi reached?' He sounds unflustered.

He is not faking friendliness. Velia Pappa, though quick to react, is just as quick to forgive. Convention often casts the older siblings as the expected bearers of forgiveness, but in their family, it is Velia Pappa and Cheria Pappa who hold the keys to absolution. He has called to mend fences.

'Yes, Amma is here. Things are all right. Elsy Chedatty does most of the work, as I am still settling in.'

'Elsy is good that way. She knows everything one needs to know. And the bookings are going okay?'

'We've had steady bookings ever since I reached.'

'All good otherwise? People from town not giving any trouble?'

'No. What do you mean?'

'Oh, it's nothing,' Velia Pappa says. His voice is nonchalant. But there is an awkward lull.

When he speaks again, he is picking his words clumsily. 'There was an incident once. Nothing big, though. So, don't worry. Okay?'

'What happened?'

'We had an Arab family as guests a few months ago. The women were in their purdahs and stuff. Then some people from the party came over and asked the guests to show their passports. Their student wing has an office at the junction, you know. When Elsy asked why they wanted to see the guests' passports, they said they wanted to make sure that they were not terrorists. The guests were angry. God knows what they must have thought about our country. Later that week at the kavala, there was a public meeting about love jihad and things like that.'

'Oh my goodness. I didn't know that.' She draws her legs together and sits upright on the sofa. 'So far, I've had no trouble,' she tells him.

'Good then. Don't worry. You know, they are doing all this because of the upcoming elections. All these people do the same. The Congress, the communists, and the BJP. They are always waiting to pick up an issue and make it political. But I don't think we will ever become a Gujarat or a UP. No one can fool us Malayalis so easily. See how far we have come. And if Kerala does become a Gujarat or a UP, I will take the next flight out of India and migrate to Canada or the US.'

Velia Pappa laughs at his own joke.

But they both know that he will not leave. He will not scrub his own toilet, mow his own grass, buff the silverware himself, or let go of the status he was born into for the so-called better standards of living abroad.

He is also laughing at himself, for once having subscribed to similar ideas. There was a time when he, along with a few members of the church, spoke to a television channel about the rising cases of 'love jihad' and 'narcotics jihad' that were happening in the state, shaking their heads over the poor Christian and Hindu women who were tricked into Muslim marriages (and in due course, terrorism) through promises made over drugs mixed into ice creams. For Velia Pappa, it was a matter of flaunting his Ray-Bans on the screen, but for some others, it was about gaining a political footing, as siding with a party with roots in Brahmanism was well suited to propagating their versions of history as well.

'I can come if you need any help,' he says.

'Oh no. That would be totally unnecessary.'

'Okay. I am busy here anyway. But I was thinking of something. I was thinking of asking Krishnan if he could help you and Elsy at the estate. I hope you have no problem with that.'

'Problem? Not at all. In fact, I am thrilled to hear that.'

She senses relief washing over Velia Pappa's voice. 'Then I will tell him that. Let's see what he has to say.' Velia Pappa is pensive again. 'Appa would have wanted that. In fact, before everything happened to Appa, he told me that I would have to make sure that Krishnan is cared for after he is gone.'

She is not surprised. Appacha cared for everyone. And Krishnan Uncle was Appacha's best friend.

The words slip from her tongue instinctually. 'Did he ever talk about me?'

She knows Velia Pappa is surprised by the question given that he falls silent. 'Yes, of course,' he says after a while. He is emphasizing his Elvis drawl to camouflage his discomposure. 'Appa talked about everyone. Made sure everyone was fine.'

That is not what she wants to hear. But she knows she cannot squeeze anything from Velia Pappa any more. He is probably rolling his good eye at her through the mouthpiece. 'I will talk to Krishnan,' he says before hanging up.

Aleyamma sits on the sofa, puts her head back, and watches the wooden ceiling. She should be grateful. Appacha has given her land on which she has not laboured, a place that she has not built. She is eating the fruit of the tree he planted. Yet he is far away. She wants to call him back to fill the empty spaces he has left behind, the hollowness she has tried to fill with cigarettes, running, Roy, morbid paintings, and those extra weekend shots. She wants to feel his hands on her forehead. She wants his laugh lines and the ears that wiggled. She wants him to keep her snug in his arms as he did when she was a child. Some would deem it foolishness to be stuck at the age of eight years. But she wants to be stuck. Stuck in a place where love and trust effortlessly embrace her. A place where she never has to seek out these treasures. A place she calls home.

Amma remained resolutely unbelieving of Aleyamma's near-death experience after falling into the pond; her disbelief stood like a sphinx-like wall, and she told Aleyamma to stop spinning yarns. The doctors called it 'near drowning'. Patients talked like this when they were in shock and when the oxygen supply to the brain was inadequate. 'She will get over it,' they said. The doctors were perhaps right, but Appacha believed her. Because Appacha believed everything she said. When she feigned a fever to skip school or when she said she spotted fulgent UFOs darting across the sky on starry nights like wobbly jellyfish, he loved and trusted her with effortless abandon.

Her eyes stray to the shelf pushed against the wall with the stuffed deer heads. There is a statue of St Joseph and baby Jesus on it, with chipped noses and stonewashed clothes. Father is holding the baby in his arms, close to his chest as if he is endeavouring to keep the hapless being warm in the crook of his armpits. Velia Pappa found it when he had dug up the front of the garden to lay tiles in his act of beautifying the entrance to the house. It was wrapped in cloth, laid upside down, and buried one foot into the ground. He first marvelled at the treasure he had unearthed from the ground and was glad that he could add it to the list of other treasures within the house: the stuffed heads, the rosewood furniture, the sepia photographs. But he was disheartened when he found out it was not that old and that it was buried by the previous owner because burying a statue of St Joseph was supposed to help with the sale of a house according to Catholic traditions. And in this case, it was a house with spectral sightings and deaths. 'Bloody Catholics. As if burying a statue can help you sell the house,' Velia Pappa said. Though he wasn't Catholic, he still placed the statue prominently on the shelf, secretly fearing the heavenly wrath he could incur if he didn't show respect to an icon of much veneration.

Aleyamma looks at the figurine closely. Joseph's face reminds her of Appa—Appa with a fuzzy French beard and a faraway look. She tries hard to recall the time he held her in his arms and wonders if she would find a picture of him doing so in one of their old, moth-eaten family albums. He might have walked out on her when she was eight, but he must have held her when she was a baby, well-pleased with what he had created. He must have tickled her toes and her belly. He must have held her in the crook of his arm while she giggled and played with his hair and held onto his ears. Nonetheless, the only time she remembers feeling his touch on her skin was a week before he walked out on them, when he held her hand while they were on a ferry to Vypin island, where Appa's office was located.

Appa did 'import-export' of dried shrimp. She was never sure if it was import or export, as the nature of the business was never clearly explained to her. They drove the Ambassador onto a ferry of questionable integrity and sat in the car as they sailed through the backwaters of Cochin. It was a school holiday, and for the first time, she was accompanying him to his office. She was grateful that Amma had gone down with a stomach bug, which she claimed she (alone) had caught after they ate the food that Appa had packed from 'some third-rate hotel' as a treat for a deal he had struck at work. Amma sank into the sofa, threw a cushion at Appa, and pointed at the door. 'Out, both of you,' she screamed. Appa had no choice but to take Aleyamma along.

It was her first time on a ferry, yet it was Appa who was anxious. When the driver moved his hand to scratch an itch on his back and the ferry shuddered beneath the Ambassador, Appa reached out and took her hand. His sweat seeped into her fingers as he watched their locked hands. When the ferry driver stopped scratching his back, Appa placed her hands on her dress again. Appa's eyes were, once again, far away.

Appa's office stood hidden in a murky alleyway that smelled of dead rats and urine. 'Do not urinate here' read the carelessly written sign on the office door. It was Appa's handwriting. It was clear that the notice was not having the desired effect. As they reached the office, Appa had to shoo away an old man who had positioned himself close to the door, about to engage in the customary routine.

'Can't you see the sign? Do not urinate here, it says,' Appa said, pointing at the notice.

'I can't read.' The old man smiled, flashing his orange teeth.

'Oh great, now I will have to draw a picture for illiterates,' muttered Appa as the old man ambled away, looking for another place to empty his bladder.

The office thankfully didn't smell the same. But it was not much better.

Aleyamma was well-acquainted with the odour—a stale, salty shrimp smell that had also seeped into Appa's armchair at home, where he sat every evening. He would ask Amma for a cup of tea, unbutton his shirt, take off his baniyan, and wipe down his sodden armpits with it. Amma would give him the tea and Appa would give her his sopping vest. Amma would retire to the bedroom with it, holding it gingerly at arm's length, muttering names under her breath.

She also smelled the same. Not Amma. But the woman. She must have picked it up from the office. Or perhaps from Appa. She was perched at the edge of a chair and working on a Remington… clack…clack…clack…her fingernails, dark and pointy like that of the sorceress from Snow White. When she saw them, she sprang up and watched Aleyamma with twitchy eyes.

'She is my secretary,' Appa said.

'What is a secretary?' Aleyamma asked.

'She types and sends letters for my company,' Appa said, pointing at the typewriter.

Eyes still twitching, the secretary walked towards them, pinched Aleyamma's cheeks with her sorceress nails, and smiled with her claret lips. 'So swed-swed you are,' she said, sounding like her typewriter. Only her lips smiled. Her eyes didn't.

Appa's eyes were on the woman; his eyes were as alive as the times he looked at his bladder stone. They had left their faraway existence and come down to earth to drink from the life it offered him.

Aleyamma wiped her cheeks on her dress sleeves. Her heart tugged with a fugitive sadness for Amma. And, at that moment, in the salty shrimp-infested confines of the room, she swore to herself that she would never be the woman with the cheap nail polish and the claret lips.

Aleyamma stares at the stonewashed statue of Joseph and baby Jesus and lets out a chortle.

'What are you looking at?' Amma asks. She has appeared beside Aleyamma. Though Amma is heavy, her footsteps are strangely light.

'I was wondering whether that resembles someone,' Aleyamma says, pointing at the French bearded face.

Amma stares at it briefly through her monkey crop. 'He never held you,' she says, and floats away on her tiny feet.

chapter 14

EARLY IN THE MORNING, ALEYAMMA pulls on a tank top and shorts, slips on a headset, and runs towards town. She steels herself, mentally rehearsing her resolve to dodge the weight of prying glares. 'Eyes on the expanding horizon, let the music in your ears drown out the world,' she whispers.

A few minutes in, she nears the building with the saffron flags. Eyes ahead, she reminds herself. But the place is a hive of activity, and she can't help but look around. There he is, arranging chairs on the dusty ground, when she hears them call his name—Soman. This time, he doesn't glance her way, and she's washed over with a wave of relief.

He's no longer the barefoot figure sweeping up dust on the veranda. Today, he's dressed for something more. He is clad in vivid white. A saffron scarf hangs around his neck and his starched shirt is forming puddles at the armpits. His mundu is folded at the knees. A red tilak adorns his forehead, and his floppy hair is slicked back with gel, the scent of which she thinks she can detect from far away. He takes the chairs piled up in the veranda and puts them in neat rows next to the building. He seems essential to the environment as people keep running to him, seeking his endorsement for their efforts, to which he either nods or shakes his head. The boys are busy stacking up pamphlets and sweeping the ground next to the building, too occupied to notice her. They carry on with their work, foregoing their usual habit of staring at her.

When she returns from the run, Soman is not there. But the boys are hoisting a banner across the gate of the ground. It flaps in the gentle morning breeze, announcing the purpose of the buzz. 'Mission Dheera—bringing up the brave women of tomorrow', it reads both in Malayalam and English. There is a steady sibilation in the air. The members of the Sports Club have been fans of such gatherings. Elsy Chedatty said that, not long ago, they had held a meeting that questioned women's entry into Sabarimala and highlighted the need to protect age-old traditions and the chastity of Swami Ayyappan, who vowed to stay celibate until first-time devotees stopped visiting his shrine.

As she passes by the building, a pamphlet floating in the air lands near her feet. She picks it up and runs on without reading it.

'What is that?' Amma asks when she reaches home. Amma is stretched out on the sofa, dunking arrowroot biscuits into a cup of tea.

The paper is damp with sweat from Aleyamma's palms, and she wonders why she even bothered picking it up. She sits next to Amma and smoothens out the pamphlet. Soman's photograph is displayed prominently on it, with rows of much smaller photos of the members of the organizing committee. He is the secretary of the Kozhikode chapter of the AJVP, the reason the worker bees flocked around him. There is a brief write-up about the need for such a meeting. On the need to equip girls to fight harassment. On how they will be taught to use keychains, dupattas, pens, and hair clips—anything within their reach to fight harassers.

Amma looks at the pamphlet and the arrowroot biscuit sinks to the bottom of her teacup. She turns her head to the television and watches an advertisement for life insurance with the pretence that she is riveted by what it offers. The pamphlet clings to Aleyamma's fingers. They are thinking the same thing—that dark passage in their lives when Amma's boyfriend made an abrupt exit from their house in Cochin.

It had started when Amma discovered Aleyamma's pillow and bedsheet in the bathtub. Her initial reaction was that of casual dismissal, as she believed they were items that needed to be washed. Usually, Aleyamma would remove her bed linen from the bathtub and put them back on her bed, leaving no trace of her bathroom escapade. But one day, she forgot, and they stayed in the tub, soaking up the dampness of the wet bathroom.

'What are these doing here?' Amma asked. She was about to commence her deep cleaning of the bathroom. Once a week, the wet bathroom would get an even wetter scrub. Amma said that cleaning the bathroom was not a lowly undertaking, though, in truth, she did it because the maids in Cochin had started to refuse the task of bathroom-cleaning. But Amma was meticulous in her task. She scrubbed the tiled floor and walls with much gusto, making sure she left no vestige of germs or slugs behind. She would kill the germs with a mephitic concoction of Dettol, phenyl, and muriatic acid, flick the slugs off the walls with her index finger like she was playing a game of carrom and brush their fat bodies into the sinkhole with delight. Sometimes the sinkhole would get so clogged with the slugs that had died in the confines of the deep, dark tunnel that Amma would need to use a plunger to get rid of the blockage.

The bathtub was not a bathtub but a big metallic basin, painted blue, giving it the appearance of a derelict swimming pool. It was pushed against the wall close to the commode, much to Aleyamma's aversion. But there was nowhere else to place it. It was either near the commode or under the washbasin, which then couldn't be used. Appa, having read about water therapy, had bought it for Aleyamma. Every day, she would be placed in the tub with lukewarm water up to her navel for twenty minutes. Although she discontinued the practice, it sat there silently and made a perfect sanctuary for slugs. And also, her.

'You need to know where to put the laundry,' Amma shouted and shoved the plastic laundry basket in her direction with her foot. Aleyamma stood silently near the bathroom door as Amma engaged in the industrious task of cleaning the dirt surrounding her. There were times when she thought of telling Amma about her boyfriend and the mischief he was up to. She wanted to tell her about her dreams. That her bedroom lock hadn't broken on its own. That she hated her newly acquired breasts and the interest they had sparked in her mother's boyfriend. She was repelled by the attention she was getting. But she was scared. Confused. Intimidated. She also didn't know how Amma would react.

Amma held the detergent and the plunger in one hand and pulled out the pillow and bedsheet from the tub with the other. She examined them, feeling the damp linen on her skin, and then her eyes met Aleyamma's through her monkey crop. Something sparked behind Amma's eyeballs. She dropped the detergent, the plunger, the bedsheet, and the pillow on the wet floor and parted her monkey crop with her fingers. The veil of her temple was torn in two and through the rip, Amma's eyes had opened. Aleyamma told her everything.

Her boyfriend was having tea and snacks in the sitting room, flashing his teeth as he chewed on stale acchappams and banana chips. Amma stormed out of the bathroom. He got up from Appa's armchair with a jolt, shaken by the thing in front of him, which he didn't recognize but had heard about from Amma herself.

'Is it true?' Amma was loud. She didn't need to say anything more. He coughed into his tea and let out a garbled sound through his acchappam-covered teeth.

'Answer me.' Amma stared at him unfalteringly, her eyes as big as the acchappams in his hand.

'She is lying,' he said like a weak-kneed schoolboy answering his class teacher.

'I didn't even say she said anything, you small-dick loser pervert.'

Amma then reached for the spice jar on the centre shelf of the showcase. She put her hand inside and picked up Appa's bladder stone that looked like a cream bun from Varkeys bakery, polished it on her copious bottom, and tossed it in the air a couple of times like Anil Kumble. She then drew her hand back and hurled the stone at the man cowering in front of her. The stone darted across the room and smote him on the forehead. He dropped to the floor, trembling. Amma pointed to the door and flared her almond eyes at his acchappam-crusted teeth. 'Never show your face in my house again.' And he left, holding his forehead in his hands.

But now, Amma's eyes are veiled, resting somewhere on the television. Ever since Appa left, Amma has kept the television on in whichever house she has lived in. It is her attempt at creating company in the house that otherwise feels empty. Aleyamma scrunches up the pamphlet, crushes the crisp paper in her fists, and tosses it out of the window.

Amma's mind is elsewhere. Otherwise, she would have said something about what the politician on TV was saying; the man has been engaged in an endless tirade about the recent Sabarimala verdict. Amma would say that all religions are the same—that they have been crafted cunningly by men to keep women in their places—tying them up like their movable cattle and immovable land; she would equate it with her own experience from when she had decided to experiment with Christianity around the time Appa left.

In Cochin, Amma was friends with Gracy Kochamma, the Achen's wife, who would come home and have tea with her in the evenings. One evening, when Amma told Kochamma that she was looking for meaning in life, a higher purpose than the ephemeral existence she led (this was a day after Appa's departure), Kochamma put down her teacup with a determined look on her face and took them to the Cochin Government Library and headed to the religion section. Together, they browsed through the dust-laden cupboards where the only living presence was that of invisible dust mites and silverfish that hid within the fissures of crumbling books. Amma ran her fingers over the titles and whispered, *'What Would Jesus Do?'*, *'The Cross and the Switchblade'*, *'The Purpose Driven life'*. Amma brought back a few books and piled them up on the coffee table in the living room. That evening, she put her feet up, picked up a book, and flipped it open. Flatness overtook her eyes which refused to follow the words. A few minutes later, she tossed it on the table like a frisbee and rolled her eyes at the disappointment it offered her.

Later that week, Amma decided she would not go to church any more.

'Why?' Kochamma asked, choking on her tea.

'See where I am now,' Amma said with a vague flourish of her hands, pointing out her state and her figure.

'Come to church. Don't we ladies have fun together at the Sevika Sangam meetings?'

'Fun is not what I am looking for. If I wanted fun, I could go and drink beer at the Seagull Hotel and dance all the way back home,' Amma said. 'The two-hour service is so predictable. It's the same every time. Sometimes we sit. Sometimes we stand. Half of it is not even in Malayalam. What do "kuriye laayisson" and "baarrekemaar" even mean? Why do we have to do it in Hebrew?'

'It's Greek. And Syriac,' Kochamma explained, as though that would help.

Kochamma tried her best to convince Amma to return to church. But Amma didn't budge. She wasn't fine with the formulaic any more. She wanted a change. She yearned for metamorphosis. And perhaps that is why she forged an unlikely friendship with the lady who booked and cancelled tickets with her at the travel agency. The friendship would lead to her experimenting with a new kind of worship.

One day, after school, Aleyamma stumbled upon a curious sight—a glistening mount of jewellery strewn across the dining table. Most of it was Ammachi's and now belonged to Amma. 'I will not wear them any more,' Amma announced. Amma had taken off all her jewellery. The diamond studs that twinkled in the sunlight. The gold chain that eternally graced her nape. The bangles that clanged with her every step. They had now surrendered their permanence on Amma's skin. Her neck was now bare. Her wrists were stripped of their metallic splendour. Her ears had holes that had turned ashen. Her fingernails had been cleansed of their fiery red hue. Amma had metamorphosed.

'Ask me why?' Amma asked her.

'Why?'

'Because women should adorn themselves in respectable apparel, with modesty and self-control, not with braided hair, gold, pearls, or costly attire. Do you understand?'

'So, we shouldn't braid our hair?'

Amma ran her fingers along her own neat braids. She looked at the pile of jewellery on the table and said, 'You should not wear jewellery. Or paint your nails. That is what it means. Most likely.'

When Kochamma saw Amma's naked face when she came over one evening, she was appalled. 'Are you also going to wear white to church, talk in bizarre tongues, and do bizarre dances like those crazy people?'

'You are an Achen's wife. You should know better. Only the Pentecostals do such things,' Amma said.

Swayed by her new friendship, Amma accompanied her companion to church every Sunday. Soon, she started taking Aleyamma along with them. 'Believer's Family Brethren Church' read an inconspicuous sign near the doorway which led to a small hall with plastic chairs. No one wore white, or talked in bizarre tongues, or did crazy dances as Kochamma had said. But there was also no altar or an Achen, no pipe organ or a choir.

Amma's friend led them to a row in the front and they sat down. Faithful to her Sunday ritual, Aleyamma opened her box of Parle-G biscuits, a little treat to fend off the impending boredom. But Amma's friend slapped her wrist and eyeballed her. She then dived into the depths of her bag, produced a scarf, and gave it to Amma.

'You forgot again,' she said.

'I also want one,' said Aleyamma. Amma was looking at the pale pink floral scarf apathetically.

'You will get one later. When you are old enough,' said Amma's friend.

'How old?'

'When you are a woman. When you realize that the man is the head of the house. Then you must cover your head to show your respect.'

Amma covered her head and sat in conformity like all the other women with bare necks and no earrings. Men got up, uttered practised prayers in reverent pitches, and expounded verses they chose from the Bible. One man got up and eyed the women's side of the congregation. 'Paul said thus, a woman should learn in quietness and full submission. I do not permit a woman to teach or to assume authority over a man; she must be quiet. For Adam was formed first, then Eve. And Adam was not the one deceived; it was the woman who was deceived and became a sinner. And in First Corinthians, Paul reminds us all, as in all the congregations of the saints, women should remain silent in the churches. They are not allowed to speak, but must be in submission, as the law says. If they want to inquire about something, they should ask their own husbands at home; for it is disgraceful for a woman to speak in the church.'

A smile, dripping with condescension, deftly made its escape from his lips. 'Yet,' he said with a note of restrained authority, 'the women have the choice to engage in silent prayer if it so pleases them.'

Amma twisted uncomfortably in her chair. She scratched her scarf and curled her toes into her Kolhapuri chappals. 'What if they don't have husbands at home?' she whispered to herself. Amma was by now used to people referring to her, under muffled breaths, as that woman who had a *dieworse*, that woman who even after the *dieworse* chose to wear sleeveless blouses. Words like those never affected her. But there was discomfiture in her eyes this time.

Amma's friend first fired an admonitory glance. Then her eyes softened, and she squeezed Amma's hand. But during the time of communion, Amma's friend passed the bread and the wine over Amma's head, handing it swiftly to the lady who sat behind them, like she was handling something hot.

'Why did she do that?' Aleyamma asked Amma when they got back home.

'Because I don't have a husband at home. But can you imagine sipping from the same glass that has passed over a hundred lips? I will not touch that thing even if they offer it to me. I very much prefer the way the Achen just tosses the stuff down your throat like an expert frisbee-thrower. Seems like a more hygienic thing to do.'

But they still continued to attend the church services, each Sunday unveiling a new layer of enlightenment to Amma. 'Maybe it was my fault that Appa left,' she said one day as she baked a marble cake. 'I was not a submissive wife. That's why he left. Women have to submit to their husbands and husbands have to love their wives.' She was trying to rein in her rebellion through words she herself didn't believe.

'Did Appa love you?'

'Love is patient. Love is kind. It never fails.'

'But Appa left.'

Amma wiped her hands on her sari and passed Aleyamma

the spoon and the bowl to lick. 'You know, you are quite mature for your age. Love is a tough nut to crack. You will understand it someday.'

One Sunday morning, perhaps jaded by the men's droning sermonizing, or by the realization that she was becoming a person she had long dreaded, Amma broke the rules. During the time dedicated for the men to pray loudly and the women silently, Amma rose from her plastic chair. A determined clearing of her throat served as the opening note of rebellion. Amma's friend's eyes grew faint with horror, and she tugged urgently at Amma's pallu in an attempt to pull her back into her chair.

'Sit down,' she pleaded as silently as she could.

'Shut up, you Antichrist,' Amma said, flicking her index finger at her friend's knuckles. She then pulled the floral scarf off her head, tossed it to the side and prayed as loudly as she could. She prayed like she had never prayed before. Men turned voiceless and headscarves slipped from women's crowns. Patriarchy ground to a halt for the ten minutes Amma implored God. Aleyamma couldn't remember what Amma prayed for because Amma was not praying but making a statement.

The next week, Amma was back in the old Marthoma church, where patriarchy was set to tunes she could bear. Decked up in her fine jewellery, with fingernails painted a flashing red, she cantillated 'kuriye laayisson' and 'baarrekemaar' without understanding their meaning, while Gracy Kochamma stood next to her, singing along in the Greek and Syriac she assumed she knew. Aleyamma was pleased because there was no one to stop her from eating Parle-G biscuits. More so because Amma's voice could not be quelled by a handful of random sanctimonious men who believed they had the right to dictate doctrines because of the gender they were born into.

PART VI

chapter 15

A RED FLAG FLEW HIGH above the bookshop all the time. Though only eleven-and-a-half people could fit in at one time, it was in a pivotal location, tucked away in the kavala on Kallai Road, near the cardinal tea shop where people gathered to gossip, not far from Town Hall and the sweeping grounds where political meetings were held and just a hair's breadth away from the solitary bus stand of Calicut. The door to the shop was always left open. Anyone could enter and drown themselves in the profundity it offered. Cyclostyled copies of *Quotations from Chairman Mao Tse-Tung*, *The Little Red Book* were placed on a folding metal table with a bedsheet cover at the doorway. On the table was also a coffee-brown Murphy radio from where the Murphy baby, finger on his chin, looked at the world through seraphic eyes.

When one of the people acquired *The Little Red Book* in the original Chinese version, they were delighted. They felt the red vinyl cover, and it caressed them like velvet on their skin. The letters on the pages were strange yet comforting somehow—267 aphorisms, written in a language that looked more like paintings than words. They mounted it on the wall next to the table. A tiny red fleck on a large beaten whitewashed wall.

The people who had started the shop did so because they wanted to educate the public about international deliberations on communism. With changing times, they knew there were many things to be debated. Like how the Soviet Communist Party had let down the working classes. And how Stalin had moved away from true revolutionary principles. Also, all the party manuals were in English, and they wanted to translate them into Malayalam. The party was not interested. 'There is no need for such thoughts. They are too radical,' the party said, forgetting its own birth pangs. However, they were not dispirited. They collected more books, printed more pamphlets, and set them up in the shop. They worked day and night to translate major articles from newspapers and publishers from English to Malayalam.

Each time they printed a work and distributed it among the people, the party condemned them with scurrilous words.

They met at the shop every day and listened to Radio Peking. When Radio Peking mentioned their works, their bodies rose with rapture. To know that someone understood them was comforting. They wrote to the Chinese Embassy for books. Packages trickled in. More books and quotations. There were also photographs, showing them a world that they had never seen before—the long marches of the student-led paramilitary—the Red Guards at Tiananmen Square, Mao receiving them personally with warm smiles and salutations; the advances of the people of Vietnam and Laos against American exploitation. Now, these, too, adorned the shop, mounted on cheap frames. People walked in and gazed at them like they were gazing into the sky on a clear moonless night, eyes filling with marvel and curiosity.

Marxist Publications had become a little red pulse that kept throbbing in the heart of Calicut.

The shop was a haven for the disenfranchised—daily wage workers, discontented intellectuals, and more recently, jobless bidi workers from Kannur, whose livelihoods had been lost to a shifting political landscape. The ruling communist party's promises to help them had turned hollow.

One day, Adivasis from Chekadi village, beaten up by their landlord for resisting land seizure, sought the comrades' help. He had pushed them to sign blank papers for a few rolls of bidis and they had refused. 'A father of three young children was beaten to death two weeks ago, and no case was filed against the landlord because the policemen always favour the high-caste men with money. We are thinking of approaching the ruling party. But we don't know how to do it. Can you help us?' they asked.

The comrades looked at each other, their eyes kindling with shared understanding.

When the communist party took root in the state, the initial assumption was that solving the issue of class would automatically resolve the problem of caste. Yet, there were those who ventured beyond assumptions; the literate high-caste members would visit the huts of the labourers and ask for a drink of water before leaving, just to earn their trust. No party had done things like these until then. They were revolutionaries. Many people at the bookshop had previously been members of the same party, but more recently, they were thrown out for swimming against the tide. For being revolutionaries. They knew that time was a true test of principles. And time had let them down.

'Politics and elections are just eyewash. Join us and we will fight for you,' they told the Adivasis. The comrades knew that their time was drawing near.

∽

Not far away from the bookshop was a toddy shop. A shoddy one that no one would notice. Except for the presence of the occasional wobbling patrons, it faded into the corner where people dumped garbage from the shops nearby. The customers didn't mind the smell because the booze was cheap, which was all that mattered.

This is where Avaran heard about the chairman. Once a week, he would venture into town, with cash tucked into a knot in his mundu, cinched with a belt for security. He had learned his lesson after passing out on the roadside, losing both his mundu and the cash strapped to it.

But there were days when the knot in his mundu had no cash because he had to buy eggs and fish for the house, and occasionally a set of glass bangles or kanmashi for Elsy when he was rueful about abandoning her at home the entire night while he bathed in the glorious scent of a woman who was not his wife. Whenever his knot turned light, he would attend the church service that Sunday and when the offertory plate was passed around, he would dip his fingers into it and help himself to a fistful of coins. It was not easy at first. Pretending to be giving when he was taking. But in time, his fingers became adept. Pilfering from the money bag was a skilled job, much like tapping a tree, something he knew he could do with his eyes closed.

Under his belt, he also placed a knife, one that he raided from the kitchen, a rudimentary blade that Elsy used for cutting fish. It was old, but still sharp, sharp enough to cut through the silver skin in a single stroke. When he first placed the knife under his belt and walked to the road, the blade bit through his mundu and the metal rubbed against his skin with a coldness and sharpness that stunned him. He froze when spots of red seeped through his white mundu. He lifted his clothing and examined his thighs. The knife had only bruised the skin. But he was careful after that, wrapping it in a piece of cloth, torn from Elsy's mundu which she kept in a metal trunk. He relished the power he had, even over her belongings.

After his headlong flight from the wolf in the superend's bungalow and his subsequent conversations with Eesho in his office, Avaran had made his way to one of his favourite haunts, the toddy shop. Having finished a bottle, he asked the waiter for another. He intended to drown his soreness in it that night. It was not a Saturday, the day for his weekly excursion to town, yet he had caught a Jeep and made his way to the toddy shop because the way he ended the conversation with the superend had left him incensed. Though the wolf had left him shaken that morning, he had confronted the superend in his office. Avaran's wrath hadn't disturbed the man. The wolf was curled up near the man's feet and as soon as Avaran walked in, it raised its head and showed him its teeth, gleaming and feral like the tushes of a wild boar. So, Avaran lingered near the door and didn't move any closer.

'I hear that my wife is staying at the Estate House,' he said, keeping his eyes on the beast.

The superend leaned back in his chair, nonchalantly. 'Is that so?'

Avaran ventured a few steps closer. 'Tell me. Is she there?'

'Yes, she is. She is working there now. We gave her a job.'

A job. What job could a girl like her do, he wondered. Forgetting about the wolf for a moment, he moved forward and put his hands on the table. The wolf bared its teeth again. He scuttered back immediately.

Some of the tappers and the workers from the factory craned

their necks and crowded near the window to see what was going on.

'She is my wife. What is she doing in your house? She cannot be there.'

'She can be where she chooses to be. She is her own woman. She needs to be treated with respect.'

Avaran looked at the workers huddled near the window. His muscles twitched. 'Who are you to try to teach me respect? If you had any shame, you wouldn't have taken her to your house. She is a married woman. And you are a married man. You are shameless.'

The superend sat back in his chair. A gentle snicker escaped his lips. 'Do you have any?'

'Any what?'

'Any shame.'

'Why are you asking me? You are trying to change the topic. Give me back my wife.'

'Your wife is not an object that can be given or taken. She is where she wants to be, earning wages that thankfully you will not be spending any more on cheap liquor.'

The workers outside hung on to every word. Someone swallowed a chuckle.

'If you are done with the collection for the day, you can leave.' The superend sat up in his chair, opened a book in front of him, and ignored Avaran while the wolf looked on as he walked away.

Avaran despised the man and his beast. But no one else did. The workers found the new superend personable; they laughed at the man's quips and fed the wolf biscuits. They told him about their predicaments when he drank tea with them, squatting on the rough red earth like he was about to take a shit wearing fancy pants. The tribals invited the superend and his wife to their hutments and even lavished on them a meal that they could scarcely afford. 'It must have cost them at least three hundred rupees. They could have used the money themselves or on the poor,' Avaran said when he heard about it. 'Leave saar alone,' some tappers responded. Avaran cursed himself for having chased away the previous superend who now seemed much more manageable than this one. At least that man hadn't taken his wife away. Avaran always believed that he had power over his wife. And now look at him!

Avaran was halfway into his second bottle when the man who sat next to him told another about a group of men and one woman, communists, who were highlighting the plight of the poor peasants in some village called Naxalbari in Bengal. Nine women and a child had been shot down by the police there when the peasants tried to protest. He said it was a few months ago, but these people in Kerala were troubled about what happened, as though it had occurred in their own land. They follow the chairman and believe that his way is the right way. Avaran wasn't sure who the chairman was. So, he asked the man whether he was the head of a big company in Calicut. The man laughed a hoarse laugh. 'If you want to know more about the chairman, then you should go to that shop,' he said, pointing to the shop, surmounted by a red flag. Avaran wasn't sure if the man was mocking him, but he went there anyway.

When Avaran entered the shop, the hair on his skin stood up. The tiny space held an air of importance, like a sacrarium. A tabernacle. He steadied his feet and walked to a table with books and pamphlets. The malodour of the toddy didn't deter the girl who sat behind it. She handed him a pamphlet and said the first one was free. There were five quotations printed in Malayalam:

> We must have faith in the masses, and we must have faith in the party. These are two cardinal principles. If we doubt these principles, we shall accomplish nothing.

> No political party can possibly lead a great revolutionary movement to victory unless it possesses revolutionary theory and knowledge of history, and has a profound grasp of the practical movement.

> Socialist revolution aims at liberating the productive forces. The changeover from individual to socialist, collective ownership in agriculture and handicrafts, and from capitalist to social ownership in private industry and commerce, is bound to

bring about a tremendous liberation of the productive forces. Thus, the social conditions are being created for a tremendous expansion of industrial and agricultural production.

A revolution is not a dinner party, or writing an essay, or painting a picture, or doing embroidery; it cannot be so refined, so leisurely and gentle, so temperate, kind, courteous, restrained, and magnanimous. A revolution is an insurrection, an act of violence by which one class overthrows another.

Every communist must grasp the truth; political power grows out of the barrel of a gun.

Avaran took the pamphlet, kept it under his belt along with Elsy's knife, fell asleep on the Jeep-ride back to Puthuloor, and forgot all about the night like usual.

chapter 16

EESHO STOOD NEXT TO THE empty spot in the corner of the garden. This, he thought, was the perfect spot for Mamma Mollykutty's mango sapling.

He had noticed it from upstairs where, every evening, he would loll in the plush Morris chair with a book or the office ledger. Across from him, Kochuthresia would sit near the window with her cross-stitch or her fabric paints.

'I love this room,' she had said more than once as she gazed at the world outside the window. 'But the sun shines right into my eyes sometimes. It would be good to have a bit of shade near the window.'

Eesho marked a spot a few feet away from the wall of the house, loosened the soil with a shovel, and lowered the sapling into the ripe red earth. He finished planting the tree and watered it.

He looked up at the study and knew that it would take a few good years for the sapling's limbs to reach the window. And another six or seven years or so until little florets popped open. But people in the family, according to Mamma Mollykutty's reckoning, were bearers of a green thumb—even the mango seeds that they threw heedlessly over their shoulders after they sucked at the fruits grew into giant trees.

Still, it seemed like a long time away. He wondered where they would be by then. Though the story of the murders had brought upon him an unsettled restlessness, in time, the house had begun to endear itself to him, mostly because Kochuthresia had stumbled upon the fragment of her heart she had left behind in Munnar as a schoolgirl. And he was glad he could give her that.

Eesho savoured every evening with her in the study, where she was surrounded by rolls of cloth, transforming them into things of beauty, her nimble fingers deftly swimming through the fabric held firmly within the tambour frame. Their eyes would meet whenever Duke, who was curled up in his favourite corner, began to snore.

Her lips would then curve into a smile as she placed a finger to her lips, cautioning Eesho not to disturb the sleeping dog, preserving the beauty of the moment.

But still, Eesho knew the house did not truly belong to them. It was a tarriance. A break in their journey. Just like a dak bungalow where people rested and left feeling resurrected.

'Saar, I would have done the work. Your shirt has become dirty,' said Pappan, appearing by Eesho's side.

Eesho rubbed the soil off his fingers. 'There is no dirt that soap can't clean. My mother will be happy now. She is the one who sent me this sapling.'

'Mothers know best, saar. My mother thinks I should get married. She doesn't seem to realize that I have a limp. Whenever I go and see girls, they smile at me first, because you see, my face is not so bad. But when I get up and walk towards them, they get scared and run away like they have seen a ghost or, worse, a leper. Saar, that is why I am still unmarried.'

'You will find the right girl someday. You can't always plan these things. I never thought I would meet Kochuthresia.'

'You had a love marriage, saar?' asked Pappan, timorously. His eyes refused to meet Eesho's.

'Yes. A strange term, though. Like there is no love in marriages otherwise.'

Elsy was sweeping the garden. The day she had fled Avaran, and in the days that had followed, her face was haunted by the troubles she had had to endure, but with time, her spirits lifted. She followed Kochuthresia around and became adept at navigating the intricacies of the kitchen and the garden.

A few days ago, Markose's hunting party had brought back a wild boar that they had shot. Two men carried the boar, its feet tied to a thick branch of a wild mango tree. Kochuthresia was traumatized by the sight and smell of the dead hairy beast and decided to make a hasty retreat to the bedroom. However, Elsy walked up to the side of the animal and slapped its shaggy skin. 'Build a skinning rack and hang the boar upside down. I will start skinning it while you make a fire outside,' she instructed the men who had carried the beast. There was authority in her voice, and the men did as they were told. Pappan offered her his services, which she subtly refused.

'How do you know all this?' Eesho asked her as she pulled off the hide with a powerful tug.

'My father used to be part of the estate hunting party before he became bedridden.' She then sawed the animal into chunks and roasted the pieces over the open fire.

Elsy, having meticulously swept the garden, gathered the dried leaves into a corner. She turned to them and smiled. Her eyes were young and yet as old as the hills. 'I will wash the Jeep before you go to the office,' she said and went to pick up the hose from the garden.

The first time she laid eyes on the Jeep parked in the shed, Eesho noticed a spark of curiosity light up within her.

'Do you want to drive?' he asked her.

'Oh no. I don't think I will be able to do it,' she said, running her fingers along the steering wheel.

'Who said you can't? Anyone can do anything if they set their mind to it.' And when Eesho showed her how to turn the steering wheel and change the gears, she took to it like a natural.

'In some marriages, love is hard to find,' Eesho said, as Elsy sprayed the Jeep with water from the hose.

'You are talking about the girl, saar? I know her husband is a bad man. First of all, he is a drunk. He married her because he fell for her beauty. But he also has a woman he keeps in the town. That is why he takes trips to Calicut very often. But now people say that he is also friends with the revolutionaries of the communist party. Someone saw him at a bookshop these people run in town. Do you know that they listen to Chinese radio, get together, and string the heads of chickens just to get the courage to do the same to people one day?'

'Avaran strings the heads of chickens?'

'Yes, saar.'

'Like your mother?'

'Oh no, I'm serious, saar. Avaran is a chicken himself. He trembles at the mere sight of his own blood, and even his own tapping knife makes him nervous. But the blood of a chicken is something he doesn't mind, saar. Because he thinks animals have no souls. Still, one can only imagine how different it must be to take the life of a person, to watch life slowly departing the body. Not that I have done it. But these people have no fear. And they believe that violence can solve poverty. Don't you think that these people are bad, almost evil?'

'Well, I don't think it is that simple.'

'It is simple for me. They are either killers or not. Either good people or bad people.'

Pappan watched Elsy as she sprayed the Jeep with water from the hose. 'But she is a good girl, saar. She doesn't deserve to be with a bad man like Avaran.'

chapter 17

EESHO KNEW MARKOSE DIDN'T LIKE his desk. Its leg wobbled, shrunk by an inch from the dampness of the monsoon. Markose shook the desk and frowned at the infirm leg but didn't make an attempt to get up and examine it. He cleared his throat and said, much too loudly, as if to himself. 'Keep a thing for seven years and you will find a use for it, Papa tells me. But if I were to keep this for seven years, it would be dangerous.'

Eesho knew that his post-lunch factory inspection would have to wait because the boy wouldn't leave the matter alone until it was resolved. Eesho got up from his chair in his office and walked over to Markose's desk. He bent down and was pleased by the simplicity of the solution to the problem. 'It is not so bad. There is nothing a piece of paper can't fix.'

Markose was still frowning at the wooden leg. 'Hope your desk is not as bad as mine. Papa made sure that everything in your room is new or refurbished.'

Eesho smiled, choosing to dismiss the spite in the statement. He brought a bundle of papers from his office, folded them neatly into a thick wad, and handed it to Markose. 'We used to do this to our desks in school. This should fix it.'

Markose took the chunky wad and waved to the old man who was squinting at some papers on his desk. He failed to attract the old man's attention. Krishnan was inscribing the daily transactions into a fat yellow ledger. 'Fix this for me,' Markose said, waving the wad of paper in the air.

Krishnan raised his eyes from the book. 'Yes, saar. I will come in one minute. I need to make a few more entries. There was a good collection of earth scraps this month.'

Markose knew that even the discarded rubber crumbs carried their worth, but in that moment, with the world spinning indifferently, they simply didn't seem worth enough to him. He clutched the side of his wobbly desk and shook it to announce its import. 'You can do that later. I am the one who taught you what earth scraps are in the first place. You need to come when I tell you to come!'

Krishnan closed the ledger and got up.

'You can go back to your work. I've got this. I can fix this in a minute,' Eesho said, reaching for the thick wad of paper in Markose's hands.

Markose would not let go of the wad. 'Why do you have to do it? I did not ask you to do it. This is not your job.'

'Neither is it his. Give me the paper.'

Markose clutched the paper tighter in his fist. His cheeks flushed. 'No.'

'Don't be a child, Markose. Give me the paper or just do it yourself.'

'You are not my father. Do you know what your problem is? It is that you don't know where people belong.' Markose opened his palm, flung the fat wad of paper across the room, pushed his chair back, and walked to his car.

Krishnan was standing behind his table, eyeing the wad of paper that had landed on it like a stray rocket. He picked it up and gently held it between his fingers.

By now, the old man who had been oblivious to the goings-on, seemed to understand that something significant was stirring in the air. 'Why did kochumuthalaly leave? What happened?' he asked.

'I didn't do something I should have. I should have fixed it when he had told me to. It was a very simple thing to do,' Krishnan said. Creases formed on his forehead and his shoulders stooped.

Eesho's heart ached. He walked over to him and said firmly, 'Nonsense. The assistant manager is young. He doesn't know what he is talking about. Don't worry about it.'

Eesho tapped the yellow book in front of him and said, 'Finish up your work soon. You are coming home for dinner. Kochuthresia is making appam and mutton stew, a favourite of mine and certainly yours.' Relief spread across Krishnan's face. He sat back in his chair, threw the wad of paper in the dustbin, got back to his ledger, and continued writing in it.

chapter 18

A WEEK LATER, WHEN A tapper asked Markose for an advance on his salary, he let out a little guffaw. 'It will be one now. Then everyone will follow suit,' he thought, looking around the room filling with people. The tappers had lined up all the way to the gate to collect the chelavu cash for the week, with which they would buy rice and vegetables at the local market. On the day they received their full salary, they would venture to the shops in Calicut and buy their children sweets, clothes, and balloons with whatever they had saved up over the months. From the window of his bedroom, Markose could see them walk back to the paadi on their day off, fathers, mothers, children, holding hands, munching on peanuts and sweetmeats, and he would be reminded of the days when he was just a boy, safe within the locked hands of his parents, sauntering on the beaches in Madras and Bombay whenever they visited relatives during his summer vacations.

Life was different now. After the stroke, his father had retired into his planter's chair and his mother to the leg-rest of the same chair, leaving Markose to steward the empire his grandfather had built.

Markose tried hard to recall the tapper's name, but to no avail. They all looked the same.

It had only been a week since they had collected their monthly wages, and yet here was a man who had spent it all, standing before him with folded hands. Had he squandered all the money on drinking or gambling? These people habitually indulged in such things even when they could ill afford it. They had very little, yet they were imprudent. Afterwards, they would attempt to persuade the superintendent to give them more money, offering excuses about their fathers, mothers, wives, and children falling ill. The previous superintendent had been fully attuned to their tricks, but Markose wasn't sure if Eesho was aware of them.

Markose craned his neck and looked through the window at the factory where Eesho had gone to inspect the drums of latex that were ready to be loaded into the trucks waiting near the gate. He was still inside.

Markose turned to the man who stood before him. 'No,' Markose said. The tapper had held up the queue and the men and women who were waiting in line wanted to move forward. 'You already collected your chelavu cash for the week. But your salary is only due in three weeks.'

The tapper did not budge, but continued to stand there, head bowed, hands folded.

This was unfamiliar and unsettling. It was the first time someone was asking him for a monthly advance; he had never had to say no before. Yet when he said it, he felt uneasy, and it surprised him that the words didn't slip out of his mouth as readily as he had assumed they would.

There was a fragility in the way the tapper remained before him, eyes fraught but still hopeful, watching Markose like his life depended on him. But Markose was well aware of the lengths to which people would go for a bit of cash—his father often fell for them.

Now, he found himself in a quandary—should he emulate his father or be more hard-nosed like his grandfather? There were times he wished he could have met his grandfather. But his grandfather had passed away before he was born. His mother's tales depicted a formidable figure who was held in awe by the local population and respected by the British elites. 'He ruled with an iron fist,' she would recount whenever she showed Markose photographs from the family album. Markose couldn't help but notice the physical resemblance he bore to his grandfather, having inherited the same sharp jawline, broad forehead, and dimpled chin. 'You remind me so much of him,' his mother would often remark.

The tapper still stood before him and the old man turned to Markose, his eyes searching for his counsel. The line of waiting tappers stretched on and the old man couldn't pay them until this matter was resolved.

'Why are you still standing there? It is simply not possible for me to give you any more money. Now move,' Markose told the tapper.

But the man didn't move. Instead, he began to cry. The workers in the room whispered amongst themselves and the ones outside peeped in through the windows.

'My daughter has asthma,' the tapper said. 'This morning, she could hardly breathe. I need to take her to the hospital. I wanted to ask superend saar for the advance. But because he is in the factory, I am asking you. I have no time left. She might have no time left.' His chest rose and fell in frantic rhythm, mirroring the very breathlessness he described, while his trembling hands fought to contain the tears welling up in his eyes.

Markose couldn't help but wonder why people didn't come up with more inventive excuses. At the same time, the man's weeping bothered him. Grown men didn't weep like schoolgirls. And so, instead of sympathy, a sense of revulsion rose within him.

'If you want to ask the superintendent, go ask him. Am I your second choice?'

The tapper shook his head ruefully, his hands shaking. 'No, kochumuthalaly, I did not mean it like that. I thought he would understand as he is older.'

By now Markose was tired of the outpouring. Why did they all conjure identical tales when their pockets ran shallow?

Markose sat upright in his chair. 'You are insulting my position. Your daughter is not my problem. I believe it is also not the superintendent's problem. He is new here. And I suggest that you don't trouble him with such requests. Take your daughter to the compounder. Or ask the local tribals to give you some herbal remedies. Then it will be free of cost.' He pushed his chair back, picked up his rifle from the table, and got up to leave.

With a thud, the tapper fell to the ground and caught hold of Markose's feet with his hands. At first, Markose thought he would fall over; the tapper's grip was formidable, and it took him by surprise. He held on to the wobbly table. The man was on the ground wetting his feet with his tears and wiping his hair against his trousers. The warm tears seeped through the linen and touched his skin. It was revolting. He longed for some hot water to wash his body. And also, some soap. His repugnance now soared.

'Chhi....' Markose let out the sound of abhorrence. He looked around the room and hoped that someone would push the tapper off his feet. But everyone was too stupefied to react. He had the sudden urge to kick the tapper free. But there were too many eyes on him.

'You cannot force me. Stop this trickery, you fool,' he said, shaking his feet roughly. The man released his grip. The tapper got up from the floor and looked at Markose. 'You are all the same,' the tapper said, his lips barely moving.

Markose couldn't quite grasp the man's words because that was precisely what he had been thinking—that they were all the same.

'Are you talking back to me?' he asked.

'I am not talking back. I am just talking,' the tapper said in a dead voice.

Blood rushed to Markose's face. His skin burned with the kind of mortification that he had never felt before; a half-naked tapper had never attempted to school his behaviour before. Fuelled by rage, he hit the man as hard as he could. The man flew across the room and fell to the floor, a streak of dark blood splashed across his darker face. Markose looked at his own hand, astounded by the ferocity of the blow. Striking the servant boys at home had never yielded such results; they only grinned back at him through rotten teeth.

Then, from the throng of people, Krishnan stretched out his arm, took hold of the tapper, and raised him to his feet. Holding the man steady, Krishnan said, 'Please saar, we can talk this out.' Krishnan took out a handkerchief from his pocket and gave it to the tapper, who brought it to his lips. The fragile piece of cloth grew red in his fingers.

The ostentatious display of concern left a bitter taste in Markose's mouth. It was a mere performance, and he despised it.

Markose walked to the centre of the room and the workers parted before him. As his anger ebbed away, he grew afraid of what might happen to him if the tappers grew violent. But he did not allow his fear to show. Brusquely, he said: 'There is absolutely nothing to talk about. The man will receive his weekly wages next week if he still has a job.'

'He will still have his job,' said Krishnan.

The commanding note in his voice shook Markose. But this was not a time for wavering. Markose took a few steps towards Krishnan. 'And who are you to say that? You seem to keep on forgetting your place. You should go back to hiking up the coconut tree like a monkey. That is where you belong. Like your father, you will always belong there. Your children and your children's children.'

Markose's breath, warm and moist, fell on Krishnan's face. Krishnan's eyes dropped to the floor. Though it pleased Markose, his heart was racing. The room was casting shadows on him, and the workers had begun to murmur amongst themselves. Whenever one of them was affected, they shoaled together like bloodthirsty piranhas.

Markose walked to his table, picked up his rifle, and made his way to the door. As he walked to his car, he glanced back. A group of tappers had gathered around Krishnan and the bleeding tapper, while others hovered around the old man and asked him for their wages. A few men came out the door and kept their eyes fixed on him.

Markose's heart was pounding. He took deep breaths, attempting to steady the uneasiness within him, as he ran the last few steps to his car. His rifle weighed heavily on his shoulders like dead weight.

He turned around. Avaran was talking to the tappers who had gathered near the door. Markose stepped into the car and closed the door. When Eesho walked towards him from the factory, he shrugged and tried to keep his voice steady. 'Shho! What a bother. Spoiled my mood completely.'

His foot trembled as he pressed against the accelerator. As he drove away, he longed to float in his parents' locked arms, feel the sand beneath his feet, and smell the brackish winds of places far away.

As Eesho entered the room, an eerie sensation washed over him. Blood trickled from the lips of a tapper. Krishnan brushed past him and walked to the gate without a word. Eesho recognized the look in his eyes. It was something he had seen before.

Seven years earlier, in Quilon, Father Goody once summoned Eesho to school. He supposed it had something to do with coursework and Krishnan's inability to manage a curriculum in English. He had already prepared what he would tell Father Goody, and he chanted it to himself on the drive to Quilon. 'Give him some more time. He is a quick learner; imagine translating everything from English to Malayalam, words like electricity, electromagnetism and wind energy—my boy is just doing the opposite, that's all; even I struggled with English when I first came here,' he spoke into the steering wheel.

As Eesho sat before the desk and waited for Father Goody in his office, he wondered if geometry was the real problem and not English, as Krishnan's grasp over polygons was as weak as his understanding of angles and manifolds. Though he was no Euclid, his accounting skills were nothing short of meritorious. The boy was bright for his age. Eesho shrugged off his thoughts because he knew he was overthinking.

Eesho couldn't help but think of Tharakan, standing in the old room, sweat pooling under his armpits, probably feeling that same gnawing impatience as he waited for Father before picking up Eesho and Georgekutty for yet another summer holiday.

'Your older boy, a fine young man you have there. I will make him the head boy soon,' Father Goody would tell Tharakan before opening a bottle of communion wine, surreptitiously stashed within a secret compartment of a wobbly wooden statue of Jesus on the cross that stood on his table.

The statue still occupied a prominent place on the table. 'Jesus, the wine bearer,' Father Goody called it. 'It's so that I will never forget Jesus's first miracle,' he had explained to an astonished Tharakan when he bore witness to the secret act the first time.

Eesho ran his fingers over the statue and wondered if it still served the same purpose when he heard Father Goody bellow at the kids who had camouflaged themselves amongst the tree branches. 'I will ascend and seize all of you. Do you take me for a simpleton? Or perhaps blind? Or, heaven forbid, dead?' The sound of chuckling drifted from the treetops and Father Goody appeared by the door. He scratched his temple, and his eyes roved over Eesho. He leaned his weight against his walking stick and trembled.

'Who are you?' he asked as he walked into the room with suspicious steps.

Father Goody was once a man with a sharp mind, and his power of recollection even proved to be perilous at times. He could not only recite entire chapters from *A Passage to India* and recall the genealogy of Jesus (both from Matthew and Luke) without batting an eyelid, but also remember every mark-sheet of every pupil—so much so that his bamboo cane made its way to the shins of the ones with the ever-plummeting numbers.

But now he looked at Eesho vacantly as he made his way to his chair. It was only a few months ago that Eesho had last seen Father Goody. A lot had changed in a short time. Eesho got up and knelt by Father Goody's side. The hollowness on Father Goody's face terrified him. Maybe there were even times the Father didn't recognize himself in the mirror. Old age was unforgiving; it crushed people and stripped them of their selfhood. It would be better to die a quick death than rot away like a vegetable.

'Father, it's me…Eesho,' he said and held his hand.

Like a slow-moving stream, Father Goody from the past emerged before him. His spindly fingers gripped Eesho's and a smile of recognition spread over Father Goody's face. 'Head boy,' he said, his words spilling with fondness.

'Yes, Father. How are you?'

'Fit as a fiddle, I must say. However, I do believe that my tree-climbing days have ended,' he said, pointing through the windows at the boys in the treetops.

'I remember climbing those trees. I remember the taste of the cane, too.'

'I do apologize if I may have been exceptionally stern in the past. Nevertheless, see what a fine gentleman you've evolved into. You may attribute a measure of your upbringing to my guidance, I dare say.'

'Yes, of course. You wrote to me because you wanted to talk to me about Krishnan.'

Father Goody drew his hands back and sat back in his chair with a painful grunt. Dark clouds floated through his eyes, and he shook his head emphatically. 'Oh! Deplorable.'

'What, Father?'

'Such deplorable behaviour. The young man's father is understandably terribly upset. He required stitches on his lip, and his face now looks like a monstrous Indian wasp has stung him.'

'What are you talking about, Father?' Eesho asked him, wondering if Father Goody was lost again.

'Your boy resorted to employing his own fists upon an unfortunate chap. That young fellow hardly warranted such treatment. I had intended to appoint him as the head boy in due course. You should see his face now. It bears a striking resemblance to having been stung by a wasp.'

'Krishnan hit a boy?'

'Indeed, right in the face.' Father Goody clenched his fist and boxed into the air.

'But why did he hit him?'

'Violence of any kind is not permitted in the school. Violence begets violence. Our lord and saviour Jesus Christ said that.'

'Well, Jesus Christ implied it. But Father, it was Martin Luther King who said it,' Eesho pointed out, though he knew Father Goody would forget it soon after the conversation. 'I apologize on the boy's behalf. Still, I need to know why he hit him.'

'Oh, he called him some silly names. Although, to be precise, he did not address the lad himself. Rather, it was your boy's father who bore the brunt of those appellations.'

'What names?'

Father Goody shifted awkwardly in his chair and adjusted the cushion under him. 'He called his father a monkey, quite likely because he climbs trees and perhaps also because he looks like one. There is a possibility that he might have also called his grandfather some names.'

'What did he call him?'

'He called him a coward who, rather peculiarly, he accused of partaking in an unconventional toiletry practice—defecating upside down. It is strange indeed. Who would dare engage in such an acrobatic undertaking?'

Eesho got up from his knees. 'Did you summon the boy's father for his behaviour?'

Father Goody's eyes darted around in confusion, perhaps because his memory was playing tricks with him again. But when he spoke, there was no confusion in his voice. He said, 'Children do utter the most careless of remarks. I'm inclined to believe that the lad did not intend to be taken seriously when he called your boy's father a monkey. See, none of us believe in evolution. It is completely unbiblical. Darwin was a fool! I have to suspend the ward for his disruptive conduct. This decision does not solely rest on my shoulders but also involves the management. Since this is an austere Christian establishment, as you are well aware, there exists a certain code of conduct that must be preserved. We can't let incidents like these tarnish the reputation we have built over the years.'

Having delivered himself of this little sermon, his face grew slack and confused again. Though Eesho sympathized with his state of mind, he knew that not all his faculties were ailing. Some things would never change. Some people would never change.

'Yes. I understand. I understand how my boy doesn't deserve to be in a place like this.'

Father Goody nodded fully in agreement. 'Yes, yes. You should have seen that poor chap's face....'

Eesho left Father Goody in his chair and walked out the door.

'Monstrous wasp. Monstrous Indian wasp...monstrous Indian....' Father Goody continued to say behind him.

It was recess and Krishnan was sitting in a vacant classroom, staring intently at the empty blackboard in front of him. Eesho put his hand on Krishnan's bony shoulders. Krishnan didn't move. His eyes were somewhere far away.

That was the incident his mind flew back to when he looked at Krishnan now.

PART VII

chapter 19

ALZHEIMER'S DESCENDED ON APPACHA LIKE a cheerless cloud. It worked its way into his heart, inch by inch, shrouding his light, swallowing his smiles, until he was reduced to nothing more than a hollow shell of a man.

When Aleyamma saw him, it felt like she was drowning once more. He was in his room, slumped in a chair on green rubber sheets, spread out in two neat layers—one for the expected, the other, just in case.

Aleyamma stood at the threshold, her eyes fixed on Appacha. He was a stranger framed within the doorway. A ghost inhabiting a room he had once called his own. She watched him and felt the earth dissolve beneath her feet and the weight of her childhood press down upon her.

Velia Pappa's 'r's and his good eye rolled as he said, 'It's an ergonomic chair, designed for people in this condition. But he cannot respond and is likely beyond understanding us too.' He told her that he had pressing matters to take care of back in his house in Kottayam and left her standing near the door.

Soon after his sixty-third birthday, a few years after Amma took Aleyamma away from Niranam, Appacha's memory began to unravel. First, he forgot people's names. Then he forgot his own. In some time, he also forgot to eat, talk, and walk. But all through his descent into infirmity and vacuity, Krishnan Uncle was by his side, walking with Appacha every step of the way. Krishnan Uncle had let go of his accounting job at the corporate bank to become Appacha's caregiver. In the early days of Appacha's Alzheimer's, he would wander around the house telling Krishnan Uncle, 'I need to go home.' When Krishnan Uncle gently reminded Appacha that he, in fact, was home, he would shake his head and say, 'No, no, how can I be home? Kochu is not here. Our home is in the hills, where her forefathers lived. She was happy in the hills. A schoolgirl with pigtails. The hills made her smile. The hills made me smile. And

Duke. My home is with Kochu and Duke.'

Velia Pappa, grateful for Krishnan Uncle's service, was also thankful that he didn't have to hire home nurses, who he believed would make off with the plates and bedsheets from the house every time they left. Velia Pappa drove from Kottayam whenever Appacha had to be taken to the hospital or when his monthly supply of farm-fresh coconuts or cashews dwindled. Cheria Pappa was still in Dubai, toiling away as a chartered accountant labourer. Amma never visited Appacha.

For a rare moment, Aleyamma found herself agreeing with Velia Pappa because she knew that Krishnan Uncle would be better than any home nurse. Better than the family.

When she walked into Appacha's room, Krishnan Uncle was standing, hunched over Appacha's waterbed, gathering soiled green rubber sheets, depositing them into a basin on the floor.

'Baby!' he cried. He hadn't seen her for more than ten years, but he hadn't forgotten. No one called her by that name any more. He called her the way he had always called her. The way Appacha had called her. It turned her into the eight-year-old who believed in magic.

He drew her towards Appacha's chair, where he sat inert, like a doll. 'See who is here!' he told Appacha. 'It's Baby.' He spoke to Appacha the way he always spoke to him. But Appacha didn't move. He sat soundlessly, hands as narrow as reeds resting on his thighs, eyes open, but removed from this world.

She reached out for Appacha's hands, wrapped them in her palms, and held them close to her chest. A decade had passed since she last saw him. His hands had become vapid and drained of life. Blue veins swelled around the back of the palm, ferrying blood that kept the body alive. She ran her fingers over them. Could Appacha feel her? See her? She hoped something of him still remained within the shell of his body, watching her, smiling within. Appacha's breath fell on her shoulders like a warm breeze and she knew that it would be the closest to a conversation she could have.

It was strange to find Appacha trapped in his own body, unable to move about the room they once shared, a room where she had been safe as a child. Every Sunday, she would wake up to Appacha humming 'Beautiful Sunday' as he got ready for church in the adjoining dressing room, standing in front of the cloudy mirror, spraying his armpits with Brut and patting on sweet-scented clouds of Cuticura. He would emerge from the dressing room, still humming, silver hair polished back with Brylcreem, jubba as crisp as a dosa, fragrant with Brut, Cuticura, and Radhas. He would pick her up gently from her cot and get her ready for church.

Now, her little cot was pushed against the window, with rows of Appacha's medicines laid out on Ammachi's embroidered bedsheet. The wall still held old photos of Appacha and Ammachi—she, elegant in cotton saris and puff-sleeved blouses, he in a waistcoat and deerstalker, like Jeremy Brett from *The Adventures of Sherlock Holmes*, with Duke by his side. The deerstalker always hung from a single nail beside Appacha's bed. 'I'm keeping it safe for you,' he'd said once, placing it on her head as she danced around, lost in laughter under its oversized brim. She remembered Appacha taking the deerstalker along with them on their first plane ride together. She had asked him whether the poop from passing planes might rain down upon them as they stood beneath a soaring aircraft zipping across the skies.

'No. It's not like a train. It works differently,' he said.

The following week, they had driven with Krishnan Uncle to the Trivandrum airport to take a flight to Cochin.

'Are you going to leave me with Amma?' she asked Appacha.

'No. We are going to see if poop will fall out of the plane.'

Krishnan Uncle came on the plane too. He sat on the aisle seat in the row ahead of them and smiled as the plane took off. 'We all need to fly. Like Phantom,' Appacha said.

'But Phantom cannot fly,' Aleyamma pointed out.

'Maybe he could have. Perhaps no one told him he could,' said Appacha, putting his arms around her and placing the deerstalker on her head because the air-conditioning was too cold and the engine's roar too loud to be ignored.

Now, Aleyamma looked at the wall where the deerstalker had once hung, and a nude rusty nail stared back at her.

'It's gone,' said Krishnan Uncle, knowing well what she was looking for. 'The termites got to it.'

Krishnan Uncle read the disappointment on her face. 'He would have wanted you to have it. But the insects. They always get to everything.'

He tucked a towel into Appacha's shirt and took a plate of appam and mutton stew from the table. He dipped the appam in the stew till it became soft and mushy in his fingers. 'It is not right to drink kanji all the time. So, we have this once a week,' he said. He said, 'we' like they were one being. Krishnan Uncle rolled the appam into a perfect marble and gently placed it in Appacha's mouth. Appacha swallowed it without any emotion.

'I always think of the day I fell into the pond. You made the car fly. I never thanked you for it,' Aleyamma told Krishnan Uncle.

'Baby doesn't have to thank me. It was Appacha who pulled you out of the water.'

'I don't think I've ever told you, but for the longest time, I thought I was dead. I saw myself, outside my own body, looking down at you all. My eyes were shut, but I could see everything. But something brought me back. Amma never believed me.'

'There are many things we don't understand.'

'Appacha believed me.'

'I also believe Baby. There are mysteries that live in the spaces no one talks about,' Krishnan Uncle said, his eyes serene, as if he, too, knew of the worlds wedged between worlds. 'You will stay for lunch? Balan will make something nice for you.'

'No. I have to catch a flight soon. I am going to Chennai for my undergraduation in Fine Arts. You were right all along—looks like I'm going to be an artist after all,' she said.

'You are like your Ammachi. Very creative,' Krishnan Uncle said, his words falling on her like a blessing.

'You know, I want to go to the house he always spoke of.'

'Yes, it was a beautiful place.'

'Have you been there?' She was surprised as she never knew that Appacha had taken him there.

'Yes. A very long time ago.'

When she left the room, Appacha was still staring at the wall.

'Are you ready to sleep now?' Krishnan Uncle asked Appacha as he got the bed ready. That was their way of life now. She turned around and looked at them. Krishnan Uncle was carrying Appacha over his shoulders like a child. Gently. He laid Appacha in bed and wiped the drool that had gathered at the corner of his mouth.

'Shall we read?' he asked him. Krishnan Uncle took the Bible from the bedside table and read from the Psalms. 'If you Lord, kept a record of sins, Lord, who could stand? But with you, there is forgiveness, so that we can with reverence, serve you....'

Aleyamma walked to the porch. Velia Pappa was strolling around a batch of coconut saplings that a couple of men had brought in a truck. 'They are dwarf trees. It's easier this way. No one needs to climb them any more,' he said before waving at her and driving away in his car.

Her taxi driver was impatiently checking his watch, and she knew she would have to leave too. It would be a long drive to the Trivandrum airport, from where she would take a flight to Chennai to begin her new life as a student of Fine Arts.

Aleyamma got into her taxi, put her head back, and watched the coconut trees roll past her, realizing she would never have Appacha back. A wave of sadness washed over her as she left him with Krishnan Uncle.

chapter 20

ALEYAMMA HAS BARELY VENTURED INTO the backyard. She is not sure where the boundary ends and wants to learn more about the property. So, she asks Elsy Chedatty about it.

'It goes all the way till the brook. No one really goes there any more,' Elsy Chedatty tells her as Aleyamma finishes her morning tea in the hall.

'I have heard about the brook. But I haven't seen it. I think I will take a walk.' She gets up and makes her way to the door.

'Wait,' Elsy Chedatty interrupts, extending her hand in a gesture of caution, her eyes hiding something profound. However, she withdraws her hand and says, 'I'll give you something.' She heads to the back of the house.

When she returns, she is holding a pair of gumboots close to her chest. 'It belonged to saar,' she says and hands it over.

The tan gumboots have waited for her all these years, tucked away somewhere in the storeroom. Flecks of red loam have now melded into its skin like an inherent pattern. Indelible stains from a different time. She wonders when Appacha had last worn them. Was it just before he left the house? She takes them in her hands. They are bizarrely warm, like they had just been worn.

'You miss him,' Elsy Chedatty breaks the silence.

It is the first time someone is addressing her feelings about Appacha.

'Yes. I miss him. Every day since I've been here. Everything here reminds me of him.' She speaks more than she thought she would.

'I heard about how you left Niranam. I'm sure that was hard.'

Aleyamma is grateful she doesn't have to recount the details of what happened twenty-seven years ago when Amma drew her away from him. The day still plays like a movie in her mind. She remembers the dress she wore—puff-sleeved with inverted pleats, and multicoloured, like Joseph's coat of many hues. She remembers the sleeve ripping off as Amma pulled her away from Appacha.

She remembers the Ambassador door that kept swinging like the pendulum of a regulator clock. Cutlet's wet snout sticking out through her bag. Manoj chasing the car that engulfed him in a swampy black cloud of smoke. Krishnan Uncle, racing to intervene, restraining him from his reckless chase. Appacha's pencil moustache collecting droplets from his eyes. His ears, like wilted leaves, hanging from the sides of his head.

Aleyamma slips her feet into the gumboots. They fit perfectly.

She walks to the back of the house, which is unkempt, unlike the much-beribboned façade. But there is beauty in the understory. Curly ferns unfold their pinnate fronds. Jungle babblers call out. Bullfrogs grumble. Laughing thrushes crack up. The brook gurgles along like an immortal song. She wonders why Velia Pappa disregarded this part of the compound when it brims with promises of a tourist honey trap. Fishing. Birdwatching. Foraging. Biotourism. He probably ran out of money well before he thought of the fluffy pillows and the flat-screen television. But Aleyamma is glad.

She walks along the brook and comes across the remains of a hut, caved in, open to the sky and the trees, vulnerable to the winds and the rains. There are signs that the hut was once occupied. There is a blackened hearth and some broken mud pots next to it. A large sunken cot occupies most of the room. A scrawny brown stray dog, ambling around the edge of the brook, lifts its hind leg and pees into the rushing waters. Aleyamma laughs and is thankful for the well that stands near the kitchen.

The land rolls out before her like a masterful canvas, meticulously painted by Mother Nature. But she knows there are bloody stories that are hiding within the peaceful scene that meets the gaze. She has heard about them in passing when relatives talked about the murder of an office employee during a labour union protest during Appacha's time. 'There were Naxals in the mountains then. We were terrified of them. They brainwashed young people to join their revolution,' they said.

Appacha spoke to her about Puthuloor, too, but never about its raw wounds—the unrest and the murder. He only told her about the beautiful estate. The ripe earth. The burbling waters. About Elsy Chedatty and her gifted hands. The impenetrable forests that started off the edge of the rubber plantation. The elephants that carried the felled trees when forest-clearing was allowed. The wild boar that his friend brought home when hunting was an acceptable sport.

When she was older, she read about the revolution that took the state by storm. She pored through the many articles about the armed peasant revolt that began in West Bengal in 1967 and trickled down all the way to the country's southern tip where the radicals shot at policemen and chopped off the heads of landlords and factory moguls. The severed heads became trophies as the perpetrators cried out in victory and beat their drums. People called them Naxals, after the sleepy village in West Bengal, where it all started.

She understood her family's shared dread of the revolutionaries, for they, too, cared for their heads. But she also empathized with the browbeaten and their struggle against oppression, their fight for freedom from exploitation, from chains that were bound too tight. It was a war that they believed was needed to set the world in order. But the policemen shot back, sometimes captured them alive and tortured them behind closed doors, then threw a piece of bread once a week into the grimy cell where more than twenty slept and shat together. They stripped off the sari of the lone woman among a band of men who had attacked a police station in the dead of the night, and paraded her in front of newspaper photographers, telling the world that she had roamed the land in scanty clothes with the men she had slept with. They plucked out the hairs of the men they caught, struck them with bayonets, crushed their knees with booted feet, and rolled thick wooden logs over their stretched-out bodies. They pushed the others into deep, dark pockets of the jungles, killing them in encounters and claiming they died in gunfights. They called it a failed movement. The captured ones became peaceniks in jail. Some revolutionaries became practical. Some lost their romance with revolution. Some turned to spirituality and others to social work, like the girl whose sari was stripped off. They are not called Naxals any more, but Maoists. Some still live in the forests, in the trijunction of Kerala, Tamil Nadu, and Karnataka, close to the tribals' hamlets. From time to time, they emerge like bats at dusk and drift through the hamlets, leaving behind leaflets, strewn with the hope that one day the land will rise, the mountains will roar, and an armed rebellion will shatter the silence of the skies.

Still, Aleyamma doesn't know what the Naxals had to do with the murder of the employee in Appacha's office. Amma didn't exactly like to talk about these things.

The only time Aleyamma heard the name 'Maoist' being used for someone was in Chennai, two years earlier, at an art show that created much furore in the city. She was invited by a friend, the owner of an upmarket art gallery on Chamiers Road. Aleyamma attended the event with Roy. Although it was a sweltering day in April, Roy was in a black suit.

'Do you want to be cooked alive in April?' she asked him.

'Wherever we go, there is an AC, isn't there? Anyway, I don't mind dressing up for you,' he said and pecked her on the cheeks.

The room buzzed with scribes and debutantes from the art world. The artist who was being featured was a young woman from Kerala, about the same age as Aleyamma, whose works some people thought would create problems in the political circuit. She was from PRDS, Prathyaksha Raksha Daiva Sabha, a religious, social protest movement that had its genesis in 1909 in Travancore. A movement that vehemently rejected the tenets of both Christianity and Brahmanism, it was started by Poykayil Yohannan, later known as Poykayil Sreekumara Gurudevan or Poykayil Appachan, a Parayar man whose parents worked as bonded labourers in a Marthoma household. When Yohannan joined the Marthoma church, the stark reality of caste divisions within Christianity became all too apparent to him. For within the sacred walls, a separate seating space was marked out for the Parayars and Pulayars—a mud floor in the far corner of the church, away from the doors, away from the windows, away from the touch of well-born skins.

Yohannan left the church and set off on a journey distinctly his own. He questioned the theologians who had adopted a caste approach to theologizing by using Biblical texts for domination endorsement, and voiced his opposition to those who said that Jesus came to fulfil the law and not to abolish it. He challenged those who invoked St Paul's words to legitimize the subjugation of Christian slaves who dared to defy their masters. Yohannan declared, 'St Paul wrote epistles to the Romans and Corinthians, but none to the Pulayars of Travancore. Their revelation comes through me.' He argued for salvation (raksha) of a visible (prathyaksha) kind, and against promises of redemption in the afterlife. He bought land, built schools, and established small factories to uplift his people, giving them a community where neither men nor gods scorned them. After his death, Yohannan's followers made him their saviour, the one who led them from the desert of slavery into their promised land. The artist's parents were part of this movement, though she considered herself secular. Leading an NGO that worked with the Irular, Paniya, and Kattunaika tribes in Attapady, she oversaw the construction of homes deep in the forest, where government aid had struggled to reach. In her rare moments of free time, she painted. Her debut show in Chennai, 'Adimamakkal Still'—'Still the Children of Slaves'—recreated the lives of her Dalit ancestors through watercolours. Her installations with wood, mud, and metal were pregnant with narratives—the adima changala (slave's chain), adima nukam (slave's yoke), and adimayola (palm-leaf documents that were used for slave transactions).

People wandered through the gallery, their eyes barely glancing at the art, too busy munching on coin-sized appetizers, fingers twirling rose-gold glasses filled with sparkling wine. The air shimmered with casual indifference. Roy nodded at the watercolour works with approval. He looked at the yoke that the artist had carved out of wood and tutted. 'Considering the bygone eras, I'm glad we live in the twenty-first century where there are courts and the rule of law,' he said.

'So, have the courts and the law fixed everything?' Aleyamma asked. Roy hadn't grasped the point of the show.

'Why do we keep saying that the world is going to the dogs? It is obvious we are living in better times. At one time, people lived in constant fear of being attacked by enemy armies. Women were mere property, people were stoned to death, and slavery was lawful. We have to agree that today's times are better than before.'

A lady who stood next to them joined the conversation. 'I agree. But did you know that the artist's father is a Naxalite? He was once arrested by the police for attacking a civil supplies store and distributing the rice to the tribals. It seems he is also egging them on to occupy other people's land in the hills?' She sipped her champagne and shook her head.

'Perhaps only because the land originally belonged to them,' Aleyamma said.

The lady gripped her wine glass and opened her mouth. But because she knew so little about the law or the courts, or about history or land deeds, she found herself at a loss for words. Roy came to her rescue.

'I'm Roy,' he said, extending his palm.

'Of course, everyone knows you. My name is Omana,' she said, pronouncing her name with a British accent, her fingers lingering on his longer than necessary.

Aleyamma introduced herself. Omana raised her sculpted chin and studied her.

'I've never met an Aleyamma before. Strange; the name is quite archaic, isn't it?'

'Yes, it is. Just like Omana.'

British Omana's Chinese lashes fluttered. She smiled warily, took a sip from her glass and disappeared into the crowd.

'Why were you so nasty?' Roy asked. His cheeks were flushed with embarrassment. 'What will she think?'

'I don't care what that woman thinks. I think I am done with phoney parties. How do you stand it?'

'This is the world we live in. Unlike you, I don't believe in being removed from it.'

Aleyamma sensed they were in for a draining argument. But it would have to wait, for the artist had taken to the makeshift stage for her speech.

She held the microphone in her hand. Without preamble, she launched into a fiery speech. 'My great-great-grandfather had two wives. When he wanted to become a Christian, the missionaries told him to give up one wife as polygamy was a sin. I am a descendant of the wife he kept. Though the missionaries said things like "It's better to convert one Brahmin than ten Pulayars", my forefathers thought that if they changed their religion, things would slowly change. They thought that they would be seen as humans and not as objects to be traded in the market. And they were hungry for knowledge. But when they tried to send their children to school, the landlords tied them up and beat them. If they went to school, learned how to read and write, who would work for them, they thought. There are times I've wondered what happened to the other wife and kids. Life must have been even harsher for them. I wonder where they ended up. I wonder if their descendants are still alive. I look at the country now and I see that not much has changed. We witness the brutal floggings the cow vigilantes engage in. We see institutional murders of ambitious students. We read about rapes—rapes of children as young as five. We hear about the cover-ups of the rapes using money and power. We hear ministers telling the world that Dalit students are anti-nationals, enemies of the government. Adimamakkal are still adimamakkal. How could you label us as foes of the government? Is it because you fear losing power if the foundation of Hinduism begins to crumble? You organize rallies in golden chariots, sow seeds of hatred among common people, and then call us anti-national. But let's remember that "anti-national" is the word that Ambedkar used to refer to the cast system during his speech on the eve of adopting the Constitution. Look at us now—we are living in a world steeped in irony.'

Her speech left Aleyamma shaken. Roy, too, was affected by what he had heard. He was looking at the young woman, eyes narrowed, wine glass forgotten. Aleyamma held his hand, and he clasped it tightly. From the corner of the room, British Omana was watching them. Roy's eyes caught her gaze and his hand drifted away from Aleyamma's to brush off invisible motes of dust from his impeccably tailored jacket.

When the artist had concluded her speech, the people who had gathered around her were unsure whether to applaud, for it was not a narrative that could be treated with claps. They took sips from their wine glasses and watched the walls, where her story lingered, silent and powerful. The exhibition had been gaining heat from the time it was advertised in the media. There were threats to the young artist's life. Rape threats on social media. Rumours of arrest for hurting religious sentiments. Outside the gallery were policemen, lathis in hand. Nevertheless, they stood around ineffectively, when a group of men wearing saffron shawls trooped in, shouting the name of a popular Hindu god and flung cow dung at the young woman. People gasped and retreated to the corners of the room as photographers clicked pictures. Roy dropped his wine glass and pushed Aleyamma towards the back door exit. Aleyamma's gaze remained fixed on the artist. The young woman didn't flinch; she stood with her head held high as the men with the saffron shawls roared, 'Bloody anti-national Maoist. Leave the country', before they were dragged away by a handful of constables.

As she recalls the incident amidst the tranquil surroundings of the Estate House's overgrown backyard, her gaze falls on the graves of the couple by the brook.

But to her perplexity, there are three of them. Two large ones and one much smaller, hidden away under a clump of ferns that have formed a green awning over them.

She was aware that the British man who built the house was buried there, along with his wife. But she didn't know they had a child. The inscriptions on the stones are indecipherable, having been steadily devoured by time, rains, and the relentless advance of weeds.

The small grave stares at her with a stony silence. Was it a boy? Or a girl? Was it a baby?

She shifts her gaze, saddened by the weight of the tragic revelation. Someone once said that the smallest coffins are the heaviest. Now she knows why Velia Pappa let nature rule over the back of the house. No one would want to see the grave of a child; it wouldn't be a tourist attraction.

She drags her feet back to the house, wanting to erase the sight of the child's grave.

Her fingers run over the familiar contours of her mobile phone in the pocket of her dress and a sudden longing stirs in her to call Roy; he is her emergency contact. Press 1 for emergency. He is a call away with a simple press of the digit 1. This is the first time since she got here that she has wanted to call him. A total of twenty-seven missed calls and fifteen messages from him have accrued since her departure from Chennai. 'Where are you?', 'Have you left the city?', 'I miss you. Call me back, my love', 'Why are you doing this to me?', 'I need you. You know that'. 'You are breaking my heart. I will make things right'. She never replied.

Roy always appreciated her for her independence. He knew that she liked it. She was the kind who relished solitary trips to the cinema and eating out without company, a preference that puzzled him somewhat, as he never did those things himself. He always went with his wife. Perhaps shared a tub of caramel popcorn and Coke. Picked from each other's plates.

Now, she takes the phone from her pocket and holds it before her face. Her index finger moves to the digit 1. But then she pinches herself, a self-inflicted reminder of discipline. The pain reminds her not only of the past but also of the future she shouldn't have.

When she gets back to the house, she finds Amma standing on the porch, her eyes wide with curiosity behind her monkey crop as she studies the unanticipated visitor in front of her. His back is towards Aleyamma. He turns around and smiles. She watches the laugh lines and the ears that move. The world with all its madness slips away. Nothing else matters any more.

PART VIII

chapter 21

THE DAY WAS HEAVY LIKE a wet blanket. Though it seemed like a remarkably habitual morning, and the tappers went about tapping the trees, and the watchers walked around watching the borders, and the Kurumbars plucked weeds and wildflowers that had sprung up in places where they didn't belong, Eesho could feel the winds of change. It hid among the fallen leaves and the weeds. Between the tapping and the tea breaks. Beyond the songs on their lips. Amongst the patchwork clothes that hung in neat rows on washing lines. In thick gruels at the beginning of the month and watery ones at the end. In milkless teas that the old ones cupped in their hands, and the dearth of dreams in their children's eyes.

Eesho drove to the far-flung block where Vishwan, the man Markose had struck and humiliated, tapped the trees in silence. Just two days had passed since the incident and yet here he was, already at work. With nimble fingers, he was pinching the dried latex that ran along the oblique cut of the trees and depositing it in a bucket tied to his waist, before using the sharpened end of his gouge to push it along the slash with a practised precision that he had earned with seventeen years of tapping. Like nearly all others on the estate, tapping was his only job. Only about 10 per cent called tapping their secondary job. But all of them knew how to cut the tree without hurting it. They knew where to stop their gouges—millimetres away from the invisible cambium, slicing through only the lactiferous vessels that would respond to pressure and release a brilliant white liquid.

When Vishwan spotted Eesho's Jeep on the road, the tapper's fingers slackened, and his eyes widened with alarm. His lip had a gash, but not quite deep enough for stitches. Markose had dampened his spirit more than his face.

'How is your daughter?' Eesho asked him.

'She is at home. Sleeping. Some days are difficult,' Vishwan said, looking down.

'How are you?'

Vishwan lifted his eyes and searched for an answer. No one had asked him that before.

'Did you put Dettol on the cut?' Eesho asked.

Vishwan raised his finger to the wound and nodded.

'Let me know when you need to buy medicines for your daughter. Come straight to me next time. Even if I am in the factory or at home,' Eesho said, taking out his wallet.

Vishwan took a step back and tightened the string on his bucket. He looked away from Eesho and moved to the next tree. 'I know you want to help, saar. But I cannot take it. I don't want charity,' he said. There was no contempt in his voice. Only resignation.

'It is not for you, but for your daughter. And this is not charity. It will be deducted from your salary next month. It is only what you wanted.'

Vishwan craned his neck and looked at the road below. 'If kochumuthalaly comes to know, it will be a problem again, saar.'

'Let me deal with that,' Eesho said, thrusting the notes into his hands. 'You can report to the conductor if you need to go early and check on your daughter. You are eligible for leaves. Tell him I told you so,' Eesho said, and walked back to the Jeep.

He drove to the office, hoping to find Krishnan behind his desk. Deep within, though, he knew Krishnan wouldn't be there. When Krishnan had walked out that day, Eesho had wanted to go after him. But the old man was overwhelmed. While some of the tappers were huddled around Vishwan trying to calm him down, others swooped in on the old man, demanding their weekly earnings. The old man looked at Eesho helplessly. By the time Eesho reached the paadi, he knew it was too late. He looked through the window of Krishnan's room. It was empty. Krishnan's tin suitcase was missing, and his mattress was rolled up and kept at the end of his bed. Eesho kicked the earth and cursed Markose under his breath. Then someone told him that Krishnan had taken the last Jeep to town. But he would have no way of knowing if he had reached Niranam till he drove to Calicut and booked a trunk call to Mamma Mollykutty.

When Eesho walked into the office, he saw that Krishnan's desk was empty except for a pile of papers that had made its way there from the old man's table. 'Have you seen Krishnan?' Eesho asked the old man, who was writing something.

'No, saar.'

Markose was sitting behind his wobbly table, drinking tea and reading the newspaper.

'It is hopeless,' he said as he rubbed his white sweater. 'We have lost all the matches in Australia. Pataudi is just a glorified face for the country and nothing more. Maybe he should be replaced.' He kept his eyes on the paper and shook his head at Pataudi.

'Maybe you should talk to Vishwan,' Eesho said.

Markose lifted his eyes from the newspaper. 'Who is Vishwan?'

'The tapper who wanted the advance. The one you hit.'

'Why? What should I tell him?' Markose's voice was jagged with bitterness.

'Tell him that you are sorry.'

Peevishness spread over Markose's face like melting wax. He bundled up the newspaper and put it down with a needless thump. 'Why should I? They must know that they can't come and ask for money whenever they need it. It will only run this business to ruin.'

'It will not. We are not giving extra money. It is only an advance.'

'Yes, from our coffers. It will affect our monthly rolling.'

'That is why we have earmarked some money for miscellaneous expenses. We should use it in emergencies.'

'Think. Just think,' Markose said, knocking his temple gently with his index finger. 'What if all of them come and ask for emergency advances? What will happen then? Will you give it from your pocket?'

He pushed his chair back, picked up his rimfire rifle, and left.

The protests began the next day.

∽

Under the feeble shelter of a flimsy blue tarpaulin tent, an array of flags cast indistinct, murky shadows. On occasions such as these, every political party and workers' union sought to assert their presence.

As the Jeep rumbled past the makeshift pandal that stretched along the office wall, Duke let out a low growl. 'He knows something is different today,' remarked Pappan from the back seat. Pappan had grown somewhat accustomed to Duke's presence, but he still kept his distance.

Eesho inched forward in his seat. The workers were cowered under the pandal, faces blue and hollow in the deflected light. He looked for Krishnan among the clustered heads, hoping he'd be there, even if it meant that he was part of a sit-down strike. But there was no Krishnan. His heart grew faint with dread.

He knew Krishnan had not reached Niranam because when he rang Mamma Mollykutty from Calicut the previous night, she said she hadn't seen him. 'What is happening there? Is everything all right?' she asked him, her voice weighty with worry. 'Oh, it's nothing, Ammo. Everything is fine here. We are happy. We love the mango sapling you sent us. We planted it in the garden,' he told her. Mamma Mollykutty's smile reached his receiver. When she spoke, her words poured out in a whisper. 'Mone, if you don't like it there, both of you just come back home. Why toil on someone else's land when you have everything here?' She said it, knowing well that nothing could sway his determination.

Eesho clutched the steering wheel tighter, his gaze piercing the sea of faces beneath the billowing blue tarpaulin. Most of the workers—the tappers, the factory workers, and the Kurumbars—had joined the strike. Some of the workers' wives had joined them too. Eesho had told the rest of the staff—the conductors and the writers—not to report for duty until the strike reached a resolution. The watchers, too, were part of the strike, except for Pappan, who didn't mind the wrath he would face from the striking workers, as he claimed to remain invulnerable to derision of any kind.

Women held their babies to their breasts, wiped their leaky noses with their fingers, and lulled them to sleep. Vishwan sat against the wall and looked at his feet. He didn't look up as Eesho drove past him. Avaran stood around a table along with the union representatives from the taluk, a move he repeated each time tensions flared within the estate. It was his first line of action, reaching out to the taluk. If disputes remained unresolved, together, they would summon district representatives. Remarkably, matters seldom progressed beyond that stage, as Ousepachan typically relented on most of the demands by then. Eesho slowed down the Jeep as he searched the faces for Krishnan.

'New superend?' one of the men from the party asked Avaran.

'Yes. New superend. But same old kind.' Avaran glanced at the passing Jeep.

'Ignore him, saar. He is just angry that his wife left him to stay with you and madam,' said Pappan as they parked the Jeep in the office shed. 'He is a bad man. That girl doesn't deserve to be with someone like him.' Though these were serious times, Pappan's conviction amused Eesho, and his forehead lightened for a fleeting moment.

Markose was early to the office that day. He stood near the door and watched the movements at the gate with a glass of cold tea in his hand. He clicked his tongue. 'They will come in now and say they want to talk, but we must not budge. Yielding to their demands at this point will only expose our weakness.'

'Don't you think we have to first hear what they have to say?' Eesho asked as he walked up to the door.

'It's always the same. Raise in wages. More bonuses. Their heads are fixed on money.'

'And what about yours?'

Markose grew red like Mary's lipstick. He looked a lot like her. The sharp jawline. The high cheekbones. The raised chin with an air of haughtiness.

'Let's first hear what they have to say. I think it won't be just about money this time,' Eesho said.

Even as the words left his mouth, he feared that Avaran might attempt to make it personal. The day Markose struck the tapper, he heard Avaran talk to some of the tappers outside. 'It is the first time he is using his fist on someone. Didn't I warn you about the new superend? I'm certain he's the one who put such ideas in the boy's head.'

Avaran's voice soared over the murmuration from the pandal. They were in the process of deciding the demands.

'The last time they staged a sit-in strike for a wage raise, we gave in. Papa had a stroke. His blood pressure kept going up all through the deliberations. Mummy was in the hospital with him. She was pale with worry. I had never seen her like that before. The doctor said he was lucky, but it can't happen again. I don't want him to put up with these theatrics at his age. I am afraid something will happen to him. And if it does, it will break my mother's heart,' Markose said, looking a little pale himself. He finished his tea, set the glass down, and eyed the gate.

'Nothing will happen to him. He is stronger than you think,' Eesho told him.

'I can't help worrying about him and Mummy. But I still think Mummy is the tougher one. She has my grandfather's genes,' he said, grinning faintly.

chapter 22

MARY SAT ON THE LEG of the Bombay Fornicator like she had never moved from it, tucked a loose strand of hair behind her ear, and broke a butter biscuit in half.

'Sundarakuttan. Such a beautiful boy. I am in love with him,' she said and held out a piece to Duke. Duke chewed on it and then licked her fingers. Mary laughed and Ousepachan nodded with appreciation.

'You should have brought your wife also,' she said and passed Eesho a cup of camomile tea from the side table, where the teapot and the tin of butter biscuits seemed to be resting forever.

'We need to talk about the matter,' Eesho said.

Mary picked up her cup and said, 'What they are asking for is impossible.' She watched her husband, who was drumming his fingers on one of the arms of the chair.

Satisfied with his non-belligerent bearing, she passed him a cup of tea, turned her eyes to her greenhouse, and rested her gaze on the white orchids that had bloomed. Her lips wrinkled as she spoke. 'My son will not apologize.' Her words were crisp, like Markose's when he had heard the demands that morning—an increase in wages and an apology. 'If my son did something, I'm sure he had a good reason to do that.'

Eesho understood Markose's childishness, but he had expected better from his mother. 'That was no way to behave with anyone,' he said.

Mary's gaze snapped towards Eesho. His bluntness startled her, but she was not a woman who could be persuaded painlessly. 'We have never apologized to anyone. We never will. First of all, what do wages have to do with what happened that day? Kallanmaru, liars. They are only taking advantage of the situation. You should be able to see that. If we give in to their tactics now, it will only make them come to us with more demands like these in the future. We can't give in.'

'Apologizing doesn't mean giving in.'

'What else does it mean?' Mary asked, her voice rancorous.

'It sometimes means doing the right thing. Krishnan is nowhere around because of what Markose said that day.'

Mary's red lips wrinkled again, and she placed her teacup on the side table. 'That boy disappeared, not because of my son. It is like blaming others for someone's suicide. You commit suicide because of your weak mind. Not because of others.'

Eesho was bilious. His mouth was acrid, and he was finding it difficult to swallow. Ousepachan was still scattily drumming on the arm of his chair.

Ousepachan caught sight of Eesho's gaze and decided to break the rhythm. He moved in his seat and violently cleared his throat. Phlegm chirred in his jaws as he cracked his lips open to speak.

'You should rest. You cannot get a stroke again,' Mary told him, pushing him back gently with the tips of her fingers.

Ousepachan stuck out his hand and moved Mary's fingertips aside. He looked at Eesho. 'You are right. What our son did was wrong. He should apologize.'

Mary's body stiffened on the leg-rest. She snatched the teacup from her husband's fingers and threw it, aiming at the side table. The cup rolled to the side and fell to the floor with a clang. Duke raised his head and watched the broken teacup with puzzlement. Mary's gaze softened as she looked at Duke, the storm within her briefly quelled by the innocence of Duke's incomprehension. But before her husband could push his luck any further, she got up and stood firmly on her kitten heels. She turned to Eesho. 'Well, for that to happen, my son should also decide the same. Avan midukkana, smart boy he is. He understands the games that these people play. I think for now, we should wait and see if their fervour will subside. We cannot revise their wages or tender an apology.'

She got up from the leg-rest and walked to the door, clicking her heels, ready to disappear into the house. But before she went in, she looked back and said, 'Their enthusiasm will dwindle when they realize they have no money to buy food. See, it is strictly business.'

Mary disappeared into the house and Ousepachan into his Fornicator.

When Eesho got back to the office that day, he distributed fruits and biscuit packets to the people who were huddled under the tarpaulin. The women smiled at him as their leaky-nosed babies sucked on the crumbly biscuits.

'What on earth were you doing?' asked Markose as Eesho walked into the office.

'Everybody has to eat.'

Markose refrained from pushing further, aware that the superintendent's actions would extend no further than doling out biscuits to the labourers; it was his mother who held the ultimate authority.

The workers huddled under the blue tarpaulin for two weeks. The men grew bluer, the women gloomier, the babies thinner, but they did not change their demands.

Avaran and the men from the parties walked out of the office every day with no resolution. Faced with fruitless deliberations, they decided to gherao the building.

chapter 23

THE POSTMAN DROPPED OFF A letter at the bookshop one evening. He placed it nonchalantly at the edge of the folding table and left. Though the address on the envelope was incomplete, he knew where to deliver it.

They opened the letter and read the blue words that were scrawled with a painful drawl, each word crying out to them like a baby, as the writer, a peasant, told them the story of his people in Wayanad—a group of more than a hundred, men, women, children, and infants, all relocated from Kottayam because they had lost their land due to a rubber development project.

However, he wrote that it didn't deter them as much as it should have, because some men had told them about the fecund soils of the Pulpally forest in Wayanad, where they could buy land with the money they'd received as compensation and start a new life. The peasants gave them the money and moved to the new land, hoping to gain rights to it, but the men never returned.

The land they now lived on belonged to the Devaswom Board. Seeing the peasants pitch their tents in what was rightfully their land rankled them, largely because the Seetha Devi temple, which the trust oversaw along with the other temples of Kerala, stood not far away from where the peasants had moved. Named after the consort of Lord Rama, it was a temple that brought the Devaswom Board much pride because it was built in the eighteenth century by the warrior prince, Pazhassi Raja, the first local leader to declare war against the ruling British. The temple also had many legends associated with it, the most famous being that of Tipu Sultan having to retreat from the temple after he had planned to destroy it, because of a supernatural force that protected the temple grounds, taking the form of a pillar of cloud, making the afternoon sky as dark as ink.

By now, the peasants had cleared the land and started farming. They loved the land and believed that it would one day belong to them as they were promised. They planted rice, bananas, tapiocas, yams, and spices. They built little huts for themselves and kept chickens and goats. Fearing that they would not leave, the Devaswom Board and the forest department filed cases against them. The government was swift with its action, setting up a Malabar Special Police camp and a wireless station in the hopes of evicting the peasants, though there was already a police station there.

'What do they think we will do? Fight them? With what? Our farming tools?' the writer of the letter questioned. 'We went to the Marxist party and told them about our dilemma. They formed a farmers' organization and promised that, if voted into power, they would ensure that we received our land deeds. So, we believed them. We voted them into power. But now, they do not remember us. It's as if we don't exist, as if we are nothing.'

The conclusion of the letter hit them hard. It read to them like a challenge. 'You talk about the injustice in Naxalbari. But do you see the injustice in your own backyard? Do you think you will be able to practise what you preach? Show us if you think you can.'

The reader of the letter bowed his head, the blue inland fluttering like a wounded bird in his hands. Silence fell over the shop. The girl sighed and rose to close the door. They all knew there was nothing left but the way of Mao.

chapter 24

KRISHNAN'S SKIN CRAWLED WHEN HE heard the stories of the landlords who beat their workers. Beat them again and again with merciless blows. Left their flesh open and raw. Broke their bones. Threw them alive into a pit and closed the opening with a stone. Shut them in a prison of misery and anguish as the water began to close over them. When their stomachs rumbled, bitter suffering was what they were given for food and drink. They were bound in chains. Made prisoners with no escape. Made targets for arrows. When the arrows sank deep into their flesh, the rich men laughed and hurt them further with their curses. Stripped them naked. Rubbed their faces into the ground. Broke their teeth on stones. Tears and blood poured out in a ceaseless stream. They died and no one cared.

He remembered his grandfather. And his great-grandfather. And his forefathers who were treated like cattle. Beaten; yoked with bulls and buffaloes; sold in the market; children separated from parents, wives from husbands; given as gifts to friends, peace offerings to enemies, dowry for daughters, or placed as bets in gambling. They were alive. But not living. Hurled outside time and space, with no past to remember, present to hold, or future to look forward to. Just there. Drifting. Discarded.

He thought of the story his grandfather had once told him when he was a boy, about a girl who had been sold in the slave market to a man who had taken her home and kept her for himself even though he had a wife and children who were older than the girl. She had been only ten. Once, when he kissed her, she screamed. It infuriated him so much that he strangled her. Then he threw her into the river. Even if people found her body, no one would question him, because he had rightfully bought her. She was his property, and in the 'Adimayola', it was written that he could 'kill, you may kill; sell, you may sell'. He was on the right side of the law and his actions were justified.

Krishnan didn't have a sister, but he thought of the girl as his own. Whenever he closed his eyes, he could hear her helpless cries, see her broken neck and her tiny body being carried away by the river. He refused to eat that night and when his father came to know of what the grandfather had told him, his father said that it was a story from another time. 'Things like these don't happen now,' he said.

'But did it really happen during Muthacchan's time?'

'Muthacchan is old. Sometimes, he doesn't know what he is talking about. Don't listen to him.'

What his father had said had quietened his soul.

But now, he knew better. His father had been wrong; people still did the same things. He understood that when he walked into the bookshop two weeks ago.

Krishnan perched in the shadowy corner of the room, his eyes fixated on the man who read the letter from a farmer in Wayanad. The man was silent now. His hands were shaking. The letter once clutched firmly, slipped through his fingers and dropped to the floor like a dead bird. The silence that swamped the room unsettled Krishnan.

A few months ago, when Avaran had pressed into his hands a pamphlet, Krishnan didn't think much of it. Avaran was wobbling as usual, and Krishnan supported him back to his house. After he dropped him on a string cot, he turned and walked to the door. 'Wait,' Avaran said. He lifted his shirt and ran his fingers along his belt. His hands ran over the handle of a knife and then they reached for a piece of paper, folded into four. He took it out and pressed it into Krishnan's hands. 'You keep this,' Avaran said and passed out on his string cot. Krishnan didn't know why he gave him a crumpled piece of paper, but he took it back to his room and kept it in his tin suitcase under his shirt with the paisley prints. He read the words before he wedged it between the layers of cotton, but forgot all about it in the morning.

Two weeks ago, he found it again. After Markose had hit the tapper, Krishnan walked back to his room in the paadi. Words stewed within him and cut through his gut like a knife. He opened the door, dabbed his eyes on his shirt sleeves, and dragged his tin trunk from under his bed. There was still time for the last Jeep to town.

He would take it and go back home. He unlocked the trunk. The paisley-printed shirt lay folded neatly on top.

He remembered the hands that had held his shoulders. Surely, Eesho would come and tell him that everything would be okay.

Krishnan climbed into his bed, pulled his knees to his chest and waited. The little girl in the next room was breathing hard. Her every gasp hurt his ears. Her sniffles brought tears to his own. What would she say when her father walked in with a wounded lip and no money for medicine?

Krishnan looked out of the window. The sun dipped into the horizon. The lights in the paadi turned on. The smell of blistering curry leaves wafted through the air. Mothers sang lullabies. Crickets chirped. Fireflies blushed. Krishnan stared at his door. He did so till he couldn't any more. He got up and threw the clothes that were drying on the clothesline into the suitcase and pressed them in. His hands touched the pamphlet, and it crackled under his skin. Krishnan stared at the words. They told him a tale that was meant for him alone. He folded the pamphlet, put it in the pocket of his shirt, and took the last Jeep to town. The Jeep dropped him off at the solitary bus stand in town. He walked to a tea shop, sat in a corner, and asked for a glass of tea without milk because he wanted to save the money for his bus fare back home. A radio played an unfamiliar song in an unfamiliar tongue. Krishnan looked outside. The door of the bookshop was left wide open. The girl who was minding the books at the table smiled at him and he walked in. The girl's parents bought him hot puttu and sweet milky tea and heard his story. That night, he slept on the floor of the bookshop, though they had told him that he could stay with them. Krishnan knew that they were the primary forces behind the shop, and he didn't want to be a burden on them. 'I will be fine here,' he told them. On the cracked cement floor, he lay on his side, gazing at the whitewashed walls bearing photographs of people he didn't recognize. A little red book sat on a shelf like a trophy. He dreamed of monkeys and coconuts as he fell asleep.

The next morning, he sat with a bunch of people who convened around the radio and listened to the news. They welcomed him and called him comrade. They said he could stay with one of them in a small room behind the bookshop because they knew he had no place to stay. The awkwardness from the previous night departed his body.

Soon, he became one of them. In the bookshop, they met every day and talked about life. They discussed the Chinese revolution. American capitalism. The war in South Vietnam. Soviet revisionism. Marx. Castro. Che. Lenin. The injustice in Naxalbari. The landlords who never paid their workers. The landlords who beat tribal labourers to death. They spoke about the way of Mao. 'It is up to us to organize the people to overthrow them. If you do not hit, it will not fall. It is like sweeping the floor: as a rule, where the broom does not reach, the dust will not vanish on its own,' they said, reading from the red book.

Krishnan's eyes opened; finally, he could see. Still, he didn't understand why they were waiting. They spoke of armed revolution, but he had not seen any arms. When he asked the girl's father about this, he sat him down, looked him in the eye, and told him about what Fidel Castro had said about waiting: 'We waited patiently because it was necessary to wait. This differentiates the revolutionary from the counter-revolutionary, the revolutionary from the imperialist. Revolutionaries know how to wait; we never despair. The reactionaries, the counter-revolutionaries, the imperialists—they live in perpetual despair, in perpetual anguish, perpetually lying, in the most ridiculous and infantile way.'

The girl rose to her feet, walked to the door, and closed it. The girl's father held Krishnan's gaze with his own. His eyes were like coals. Then he got up and cleared his throat. 'Now is the time,' he said. And so, they began to make preparations.

∽

Markose threw his head back and laughed as Avaran walked over to close the thick iron gate, cutting off access to the office. He did not believe a gherao could happen on his estate. He had only heard about this form of worker unrest from other planters who talked about a certain powerlessness that overcame them when they were locked in their offices and homes by those who never had any power over them.

'Everything changes with time. Perhaps, everything should,' they said. But Markose had never found their argument persuasive. Power structures were clearly defined in his eyes. It was a requisite to keep the world going. What if governments ceased to exist? What if the military lost its hierarchy? What if moneylenders were rendered penniless and proprietors lost their power? What if workers refused to till the land, and the police relinquished their lathis? What if the hangman parted ways with the noose? The world would only descend into death and decay.

Though the men had raised flags of protest before, they had gone no further. All the sit-down protests had ended peacefully, following his father's acquiescence in their demands. However, now, as the workers began the blockade of their office, doubts began to creep into Markose's mind. Was it his father who was truly devoid of power? And was that the reason he yielded so easily? Markose peered through the front room window. The men behind Avaran—union representatives in the white garb of politicians and tappers in their threadbare clothes—seemed determined, driven by their desire to coerce the management into meeting their demands. Avaran produced a chain from a gunny bag and proceeded to secure it around the iron bars of the gate. He fished out a lock from the same bag, ran it through the hoop, and pressed it in place with a resounding click. Markose's eyes drifted to the lofty walls of the compound with the barbed wire on top, and his thoughts wandered to the cliff in the back. Absentmindedly, he scratched his sweater, and his sardonic laughter turned into a nervous chuckle.

'Who do they think they are?'

'That's what gheraos are like,' Eesho said.

Markose was irritated by Eesho's response. He banged the stock of his rifle into the cement floor. The stock did not break but a fine crack appeared on the floor.

'Be smart. I don't think that's any way to treat your weapon,'

Eesho said. He was sitting on Krishnan's empty chair, and Duke was standing near the front door like a sentinel, ears upright, eyes glued to the gate.

'See, the dog understands that it is a serious situation,' Markose pointed out.

'It is undeniable that the situation is serious.'

'They cannot keep us from leaving. It is unlawful.'

'Yes, that is true. It is also unlawful to hit people.'

Markose got up and walked to the door. He leaned against the door-frame and noticed that a tremor was pulsing through his legs, betraying his anxiety. It was reminiscent of the times when he was playing cricket, and a spin bowler was bowling to him. He found them hard to read, and this made him nervous. He preferred facing the seamers; they were more predictable. Markose drew closer to the window, looked out, and longed for the distant comforts of Colombo. He yearned for the carefree days of walking along Beira Lake, drinking rum and soda with his mates in his dorm room and flying kites on the rooftop. 'We should call the police,' he told Eesho.

'Yes, we will when they decide to lay phone lines in these hills.'

Markose's irritation grew at the scorn on Eesho's face; he was not being sympathetic towards him.

He felt the walls of the room closing in on him and imagined that the susurrations from the pandal were pressing against his eardrums.

Perhaps he merited being in this quandary. However, never in his life had he envisioned a day when he would find himself the imprisoned bird, caged and yearning for freedom. He could now somewhat sympathize with the servant boy he had locked in the bathroom after a game of cricket, back when he was nine years old. 'I was not out. Do you hear me? You bowled a wide, and the stumps fell because of the wind,' he had shouted, though it had not been a windy day. He had then locked the boy in the servant's bathroom, strategically placed in the farthest reaches of the compound to muffle the sounds of daily ablutions. The air in the dark little chamber was foul with the stench of human waste. The boy had wept and pleaded with him to release him, but he had walked away. When the boy's mother finally opened the door in the evening, she discovered the little boy unconscious on the floor. Yet, Markose had never apologized for his actions, and Mary had brushed the incident aside as nothing more than a typical boyish prank.

The workers had provided them with packets of biscuits before they locked the gate. Now, Markose said bitterly, 'What do they think we are? Dogs?'

Eesho bit into a biscuit and held one out to Duke. 'Maybe they will treat us to a three-course meal later.'

Resentment washed over Markose. 'Whose side are you on? Are you not worried about being locked in here? Are you not worried about your wife at least?'

'My wife is not your concern. But since you asked, let me tell you she'll be fine, because she is the strongest woman I have met.'

Eesho got up from Krishnan's chair and walked towards him. Eesho looked imposing, even menacing, as he was at least a foot taller than Markose. 'What you did was wrong,' Eesho continued. 'I hope you realize that. You should apologize to Vishwan. And to Krishnan...when he comes back. They deserve to hear that. We can discuss the raise in wages once you do that. Your father also thinks the same.'

Markose advanced a stride and spoke into Eesho's chest. 'My father never told me that. And my mother agrees with me. And I am glad that she is staying as strong as me. We are the only ones who can call their bluff. You don't understand these people. We have dealt with them for years.'

'Listen, Markose, if you apologize, we can easily put this behind us. Believe me, it will only get worse otherwise. I don't want you or your parents to regret it.'

Although Markose agreed with him partly, he was determined not to show it. 'No,' he declared, and began to pace restlessly around the room.

∽

Eesho sat back in Krishnan's chair and silently thanked Mamma

Mollykutty for liberally applying her bamboo cane to his shins whenever his cheekiness crossed the line. He couldn't help but wonder—if Mary had applied the same discipline to her son, would he have turned into such a rapscallion? Then he remembered Georgekutty.

Georgekutty was still in Guntur, exhausting the last coppers on local brews, and likely, women. Mamma Mollykutty still held on to Georgekutty's first swaddling cloth, tucked away in a trunk alongside her chattas and mundus. Every night, she would open the trunk, take it out, and weep into it as she said a prayer for her second-born.

Would Mary shed tears if she heard about the gherao? Would her anxious tears fall for her son, locked up until he yielded? It was only a matter of time before someone went to Calicut with fresh news from the estate. Still, there was not much anyone could do, not even the police, who, averse to being wedged between party men and proprietors, left such matters alone.

As Eesho fed biscuits to Duke, he dreamed of the four-poster bed in the bungalow and longed to sink his weary bones into the mattress.

Markose paced restlessly around the room. He stole glances through the window, his eyes darting over the lock and the chain on the gate. His ears would perk up at the sound of every passing vehicle and disappointment would show on his face when he realized that it was the estate Jeep making its way to the paadi. He was searching for his mother and father. At times, he turned his face towards Eesho as if seeking solace. But Eesho ignored him. Markose didn't warrant his attention. He wouldn't give him what he couldn't give Krishnan.

But by evening, Eesho had reasons to worry. There was a desperation to Markose's stride. He looked wildly around at the empty walls and muttered under his breath as he paced around the room.

'Just eat the biscuits,' Eesho told him. But his pleas fell on deaf ears.

Markose began to pant heavily and clutch at his chest. Puddles formed in his armpits and his legs buckled under him. He sank to the floor and dug his fingers into his creamy white English sweater.

Eesho rushed across to him. He spotted an empty biscuit packet on the floor. 'Here, breathe into it,' he said, holding out the packet.

'I am getting a heart attack. Or a stroke. It runs in the family. I am going to die. It will kill my mother. I can't die.'

'It's no heart attack. It is only a panic attack. It will pass. But you need to go home. Let me talk to them.'

Eesho hurried to the gate with Duke by his side. The workers sprang to their feet upon seeing him. Avaran got up from his plastic chair and walked towards Eesho, keys jingling from his waist.

'So, have you decided to listen to us?' asked Avaran.

'That decision isn't entirely up to me. I promise you, I will talk to Ousepachan sir again. I want this resolved as much as you. But now, please open the gate. Markose is not well.'

Avaran clutched the keys possessively and turned to the workers. 'Superend saar shows up. But it is to take the bourgeois son back home. Didn't I tell you how they all are? They want to go home, it seems. Back to their comfortable beds and lavish spreads while we sit here and beg. Did we ask for too much? We are merely asking for what we rightfully deserve.' The people nodded in agreement.

'Now is not the time to talk about this. I am telling you the truth. Markose has to be taken home. Maybe even to a hospital. You can come and see for yourself.'

Avaran grabbed Vishwan from somewhere within the sea of bodies and thrust him forward. 'Did the bourgeois boy let him take his daughter to the hospital? Did he? Now why should we let him go?' Vishwan looked at his feet.

'Because we all are human beings. We make mistakes. You can't make the same mistake because someone else also made it.'

'Then tell that boy to apologize. We will let you go,' said Avaran, pressing his nose through the iron bars.

'I apologize on his behalf now. Also, I will also ensure that he apologizes once he is better.'

'That is not good enough.'

Eesho turned around. Markose was walking to the gate, clutching his chest, breathing hard. The workers murmured amongst themselves.

'We have to let them go,' Vishwan said. He pulled the key from Avaran's waist and clicked the lock open.

A look of betrayal washed over Avaran. He hadn't expected his own men to play Judas. He held the gate together with his hand and spoke to the people behind him. 'Can't you see he is acting? The boy is fooling us all.'

'Enough, Avaran. You need to stop it right now. Let go of the gate. What you are doing is not right,' Eesho said, and pushed against the cold iron bars.

The gate swung open and Avaran fell over backwards. He stared at Eesho in disbelief. His eyes fell on a rock, heavy enough to knock a man out. He grabbed it, sprang to his feet, and raised it high above his head. He aimed at Eesho's temple and was about to hurl it when Duke sank his teeth into Avaran's descending wrist. Avaran dropped the boulder and cried out, more in shock than in pain, because the bite did not draw any blood. Duke pinned him to the ground and stood on his chest. The workers refused to help the man on the ground because they understood that the wolf had bitten him for a good reason.

Eesho got into the Jeep and helped Markose in. He whistled and Duke hopped into the back seat. They drove to Calicut, and Mary decided that there was no option other than an indefinite lockout.

chapter 25

WHILE SOME SLEPT WITH THEIR eyes open under the thick canopy of trees, others kept guard around the camp. They took turns and changed camps as they inched forward towards the Seetha Devi temple, which sat at the edge of the Pulpally forest like a beautiful mirage. But within this beauty, there was a disquieting truth. The dining hall of the temple was where the government had set up the Malabar Special Police camp and wireless station.

The Devaswom Board knew their victory was assured because there was now a battalion of policemen in Pulpally, watching over their land, preventing farmers from engaging in any more agricultural activities. The policemen watched the land and also the women. They took the women to their beds at night and returned them to their husbands and their fathers in the morning, while the Namboothiri priest continued his pujas in the adjoining room, ignoring the stifled sobs of the victims. The men at home didn't know to whom they should complain, because the complaints were about the police themselves. Helpless, the farmers were delighted when the comrades came forward to help them. They welcomed them with open arms. No one had helped them before. The comrades told them that the time for negotiations was over. They promised that they would fight for them, not with words or empty slogans or deliberations, but with weapons. Together, they bought cracker chemicals, jute, yarn, and cardboard and made country bombs. They plucked stout branches from trees, whittling them into menacing daggers, while practising shooting with crude bows and arrows.

After several days of preparation, a motley group of sixty people made their way to the temple. Peasants, farmhands, intellectuals, tribals, bidi workers, and weavers—it wasn't just those from the bookstore, but also people from across the state, who had come together in the preceding days. However, as the band made its way towards the temple, its numbers dwindled. Some went back home to their wives and children, others resumed their toil on the land, as if the events they were experiencing were but a passing dream. They were uncertain about resorting to violence, despite understanding that it might be the only remaining option.

One morning, Krishnan sat cross-legged on the forest floor with the comrades who remained and listened to the radio. They were waiting for the news. A group had ventured forth to Thalassery, ready to strike at the police station. Yet, those in Pulpally had to remain patient, awaiting confirmation of the attack from the news. Only then could they set their own plans in motion.

Their strategy was set in stone: attack the temple, seize the guns from the MSP camp, and destroy the wireless set, so their actions would remain hidden from the world. Then the two groups would unite and march to the villages. There, they would rid landlords of grain in the granaries and distribute the grain among the peasants and the tribals, who were denied their share. Safes would be opened, wealth seized and redistributed to the suffering families. They would grab the rich men's rifles and continue the revolution because that was the way of Mao—start with the villages and then close in on the towns and cities. Guerilla warfare had wrought change in distant lands like Vietnam, Cambodia, and China. Here, too, they believed, it would find fertile ground.

The morning news had mentioned nothing about the attack, but they believed they would receive the good news at least by afternoon. As the radio played songs from the movies, Krishnan looked at the girl who sat next to him. Her father was leading the attack in Thalassery. But there was no fear in her. All he could see was grit. She kept her eyes on the radio, bunched up her cotton sari over the pair of khaki pants she had worn underneath, and hummed a song under her breath.

She was the only girl in the group and some of the comrades had unresolved feelings about her involvement in the attack, as they deemed that violence was not right for a woman, especially a young woman. 'A woman must learn in quietness,' they would say. But she dismissed their words as effortlessly as their lecherous gazes.

On the first night in the forest, when it was time for dinner, a man emptied a sack of rice into a pot and looked at her. But she walked away to practise shooting with her bow. Krishnan despised the comrades who belittled her just as much as he despised the deserters. There was courage in her eyes, a courage he knew he didn't possess.

Krishnan plucked at the grass beneath him and contemplated the journey that had led him to this moment. After he was sent back from the school in Quilon, his father had told him that he was too quick to anger. Yet, it was not anger that had led him to the forest. It was clarity. He wanted to break the shackles that still bound people to the soil, shackles that people believed had been loosened with the passage of time. To him, these bonds were palpable, draped around his hands and feet, like ribbons on cruel gifts from the unbroken past.

'A deserter is a pseudo-revolutionary who just wants to play at revolutions,' said the girl. Krishnan wasn't sure if she was addressing him; her face was still turned towards the radio. He kept looking at her in the dappled light and feared she knew his story. His grandfather's story that he had heard so many times. People would whisper it around him, and it would hurt his ears. He didn't want to be known as the grandson of the man who ran away from the Vaikom Satyagraha. But he couldn't escape it. The remnants of rebellion clung to him like thorns in the flesh.

It was 30 March 1924. Long before he was born, before his father was born and when his grandfather was still a young man, three men walked hand in hand towards the Shiva shrine in Vaikom—Kunjappy, Bahuleyan, and Venniyil Govinda Panicker—three men from three different castes. Kunjappy's younger brother watched on as the police stopped the men at the entrance of the road that led to the temple. Next to them was a board that read, 'Ezhavas and other lower castes are prohibited from using the road'. The policemen asked them their castes. Bahuleyan said Ezhava. Panicker said Nair. Kunjappy said Pulayar. The policemen shooed away Bahuleyan and Kunjappy. But the three men didn't budge; they stood before the policeman, holding hands. They took one step forward. And two. And three. They marched towards the temple gate. The men in khaki raised the lathis into the air and brought them down on the backs of the marching men. One. Two. Three. Blows rained under the heavy Vaikom skies. Kunjappy's brother couldn't bear to see them being beaten like dogs. He rushed forward to shield the blows. So did a couple of other men. No one was spared. The policemen bundled them into bullock carts and took them to the station. They stripped off their clothes and hung them upside down. They pulled out their fingernails and asked them to apologize. When they brought burning coals close to their eyelids, Kunjappy's brother shuddered. Fumes singed his brows, and he remembered his childhood. Fear conquered his body; ordure trickled down his belly and onto his face. He cried out an apology. The policemen smirked, held their fingers to their noses, undid the knot, and told him to leave. People forgave the young man. But no one forgot. He came to be known as the man who let fear overcome his body. Even after the Shiva shrine was opened to all castes years later, Kunjappy's brother still didn't visit the shrine. Kunjappy's brother's son didn't. Kunjappy's brother's grandson didn't. It would be too shameful a thing to do.

'I like your shirt,' said the girl, pointing at the paisley-printed shirt he was wearing. She was oblivious to his past. It had only been a month since he had joined them, and no one knew him well enough. He gently breathed out and then found himself blushing at her observation. It was the first time he had received a compliment from a girl. He had barely gathered enough courage to whisper a thank you when the newsreader's voice crackled through the radio. A shiver ran down his spine. A group of men had attacked the Thalassery police station in the early hours of the morning. Though nothing was described in detail, it was all they needed to hear. He knew that their time was approaching. There would be no sleeping that night.

At around midnight, a couple of comrades went ahead of them to survey the temple grounds. They came back with the news that the camp wore a deserted look and that there was just a handful of men there. Most of the policemen had gone to the Sultan Bathery police station, carrying all the guns with them. 'Why attack them now? They have taken all the weapons,' the men said.

'No, we can't go back now. We need to send them a message. Let's destroy the wireless set and attack the men who are there,' said the girl. They agreed. Even the men who found her presence questionable.

They marched forward in the dead of night. Krishnan cleared the thick grass with a knife that a comrade had given him and trooped along with the rest of the group. Through a clearing, the temple spire appeared. A comrade ahead of them signalled for them to halt and remain silent.

Krishnan looked down at his hands. They were trembling. The knife was sticky on his skin and the dead weight of the metal hurt his wrist. The knife reminded him of the coconut tree cleaver that his father used to fell the nuts with—the one with a smooth wooden handle and a black shiny blade that curved gently on top. His father would tuck it into his lungi as he ascended the tall trees to gather coconuts. Krishnan remembered the time he had played with the blade when he was a boy. Drawn to its deep black glint, he swished it in the air like a sword. 'I am the king. Down you fall,' he shouted as he waved it about. His father saw what he was doing and grabbed hold of him. He plucked the cleaver from Krishnan's hands and gave him a rough shake. 'We don't play with our tools,' he said and smacked his behind. 'We respect them. They are our bread.'

The night shattered with a gunshot. It rumbled through the air like an alien song. Krishnan froze when he heard it. Someone said a policeman might have shot at them from the camp.

'Charge!' those ahead of him shouted. The people ran forward, raising their crude weapons high above their heads. They cried with one voice and tore through the trees. Krishnan couldn't move his legs, but he felt his body being pushed along by the people behind him. They swarmed into the camp, chopped off the arm of the sub-inspector, and hacked the wireless operator to death. Krishnan's body was limp. He felt his father shaking him by the shoulders. He heard Mamma Mollykutty lamenting the ways of her younger son every night as she sat in bed, wiping her eyes on a white cloth, saying, 'I had planted you like a choice vine of sound and reliable stock. How then did you turn against me like a corrupt wild vine?'

Krishnan looked down at the dead man, and his mind became an empty abyss.

He dropped his weapon and ran into the forest. As he fled, he could hear the rest of them shouting, 'Inquilab Zindabad, laal salaam, red salute to Naxalbari, long live the armed revolution, long live Chairman Mao.'

As he disappeared into the thick of the trees, he heard the girl shout behind him, 'Coward!'

PART IX

chapter 26

THEY SIT AROUND THE BREAKFAST table, discomfort apparent in their bearings. Amma does not ask her anything about Roy because she does not know where to start. If she has to make enquiries about her life, then she would have to start from a few years ago. When Aleyamma introduces Roy as a friend, Amma lifts her face from her plate and looks at him, questions chewing their way through her monkey crop. Amma butters her already-buttered toast and inspects Roy. He is sitting across from her, drumming his fingers on the wooden table. Words ripen in his mouth, but his lips don't move. Aleyamma wonders what sort of support she can lend him in the situation, but she comes up with nothing.

Amma eyes the jar of banana jam sitting close to Roy's drumming fingers. He abandons the drumbeat and promptly grabs it, wanting to be of service somehow. He wants to oblige Amma like he tries to please the scribes and critics of Chennai.

'It's so great to meet you finally. I have heard so much about you from Aleyamma. She never stops talking about you.'

Amma watches him, squinting through the monkey crop. She doesn't buy anything he is saying. But Roy presses on. 'I now know where Aleyamma gets her looks from.' He is saying all the wrong things.

Amma looks at her body overflowing the chair. Her eyes meet Roy's, disdain in them. A kingdom lost. He briefly stares at Amma's rolls of belly fat spilling through the gaps of the armrest like melting butter. He cuts his rambling short; he knows he has annoyed Amma. Aleyamma hears Roy swallow his spittle, a habit he indulges in each time he contemplates a weighty statement. 'Capital punishment. Yes, or no?' Gulp. 'Depends.' Gulp. 'Depends on the kind of crime, you see.'

Now he has nothing left to say.

Though she feels sorry for him, laughter arises from her belly unrestrainedly. She doesn't laugh because it is humorous or because she senses inelegance in the situation. She laughs because she doesn't know what else to do. She laughs like the times she used to laugh when she was with Appacha, when they would find laughter even in the silliest of things. They laughed about things they shouldn't have really laughed about. Like when people tripped over and fell, their eyes clouded more by embarrassment than ache, or when someone let out a sneaky fart at weddings. When men and women fell asleep in the front row during the church service, head still in hands, feigning prayer, disregarding decorum when the congregation dutifully rose to their feet. When the old guard told Appacha to 'bark' his car outside a restaurant. When they read the stories of Suppandi, Shikari Shambu, and Mayavi. And when Luttapi fell off his flying arrow, red with fright and red because it was really his skin colour. When they watched Ducktales on television. When the milkman frantically looked for his cycle after Appacha hid it with his magic.

'Jam,' Amma says, looking at Roy, ignoring Aleyamma's laughter.

'What?' Roy asks her.

'Pass me the jam you are holding.'

Roy realizes he is still clutching the jam jar. He looks at it witlessly, then utters an apology and swiftly passes it to Amma. The rest of the breakfast takes place in silence, periodically interrupted by the clink of cutlery meeting plates.

'I'll leave you to it, then,' Amma says after breakfast and disappears into the house.

They finish breakfast in a hurry. They then make their way to the hall, where Roy settles heavily onto the sofa beside Aleyamma. 'Your mother is formidable. No wonder you left her after school and made your escape to Chennai,' he says, throwing his head backwards onto the headrest.

A sudden urge to shield Amma grips her. 'Roy, it is my mother you are talking about.'

Roy shrugs. 'Don't you want to know why I am really here?'

Her skin is a-tingle. 'Yes, tell me,' she says, trying to hide her enthusiasm with a clinical gaze.

They hear Amma's bedroom door close. Roy gets up and plucks

Aleyamma from the sofa and draws her into his arms. She welcomes his body into hers and rests her face against his chest, warm and plump with perspiration. There is a faint trace of cigarettes and stale beer on his skin.

'I know what happened. She told me about it.'

Roy never uses the word 'wife', as he doesn't want to confront reality. There are a few things he doesn't like to talk about. His wife. His bruises. 'I'm sorry. She shouldn't have treated you that way. I tried reaching out to you so many times. Do you still think about me?'

Aleyamma doesn't want to give in too easily. She takes her time. 'Yes,' she tells him.

'Yes?' Roy's eyes wander, surveying their surroundings in a slow, deliberate circle. 'It seems like you are pretty happy here. In this grand house.'

'My grandfather left it for me. Yes, I am happy here.'

He lets go of her and looks around. 'Maybe he felt guilty. That is why he left you this place.'

An unsettling tremor creeps up from her feet. Roy always had disparaging words for Appacha. In his eyes, she was tethered to a past replete with memories far too ancient and fragmented to retain any real significance. He'd once challenged her, saying, 'Imagine what your cousins must have felt when he called you his favourite grandchild. That is not how a grandfather should behave. Don't you think he should have tried connecting with you after what happened?' 'He did try,' Aleyamma had said. 'But didn't he go around fixing everyone's lives? The poor people's kids, sending them to colleges and finding them jobs? He was an exemplary man and what he did was commendable. But he should have tried harder with you'. *Life is an undying symphony of mistakes. Everybody makes mistakes. Just like us. Over and over again. Every dinner together. Every sleepover. Every stealth getaway. Seven times seventy*, she longed to confess. But she didn't. She didn't want to give voice to those thoughts and breathe life into their existence.

Roy takes in the tall ceiling, the ancient furniture, the giant windows, the antiquated photographs, and the stuffed heads on the walls. She knows she can't blame him for his apparent petulance; he is reacting to the fact that she had left him without even saying goodbye.

She has always been quick to forgive Roy. She forgave him because, among other things, she didn't want to be like Amma, who forgave no one.

'You left me, and it broke my heart.' His face is turned away from her. The back of his ears is flushed red.

'Does your wife know you are here?'

His shoulders quiver at the mention of the word 'wife'. He doesn't want to talk about the woman he carries within the transparent plastic slip of his wallet stuffed into his butt pocket. 'No,' he says.

'Are you afraid, Roy?'

'I'm afraid I'll lose you.' He turns around and looks at her. 'I will make everything right in its time. For both of us.'

'What is the right time?'

'Now,' he says. There is truth in his eyes.

'Take me to your room,' he says, clasping her hands tightly.

She leads him up the rosewood steps into Appacha's study.

A smile spreads across his face when he sees the wooden easel next to the window. He runs his fingers over them. 'Casabianca,' he says. 'He kept you company.' He takes off his shirt and hangs it on Casabianca that now looks like a coat hanger.

His skin is ravishing—glossy with sweet perspiration. She draws closer to his chest and brushes her lips against his skin. It leaves a salty taste on her tongue. There are bruises on his left wrist. She kisses them, holds his face in one hand, and unties his hair knotted at the back of his head with a blue rubber band. She has always liked the way his hair forms a halo around his head when he lets it loose and how the soft locks rub against the curves of her body, arousing her and tickling her at the same time. He buries his head within her breasts and tenderly tastes her nipples through her gauzy top. She pulls him to the mattress on the floor and draws his face to her hips. His breath sweeps through her skirt, and his plump lips burrow into the wetness between her legs. She cries and forgets what stands between them. She forgets the friction. The awkwardness at the breakfast table. The unconventionality of their relationship. The scarlet bindi. She is home again.

∽

The next morning, they rise at daybreak. It's too early for breakfast. When they find themselves in the hall, Roy picks up the newspaper and hands her the inner page. They always share the paper. Aleyamma goes through the world news while Roy immerses himself in the front page. His observations coalesce into a sigh, and he swallows his spittle.

'We are still living in the dark ages. You people should know better than anyone else that women are to be treated equally. It is an embarrassment for the entire country. This Sabarimala issue is preposterous.'

'My people?' Aleyamma asks him.

'Malayalis, I mean. No point having cent per cent literacy.'

'This had nothing to do with literacy. And the issue is nothing that concerns me.'

'But doesn't it anger you? Doesn't it anger you that women still have to fight for their rights?' Roy has put down the newspaper and is looking at her. He wants her to react.

'I don't think I am in any position to talk about another person's faith.'

'So, you won't say anything?'

'Even Gandhi advised the Syrian Christians to refrain from participating in the Vaikom Satyagraha when some of them had joined the fast, as it was an issue that needed to be resolved internally.'

Gandhi doesn't convince Roy. 'But don't you think this is just like what happened back then? Back then, it was the lower castes who fought for the right to enter temples. Now it is women. What if someone asks you your opinion about the whole thing? What will you say then?' It sounds as though he has been asked to formulate a response to the situation. Maybe he is surprised that no journalist has asked him for a quote yet.

'That I am entitled to not have an opinion about every political circus that happens in the country. Roy, we all know what this is really about.'

Roy leans back on the sofa and picks up the paper again. 'If you say so. But I could never watch women being treated this way. Like they are inferior. Like they are dispensable.'

Elsy Chedatty comes in with two cups of tea and places the tray gently before them.

'Hello,' Roy says.

Elsy Chedatty nods and leans against the doorframe.

Roy picks up the teacup and turns to Aleyamma. 'You need to tell her that she needs to smile more. She looks a bit morbid. Don't you think she has to seem appealing to the guests?'

'All the guests love her. She smiles at them.'

Roy searches for a smile on Elsy Chedatty's face, but he gets nothing.

'Ask her if you think I look Malayali.'

'Ask her yourself. She understands English.' Roy becomes mindful of his surroundings. A shade of crimson creeps up to his cheekbones. He drinks the tea in silence. Once he reaches the bottom of the cup and there is nothing else he can do, he taps Aleyamma on her thighs. 'Shall we go for a run?'

'Yes. Let's do that.' She, too, wants to escape the unpleasant situation.

'Good that we believe in barefoot running. We can run anywhere. No special shoes required.' Roy laughs and expects Elsy Chedatty to laugh along. But she shows no emotions as she leaves them.

They run to the part of the town she is familiar with. As they cross the two-storey building with the saffron flags, the boys from the sports club are perched on the balcony as is their routine, brushing their teeth and reading the newspaper. They eye Roy with a narrow, suspicious glare. In the corner, Soman is concealed behind the pages of an English weekly. He doesn't look at her, but she knows that he can read her through the pages.

She senses her body stiffen every time she crosses this part of town, though her mind has apprehended the wash, rinse, and repeat pattern. The tension departs from her limbs as they run past, though she knows she will have to sink into it on the way back.

There is a sense of elation in Roy's gait. His shoulders are relaxed, and his steps are springy. He runs closer to her than he ordinarily would, his shoulder touching her, the smell of his sweat and deodorant stronger than usual. He gently touches her arm from time to time and makes little observations about the new place he has found himself in—the shape of the clouds, the scent of the rubber sheets, the pigtails on a passing girl. He is a person who would do well in a small town, for a while at least, immersed in the small and mundane things of life that he might later translate into colourful thoughts strewn across giant canvases.

And when it's time to unveil these paintings, he will make the rounds, attend parties, shake hands with monied buyers, drink wine from corked bottles—swirl, sniff, sip—and smile at photographers. Roy is seeking to shroud his scars behind the mask of sociotropy; needing to be liked is his way of seeking safety. But she knows he is more complex and nuanced than that. He is tender, and she glimpses it in candid moments like these.

The first time she saw his fragile self was after he had cremated his mother. He came home to her from Manikarnika ghat, the holiest of holy ghats in Varanasi, where the Ganga flows backwards to the Himalayas. Being cremated there guaranteed that one would attain moksha without having to endure the daunting cycles of reincarnation.

Roy carried the smell of death and dejection on his skin.

'Will I see Ma again?' he asked, leaning on Aleyamma's shoulder. A desperate plea from one cynic to another.

Her dreadlocks turned wet with tears and ashes.

She clasped his face and kissed his cheeks.

'Will you be sad if I die?' he asked.

'Not *if*, but *when*. We all die,' she said, trying to lessen the sombreness the air had come to acquire. Her attempts at humour mostly floundered. Sometimes they were well-timed, and Roy laughed at them. But most of the time, they merely made things awkward.

'Will you be sad when I die?' he asked her, indulging her lack of wit. He didn't find her statement witty because perhaps it wasn't witty to her either. Death was a slippery subject. Perhaps it was the end of everything, she thought. It was paradoxical for someone like her who had had a brush with death. But she wasn't eight any more. After her fall into the pond, she had thought she'd glimpsed what some might call a near-death experience. But now, she saw it as the doctors had suggested—a hallucination born of oxygen-starved delirium, a bizarre trick played by her waning consciousness. Religion, magic, faith, God, Satan, angels, demons, seraphim, cherubim, Beelzebub, heaven, hell, souls, eternal life—they were nothing but illusory shrouds, crutches for broken hearts. Sometimes even excuses for despicable human actions and the inexplicable suffering in the world.

She refrained from contemplating death any longer; it had become a source of great trepidation. People like her would have been stoned to death once upon a time. People like her were still stoned to death in some parts of the world. A slow, biting, and dishonouring death, one stone at a time, where her blood would be upon her hands, with no one to acquit her by writing in the sand.

'You will not die anytime soon, Sarvamayavibhanjana Roy,' she said. 'And when that happens, if I am still around, I will light a candle for you.' And then, he smiled.

Roy holds her hand and stops her. They are on their way back to the house. He looks at the tea shop opposite the building with the saffron flags and sniffs the air.

'I like the tea shops in Kerala. They're places where social relations are openly challenged. Anyone with money can walk in and ask for tea and snacks. Come, let's get something to eat.'

She doesn't want to kill the gaiety in his steps. She walks in with him and finds a place at the end of a long wooden bench.

The boys from the sports club have a full view of them. Aleyamma draws her legs back and thrusts them under the table.

She doesn't pay attention to what Roy is saying. 'You know, tea shops even strengthened communist thought at one point in time. If any problems arose in the village, people ran to the tea shop.' Roy notices Aleyamma's inattentiveness.

'What happened? Are you uncomfortable?'

'It's them,' she says, raising her eyes to the balcony. 'They always keep staring at me when I run. At my breasts. My legs. It's not that people haven't done it before. But it's unsettling when it happens every morning. Like clockwork.'

'What a bunch of losers.' He glares back at them.

Roy turns to her and runs his fingers along her cheek. 'I don't blame them, though. They are just admiring something beautiful.'

'Liar.' She laughs at the cheesy line.

'All right. Then they might be staring at my legs, actually,' he says, stretching out his legs from under the table. 'I have thunder thighs.'

'Yes, you do,' she says, tapping his robust thighs. 'You know, I am really glad you are here.'

'Me too,' he says, and draws his lips to hers.

There is no one in the tea shop except a gaunt man who is minding the tea on the stove. He turns his face away from them and watches the tea boiling away.

'You always say I am not forthright about my love.' Roy takes her hands in his and kisses her fingers. He never did that in Chennai. He would always hold her hand under the table.

She pulls her hand away. 'Would you do the same if we were in Chennai?' She doesn't mean to hurt him with her words, but they tumble out interrogatively.

Roy's eyes darken. She has killed his joy. He turns to his puttu and kadala, and busies himself eating.

Soman crosses the road with the rest of the boys from the Sports Club. He walks into the tea shop and plucks a banana from the bunch tied to the roof with a coir rope, eats it, and leaves the peel on the table. Roy eyes the peel with aversion. Soman drags up a chair, places it across them, and sits. The smell of banana and cheap hair gel waft down Aleyamma's nostrils. 'This will not be allowed,' he says in Malayalam. 'Such acts will not be tolerated.'

Roy grips her elbow. 'What did he say? What do they want?' But she doesn't know what to tell him because she doesn't understand either.

'This is a public space. You cannot act the way you both are acting.'

Panic rises in her stomach. 'What are you talking about?'

Roy tugs at her tank top now. 'What does he want?'

'Is he Muslim?' Soman asks.

'What? Why does that matter?'

'Because many cases of love jihad are happening in this constituency.'

'I would know if things like that were happening to me. But what is the problem here? What do you want?'

'He is kissing you, and you are doing unspeakable acts in broad daylight in front of everyone. This will not be allowed. This is India. This is Kerala.'

Roy shakes her arm, seeking an explanation. 'I don't understand what you are saying. Why does everyone talk to me in Malayalam? Why does everyone think I am a Malayali?'

'Are you both married?' Soman now asks in English.

'Yes,' says Roy.

'No,' she says, at the same time.

Soman smiles. 'Oh, affair! That is what is happening. I thought as much.' All the boys from the Sports Club are now in the shop, and a small crowd has gathered outside. Some of them take their camera phones from their pockets.

'Please explain what is happening,' Roy says, looking at Aleyamma.

'You still don't know what is happening? It's the moral police. They say we are acting inappropriately,' she snaps. She is now more irritated with Roy's obliviousness than the bigger matter in front of her.

Roy gasps. Words have left him for the second time in two days.

'So, you know what morals are, after all. We should take you both to the police station. We have arrested people indulging in indecent activities before,' Soman says. He is now poker-faced and determined.

'We are not doing anything indecent. You have no right to pass judgement,' she tells him. By now, she has recovered from the shock of the accusation.

'The police can decide that. It is a matter of law and order. We have reported people before, based on Section 294, for obscene acts. Didn't you see what was happening here?' He turns to the gaunt man who minds the tea. His eyes dart between Soman and the tea bubbling on the stove.

'Didn't you?' he asks again, his voice laced with menace.

'Yes, saar,' the tea shop owner responds promptly.

'See. We are not making anything up. We have witnesses.'

A voice escapes from inside Aleyamma. It is louder than she had expected. 'So, this is what you do. This is what your party and your Sports Club do all day. Stare at women, their breasts, their legs, and then tell them how they should behave by citing sections from the law. You call this law and order?'

Soman plucks another banana from the bunch and peels it. He is unfazed. Her voice, no matter how loud, appears to be swallowed by a vacuum. He takes a bite and chews unhurriedly. 'Our party and our people won't tolerate Western culture. They are detrimental to our traditions. Once you spend a night behind bars, on the cold cement floor, you will think twice before you feel like giving in to your urges.'

'Yes, I would like to go to the police station you have been threatening us with. In fact, we are the ones who should complain about harassment. And eve-teasing. There are laws for it too. And they will protect the deserving.' She walks to the entrance of the tea shop and waits for Roy to join her. Roy hasn't uttered a word since he realized the nature of the conversation.

'Roy!' she calls him. 'We can't let them treat us like this. Come, let's go to the station.'

But Roy doesn't move. A larger crowd has gathered outside the tea shop. Some have started recording videos of them. Roy shifts uneasily, his eyes darting, and his throat bobs as he swallows his spittle. 'Shall we settle this instead? Let us not get the police involved. People are looking,' he tells her.

'Roy! Right now, I don't care if people are looking. Stop acting like this.' Her mouth is trembling, and her tongue is heavy.

'Please,' Roy begs her like a teenager. He has become the Roy that tries hard to get people's love. People's validation. He is the Roy who wants to maintain the sacrosanct image he has built after years of mingling with the swanky townspeople who buy his art, praise him in his presence, and then call him 'overrated' behind his back.

Roy pulls a couple of chairs deeper into the darkness of the tea shop, away from the people and their camera phones and turns a pleading eye to Soman. 'I am really sorry. Could we go to the other side? Actually, I am leaving Kerala in a few hours. So, this will not happen again. You will never have to see me again.'

Her heart skips a beat. She can taste vinegar in her mouth.

Soman gets up from his chair with a surprising grace. The lines on his face have relaxed. He didn't think he could break the man so easily. He looks outside the tea shop and gestures to the lingering crowd. 'Show's over. Everyone, please leave now,' he tells the people. But they hold on to their camera phones and continue to film the scene. There is a new gentleness in Soman's voice, and she finds herself welcoming it wholeheartedly, though she doesn't want to. It is Roy who fails to meet her eye. His pockmarked chin is pointed to the floor.

'Are you leaving?' she asks him. Pain makes her voice unsteady.

'Yes. This was a mistake,' he mumbles to the floor of the tea shop like she is not present in the room. Like she is dispensable.

Aleyamma's heart cracks in two. She wants to scream. She runs out of the tea shop, towards Appacha's house, dying one stone at a time.

chapter 27

ROY DOES NOT LOOK FOR her after he comes back from the run. He calls a taxi and waits under the shade of the Eastman Maavu, irresolutely shifting his weight from one leg to the other, backpack slung across a single shoulder like a college girl, hair released from his perfect bread roll, eyes glued to the phone as if he is waiting for an important call. His kurta clings to his slender frame in the morning breeze as she watches him from the study. When his phone rings, he gives the taxi driver directions to the house, and does not look back when he gets into the car and leaves.

A few months after she had met him, intoxicated by love, lust, and late-night whiskies, she started dreaming about him. She pictured travelling with Roy, a happy honeymooning couple, garbed in careless beach clothes, caressing each other impulsively when they sat in the back of a taxi, or when they ate breakfast, taking desultory steps to nowhere in particular, just walking, over cobbled stones or on sandy beaches in flip-flops that didn't fit them perfectly, but in perfect unison. In her dreams, they scaled the heights of Machu Picchu, watched the Northern Lights, and scuba-dived with great white sharks. They smiled back at the Mona Lisa, drank wine and ate coq au vin near the Eiffel Tower, backpacked across Europe and stayed in cheap hostels that they shared with dopey hipsters, ran the Boston Marathon barefoot, and roamed the Masai Mara and the Great Barrier Reef.

'Let's go,' he said enthusiastically when he heard her fantasies. They didn't go to any of the places she had dreamed of. But they did go to Gokarna. They could have gone to Goa like everybody else, but they craved the unspoilt embrace of nature: the sandy beach that looked like an Om as shown in the aerial shots from the pictures they had seen on *Lonely Planet*. They longed for noiseless nights free from the revelry of the neighbouring shack that reeked like locoweed and sounded like orgies and sex.

It was raining the day they reached Gokarna. They got out of the bus and ran to the solitary bus shelter with a leaky roof where it was pouring more than it was outside. So, they walked to the hotel, wet backpacks getting wetter and heavier with every step, flip-flops slipping dangerously under their feet, up a hill that stretched out before them. When they reached the top, they realized that the hotel was nothing like the online advertisements: it was merely a shack, lacking both a real roof and a floor.

'Did you forget to cement the floor?' Roy asked the manager-cum-bellboy-cum-waiter-cum-owner, who opened the tin door of their room and deposited their sodden luggage on the sandy floor.

'Oh no, it's supposed to be this way. Nature at its best. Romantic, you see.' He smiled sheepishly and tapped his bare feet on the sandy floor.

'And what about the roof? Will it leak?' Roy asked. The pervious-looking coconut-leaf roof quivered unrestrainedly in the wind.

'No, sir. Not at all. If it leaks, I will give you a refund,' he said aggressively.

'It's only 750 for the day. You can keep it if you want. But make sure the roof of this cowshed doesn't fly off while we are sleeping.'

Roy was already disgruntled. Nothing was going according to plan. Roy always radiated the air of a carefree artist; but the cotton kurta and bread-roll hair were façades. It had been three months since she met him, and she knew there were many layers to him underneath the impeccable layer he presented to the world. She couldn't wait to explore more. She wanted to peel them off one by one the way she peeled off his clothes.

'I need a bath,' said Roy, grabbing wet clothes from his wet backpack.

'I'll join you,' she told him. She dropped her clothes in the corner of the bathroom and walked to him.

Seeing her naked body pacified him. He pulled her close to his bare chest, cold and moist, and kissed the wet nape of her neck.

'I've never had shower sex with you before,' he said, anticipation making his voice tremble. Aleyamma looked around. There was no shower, only a bright orange bucket placed under a tap with a mug hanging from its cracked rim.

'We'll have to improvise,' she said, as she filled the bucket. She ran her fingers along the length of his skin. He turned hot in her embrace. He swelled under her like a slow-blooming flower.

'You make me go crazy. I could live anywhere with you. Even in a cowshed, as long as it is with you,' Roy said.

He plunged the mug into the bucket of water and splashed it on them in an attempt to improvise shower sex. The frigid water shocked their skin. Roy's flower shrivelled up like a touch-me-not.

'Madarchod!' Roy cried, his voice sharp. 'This is supposed to be the bloody tropics. How on earth is this water so cold?'

They hastily wrapped themselves in towels and returned to their room, only to discover that the romance the bellboy—in short—had promised was elusive when they settled into bed. Sand clinging to their feet now covered the bedsheet.

'In what world is this romantic? Bloody chootiya. I will ask for my money back,' said Roy.

'I think he will return the money only if the roof leaks,' she pointed out. 'Plus, we don't even have to go near the sea to experience the beach. We can do it right here on the floor.'

Roy stopped his rant and looked at her. She was on the floor, lying on her back, legs crossed in the air, sipping on an imaginary cocktail, towel cast aside. She wanted to make it easier for him. Roy joined her on their imaginary sunbathing scene while rain battered the roof. They didn't mind the drippy coconut-leaf roof that could take flight at any moment or the grains of sand that had found their way into their mouths as they made love on the powdery floor.

'I want you to be my wife,' he said as she lay in the crook of his shoulders.

Aleyamma sat up.

'Yes, you heard me right.'

'How?'

He looked up at her and cupped her face in his hands. 'Everything at the right time. You are my soulmate. I can never leave you.'

She snuggled into his shoulders and touched his ears.

∽

Roy departs on Onam day. Aleyamma sits on the floor cross-legged in front of a plump green banana leaf Elsy Chedatty has spread out before her. She has not eaten from a leaf in a long time. Whenever she celebrated Onam in Chennai at their usual restaurant in Anna Nagar, she would pull a plastic plate to her bosom as others sprinkled their leaves with water from their steel tumblers, wiped them with the back of their hands, and prevented the parippu curry and pacchadi from escaping the confines of the leafy green plate.

The leaf stings Aleyamma more than the fish. It is sharper than its bones, muddier than its meat. It leaves her aching to go back to the study and sink into the comfort of a cigarette. But it would be too churlish to complain, as Elsy Chedatty has spent hours in the kitchen working on the feast she is serving up.

Elsy Chedatty approaches with a steaming bowl of rice, so hot that she protects her hands by holding the vessel by the edge of her pallu. She serves Aleyamma a generous portion and then makes her way to the dining table. The dining room is humming with small talk. The Russian guests are leaving, having stayed barely a day. From their choice of apparel and luggage, Amma surmises they couldn't afford a high-priced holiday and are most likely to move to a tawdry lodge and get cosy with bed bugs and cheap coffee. A boy runs around the room, picking his nose and dipping his fingers in the curry bowls. His parents and grandparents hover around the table, taking selfies with the food and the pookalam, wrapped in kasavu saris and mundus. The boy picks his nose, puts it behind his teeth, and sticks out his tongue at Aleyamma. Amma pinches him playfully on the cheeks. Aleyamma gags a little.

Amma chose to be at the table with the guests as, she said, it would be unpleasant for foreigners to sit on the floor. She had instructed Elsy Chedatty to pick up the leaves from the floor and arrange them on the dining table. In her concern for the Russians, Amma was also able to avoid sitting on the floor—a posture her obesity rejected. When Aleyamma made herself comfortable on the floor, Amma shrugged. Amma also thinks sitting on the floor is below her status. The only people who did that were people she wouldn't generally sit with at the dining table. There is a leaf marked for Elsy Chedatty on the floor.

'Let's begin,' she tells them.

Amma holds her head high and folds the left side of her leaf. A glint of pride creeps into her eyes as she folds the crispy green edge and presses it. She does it religiously every Onam.

'It was an honour given to the Syrian Christians by the king of the land once upon a time. So, all of us fold our leaves,' Amma educates the guests with a good deal of bonhomie. 'You can also do it. I think it's fine.'

Amma has not celebrated Onam with white people before, but she believes they are eligible to press the end of their leaves.

Through bites of food, Amma expounds their history—that they hailed from a place where St Thomas had planted one of his seven-and-a-half churches. That they are some of the first Christians in the world, unlike the more recent converts from impoverished, lower-caste communities who fished or cleaned sewers and were enticed by missionaries with sacks of rice in exchange for their faith. That they would still have one of the oldest surviving copies of the Aramaic-Syriac Peshitta Bible, had not a certain Claudius Buchanan donated it to the Cambridge University library in the early nineteenth century. That their family name, Tharakan (like the Mappilla and Panikkar), was a position bestowed upon them by the king of the land as an act of appreciation for fighting along with him against many opposing factions. That they were the only ones allowed to fold their leaves—no one else was permitted (except for white people on the odd occasion).

Aleyamma doesn't fold her leaf. It stays unfurled.

'Your friend. Is he gone?' Amma asks once she is done explaining their history.

'Yes, he left in the morning.'

Amma raises her eyebrows. 'That was quick. He could have at

least waited till lunch. It's not like he didn't know it was Onam.'

'He had an urgent matter to take care of,' Aleyamma says. She surprises herself with her quick rejoinder to defend Roy.

'Yes, they all do,' Amma says nonchalantly, spooning rice from the bowl. Amma eyes the fat round grains that fall onto her leaf with gratification.

A dull ache ripples across Aleyamma's forehead. 'Roy is not Appa. Not everyone is the same.'

Amma's hand freezes midway. She drops the spoon into the bowl of rice with an unwarranted force.

'I did not say he was,' she says sharply. The Russian parents and grandparents swivel their heads towards Aleyamma.

Amma reaches out for the sambhar, pours a ladleful into the heart of her rice, and is pleased by the peace it offers her. The mere sight of food can solve most of Amma's problems. Aleyamma doesn't want to talk about Roy any more. The time to discuss matters of the heart has already passed.

Amma digs her fingers into the food and centres her energy unreservedly into making an impeccable ball of rice. 'Are you planning to get married to him?'

Aleyamma's mouth dries up. Amma doesn't know that Roy is a married man. She wonders what Amma will say if she ever finds out. She might act her dramatic self, drop to the sofa with a violent thud, shake her head like an overwrought heroine, and tell her to grow out of her jejune self. 'Married man,' she might repeat the words as if they were synonymous with leprosy. She might say that it was nobody's fault but her own. Or she might say something entirely contrary and suggest that Roy's wife may have looked down at her feet and had, therefore, ended up marrying him.

'I don't know.' Aleyamma's leaf is still untouched. She wasn't feeling hungry when she sat down, and now, she is nauseous.

'I'm going to my room.' Aleyamma gets up and walks to the door. Elsy Chedatty has emerged with more rice from the kitchen and her eyes follow Aleyamma.

'I can get you a plate,' Elsy Chedatty says.

But Aleyamma has already left the room. As she walks away, Amma picks up Aleyamma's leaf from the floor, takes it to the table, folds the side of the leaf, and digs her fingers into the lofty mountain of rice.

chapter 28

TWENTY-SEVEN YEARS AGO, AMMA SLAMMED her Kolhapuri chappals into the Ambassador's accelerator and left Appacha behind in a funereal cloud of smoke. The reason was a leaf. Not the kind speckled with colourful comestibles or the sort that gently cups a hill of rice, but a leaf of a different kind, one that was birthed as the result of an event that had transpired the preceding week in Niranam, with Mouse Appachan's and Happy Kochamma's impromptu arrival during lunchtime.

Appacha, Manoj, and Aleyamma were engrossed in conversation around the dining table when Mouse Appachan sauntered in, a peculiar mouse in human form, black Aviators perched upon his head like a hairband. He waggled a mousey head at Appacha and sat next to him. Huffing and puffing, Happy Kochamma followed and heaved her generous bottom into a chair next to Aleyamma.

Finding herself at the mercy of Happy Kochamma's exhalations, Aleyamma subtly inched to the edge of her chair. Manoj grinned, held his neck with both his hands, and acted out Happy Kochamma's dyspnoea as subtly as he was able to. But Mouse Appachan caught sight of it and glowered at him while nibbling on his meal with his prominent incisors. 'Can I wear those?' Manoj asked, pointing at the black Aviators that gleamed on Mouse Appachan's head.

Mouse Appachan raised his hand to his head protectively and winced. 'No. It won't look good on you,' he said, belching—a foul smell of mouldering coconuts and curried chicken eddied in the still air.

He observed Manoj with a face that looked like he had bitten into something distasteful.

'Does this boy always eat with you?' he asked Appacha.

'Yes. He does,' Appacha said.

'And he goes to school with me,' said Aleyamma.

'The roof of the school leaks when it rains,' Manoj said, still grinning.

Mouse Appachan looked at Aleyamma and pointed a curried finger at Manoj. 'People like him didn't even go to school once upon a time. Did you know that they were once served food in the backyard—on the ground? They would be served kanji in banana leaves. The banana leaves would be rolled into cones, and these would be planted in the soil. The kanji would be poured into the cones.'

Mouse Appachan gazed at Aleyamma expectantly, as if hoping she would press him for further details on how the world had functioned in ancient times. But she did not want to talk to him. She didn't want the breath of foul coconuts and chicken to waft towards her face again. She hoped he would leave the table. She averted her gaze, and Mouse Appachan's face fell.

However, he was not finished.

'See, nobody served them food in plates as they believed that even their plates would contaminate them,' he said, licking his brinjal fingers.

Though Aleyamma didn't know what 'contaminate' meant, she chose not to ask him anything.

'Con-ta-mi-na-ting means polluting, making dirty, just in case you are wondering. I, my dear, am a walking dictionary,' he said.

Happy Kochamma bobbed her head, and her sweat landed on Aleyamma's arm. Aleyamma flinched; she wiped her arm on her dress and pushed her plate away. Con-ta-mi-na-ting.

'And if they touched someone from the upper caste, they'd summon us, Syrian Christians, to absolve them of their contamination. We would touch the people from the upper caste, and they would become clean again,' Mouse Appachan continued.

Aleyamma, unable to resist the temptation to inquire, looked up from her food and blurted out, 'Couldn't they have just used soap?'

'You see, my dear, soap was utterly ineffective at purifying this particular brand of impurity. This ran much deeper than mere skin dirt,' Mouse Appachan said with a cloying smile.

Manoj was staring at the empty plate before him. Aleyamma knew that he had heard these words before, perhaps from Mouse Appachan itself. Appacha, for his part, remained a silent observer.

After lunch, they made their way to the sitting room where Happy Kochamma believed the cross-ventilation to be most effective. She turned on the fan, and her sari puffed around her like a balloon.

'Always feeling hot,' Mouse Appachan said, smiling at his wife, who looked less hot and flustered now. Seated on the sofa beside Appacha, legs casually crossed, Mouse Appachan watched Manoj, who was standing near the door. Mouse Appachan raised his hands to his head to check his Aviators and was pleased by their existence.

'So, was it the right way to behave?' Appacha asked Mouse Appachan. His voice was firm.

Mouse Appachan clawed at his mouse-ears and thought hard. He had forgotten that he had mentioned anything at all. 'Oh, that. Yes, I think, for that time, it was fine,' he said. 'There is nothing wrong with eating out of the ground. We all get our nourishment from the soil anyway.' He laughed like he had cracked a fine joke.

Happy Kochamma emulated her husband's amusement and chuckled along. Their mirth rippled through the room, and the walls silently absorbed it. Aleyamma turned around and saw Manoj darting to the back of the house. Appacha sat on the sofa, without moving a muscle, without saying a word, a still speck amidst the tongues of laughter that clapped through the room.

∽

A languid week drifted past until Christmas Eve, also the eve of Appacha's birthday. Appacha had invited the extended family for dinner. A few days before the celebration, he sat with his phone book in the hall, leafed through it, and dialled his family in alphabetical order, as Aleyamma sat on the bed and made him a birthday card with a big red heart. Most of their kinsfolk still lived in the neighbourhood, on land they had inherited from their forefathers, in houses that weren't built with new money, which they believed could never buy class.

The night before Appacha's birthday was much like the night before a family wedding. Men who had pitched up for imported liquor huddled around the drinks table, gazing at the crystalline bottles with thirsty eyes. A brave lady stole a bottle of beer from the table, tucking it stealthily into her oversized handbag. Old people sat on sofas, nursing glasses of lime juice without sugar or salt. Middle-aged men laughed at well-worn jokes. Middle-aged women shared stories about their growing body aches, their eyes fearfully flitting over the old ones bent over on the sofas. Young men watched the young women, and the young women enquired about each other's children. The children scampered around, bumping into everyone, spilling their drinks, and not being sorry about it.

Mouse Appachan walked in, Aviators still on his head, still grinning, perhaps savouring the memory of the joke cracked a week ago, and joined the men who had congregated around a table, discussing politics, church, and the politics in church. Happy Kochamma, huffing and puffing and fanning her face with her pallu, continued her diligent efforts to combat the unyielding heat as she sipped on a glass of chilled lime juice.

Mouse Appachan had a camera with him. It hung around his neck on a long pink strap that looked like an accessory he had bought from the girl's section at a toyshop. 'To get everyone together, there has to be a wedding or a funeral. But this is new,' he said, going around the room clicking pictures. 'I need a photo of the two of you,' he said, and gently pushed Aleyamma towards Appacha. Appacha picked her up and stood in front of the Christmas tree. They laughed as Mouse Appachan said 'cheese' and blinded them with his flash. 'That will be a good one,' Mouse Appacha said and walked to the drinks table, running his fingers along the pink strap.

Before the men descended into inebriation and before the women began casting baleful glances at their spouses, Appacha announced that dinner was ready. He ushered everyone outside into the backyard. The backyard was festive. Yellow fairy lights festooned the coconut trees. From a stereo placed on a tall stool in the corner of the veranda, Jim Reeves sang 'Whispering Hope' from the pit of his stomach. But there were no tables or chairs. No plates or silverware.

Under the twinkling stars, on the naked sandy floor, Appacha had dug little holes and placed banana leaves twisted into tiny cones.

'We can eat now,' he said, squatting on the floor. He spooned kanji into his cone from a tumbler placed on the ground. 'I will wait for you,' he told Mouse Appachan, his jaws setting into a razor-sharp line.

There were murmurs in the air. Jim Reeves still sang, and the fairy lights still shone. Mouse Appachan coiled his fingers around the pink strap of his camera. He ran his eyes over the arrangement on the floor and then over his wife. Happy Kochamma's bulbous butter-face had turned a deep shade of red. She looked like she was about to faint. Mouse Appachan wrapped his tiny hands around her tremendous waist and said, 'We didn't come here to be insulted like this. Just look at my wife. You can't do this to us. This is absurd.'

Appacha continued spooning the kanji into the cone like it was something he did every day. When he spoke, his voice was laced with rancour—it bewildered Aleyamma.

'Why so? The soil gives us nourishment, you feisty little rat,' Appacha said.

Only Appacha and Aleyamma ate that day. That was the last time she ever ate with him, because as the sun rose the next day, before she could wish him happy birthday or give him the card with the big red heart that she had hidden under her pillow, Amma dragged her out of the house by the wrist, pushed her into the old Ambassador, and stepped on the pedal.

As Amma drove away, Aleyamma pressed her knees into the tiger-printed seat, stuck her head out of the window, and watched Appacha trying to fly, like an angel with a broken wing, his body growing tinier and tinier under the Christmas tree, fingers embracing her torn dress-sleeve of many colours, bare toes brushing against the presents, unopened and fulgurant in the haunting morning light.

PART X

chapter 29

THE EARLY-MORNING LIGHT CAST GLOOMY shadows under the blue tarpaulin. The gate was shut, bolted from the outside, with a rococo made-in-England lock that sparkled in the sun. There were only men left under the tent. The first couple of weeks, the families sat together, men, women, children, and infants, clutching their knees and ignoring the sounds of their hollow bellies. The first week, the men from the parties took money from the party funds and bought them tea, lime juice, and glucose biscuits, once a day. Then, after a week, fearing needless questions from the leaders, they could only hand out glasses of sweetened water. One teaspoon of sugar to one litre of water. They knew lockouts could go on for months and they were cautious not to take out their own wallets as there were more than 200 workers and their substantially large families to take care of. The Kurumbars retired to their dwellings at the fringe of the forest and went back to foraging the land. In the third week, the women under the tarpaulin took the babies back to their rooms in the paadi, left them in their cloth cradles tied to the roof, and joined the Kurumbars in the forest to try and seek sustenance from the wild. It was imperative to go with someone who knew the lay of the land if they wanted to avoid the haunts of the green pit vipers or the mustard tarantulas. On the days they were lucky, they came back with a handful of mushrooms that grew along the termite hills or the leaves of the akkalkara that could be cooked as a vegetable. But they were not always lucky, as the mono-cropping culture was eating its way through the foliage like a slow cancer, stripping the soil of fecundity. The forest was beginning to bleed.

Avaran sat with the rest of the men who, like him, had begun to lose faith.

On the day following the escape of the superend and the boy from the gherao, someone told Avaran that Markose had promptly boarded the next flight to Madras. He was probably vacationing on a sandy beach, picking out the bones of fresh fried fish and drinking fine rum and soda.

The sentiments toward Markose and his mother were far from warm amongst most estate workers. As for the boy's father, well, he didn't bother many. In fact, a few years ago, when the elderly man had suffered his debilitating stroke amid a strike, some tappers had even paid him a hospital visit. They remarked that it's not the bourgeoisie that's inherently flawed, but rather people. The old man was not evil, though he often ignored the problems of the workers. But was it equally reprehensible to turn a blind eye to suffering as it was to actively cause it?

Avaran was suffering. He hadn't touched alcohol since the strike had begun and, at first, there was a quivering at the tips of his fingers and toes. The tremor was now climbing up his digits to the rest of his body. If his mother were alive, she would have called him feeble and laughed at him just as she had laughed at his father whenever she found him too frail. Basting in shame, his father could do nothing but avert his gaze from his children. He died before his time. At the funeral, some claimed that she had killed him with her cruel mirth and careless words. Avaran was fifteen at that time.

The day he buried his father, he had his first taste of arrack from the local brewer, and it numbed his restless mind. At night, he ascended into a foggy slumber on his straw mat. Late in the morning, he awoke to a macabre discovery. His body was drenched in crimson and his wrist bore the evidence of a self-inflicted gash—a frantic appeal for release from the clutches of grief.

'Next time you try to kill yourself, choose a knife with a keener edge,' his mother said, her words slicing through his heart. At that moment, he pondered the mystery of maternal cruelty. Did mothers, too, harbour the instinct to devour their own, like feline matriarchs who, in moments of primal instinct, devoured their offspring? Were humans, in their damaged existence, merely reflections of the animal kingdom, bound by the same unforgiving laws of nature?

As he grappled with these unsettling thoughts and speculated where the lines between humans and beasts blurred, the taste of arrack lingered, pungent and intoxicating, a reminder that even in the depths of despair, the soul could find rest in the numbing hug of the forbidden spirit. He grew thirsty again.

But blood had scared him since that day. It scared him particularly because he had no recollection of slicing open his wrist, leaving him to wrestle with the new knowledge that he could be both the perpetrator and the victim of his own pain.

However, it was also the day he resolved not to follow in his father's footsteps. The resolve to break free from the shackles of ridicule, to ascend from the pit of powerlessness, gripped his heart. He wouldn't be the one subjected to mockery. And for that to happen, he would have to be the powerful one.

But now, Avaran was powerless. There had never been a lock out at the estate. The day they saw the locked gate, they all knew that the battle had only begun. Since the boy had disappeared into the unknown, Avaran and the men headed to the Estate House to meet with the superend. Before they left, Avaran had told them to stand together. 'Do not fall for his silver tongue,' he warned them. 'It is us against them.' The men affiliated with political parties wanted to carry the flags of their parties and shout Inquilab Zindabad as they walked to the Estate House. So did he. It would be the first time he would hold the Kerala Congress flag—red and white in equal parts, a coming together of violence and peace. He had joined the party union because it represented a young party, not yet jaded by the cares of the world, a party that was brave enough to show the Indian National Congress the middle finger, walk away and form a faction with just fifteen rebel MLAs. Kerala Congress didn't have many union officials in Calicut; its activity was concentrated in central Kerala, particularly Kottayam. In Calicut, where the party's roots were still budding, Avaran perceived potential. What he saw was a blank slate, one on which he could write his own story.

When Avaran told the workers about carrying the flags, some of them nodded, but there were others who shook their heads. 'We have nothing against superend saar. He wants to solve this as much as we do,' they said.

Bloody lickspittles, Avaran thought as he walked to the Estate

House, curling his moustache. He wasn't sure who he was more wrathful about. The man who had stolen his wife or the men who stood by him, kissed him on his cheek, and played Judases.

When they reached the door, the beast bared its teeth at him again. A stinging pain rose to his wrist. But he stood his ground. He wanted to pick up a stone, hurl it into the beast's mouth, and watch its teeth shatter like glass. But he knew he wouldn't be able to do it.

Avaran ignored the beast and looked through the window. Elsy was who he wanted to see. He acknowledged the times he had treated her poorly, and he wanted to apologize. He wanted her in his arms again, tell her that he would change, though he was a man, and men often went astray.

He remembered the day he had first seen her, walking behind her father, a cloth bundle in her hand. She was twelve, and he was already a young man. Her father had found a job as a tapper at Eastman Estate and emptying his nest egg, he had bought himself a bald patch of land on the hills that nobody wanted.

Avaran watched her at every weekend market and followed her back home whenever he could. She never looked back at him. She always walked in briskly and closed the door behind her. She was not like his mother or the other women who smiled at men and lured them back home. She was a good girl, and he knew she was the one he had to marry.

His mother cursed him when she heard this. 'Marry a Parayar? How can you bring such impurity into my kitchen? She will pollute everything,' she said. Avaran gulped down the toddy and held his mother, frail and haggard now, by the neck. 'Stop shouting like a fishmonger woman. You don't have to worry about pollution because I am moving into her house. That woman is mine. She will always be mine. I love her. You will never understand it because you never loved anyone,' he said, pushing her onto the floor.

'Love? You think you love that girl? You just want to have someone to rule over. You want to feel powerful. That is why you want to get married. That is why you are trying to play petty politics. But you are like your father, weak. With or without toddy.'

'If you hated him so much, why did you marry him?'

'You think we had a choice back in the day? I did not even see your father until the day of the wedding. I married him because my father decided it for me. Or I married him because maybe, for once in my life, for a change, I knew I could be the formidable one.'

Avaran heard footsteps, and it was not Elsy but the man who took her.

The superend looked coldly at him. The wolf stood near the man's feet and growled at him again. A smile curled around the man's thin moustache as he patted his beast's fur. The superend was a coward. He needed a beast for protection, like the boy who hid behind his rimfire rifle and his father behind the boy's mother and the mother behind her fancy English and short immodest dresses. Rich people were the weak ones. Yet his wife had picked this man. He was her refuge from the storm. Bitterness rose to Avaran's lips.

The superend said that though he wanted to help, he couldn't do anything. Bloody bourgeois.

'Didn't I tell you how they all are?' Avaran told the men when they got back to the tent.

Now, Avaran sat on the floor and held his rumbling stomach. The sun inched its way up to the zenith. Some of the men had dozed off.

Avaran licked his lips and thirsted for some local brew. He wanted the numbness the spirit offered him. But when he ran his fingers over the knot in his mundu, it offered him disappointment. He spat at the knot that was flaccid under his fingers. What he had pilfered from the money bag last Sunday wouldn't even be enough to buy half a measure of rice. It was with the chelavu cash that he survived every week, like everyone else.

He looked at the men around him and knew that he had to put them above his ego. What if one of their children died? They might point their fingers at him. Maybe, in their hysteria, some would even laugh at him.

He turned to the men and cleared his throat. 'What if we changed our minds about some of the things?' The men sat up and listened.

chapter 30

THE STEAM ROSE FROM THE appam and mutton stew on the table. But it failed to rouse Eesho's appetite. He always had a healthy appetite, and it was something that Mamma Mollykutty took immense delight in. Warmth would spread over her face every time his fingers lucked upon the soft-boiled duck egg hidden within the plump grains of rice. Her eyes would smile as he mixed the runny yolk with the rice and moulded it into a lime-sized ball. She hid no duck eggs for Georgekutty and Eesho hadn't noticed it till one day, his brother questioned his mother during lunch. 'Why this lopsided love?' he asked her, digging his fingers into his rice. Mamma Mollykutty's face rumpled with discontent. 'Next time you catch a bird, try getting some eggs too, little thief.'

Eesho pushed away his plate with the appam and stew that Kochuthresia had served him and sat back in the chair.

'Are you not going to eat? Elsy made it.'

'I am not hungry. But you should eat,' he said, sliding her plate closer to her.

'I will eat when you eat,' she said, her demeanour composed though he had given her enough reasons to worry.

He didn't sleep well at night. He would toss and turn for hours, get up, light his pipe, and float along the corridors like the spectre of the bygone white man, till his eyes became heavy with sleep. Early in the morning, he would wake up to find himself on the sofa in the hall or on a stone bench in the garden, with a blanket that Kochuthresia must have thrown over him sometime during the night, and Duke lying by his feet.

Ever since Krishnan's disappearance, something festered within Eesho. He feared Krishnan had run away to a place from where there would be no return, and perhaps, like Georgekutty, he, too, would become a drifter.

A week after Krishnan's disappearance, when Eesho went to the local police station, he was told that Krishnan was not a missing person because he had taken his belongings with him.

'They always turn up,' said the sub-inspector. 'The kid must be off venting his anger somewhere.'

He scratched his hairless head and gave a felonious smile. 'How is the lockout going?' he asked.

'Over a month and nothing new.'

'You know how we don't really get involved in these things. We believe that these are issues you should solve at the management level. But don't worry, Kerala Police is very good at checking violence. We will come if we even smell something violent. Our noses are very sharp.'

Kochuthresia was watching Eesho with concern.

'Ok. Let's eat then,' Eesho said and served her.

He wanted her to eat, though he himself wanted to starve and waste away like the babies with the leaky noses and the children who had dropped out of school. He remembered the scraggy bones that stuck out of their mother's breasts and blamed himself for their suffering. Had he been a better negotiator, they wouldn't have their stomachs cleaving to their backbones. His father was a good leader. He was better equipped at handling the labour union activities on his farm. In such a situation, he would have used diplomacy. And he would have been fair. But even if Eesho wished to adopt the role of a diplomat, circumstances had confined him to a different path. Ousepachan, Mary, and Markose were in Madras, awaiting the resolution of their own ordeal, leaving Eesho to grapple with the situation on his own. Eesho had driven to Calicut to find a locked gate. 'They will come back once the lockout is over,' said the watchman. Eesho sat in the Jeep and put his head in his hands. He then booked a trunk call home just to hear a familiar voice.

'Come back home. There is nothing for you there.' Mamma Mollykutty's voice fluttered over the phone. Someone had told her stories of black magic being performed on the owners and staff of the nearby tea estates, their children being threatened on their way to school, and their dogs being struck down with poisoned meat. 'What if they do something to you?' she asked him. 'Nothing will happen to us. But I can't just leave. People depend on me.'

And so Eesho stayed. He waited for Krishnan to return and for the troubles to end. He waited for the babies to be fed and the children to return to school. He wouldn't run away like the previous superintendent.

Elsy brought tea and biscuits from the kitchen and laid them on the table. A gentle smile escaped her lips when she saw them eating. Duke was walking beside her, his eyes fixed on the biscuits on the tray.

'I will give you your share. You need to be patient,' she said, patting him on the belly.

Ever since Elsy had come home, Duke had a clear understanding of his protective role. After Avaran led the group of men to their home, the man's eyes searched the fluttering curtains for a shadow of Elsy. Duke had growled at the man as he inched closer to the windows. As the men walked away, Avaran had turned around and hissed at Eesho from the distance, spit bubbling from the corners of his lips.... 'Thief.' The word unsettled him. No one had ever called him that before. He had never been the thief. It was always his brother.

He walked into the house. Elsy was standing near the door, watching the men as they walked down the hill.

'Do you want to go back to him?' Eesho asked her.

'No, saar. Never. He sometimes cares for me when he isn't drunk. But when he is, it's like I'm with another man,' she said, looking at her feet.

'All right. Then look up. There's no reason to look down any more,' Eesho told her.

Kochuthresia finished the appam on her plate and got up to clean the table with a kitchen cloth. 'Now that we've eaten, do you want to sit with me in the study for a while?' She was gently pushing him towards acts of normalcy. She watched his eyes, drew closer to him, and placed her hand on his shoulder. 'I know you're worried about Krishnan. But he'll come back. I know it in my heart. He always turns to you.'

'I believe you.'

Duke growled at the window, and Elsy stiffened. 'Saar, saar.' Pappan's voice echoed through the morning mist.

'Come in. We are in the dining room,' Eesho said.

Pappan's limp was more pronounced when he walked in. It happened every time there was something exciting. 'Saar, they are ready for a compromise,' he said.

'Did you speak to them? Do you know what they want?'

'No, saar. Avaran told me he will speak only to you. They are waiting near the office. But this is good news only, no? I think very soon we can all get back to work like normal people.'

The only thing Eesho needed to hear now was that of Krishnan's return.

He drove with Pappan and Duke to the office and found the men waiting for him under the blue tarpaulin. Avaran and the men from the parties were behind a table, their heads together in communion. Avaran rose to his feet as he spotted the Jeep. He ran his fingers over the faint lines on his wrist as he laid his eyes on Duke perched on the front seat. But Eesho sensed no fear in Avaran's eyes. There was only loathing. Avaran looked at the men behind him and cleared his throat. 'We cannot let the children starve any more. That is not right. So, we have come to an understanding,' he said. 'We have decided to let go of the issue of wage increase. And we will come to work from next week. But only on the condition that the assistant superend will apologize.'

The men watched Eesho with anxious eyes.

'Do not fear. I will make sure he does,' Eesho said.

chapter 31

MARKOSE SAW THE JEEP FROM the window of his room and fell back into his bed. The sight was an intrusion into the quietude of his morning routine. Markose got up from bed, resolute, and walked to the dining room. The servants were setting the table, and his mother appeared from the kitchen, wiping her hands on her curry-spattered apron.

'Ente kuttan...my boy,' she said, patting his cheek. 'I made breakfast today. Brush your teeth and come to the table.'

'I think we have to wait a bit. The superintendent is here. He is talking to Papa.'

Her face turned cloudy, but then she looked out of the window, and it brightened again. 'I wonder if he brought the dog along. I will get some butter biscuits for him if he is here,' she said and went back to the kitchen.

Markose went out on to the veranda. He found the superintendent sitting there with his dog. Eesho's eyes narrowed as he saw Markose.

'How was Madras?' he asked him. Markose sensed mockery in his voice.

'Madras is always good. It was a pleasant change for Papa and Mummy.'

'I'm sure it was,' said the superintendent, lighting his pipe.

'You shouldn't smoke in front of Papa. You know he has had a stroke.'

'It's okay. I told him he could. It is not that easy to get rid of me,' said his father, sitting upright in his planter's chair. 'And Eesho comes with good news. Call Mummy.'

'I'm here.' His mother emerged from the sitting room with a butter biscuit in her hand and the dog wagged its tail. 'Here you go,' she said, putting the biscuit into his mouth.

She went to the leg-rest and sat on it. It was only after the stroke that she took a liking to the leg-rest. It wasn't the most comfortable piece of furniture, carved from unforgiving wood, but it mattered little to her. She bore the discomfort stoically because she wanted to be close to his father, so that she could catch his every breath and watch his every move. She would throw out the morning newspaper if it carried anything foreboding, make sure that he didn't sneak too much sugar into his tea, or send the servants to buy the much-too-salty lime sodas from the neighbourhood tea stall.

His father cleared his throat and looked at the leg-rest. 'Eesho says they are ready for a compromise.'

His mother clapped her hands in delight. 'Whoops-a-daisy. Didn't I tell you they would come around? So, they are willing to get back to work?'

'They are ready to let go of their demand for the wage rise.'

'Of course, that was just an excuse to milk us.'

'But they still want Markose to apologize.'

Her body stiffened on the leg-rest. 'Orikkalum illa, no way. We should wait more. They will come around.' Her face was cloudy again.

'What they are asking, I think, is only fair,' the superintendent said.

'Is it fair that my son apologizes?'

'Yes.'

She snickered. She wasn't the kind who would let men rule over her. She turned to his father to gauge his reaction. He had sunk deep into his chair. Sweat covered his brows as he clutched his chest.

'Mathave, is it back? Where is it hurting? I am calling the doctor.' She rose from the leg-rest and touched his chest.

'No need. I'm okay. But I can't take this any more. We cannot let this go on forever.' His father looked him in the eyes. 'You must apologize. It's been too long. People are suffering. The boy is missing. Children, women...please, son....'

His mother was holding his father by the shoulders, rubbing his chest. Her eyes were dry, but he could sense her pain, the weight pressing down on her. He would do anything at that moment to relieve her from this burden.

'Yes, I will apologize. Of course, I will,' he said and felt his mother's heart quieten.

chapter 32

IT WAS A FEW HOURS after dusk. The wait would be over by the time the sun rose. Earlier, the workers had thanked Avaran, their words charged with deep sincerity. It was never about the raise in wages, but about respect, they said.

The day was supposed to be a happy one for him. But his wrists still stung, and the house was empty except for the green bird uttering throatily from its cage. Its squawks were not as powerful as before. The bird had grown skinnier, much like him.

The day he had brought the bird home, she had smiled. It was a few days after her father's death, but she smiled. It warmed his heart as she took the bird into the house, holding the cage close. When he walked in, she was near the hearth, thrusting long green chillies into the cage. 'Do you want to kill the thing?' he asked her. 'Oh, parrots cannot taste the spice in the chillies like we can,' she said. He felt stupid. But he was happy.

Now, when the bird cackled, his face turned hot.

'Oh, shut up. Don't you see she doesn't love you? She left us both,' Avaran said, getting up from his cot. 'I cannot sit here any more.'

He looked at the alarm clock on the table and knew that the Jeep to town would be waiting at the stop. Wasting no time, he changed out of his lungi into a crumpled shirt and mundu, tied his belt around his waist, picked up Elsy's knife from under his pillow, tucked it into the belt, and walked to the stop near the paadi.

The Jeep dropped him off in Calicut, and he made his way to the toddy shop. Avaran ran his fingers over the knot in his mundu and spat into the air. He had given the last of his coins to the Jeep driver. It was a pointless excursion, and he didn't even have the money to go back.

There was one person who could help—one whose money bag always jingled with coins, putrid with the scent of many men.

He picked up his pace and reached the door that was so familiar to him. She opened it after making him wait longer than he would have liked.

'Are you coming in? Or are you just going to stand there?' she asked him.

'Is your brother home?' he asked, peeping through the open door.

'No. He got a job in Vadakkara. He left two weeks ago.'

'Is someone else here?'

'Nobody,' she said. There was an air of irritation in her voice.

'Can you give me some money?'

She laughed. A cruel laugh that had her middle-aged spread jiggling. 'Wait here,' she said. She went in and came back with two notes. 'Buy two bottles and come home,' she said, closing the door.

'Whore,' he said and walked to the toddy shop. He didn't want to beg for money in front of a woman, but he did as he was told.

The first bottle they shared numbed his mind. The woman was sitting next to him on the bed. He pulled her closer to his chest. She was not all that bad.

'You help me in ways you don't realize,' he told her.

'How so? Every time you are here, you are in a hurry to go back.'

'I am in no hurry today. I will stay the night with you,' he said, reaching for the second bottle.

She undid the hook of her blouse and watched him pour her a glass. 'I am in no hurry either,' she said, running her fingers along her breasts. The blouse had fallen away from her breasts, and she played with her nipples as she drank. She always liked to tease him. Experience made her good at everything she did.

He brought his face close to her breasts and bit her nipples. She cried in pain and fell back onto the bed. Her glass rolled over and fell to the floor. 'You are a madman,' she said, laughing as he pressed his body into hers. She bit his ear as he tried to undo her mundu.

'Bitch,' he cried and held his ear. 'You are drunk.'

'Not any more than you are.'

'No more of this.' He sat up on the bed and reached out for the bottle on the table.

She laughed again. 'Are you planning to kill yourself with that poison?'

'It's a slow poison. Never heard of it killing anyone in a day, unless they throw in batteries and dead snakes while brewing it.'

'You are a madman. You picked up the wrong bottle. What you are holding will kill you in less than an hour.' She pointed at the bottle in his hands and the bottle of arrack still on the table.

Avaran looked at the bottle he held in his fingers and flinched. Bright green liquid shone like emeralds in the light of the kerosene lamp.

'What is this?'

'Rat poison.'

'Why do you have it?'

'To kill rats, silly.'

'Who gave it to you?'

'A man who works at a mechanic shop. He used to make this for his own house. A mix of engine coolant and crushed glass.'

'What else does he give you?'

She sat up. Her words were sharp as she spoke. 'It's none of your business.'

He didn't want her to throw him out. He hadn't even managed to undo her mundu yet. 'Sorry,' he said.

'Does it work?'

'Of course, it does. I've seen the creatures walk around, drooling, vomiting blood and bile, pissing all over the floor like crawling babies. Then they roll over and die a dreadful death.'

'Does it taste bad?' he asked, pulling the bottle towards his nose.

She raised an eyebrow at him. 'Madman. How am I to know? I haven't tasted it. But the rats will drink it without a problem. So it can't be that bad.'

She tapped the bottle with her fingernails. 'Just one drop to kill a rat. A few more to kill you,' she said, laughing maniacally, her eyes rolling.

'Maybe I will kill you first, drunk whore,' he grunted under his breath. But she was too drunk to hear anything.

'The trucks. Watch out for them on the road,' she said and sank into bed.

'Stupid woman. On and on about the same thing. You think I am blind?' he said, getting up from the bed. He picked up the bottle of arrack from the table. 'I will not waste this on you,' he told her, slipped it into a cloth bag he found in the kitchen, and left the house.

He walked to the bus stop where he found the Jeep to the village. 'Wait. One more person,' he said, hopping into the backseat. He held the cloth bag close to his chest and thought about Elsy. Her big innocent eyes. Her guileless mien. He always thought about her after he left the whore's house. Elsy's face calmed him. It gave him clarity when everything else seemed fuzzy. The Jeep dropped him off at the stop next to the paadi and he walked to his house. He longed for her to be waiting near the doorstep, squatting on the floor, playing with the silver bells on her anklets, talking to the green bird.

'Elsy, Elsy,' the parrot cawed from the cage. He stuck his fingers into his ears and tried to drown out the bird's cry. 'Why do you still call out her name? Don't you know my name? Can't you ask if I am okay?' he shouted and sat on the floor next to the birdcage.

'I will go to work from tomorrow and then come back to an empty house? Is that any way to live?' he asked the bird. He reached for the bottle of arrack in his cloth bag. When he pulled out a bottle with green liquid, he winced.

'Oh God. The whore wanted to kill me.'

'Elsy, Elsy,' said the bird.

'Oh, shut up. Do you also want to kill me? With your racket?' He stared at the bird and wished for it to die.

'You are the same colour as the poison,' he said, raising the bottle closer to his eyes. 'But I don't need the poison to shut you up.' Avaran got up from the floor and opened the tiny door of the birdcage. He took the feathered creature in his hand and gently twisted its neck. He placed the bird on his cot. It flapped its wings feebly. It annoyed him that the creature didn't die in one blow. A sudden hunger for meat overcame his being. He had not eaten the entire day. The money the whore had given him was enough for the two bottles and the Jeep fare back home.

'Maybe I should roast you. You won't be very different from a chicken, I presume,' he said and walked to the hearth. There was a piece of bread that he had bought a week ago. It was pale blue with fungus and hard to the touch.

'It's definitely bird today,' he said.

He picked up the dying bird from his cot, its fragile body trembling in his grasp, while his other hand traced the familiar, cold edge of the knife at his waist. His gaze drifted to the bottle of rat poison on the floor. 'You know,' he said, a dark thought blossoming in his head, 'I know someone who will like you more than I do. That glutton wolf.' He smiled, brought the knife to its throat, and watched life ebb through his fingers.

chapter 33

SEVERAL KILOMETRES AWAY, KRISHNAN WAS walking back to Puthuloor. The dawn was yet to break, and the air was frosty. At first, he had run. When he was too tired to run, he walked.

The cold air wrapped itself around him, and his hands still trembled from the noises of the night. He draped his arms around his shoulders to stop them from shaking. His tin suitcase was still in his room behind the bookshop. It was a room he had shared with a man who might have been his own age. He never told Krishnan his name. He called him comrade. He was a zealot who had cast his lot with the revolution after completing his intermediate studies. His father wanted to send him to Ceylon to do Economics, but he wanted to pursue what he called 'voluntary poverty'. Whenever he was moved by something someone had said at the bookshop, he would pat Krishnan on the back, his bellbottoms flapping as wildly as his hair.

'Don't be possessed by your possessions,' he had told Krishnan when he first walked into the room with his tin suitcase. The man had no suitcase.

Krishnan didn't have much in his suitcase. There was only the paisley-printed shirt, a couple of lungis, and a pair of trousers. The man didn't know that. And Krishnan didn't tell him either. He liked his tin suitcase and kept it close to his chest because Eesho had bought it for him when he first went to the school in Quilon, a world of shoes, English, knives, forks, and bunk beds.

Krishnan walked along the road till he couldn't feel his legs any more. He stopped and rubbed his hands over his calves, hoping to pump feeling back into them. But his fingers were as cold as his legs and the numbness wouldn't go away. Estate House was only a few furlongs away, but he wasn't sure he could make it. It was the longest he had ever walked.

After the attack, he had fled from the temple grounds, deep into the forest's refuge. He wanted to get as far away as possible. He ran through the thick frondescence with no starlight to guide him, hoping that he wouldn't encounter a wild elephant or a leopard. He tumbled again and again, but he sprang back up—bruised but relentless—and ran until he reached a road. After walking for a few hours, a distant rumble echoed through the air, signalling the approach of a vehicle. He scurried into the undergrowth at the side of the road and crouched down as the headlights pierced the darkness. Maybe the police were after him. But it was a goods lorry. Emerging from the shadows, he extended a shaky hand, soundlessly pleading for a lift. The lorry dropped him off in Calicut.

Everything looked different. The door to the bookshop had been shut, its welcoming warmth a distant dream. There was no radio playing songs. The town was different in the dark. He walked over the hills to make it to the village. As he walked, he remembered the sounds from the night; they rang like a raw tune in his ears—the crushing bones, the wireless operator's last breath, the thud with which the sub-inspector's sliced arm landed across the room and was left in the corner like a rotten piece of meat. Krishnan remembered the sight and sounds from the butcher shop near his house, and he felt acrid bile rise to his lips. He clung to a rubber tree and retched into the coconut shell.

He wiped his face with his sleeve. There were spider webs mixed in with the bile. The tappers hadn't tapped the trees recently. The troubles hadn't ended here either. He sank into the earth and rested his head against the tree trunk. One day, someone had walked into the bookshop and told them about the troubles at the estate—the strikes, the gheraos, and the lockout. The comrades shook their heads with sympathy. 'It never stops. Does it?'

Krishnan lay down under the tree. Moonlight streamed onto his face. When he had slipped into his shirt the previous day, he had asked his roommate, 'Do you think this will be all right to wear tonight?'

'It's too good for a night like this. A little too bright for a covert endeavour. Maybe you should rub some mud on it like I believe they do in the army.'

Krishnan said he wouldn't. It was too precious to him. 'The moon won't be up until later tonight,' he said.

'True. But do you want blood on it?' asked his roommate.

In that moment, Krishnan finally found himself confronting the magnitude of what lay ahead. Would it be another man's blood? Or his own? They had, on countless occasions, read Mao's essay, 'Serve the People':

> All men must die, but death can vary in its significance. The ancient Chinese writer Ssu-ma Ch'ien said, 'Though death befalls all men alike, it may be weightier than Mount Tai or lighter than a feather.' To die for the people is weightier than Mount Tai, but to work for the fascists and die for the exploiters and oppressors is lighter than a feather.

He had thought the essay nothing short of brilliant.

But the man's question befuddled him. Krishnan's lack of response softened his roommate's face. He said gently, 'We are advocates of the abolition of war. We do not want war, but war can only be abolished through war, and in order to get rid of the gun, it is necessary to take up the gun.'

Krishnan sat under the rubber tree and ran his fingers along the shirt. Though it was a cold night, his chest was drenched with perspiration.

He knew he would catch a chill if he stayed out for too long. With heavy steps, he made his way to the Estate House. When he caught sight of the hill tucked into the clouds in the distance, he felt lighter. The weeping willows called out to him, and he sprinted. The mist lay heavy at the bottom, and through the haze, he made out Pappan at the foot of the hill, his hands covering his mouth. Eesho was crouched next to him. His shoulders were slumped and gently shaking. Krishnan walked closer to him. There were tears running down his cheeks. It collected on his pencil moustache like a swelling dam. He was hugging something close to his chest. Krishnan drew nearer. Eesho was holding Duke. His eyes were closed and motionless like a stillborn baby.

∽

Beneath the louring morning clouds, the earth was in mourning.

A praying mantis stood with folded arms on the grim, grey graves. The brook grumbled like a hungry child and the wind brought with it the taste of blood. The old headstones swelled out through the undergrowth, two blisters soundlessly retelling stories from the bygone times.

Eesho pulled out the knotted weeds from the abysmal ground. He pressed his hands into the moist soil. The earth was ripe under his skin. Red mud smiled back at him. He dragged his index finger through the mud and marked a space next to the two lonely graves. A square one. Like that for a small person or a child.

He struck the shovel into the ground and the earth gave in. The first drop of rain fell and then the skies wept. The rain stung his skin as he ploughed through the rust-red loam. Soil slapped against his gumboots like viscous blood. The last time he had dug the earth was for a mango sapling.

Krishnan extended his hands towards him. His shoulders had become skinnier. Flesh clung to his bones. There were bruises on his temples and cheeks. His eyes were hurting with many stories. He looked older, hunching over like a sickly man as he stretched out a trembling hand.

'I can do it,' Krishnan said feebly, reaching for the shovel in Eesho's hands.

'This is something I have to do myself,' said Eesho. He tried to smile at him, tell him that his presence comforted him, ask him where he had been, if he had eaten anything, and how he got the bruises on his face. But his lips were heavy.

He kept digging until the pit was deep enough. Eesho lowered himself into the hole and looked up at Kochuthresia, who stood next to the heap of mud he had dug out, eyes pained, rivers of earth lapping around her feet like ribbons from her embroidery box.

Her sari caught the pellets of rain and weighed her down. He understood that the pain she felt was no less than his own. She had cried when he had brought Duke's cold and limp body home earlier that night. Together, they had scoured the estate. She hitched up her sari deftly, as she once had on the netball court, walking over ferns and wading through the brook, calling out Duke's name. Duke had never strayed far; his presence had always been their faithful companion.

Elsy was the first to take notice of Duke's absence. Ever since she came home, Duke had taken to sleeping by her door. However, when Elsy awoke in the middle of the night, Duke was nowhere to be found. She searched the house in vain. Her eyes fell upon the slightly ajar kitchen door, the broken lock confirming her worst fears. She woke up Eesho and Kochuthresia and showed them the open door.

Eesho called Pappan, and they looked around, calling out Duke's name. 'Don't worry. We will find him, saar,' Pappan told him.

When he first saw Duke's body at the bottom of the hill, a peculiar disquiet clenched his chest. It looked like an animal Markose would bring home after his hunting expeditions. Soulless. Wooden. From another world. His mouth was frothy with green liquid, and his eyes were open. Eesho felt Duke's forehead. It was icy cold. He picked him up and held him close to his chest.

Now, Eesho stood in the hole and trembled with fever and regret. His mind, clouded with sorrow, seemed incapable of conceiving what could have happened to Duke. He climbed out, picked up Duke's body and lowered him into the earth. He sat next to him, enveloped by the swelling earth, and felt his velvet fur soak up the rain that had begun to descend on them. He thought of the first time he saw him, a tiny piece of fluff sitting in Philipose Achen's armpits, aching for an escape. Duke should have stayed there. He would still be alive then, frolicking somewhere on the white sands in Niranam, teasing Philipose Achen and troubling Mamma Mollykutty when they visited her every evening for tea and snacks. She would throw him biscuit crumbs and carp about how fat he was getting. She would tell him not to chase the chickens in the yard and shoo him away when he would try to nibble her feet.

Eesho rubbed Duke's belly one last time. He climbed out of the hole and walked to the house. Krishnan watched him as he walked away.

Eesho climbed into bed and drifted into a restless dream. In the quiet night, the faint whiff of cigars wafted through the air and the distant sound of footsteps echoed on the veranda.

chapter 34

THE NEXT MORNING, FOUR MEN stood on plastic chairs and loosened the blue tarpaulin tied to the bamboo staves.

'Isn't it too early to bring it down?' the people from the parties asked Avaran as the blue tarpaulin fell to the earth. The liquor from the night had left him dazed, and he squinted at the sun. Avaran shook his head. 'Everything will be resolved today.' He told the four men to fold the tarpaulin and store it in the shed behind the factory. 'But we don't know when we will need it again. So, keep it safe. Don't let the rats get to it.'

Krishnan walked up to the gate as the men carried the tarpaulin away. He saw Avaran talking to a group of people dressed in white, his eyes red with traces of liquor. Avaran caught sight of him, and his eyes widened. 'You are back? Where were you?' he asked, walking towards him. Avaran's gaze brushed over the bruises on his cheeks and temple, but he didn't probe any further.

'That boy will apologize today. You deserve to hear that. So does Vishwan. And you are back just in time.'

Krishnan gave a faint nod and walked to the office building. The front room was packed with people. All the workers had assembled there. Some came with their spouses and children. Vishwan stood in a corner of the room and held his daughter close to him. She was not breathing hard now. But she was skinnier. Much like the other children in the room.

The old man sat at his desk and looked at the world through clouded glasses. There was a pile of papers on Krishnan's desk.

As he walked in, people turned their heads and watched him pass. Some smiled at him and raised their hands in acknowledgement.

'What happened to your face?' a man who stood next to him asked him.

Krishnan touched his temple and turned his face away. 'A small accident while I was on the way.'

'Where did you go?'

'I had something to take care of back home.'

'But I heard you were not at home.' The man pressed on.

Krishnan moved away from the man and walked towards Vishwan and his daughter. The daughter sucked on her thumb. She looked at Krishnan and flashed him a toothless smile. The smile warmed his heart, and his cheeks stretched into a smile.

Krishnan looked out of the window and hoped to see Eesho drive in. But he knew he wouldn't come. There was a numbness in his eyes he had never seen before. Duke was his baby. His and Kochuthresia's. The day Duke had come to Niranam, they were celebrating their third wedding anniversary and Kochuthresia had made semiya payasam for the entire neighbourhood that night. Krishnan had joined them as they walked from door to door, hands overflowing with little tins of piping hot payasam. Eesho had held Duke by a leash he had bought the same day, and he rubbed his belly every time they stopped at a house. Over the months, Krishnan had overheard people whispering about the couple's inability to have children. Sympathetic comments flowed, suggesting that it was a pity there would be no one to carry on the family bloodline. But Krishnan, in his heart, believed that their love was perfect. They needed no child to complete them.

Still, he once overheard Mamma Mollykutty tell Philipose Achen that Duke had completed them in many ways. 'Why do you think I let the dog walk around in the house? I think my son believes it is his first child. And it will break his heart if I were to ever take that dog away from him.'

Krishnan looked around the room that was exploding with bodies. He could still feel the heaviness of the metal in his hand; the knife clung to him like a phantom limb. He looked down at his hands and they were still trembling. They had first trembled because of the fear of unfamiliar violence. But now they also trembled in shame. *Coward, coward, coward.* He heard the girl whisper into his ears.

He closed his eyes and tried to think of better times. The time the girl smiled at him and told him he looked good in his shirt. The time he could string together the words in *Phantom* and read them out to his parents. The time his father held Krishnan's diploma certificate with the care and awe reserved for precious things. The time Eesho clapped him on the shoulder after he had received his driving licence.

The sound of a car stirred him from his thoughts. He opened his eyes. Markose was making his way through the sea of bodies. He was hugging his rifle and contorting his body to avoid touching anyone. He pulled out his chair and sat behind his desk that still wobbled, held his rifle like a walking stick, and looked around the room crowded with bodies.

Avaran walked into the room with the people from the party, his eyes searching through the crowd. Krishnan knew he was looking for him and Vishwan. When he found Vishwan, Avaran took him by the hand and guided him towards Markose's desk. Krishnan tried to become one with the wall. The little girl still sucked on her thumb, but her eyes teared up as her father was led away. She edged closer to the wall.

Avaran was pulling Vishwan away from the teeming bodies and thrusting him towards the desk that wobbled. The little girl started crying.

'Apologize and we will get back to work,' Avaran told Markose. The workers in the room had fallen silent. The girl's cries rose into the air.

Markose leaned back in his chair. He looked at Avaran and took a deep breath. 'Over my dead body.'

Avaran let out a little gasp. The crowd gasped in disbelief. No one was prepared for Markose's words, let alone Avaran. 'But you said you would apologize. We will get back to work only after that is done,' Avaran said, forcing his way forward.

'Who are you to make the rules? You are a mere tapper like everyone else. You will get back to work anyway. You are the ones who need to feed your families,' said Markose, his voice rising over Avaran's. The little girl continued to cry.

Markose slammed his fist on his desk. 'Will someone shut that thing up? Or do I have to do that myself?'

Vishwan reached for his daughter, took her into his arms, and put her over his shoulders.

Avaran wasn't ready to give up. 'We won't let you go without an apology. So, you'd better do it now.'

'Is that so? What will you do? Lock me up again?'

Avaran lifted his shirt and exposed the knife tucked into his belt. Only its handle was visible. The metal was wrapped in cloth. Krishnan recognized it from the time he had a glimpse of it when Avaran had given him the pamphlet from under his shirt.

'No. We will have to resort to other measures.'

Markose looked at Avaran's midriff and took in the piece of metal wrapped in cheap cloth. He turned his gaze to the rifle in his own hands and laughed. 'Fool. You look like a fool with that kitchen knife stuck up your bum. Pull your shirt down. All I smell is fish. Get back to work, all of you,' he said.

Avaran's face dropped. He let his shirt fall back in its place. He was only as strong as the previous night's alcohol.

'Coward,' Markose said under his breath.

Krishnan knew no one would react. They were tired. They had no choice but to get back to work. That was the way of the world.

Markose sat back in his chair as the workers dispersed like ants. Krishnan was one of the few who stood his ground. Avaran, too, hadn't moved, possibly because he was still in shock at the way Markose had reacted.

'Go', Markose said to Avaran. Markose then turned to Krishnan. 'You, too, get out. Move. Didn't you hear me?'

Krishnan stood still.

Markose got up from his chair. 'I am talking to you. Move your filthy body away from me and get to work. I have decided to be merciful to you and let you keep your job so that you don't have to be an animal and climb trees like your forefathers.'

Krishnan's body trembled. Like the time before he had hit the boy in school, the boy who had called him the seed of a weakling. 'Did you know his grandfather was once arrested by the police?' he had told his friends. 'When he was put behind bars, he cried and shat in fear. Like an animal.' The boys pointed their fingers and laughed at him. Their collective roar wafted through the corridors and left his ears ringing. He had caught the boy by his collar and thrown him against the blackboard. Blood and tears. Reparations for sufferings unatoned for. Then he had heard Father Goody's voice reverberate in his ears. 'Boy, you shouldn't have done that. His face looks like a giant Indian wasp bit him. His father is a minister in the ruling party. He will put you in prison now. What will you do? Can *your* father get you out of prison? You need to understand how the world works.'

Krishnan reached for Avaran's waist. In a swift move, he pulled out the knife from the belt and unwrapped the flimsy cloth that clung to it. He ran his fingers along the cold metal, and it felt good. He wasn't trembling any more.

Avaran's eyes darted around with confusion. The people who were dispersing turned around to watch.

Markose watched the blade in Krishnan's fingers. 'What do you think you are doing?'

'What the world needs. A war to set all wars right,' Krishnan said and moved closer to him. There was a kind of terror that Krishnan had never seen in Markose before, the same kind he had seen in the eyes of the wireless operator and the sub-inspector when they had glimpsed the sickle in the farmer's hand.

Krishnan plunged the metal into Markose's white sweater, the blade splitting wool and flesh with an appalling simplicity. Warm blood trickled over Krishnan's hands. Redness spilled over Markose's white sweater. His face crumpled in pain. He sank onto the cold cement floor, clutching the fish knife. A long breath filled his lungs, a final puff, and then it was over.

Krishnan turned to the little girl, who clung to Vishwan's shoulders. Her father had turned her face away from the public execution. Krishnan patted her on the back and said, 'Don't worry. You are safe. No one will harm you now.'

chapter 35

A WEEK LATER, IN CALICUT, men in khaki walked around the empty bookshop, twirling their handlebar moustaches and flailing their lathis, well pleased with the reign of terror they had begun when they arrested a group of men who had attacked the police station in Thalassery. Baby Murphy watched the world from the ground, crushed into the soil like the books and pamphlets around it. The Little Red Book had surrendered to the red earth and the folding table had fallen over and cracked. And in the sit-out of his house, Ousepachan dissolved into his Bombay Fornicator.

He looked like a man with a missing body part. White stubble sprouted on his face. Every breath that he took was laboured. He ran disconsolate hands over his leg-rest, now vacant, fingers searching for a presence he couldn't feel any more.

'Was he really a part of the group?' Ousepachan asked Eesho.

'That is what the police are saying. They have evidence of his involvement.'

'Where is he now?'

'In the Calicut special sub jail. They have charged him with 120A and 302. Conspiracy and…murder.' His face hurt as the words left his mouth.

Eesho couldn't bring himself to face Ousepachan. He kept his eyes on the greenhouse, but his mind was elsewhere—Pappan's distressed shout jolting him from his nightmare, his encounter with Krishnan in the office. He remembered Krishnan's eyes; they were cold and withdrawn from the world. The tappers had confined him to the room, fearing he might attempt to escape. But he wouldn't have run even if the door had been left wide open. Eesho called out to him from the window. But Krishnan couldn't hear him. He was on the verge of flinging open the door when the sub-inspector with the felonious smile drove in with his constables. 'The boy came back, eh?' He inhaled deeply, searching for violence in the air as he pushed the door open. He took off his cap as he saw Markose's body on the floor and winced at the pool of blood he had almost stepped into. He grabbed Krishnan by his collar, put him in the backseat of the police Jeep, and slapped handcuffs on his wrists. Eesho held his shackled hands as a constable started the engine. 'I will come to get you,' he told Krishnan. The Jeep snaked through the rolling hills until it disappeared from view.

'I could offer you tea,' Ousepachan said and looked at the empty leg-rest.

'It's okay. I'm fine.'

The teacups and the bag of camomile tea were still on the table next to him. But dust had formed a thick layer over them and on the leg-rest. Eesho thought he could still see Mary, perched half-tush in half-tush out, handing out butter biscuits and cups of tea.

'I thought it would be me. That I would go first. But they left me. Without any warning.' Ousepachan pointed an unsteady finger at the mosaic floor and choked on his words. 'She fell right here. And I thought I was the one with the weak heart.'

When Mary fell to the floor and collapsed after hearing about Markose's death, a part of Ousepachan died too. People tried to comfort him. They got together and mourned with him. They lifted their voices and wept, tore their robes and sprinkled dust upon their heads. 'It was a quick death,' they said, hoping that the words would bring him succour.

It was a funeral for two. Markose wore his white Geoffrey Boycott sweater. Mary wore her red lipstick. Ousepachan stood over them and cried convulsively, his jubba glowing with the fat tears that fell on it. The priest said that Mary had 'lived a full life' and that Markose had been 'a beautiful young soul whose life was taken away too soon'.

After the funeral, when the tears still didn't stop, people reminded him about the story of Job, who had many children, many servants, and livestock that numbered in the thousands:

> But one day, the Lord said to Satan, 'Everything he has is in your power.' So, Satan took it all away—his children, his

servants and his livestock. And Job's friends said, 'Think now, who that was innocent ever perished? Or where were the upright cut off? As I have seen, those who plow iniquity and sow trouble reap the same.'

People were cruel. Like Job's friends.

'I am sorry. I know nothing I say will bring you comfort,' Eesho said. Those words were his guilt offering. He was blameworthy. For introducing Krishnan into Ousepachan's world. For taking Krishnan away from his. For not holding his shoulders. For wallowing in his pain and turning blind to the world around him.

'You have nothing to apologize for. You lost a lot, too. The boy. Your dog. Mary loved the dog. The morning she died, she asked me if I could give her a dog for Christmas, like the one you have. But I said no. I said we are too old to take care of dogs, and I don't want servants to raise them. I wish I hadn't said that to her. I want to give her a dog. But now I can't. Everything is gone. Everything.'

He brought his hands to his head. 'I have no peace. No quietness. No rest. It should have been me. I should have died. I am responsible for everything. I should have made my son apologize. I could see it in his eyes that he wouldn't. He was too proud, like his mother. I was too weak to teach him right from wrong. But I hope he didn't feel anything. I hope my son didn't feel the pain when the knife....' He cried like a child in pain.

Eesho drew him close to his chest and held him like a father would hold his son.

∽

A few days later, back in the Estate House, he smiled for the first time in over a month as he told Kochuthresia about his decision. He took her in his arms and told her to start packing.

'Are you certain?' Kochuthresia asked him.

'Don't you think it's about time you enjoyed Mamma Mollykutty's pampering? I will drive to Calicut and tell Ousepachan that we are leaving.'

Ousepachan's younger brother and his wife, from Madras, were now living with him.

As Eesho packed, he thought of how he would begin telling Mamma Mollykutty the story of the land in the middle of nowhere. Though she knew of the strikes, she didn't know everything that had happened. She would be thrilled to have them back home. She would peer through the windows, stand excitedly on tiptoes when the Hillman rolled into the yard, run to Eesho and Kochuthresia, and wrap them tightly in her arms. 'Where is the naughty boy?' she would ask, waiting for Duke to emerge from the backseat of the car to sniff her toes. She would have tucked a biscuit or two in her chatta to give to him in secret. Then she would listen to his story and weep for days. But she would never even once say, 'I had told you to come back. You should have listened to me.' She was not that callous. And her sadness would be short-lived because when they would tell her she would soon be a grandmother, she would shed tears of happiness. She would embrace Kochuthresia, hide duck eggs within her plate of rice, and tell her to put her feet up and rest. 'You are the daughter I never had. And now, you will make me a grandmother. This is the best day of my life.'

They would laugh, and everything would seem all right. But Eesho's heart would still ache.

PART XI

chapter 36

APPACHA WENT IN HIS SLEEP peacefully, Velia Pappa informed her when she reached Niranam. She paid her taxi driver and walked towards the porch with Velia Pappa, her feet getting heavier with every step.

'It is a relief that he didn't suffer more. All these years, he didn't get bed sores even once,' he said, lifting his double chin in triumph. There was contentment in his human eye, and his goat's eye, vacant and catatonic, was directed towards the porch. Overall, he was pleased with the ergonomic chair and the soft side water mattress that he had bought for Appacha and desired to take credit for Appacha's lack of pressure sores. However, the real reason was Krishnan Uncle, who had stood by his side at all times.

Aleyamma looked around the garden. There were people as far as the eye could see. She walked through the swarm of bodies and tried to tune out the nagging hum of grief that suffused the air. Even the stray dogs had gone wild. Psychologists would call it confirmation bias because, on an ordinary day, she wouldn't have perceived the echoes from the streets. Even so, was there something the dogs could see that others couldn't? Did a donkey once see an angel of God, and did it open its mouth to speak in a language that a man could understand? Did a serpent once whisper into a woman's ears and lead her to the big fall? Did the animals sense the coming storm and walk into the ark by themselves? Did a raven feed a hungry man? Did a whale know when to swallow a man and when to spit him out? Did the lions in the den know when to seal their mouths? Weren't they fables, allegories, cultural anxieties? Or did there linger a possibility that these wailing dogs could see Appacha's spirit, hovering over the sea of bodies, looking down on Aleyamma with a longing to return to his own? And would he, like Lazarus, walk out of the cave, wrapped in the clothes he was interred in? Would he, like Jesus, rise from the grave, leaving the cerement whole? Would he, like her, slip back into his body and wake up on crisp white sheets that smelled like disinfectant and death?

His body was kept in the portico for everyone to see, in a freshly lacquered coffin carved out from East Indian rosewood, his nostrils and ears replete with plumose white balls of cotton, silver hair polished back with Brylcreem, winding sheet rolled around his body. Pallbearers, who pulled out sorrowful faces solely for weddings, funerals, and report card days, sat around him, crying and singing synchronously, holding black Malayalam hymn books with a fading cross in the centre, leafing through the pages without looking into them. They nudged each other and telepathically decided the order of the warbling. Most of them knew the words by heart. They used their hymn books as an excuse to avoid protracted meetings of the eyes that would otherwise make them uncomfortable. The women cried and wiped their tears with the ends of their salty pallus that shivered disturbingly like severed lizard tails.

Mouse Appachan and Happy Kochamma smiled at her. They were sitting on plastic chairs lined up near the coffin. Mouse Appacha still wore his Aviators on his head like a hairband, and Happy Kochamma still huffed and puffed. Aleyamma offered no reciprocation, her gaze instead seeking out Manoj, though she knew he wouldn't be there. Appacha had planned Manoj's life before he lost his memory; he was sent to a college in Bombay and now he was in Pretoria working as a chemical engineer.

She caught sight of Amma sitting at the end of a diwan in one corner of the room. Amma was not crying, but for a fleeting moment, she looked sad. Were there tears in her eyes? Was she bemoaning the loss of her father, whom she couldn't ever pardon?

Amma was about to turn eight when Ammachi passed away. She died in hospital after giving birth to Cheria Pappa two weeks before Amma's birthday. Velia Pappa was four. The two of them had waited expectantly near the door, awaiting their mother's return. But she didn't come home. Instead, Appacha brought home a tiny babe swathed in cotton, kept the squalling ball of limbs on a sofa, went to his room, and closed the door.

People said that Appacha shook Ammachi after she had breathed her last, as though he was trying to rouse her from an afternoon nap. When she didn't wake up, he clutched her close to his chest and cried. Talitha Koum. Talitha Koum. But the slumber from which one cannot awaken held her in eternal captivity.

Appacha withdrew into a cocoon, days of silence stretching into weeks. He forsook food, razors, baths, and even the payasam the servants had prepared for Amma's birthday. And one day, when someone told him about a job at a coffee estate in Coorg, he packed his bags and left. Amma, Velia Pappa, and baby Cheria Pappa stayed with Appacha's parents till they were sent to a boarding school in Ooty after Appacha's father, Tharakan, had died. Tharakan was watching his men climb the coconut trees when he clutched his heart and collapsed under one. The men rushed down the trees and carried his body into the house, wailing and beating their chests.

'Ketto, I don't want you to go so fast, like poof.... You can't keep doing this to me,' Appacha's mother, Mamma Mollykutty, said. But Tharakan breathed his last in her arms and Mamma Mollykutty wept uninterruptedly for two days. When Velia Pappa asked her if his grandfather had gone to the same place as his mother, she wiped her eyes and hugged the grandkids. 'Oh, he has just gone to count the coconuts. That man loves his coconuts a little too much,' she said and got back to life. People said Appacha's mother was a vociferous woman who had mellowed with age and arthritis. With her daughter-in-law's passing, she had taken to mothering young children again. She never beat her grandkids. She displayed love in forms that didn't require a bamboo cane that people said she once famously brandished. When Appacha decided to send her grandkids away to a boarding school in Ooty, she said that if Appacha took the kids away, she would die from heartache and slowly rot away in a corner of the house with no one to even notice. His mother's emotional blackmail did not persuade Appacha. He said what the children needed was an education that the leaky-roofed school in Niranam couldn't give. Mamma Mollykutty broke her fast when Amma brought her a glass of milk, pressed it to her lips with a firm hand, and flared her almond eyes at her. Appacha always believed that his mother's chutzpah had rubbed off on all three kids, who turned out to be just like her from her younger days—loud and mulish but lacking visible expressions of love.

Mamma Mollykutty lived long enough to cross a hundred. When Aleyamma was born, though Mamma Mollykutty's bones creaked and her flesh sagged, she sat on her throne and bellowed instructions to the servants. 'Rub chicken fat on the C-section wound. It heals all wounds,' she said, as the servants giggled amongst themselves. 'Rub some chicken fat on the baby too.' A month later, when Indira Gandhi was assassinated, Mamma Mollykutty cried. When Salma Sultan came on television without a rose in her hair to read the news that evening, Mamma Mollykutty pointed at the screen and said, 'Strange. Isn't October the best time for roses? Maybe she forgot. You know, she reminds me of my daughter-in-law. She also used to wear a rose in her hair.' She then listened to the news and cried along with Salma Sultan.

Aleyamma was four when Mamma Mollykutty passed away. The only memory she has of her great-grandmother is of the old woman seated on a stool by a giant pot of steaming water, staring unblinkingly into it, while the servants undressed her for a bath and smeared coconut oil on her wrinkled skin.

Though Aleyamma never had conversations with Amma about Ammachi, she knew that Amma missed her and her passing still brought her pain. She had saved all of Ammachi's paintings, embroidery, and recipe books and kept them in her Godrej almirah in tidy piles. Throughout Aleyamma's childhood, the stillness of the night was occasionally punctuated by the sound of Amma's cupboard door opening, followed by heavy sobs that sometimes went on till the sky blushed pink. The next morning, Amma would emerge from her bedroom like nothing had happened, head to the kitchen, and begin her experiments with food. Aleyamma once overheard Amma tell Gracy Kochamma that though she and her brother were sometimes made to wear matching clothes that neither of them liked, she had eight beautiful years with her family. 'I sometimes hate my youngest brother for taking all that away from us. But I forgive him because he was only a baby. But it is difficult to forgive Appa. He was stubborn. He never changed. Never learnt from his mistakes. Amma's passing brought me the same pain that it brought him. He was wallowing in his own and forgot to see mine. He thought Amma was just a passing memory for me. I grew up in a hostel all my life, while my father took care of the children of the people who worked for him. How is that fair?'

Appacha's actions had shaped Amma. The seeds for Amma's contempt for Appacha were sown a long time ago, though it materialized only years later when she turned her back on him forever. The banana leaf wasn't the reason for Amma's rebellion, but her pain, the very cause.

Aleyamma sat on a chair at the foot of Appacha's coffin and watched Amma. Her eyes were hidden behind her monkey crop. Even if there were tears, she had sucked them back in as she didn't want to weep for the father who had abandoned her as a child.

The only one hurting was her. Aleyamma knew that Appacha had called Cochin many times after Amma took her away from him. Each time the telephone rang, Amma would hastily answer, mumble words into the mouthpiece, and then retreat to a far corner of the sitting room, seemingly dissolving into the very walls to shield her conversations from prying ears. The phone stood on a tall wooden stand, with a single shelf at the bottom for a fat yellow directory that had to be changed constantly because of the ever-growing digits that the telephone exchange threw in front of phone numbers. It was a dirty grey phone with a lock and two keys. Two keys just for insurance. After a flurry of curt responses, the receiver would eventually descend with a resounding thud. Amma would then lock it and walk away. A few seconds later, she would walk back, remove the receiver, and leave it dangling on the side of the table like a hangman's noose.

Appacha had also come home with gifts for Aleyamma, the ones he had wrapped and kept under the Christmas tree the day Amma took her away. Amma never told her about it. Aleyamma found the stash hidden away in the secret side locker of Amma's dust-green

Godrej almirah when she went foraging for her old mark sheets before she left for Chennai for the first time. She was sure there were sweets too, but with her lack of self-control, Amma had probably devoured them all. Appacha had bought them from the same place where they bought the Christmas decorations—the stationery shop that sold chilli powder and spices in newspapers shaped like cones. Within the shimmering wrapping that had come loose, there were the gifts that Appacha usually bought her. Amma never told her about them. Aleyamma didn't ask her either because she knew it was too late. She shut the steel door of the compartment and took a taxi to Niranam, where she saw Appacha, removed from the world, resting on rubber sheets.

The singing continued through minor interruptions of sniffs and sobs. 'Yatra cheyum njan crusshe nookki…Ninnoden daivame njan cheratte…As I journey, I turn my gaze toward the cross…Nearer my God to thee, nearer to thee.'

The women were singing with all their might, mimicking melancholy in their pitch that had veered unpredictably. Aleyamma got up, went into Appacha's bedroom, and sat on his bed. There was still a depression on the pillow where he had laid his head. Krishnan Uncle had folded Appacha's bedsheet and rubber sheets and kept them in a pile at the foot of the bed. The ergonomic chair stood in the corner of the room—rust had developed on its armrest. In the dressing room next door, the dresser mirror creaked gently in the wind. Aleyamma closed her eyes and let the smell of Brut, Cuticura, and Radhas envelop her.

After a while, she walked back to the porch and took a seat. Amma was still ensconced on the diwan, and Velia Pappa and Cheria Pappa were bustling about, as usual. They balanced their bottoms at the edge of their chairs and got up every so often to run the daedal business of burying their father. There was food to be arranged, a church to be prettified, a grave to be organized, and Achens to be called. There was also a rumour that the Marthoma metropolitan would visit Appacha. He lived in a sprawling abode on top of a hill in Thiruvalla and, being the spiritual head of the entire Syrian

Christian Marthoma denomination, he was an inaccessible man, busy rubbing shoulders with chief ministers and prime ministers. But if he found time to visit Appacha in the church later, it would be the icing on their cake.

A woman came forward, stood beside Appacha's coffin, and cried. Seeing her cry, the singers cried louder. But unlike the performers, there was something true in the tears the woman shed. She slipped into the crowd and vanished into the sea of mourners.

As the singers chorused the last song, the MLA of the constituency came to pay his respects. He walked in with his band of minions, dressed in starched white cotton, smelling of imported perfume and coconut oil, overpowering the smell of death. He placed a wreath with his party's name printed on it and stood by Appacha's feet in practised humility. The gold Parker pen in his left breast pocket matched the sheen of his gold tooth, which he flashed when he performed a half-smile, as he was well aware that he couldn't execute his full smile during a funeral.

A nod here and there, a few perfunctory acknowledgements to familiar faces, and he left, leading his entourage of minions away. Velia Pappa and Cheria Pappa swiftly rose from their seats and unctuously saw the petty politician out.

༄

Appacha's funeral was a magnificent affair. Ironically, he would have never approved of such a grandiose event. It was a tribute orchestrated by others, leaving him without a voice in its grandeur.

Krishnan Uncle drove Appacha to the church for the last time. He sat behind the wheel of the Jeep and drove the way he always drove, eyes on the road, speedometer not going past 40 km/hr, hands cradling the steering wheel like he was cradling a baby. Aleyamma sat wedged between Velia Pappa and Cheria Pappa in the back seat with Appacha's casket. Amma followed in the Ambassador.

Appacha was buried in the cemetery Appacha's father had bought for Jerusalem Marthoma church years ago. It stood flanking the church and the parsonage, lush with prickly touch-me-nots and wild lilies. The land for the cemetery hadn't cost Appacha's father much back then. But now, people said it was 'prime' property, an extravagant designation for the final resting place of those who had no use for road frontage. Appacha's father was buried there too. So were Appacha's mother and Ammachi. The cemetery had reached its limit, ushering in the era of double and triple burials. Bodies upon bodies. Since they had money, they could book the land for the entire family in advance. Bodies next to bodies.

Appacha's grave was next to Ammachi's. People stood around the graves, eyes on the ground, their expressions of mourning serving as a facade for their concealed fear of the snakes that lurked among the weeds. Velia Pappa elbowed Cheria Pappa and pointed at Ammachi's headstone. 'The granite we ordered is a shade darker. They won't look good together,' he remarked, his Ray-Ban-clad eye assessing the situation. Cheria Pappa studied Ammachi's grave and whispered back, 'It's okay. The rain and the sun will lighten it in no time.'

Two generations had passed, each one resting in the same earth, except for Georgekutty Appachan. Some said he was still alive, living in an ashram as a swami in the foothills of the Himalayas. Others claimed he had died due to liver cirrhosis. However, it seemed unlikely that he would swing by anytime soon.

∽

Ashes to ashes, dust to dust...the Achen said to the people gathered. Each held a handful of soil, letting it slip through their fingers to fall upon the gleaming coffin below. Within his closed rosewood casket, Appacha rested, as people hurried off to the Puthenpurackel Thommi Tharakan Memorial Auditorium for cold Rasna, hot tea, and snacks. As they mingled, they shared stories of Appacha's openhandedness, not because customary praise was reserved for the deceased, but because he had truly been a good man.

After he retired from his job at the coffee estate, he came back to Niranam and immersed himself in the welfare of the society he was part of. He donated land for an old-age centre, an anganwadi, and a home for women from troubled domestic households. He sent money to the kids of the tappers who once worked at the estate, and arranged for their education and weddings. He also took care of the leaky-nosed kids from the neighbourhood. He took care of their school fees and later sent them to colleges. He bought them *Balarama*s and told them Suppandi and Mayavi stories. They laughed together when Luttapi fell off the arrow.

Aleyamma wandered into the church and sat on a bench at the back. Doves fluttered over her head, making cooing sounds. Some were sitting on the gold (plated) baptismal font that stood by the old blue door. Three generations had been baptized in it, including her. Appa had let Amma decide where the baby would be baptized as he didn't value churches and baptisms. Aleyamma had wrapped her fingers tightly around Appacha's thumb during the service, while Amma held her, and the Achen dipped her in the cold water.

There was a tap on her shoulder, and she turned around to find a woman standing next to her. It was the woman with the real tears in her eyes. She was smiling now. 'I wanted to say goodbye before I left. You don't know me. But my father was a tapper at Eastman Estate. I was only a child then. Superend saar was very good to our family. He paid all my hospital bills,' she said.

'Oh. What was wrong?'

'I had asthma. But I am fine now. I have three grandchildren of my own.'

She stood near Aleyamma for a while and watched the doves with her.

'I have to go. Don't want to miss the bus back home,' she said.

She walked to the door and turned around. 'You look just like Kochamma. He must have loved you so much.'

She walked away, through the blue doors, through the tall gates and to the bus stop from where she would take a bus and go see her children and her grandchildren. Aleyamma returned to the company of the flapping doves. One flew down and sat on the rim of the baptismal font, studied her with its cocked head, and cooed at her. Aleyamma gripped the cold wooden bench and cried.

There was no one to stop her from crying. Amma was busy eating crispy parippu vada and drinking lukewarm tea in the auditorium. Velia Pappa and Cheria Pappa were wrapping up the business of burying their father. Their wives were talking about how beautiful the ceremony was. Everything was good. No glitches at all. Rain clouds threatening from the sky like the ones that appear on Good Friday. But no rain. Doves on the church ceiling. The German car the Marthoma metropolitan came in. The lingering smell of the French perfume he wore. Their children were checking their phones. Grandchildren who were not Appacha's favourite. Grandchildren who had more time with him. Strangers were drinking Rasna and munching on glucose biscuits. They would all go back home and get back to their routines. People might name something after Appacha. A memorial hall. An ever-rolling trophy. A seat in a local college. And Appacha's grave would be covered with sturdy cement by the workers soon. Sealed shut until there arose a possibility of a double burial far into the future.

chapter 37

THE BURIAL GROUND BRIMS WITH life. Red ants march through muggy moss. Black beetles laze on sun-warmed boulders. Chameleons slip away into the tangled undergrowth, vanishing like smoke. Leeches lurk in the thick grass, poised to latch on to skin. Crickets rub their wings with stridulating songs. And a praying mantis folds its hands before the three forgotten graves.

Aleyamma pulls away the weeds that cocoon the tiniest grave. She needs to see it to believe it. By thirty-five, the world has left her jaundiced. She doesn't believe in magic any more. She needs proof. Sharp signs from heaven. How many signs till one believes? Seven times seventy. She needs them all. The burning bush. The Urim and the Thummim. Angels to wrestle with. Wet fleece and dry ground. Dry fleece and wet ground. Still waters to walk on. Holes in the hands and feet. The pierced side and the folded grave cloth. She is Moses. David. Jacob. Gideon. Peter. Thomas. Mary. Those who loved and yet sinned. Those who doubted and yet believed.

The touch-me-nots sink their thorns into her arms and the climbing nettle prickles her skin as she tries to bring the inscriptions to light. As she plucks away the weeds, she ponders whether Elsy Chedatty's disclosure of Duke's resting place was a ploy to lure her from the study where she had sequestered herself after the Onam meal. Elsy Chedatty had initially attempted to coax her out with tales of disrupted bookings, prompting Aleyamma to instruct her to close all reservations. Subsequently, Elsy Chedatty told her about Duke's grave in the backyard.

When the words come to light, Aleyamma trembles. The engraving on the headstone has faded with time, but she can still read the words that Appacha chose, carved into stone, whispering secrets from the bygone days.

Duke
A Faithful Friend
Always Loved, Never Forgotten
1965–1968

'Saar carved the letters himself just before they left,' Elsy Chedatty tells her. She is standing next to Aleyamma, and her eyes are misty.

Aleyamma's fingers trace the grooves that Appacha had etched. The cold granite bites into her palm. Duke was only three when he died. She should be relieved because she now knows that the Hitchcocks didn't have a baby. But the words don't bring her rest. Duke didn't live to see old age, and he wasn't laid to rest near the sea where Appacha and Ammachi's love story had unfolded.

'Everyone thought he was a wolf. But he was the kindest animal I have ever seen,' Elsy Chedatty tells her. 'My husband was afraid of him at first. He was lame in one leg and thought Duke would bite his good leg and cripple him completely. But soon he got to like him. He is the one who found the body and told saar about it.'

'The body? What happened to him?'

'Duke...he was killed,' Elsy Chedatty says, her words emerging with hesitation.

'What? Who killed him?'

'It was my first husband. Duke bit him during a labour union protest. It shook him hard. Once when he was too drunk to think clearly, he poisoned him,' she says, her words halting.

Aleyamma sits next to Duke's grave and watches it with a new perspective. Appacha had filtered some of the truth about his life in Puthuloor. He had narrated the PG version of it to the eight-year-old. Poison and murder were sempiternal themes in fairy tales. But they never appeared in Appacha's stories. His stories were whimsical and crafted to assuage her fears, such as her dread of the Achens, whom she believed would spirit her away in the deep pockets of their robes—an idea the milkman had planted after frantically searching for his hidden bicycle. Perhaps the milkman had sought retribution that way. But he had told her that the Achens kidnapped little children to sell them later for a handful of silver coins in lands far away.

'I will shout and cry for help. I will go to the police and then Appacha will come and get me,' she had told the milkman.

'How is that possible? They snip off your tongue first. Then you won't be able to talk,' he said with a crooked smile.

Aleyamma hid behind Appacha that Sunday during the church service as the Achen stood at the altar and gutturalized the liturgy behind his prayer book through a formidable cloud of frankincense.

Then he read from the book of Genesis:

> Now Israel loved Joseph more than any of his other sons; and he made a tunic of many colours for him. When his brothers saw that their father loved him more than any of them, they hated him and could not speak a kind word to him. Now his brothers had gone to graze their father's flocks. When Joseph came to his brothers, they stripped him of the tunic of many colours that was on him. And then they took him and cast him into a pit. As they sat down to eat their meal, they looked up and saw a caravan of Ishmaelites coming from Gilead. The brothers pulled Joseph up out of the pit and sold him for twenty shekels of silver to the Ishmaelites, who took him to Egypt. There he became a slave.

Aleyamma breathed hard, crushing Appacha's crisp jubba in her perspiring palms, and wondered how far Egypt was from Niranam. Appacha picked her up, walked to the car, and Krishnan Uncle drove them back home. When Appacha came to understand the story behind her fear, he regaled her with a tale of his own.

'Once, there was an elderly Achen who had an insatiable appetite for ethakka appam and milk-water. He consumed so much that his stomach expanded to the size of a football. Eager to conceal his growing belly, he grew a beard. This soft, white beard was as delicate as cotton candy. However, it didn't take long for it to lengthen to the point where it resembled Rip Van Winkle's beard. He began stumbling over it every time he walked. To resolve this predicament, he enlisted the help of some children who would hold his beard for him wherever he went, listening to his enchanting stories of kings and queens as they escorted him home. The children adored the old Achen, enchanted by his cotton-candy beard and the stories he had tucked up his sleeve.'

Aleyamma felt the fear dissipate. From that moment on, the Achens held no more terror for her. But curiously, the milkman never made another appearance. He vanished mysteriously along with his bicycle.

Elsy Chedatty clears the ground and sits next to her. 'When I first came to the Estate House, I was a frightened little girl. But saar and Kochamma taught me to stand on my feet. If they hadn't taken me in, who knows, I too might have died at the hands of a drunkard.'

There are many stories in Elsy Chedatty's eyes. She has never spoken much about her life or her family. Aleyamma would have never guessed that she was married twice. She knows nothing about her, though she sees her every day. She is like Amma, who keeps most people at a certain distance.

'After saar and Kochamma left, they got me a job at the house of Ousepachan saar, the estate owner. I married Pappan, the watcher of the estate, after Ousepachan saar passed away. We ran a catering business for a long time. We lived in that house there.' She points at the ruins near the brook. 'We have two sons. Both are in the Gulf. One is a chartered accountant. The other is in the business of organizing trade shows. Ettan died a few years ago. Around that time, saar bought the Estate House and then your Velia Pappa asked me if I could be the manager here. My sons keep asking me to join them in the Gulf. But I don't want to go. There is no place like these hills. There is no place like home.'

Elsy Chedatty runs her hands over Duke's grave. 'You know, I think saar bought this place because Duke is buried here.'

'I didn't know all this,' Aleyamma says. 'What happened to your first husband?'

Elsy Chedatty's eyes are far away. There is peace and pain in them. 'He ran away after the assistant superend was killed. Someone found him lying dead outside an arrack shop in Calicut. A truck had run over him.'

∽

When Aleyamma tells Amma about Duke's grave, she is not alarmed. She has always known how Duke died, and it doesn't matter to her.

'So many graves on the property. Did you know graves bring down property prices? Maybe we should think about covering them up.'

Amma is sitting in the hall, poring over the newspaper, soaking in the world's events like a sponge. It has been a few days since she has seen Aleyamma, but she is unconcerned. She sips her tea noisily and continues to turn the pages of the newspaper. Aleyamma regrets telling Amma about her discovery. She had forgotten how unmerciful Amma could be. Her face is now as obdurate as the time she threw away Aleyamma's torn dress of many colours, the day they had returned from Niranam, stuffing it into the plastic bag with the kitchen waste. 'What is the use of a dress with only one sleeve?' she had asked.

'I am not covering anything up,' Aleyamma says.

'Then it won't be so valuable on the market,' Amma says.

'There is no market. This is Appacha's land. Mine now. Why should there be a market?'

Amma's hands curl around the newspaper. 'You have to think about things practically. That is all. I have always tried to be practical. That is why I did a lot of things. That is why I gave you space when you said you wanted to move to Chennai after school. That is why I took you away from Appacha.'

It is the first time Amma is mentioning the incident she has avoided speaking about. Now she unceremoniously slips it into the conversation.

'Practical? Why was it practical when you took me away from Appacha?'

'Because I thought he was corrupting your mind with things he thought were right. Maybe he was right. But he was too forceful. Also, I didn't want you to live in that house with that murderer any more.'

'What murderer?' Aleyamma thinks Amma is making up stories now.

Amma folds the newspaper and puts it on the coffee table. 'Krishnan...Appacha's driver. You didn't know that he murdered someone once?'

Aleyamma takes time to soak in the latest piece of information. Appacha said he killed cockroaches, walking around with a newspaper rolled up like a bat, punishing them one by one and throwing them under the coconut trees.

'He killed the assistant superintendent of the estate when he was working here as the clerk. Appacha had practically raised him. He then gave him a job and everything. But that man was ungrateful. There was a strike here at the estate. Around the same time, he joined the Naxals. Long story short, he ran away from the Naxal camp and then killed the estate owner's son. Krishnan was in prison for a long time. Appacha even arranged a lawyer for him. And once he got out of prison, it was like they were best friends again. We all were against their friendship. But no one could change your grandfather's mind. We knew he would do anything for the people he cared about, even if they were killers. Appa was a stubborn man.'

Amma's words cascade around her, starved of sense. Krishnan Uncle was not a murderer. He was Appacha's most trusted companion. His right hand. The man whose assuredness had comforted Appacha when he thought he had lost Aleyamma to the deceptive pond. The man who carried Appacha to bed, wiped his drool, and changed his soiled sheets. He was Krishnan Uncle. The gentle killer of cockroaches.

'He just killed cockroaches.' She realizes it sounds naïve as soon as she says it.

Amma slaps her thigh and chuckles. 'Cockroaches? Seriously?'

'But how come no one told me about this? How come I didn't know?'

'I thought you knew. Everybody knew. Appacha told everyone not to mention these things when you were around. But I thought you would have eventually come to know about it.'

Amma points at a photograph on the wall. The one where Appacha stands next to three people, one with bony shoulders, the other with a rifle, and an old man with thick glasses. 'I've wanted to take that picture down ever since I first laid eyes on it. That boy with the gun was the Eastman Estate owner's son, the assistant superintendent, the one who was killed. And just look at Krishnan, standing right next to him. Who thought he would do that to the poor boy?' Amma's lips curl with aversion.

Aleyamma walks closer to the picture and wipes the thin layer of dust that has settled on the glass frame. She looks at the boy with the bony shoulders. She looks into his eyes. She knows them. 'Baby will be fine....' She remembers the steadfast voice. She remembers the foot that kicked against the speed limits and made the silver Contessa fly like the car from *Chitty Chitty Bang Bang*.

Amma clears her throat. 'Anyway, that is in the past. Now you need to think about what is ahead of you.' Amma has put down the paper and is looking at her.

Aleyamma is in no state to discuss the price of the property with Amma because she is not planning to sell it. But now she is unsettled by the new piece of information that Amma has imparted. She speculates whether Amma's arrival in Puthuloor had an ulterior motive. Maybe she is here to persuade her to sell the acreage that they all considered prime property. Too prime to be a graveyard. Too prime for a starving artist. Perhaps Amma wants to sell it back to Velia Pappa. She is being fooled by all of them.

Amma has picked up the newspaper again.

Aleyamma walks towards Amma and says, 'Really? Is that why you are here? Do you want me to sell this land? This house? I am such an idiot for thinking you were here for me. To spend time with me. But why would you do that? You are here for the soil. For the moolah. All my life, I looked for affection from you. From Appa. I looked for it in other people. But you both failed to give me what

I needed. So, I clung onto what Appacha could give me, even if it was for a brief time. But you are here to erase him completely. You are here to take me away from him again. Aren't you?'

She can hear her voice crack as she struggles to complete her words. She has pictured this conversation all these years. But now that she has said it, she is weak. It doesn't lift the burden she has carried for so long. She sinks to the floor and lets vulnerability take over her body. She is open to the world. And to Amma. She hopes for her to pick her up and spoon her like a mother would. She hopes for her to wrap her hands around her, pull her to her enormous breasts, kiss the top of her head, and console her. She wants her to gather her broken pieces and fix them with her loving fingers. 'Baby will be all right…Baby should be proud….' she wants to hear her say.

Amma gets up from the sofa. 'How quick you are to judge me. But again, I deserve it. Don't I?' She disappears into her room, leaving Aleyamma sprawled on the cold, unmoving floor.

chapter 38

THAT NIGHT, A TEMPEST UNFURLS its wings. It besieges the Eastman Maavu. Twigs assail the windowpanes. Green leaves turn silver under the sparkle of the lightning. Magpies and squirrels disappear into hidden hollows. Raindrops cannon into the roof. Thunder rolls through the skies. The wind is swift, and the air thickens like blood.

Aleyamma watches the storm and waits for it to dispel her ache. From her mattress, she can see the mango tree shaking in the wind.

Casabianca still stands by the window submissively like the boy in striped brown-and-green. The urge to snatch it and cast it into the maelstrom teases her thoughts. But she doesn't do it. Instead, she continues to watch.

She can smell the storm now. A smell stronger than that of the wet earth during the first rain. The smell of violence that nature sometimes surprises people with. The smell she smelled after she fell into the pond.

She hears the plaintive cries of a dog lost in a storm. She sees cockroaches scampering over the walls. A broken chappal buried in the sands of Om beach. A pencil moustache aquiver in the wind. David and Goliath locked in an eternal game of rock, paper, and scissors. A burning ship, she in the cold embrace of the sea, watching as Appacha reaches out from a lifeboat to grasp the flailing hand of Krishnan Uncle. He climbs in and they row away. She remains in the water, drowning once more, alone now, again, always.

She must have fallen asleep at some point for she feels her stertorous breaths when she opens her eyes to a sound louder than the clap of thunder. Like the sound of a trumpet. Like the sound of many waters. Aleyamma sits up on the mattress. A shadow falls across the room, inching its way through the sky, crashing into the windowpane, shattering glass, sinking into the study. She bolts to the back of the room, feeling the wooden floor shudder. Eastman Maavu has fallen into the study like a slain king.

It is glorious even in its death, leaves still breathing.

But in its death, it has brought down something with it, like Samson, who, in his final breath, brought down the pillars of the temple on more than 3,000 Philistines. Casabianca is dead. It has cracked into countless empty pieces and lies lifeless beneath the giant that has overpowered it with a single blow. Its solid body has now shattered into fragments, disfigured leftovers from a carpenter's shop, destined to be swept up and used as firewood.

Amma has now climbed the stairs, accompanied by Elsy Chedatty. Amma's hair is tousled. Her monkey crop is dishevelled. She looks at the ruination on the floor with disapproval and mumbles something unintelligible under her breath. She kicks at a breathing branch with her tiny feet and tuts.

'Good that we have no bookings,' she says finally. 'You should come and sleep downstairs.' She holds her knees and embarks on a dangerous descent.

Elsy Chedatty watches the mango tree on the floor. Her eyes are pensive and her lips tight. 'It was not the lightning. It was something else,' she says.

'Saar planted it soon after I started living here. Krishnan brought it with him from Niranam. It was your great-grandmother's gift for saar.'

She walks up to Aleyamma and holds her close. 'Are you all right?'

Aleyamma sits back on the mattress and draws her knees to her chest. Cold air wraps around her unkindly and her hair stands up on her skin. 'I think I might be running a fever.'

Elsy Chedatty bends over and presses her palm against her forehead.

'You are very warm. I will get you a Crocin.'

'There is no need. I will come downstairs in a while.'

She squeezes a pillow and continues to look at the shattered easel and the mango tree as Elsy Chedatty retreats downstairs. The view outside the window is now empty. But her room is full. The florets on the branches are now little fruits. She pines for the taste in her mouth again, that of something tart and sweet, one she knows she cannot have any more.

Elsy Chedatty has made up the four-poster bed in the bedroom downstairs. She has kept a jar of warm jeera water, a steel tumbler, and a strip of Crocin on the bedside table. Aleyamma eyes the Crocin but slips under the duvet and turns off the table lamp. From the warm glow of the light in the hallway, she can see Elsy Chedatty standing near the door. 'Just call me if you need anything,' she says and leaves, leaving the door slightly ajar.

Her thoughtfulness touches Aleyamma. She turns to her side and watches the rain. The storm is now retreating. The sky simmers down. Thunder grumbles far away, and the lightning is fading into the moonlight. She closes her eyes.

It is perhaps past midnight when she feels them.

They run over her forehead in tender strokes. It is deeper than a dream, more lucid than a longing. She feels the hands that pulled her out of the deceptive water. The hands that ran over her forehead when she ran fevers. She welcomes the mellow waft of Brut, Cuticura, and Radhas enveloping her burning frame. She feels the fever leaving her body. Like magic. Love folds itself around her like an old, worn blanket, and she sleeps like she has never slept before.

∽

The early morning light gently trickles in through the windows. Aleyamma sits up in the four-poster bed, moves the mosquito net from the corner, and inhales the mellow morning air. She recalls the promise Appacha made her years ago, after Amma had left her with him.

Amma had climbed into the Ambassador and driven away, the same way Appa had left a week earlier. Without looking back. Without saying goodbye. A knot tightened in her belly.

'Is Amma coming back?' she had asked Appacha.

'Of course. She will come and get you once she is ready.' Appacha put his arms around her and drew her to his chest. 'Baby is strong. Baby is like Ammachi.'

The Ambassador disappeared into a gust of black vapour.

Appacha lifted her and settled her on his shoulders. The top of his head was shiny and silver like the moon. She held his ears and his cheeks. She ran her fingers over his laugh lines. They comforted her. Appacha held her solidly by the ankles. She was safe in his grip.

'Will *you* ever leave me?' she asked.

'I may not always be near you, but I will always be with you. I will make it right this time. I have to. That is a promise...you are the light of my life.'

Appacha's cheeks had become wet. She had looked around and seen that it was not raining.

Aleyamma runs her fingers along her forehead. Her mind is clear. She gets up from her bed, walks to the study, and sees the wreckage from the night before. A gift passed down over time. A sharp sign from the heavens.

She sits near the broken branches, draws the cell phone from her pocket, and presses 1. 'Hello,' says a stifled voice from the other end. Roy has taken refuge in the bathroom as always, palm over the phone.

'Casabianca is dead. I am going to light a candle.'

His breath slips through the phone.

She switches off her phone and discards it somewhere within the ruination on the floor.

Elsy Chedatty is busy near the stove when she walks into the kitchen downstairs.

'Could you make fish curry for lunch?' Aleyamma asks her.

Elsy Chedatty nods and her fingers search for something in the cupboard under the stove.

'Are you surprised?' Aleyamma asks her.

Elsy Chedatty brings out a clay pot she had hidden under the stove and shakes her head. 'Not at all.'

∽

Amma leaves that morning. She gets into her Ambassador and starts the engine. The Ambassador is resisting Amma's driving yet again. The tyres shriek like an infant, crushing the red soil underneath it into a fine powder. A thick black cloud of smoke emanates through the exhaust pipe and engulfs Aleyamma and Elsy Chedatty. Elsy Chedatty takes the end of her pallu, puts it over her nose, and waves to Amma, who has not acknowledged her even once. Amma's eyes are on the road ahead of her. Aleyamma doesn't wait for her to drive away; she knows Amma will not look back.

She walks back into the house and that is when she sees the package Amma has left on the centre table in the hall. The one that has been waiting for her all these years. It is everything Appacha had bought for her. The secret stash Amma hid in the secret side locker of the dust-green Godrej cupboard. Unruled books with pages stained an Ujala blue that turned bluer under the tube light. Colour pencils that could be sharpened on both sides. A tin car with a plastic light on top. Balloons in two colours. A toy gun with pink potash strips, that goes pop when placed precisely between the spring hinges that the trigger was invisibly connected to.

She runs back to the garden and sees the Ambassador vanishing into the thick gust of smoke.

A man emerges from the smoke. His shoulders are hunched. In one hand is a tin trunk and in the other a sapling.

Krishnan Uncle walks up to her and smiles. 'Baby,' he says. He sets down the trunk and the sapling at his feet, his gaze drifting towards the fallen mango tree in the study. His forehead broadens with stories from the past. But there is hope in his presence and promises within the tender mango leaves near his feet.

He opens the tin trunk and takes out a plastic bag. 'I found it when I was clearing the room. It was in the drawer of the dressing table. I thought you should have it,' he says, holding it out to her. Elsy Chedatty welcomes Krishnan Uncle with a smile of familiarity. 'I will show you to your room,' she says and takes him inside.

Aleyamma opens the bag. The torn dress sleeve of many colours slips into her fingers along with the birthday card with the big red heart she had made for Appacha. And there is a photograph, the one that Mouse Appachan took on Christmas Eve, twenty-seven years ago. The picture has faded with time and humidity. But it is still fresh with memories. Appacha has her in the crook of his arm and she is holding his ears that wiggled when Mouse Appachan said 'cheese'. She runs her fingers over his face and feels the laugh lines through the paper.

Aleyamma walks into the study, over the broken floor, and finds her suitcase. She opens it, slips into her running gear, and sprints towards town, shorts still short, feet still naked, and hair heavy like that of a hippie, humming 'Beautiful Sunday' under her breath. She is Baby again.

ACKNOWLEDGEMENTS

This book would not exist without the support, guidance, and inspiration of those who have been an integral part of this journey, to whom I am deeply grateful.

To my publisher, Aleph Book Company: thanks to David Davidar and Aienla Ozukum for believing in this story, offering invaluable editorial guidance, and bringing this book into the world. My gratitude also goes to Shatakshi Singh, Aayushi Gupta, and Sheeba Thattil for their meticulous attention to my words.

I am deeply grateful to my agent, Kanishka Gupta, for his steadfast belief in the novel from the very beginning. His unwavering support and insightful advice have been invaluable throughout this entire journey. To Janani Ganesan, who first guided me through the initial steps of shaping this manuscript, and to Tara Khandelwal of Bound for her thoughtful manuscript evaluation—thank you both for your support.

To Jerry Pinto and his workshop at The Himalayan Writing Retreat: thank you for your valuable feedback on my work and for helping me refine my understanding of publishing.

I would also like to thank my fellow participants for their thoughtful feedback and encouragement.

To Koshy Abraham, for sharing his knowledge about the inner workings of a rubber estate, which lent authenticity to this narrative.

To Philip M. Prasad, for sharing his experiences from the frontlines of the Naxal movement and guiding me towards the resources essential for my research.

The books *Kerala's Naxalbari: Ajitha, Memoirs of a Young Revolutionary* by Ajitha and *Modernity of Slavery* by P. Sanal Mohan provided invaluable insights that helped me deepen the historical and social layers of this story. I am grateful for the wisdom these works offered me.

To my family, the foundation of everything I do: my mother, my first and most trusted reader, who always believed in my words; my brother, who not only encouraged me to write this story but also showed me how to tell it; and my father, whose daily question—'Have you finished writing it yet?'—kept me moving forward. To my children and my husband, for being the home I needed while creating this world—you are my greatest support and joy.

To Arun Shimoga, my editor at the *New Indian Express*, for encouraging me when I first shared my intention to write this book, even though it meant leaving my job. It took me a decade and a half to get to this point, and I've made it. Finally, to my friends, my constant cheerleaders—who know who you are—your encouragement, love, and belief in me have carried me through.

This book was as much a rebellion as it was a surrender, and I could not have walked this journey without each of you.